GENDERED LANDSCAPES

To the memory of my parents

The Cornell East Asia Series is published by the Cornell University East Asia Program (distinct from Cornell University Press). We publish books on a variety of scholarly topics relating to East Asia as a service to the academic community and the general public. Address submission inquiries to CEAS Editorial Board, East Asia Program, Cornell University, 140 Uris Hall, Ithaca, New York 14853-7601.

This publication was supported in part by a generous subvention from the Korea Literature Translation Institute and the Center for Korean Studies, University of Hawai'i at Mānoa.

Number 187 in the Cornell East Asia Series
Copyright © 2017 Cornell University East Asia Program. All rights reserved.
ISSN 1050-2955
ISBN: 978-1-939161-67-3 hc
ISBN: 978-1-939161-87-1 pb
ISBN: 978-1-942242-87-1 ebook
Library of Congress Control Number: 2017941817
Printed in the United States of America

Cover image: Olga Tagaeva. Korean Landscape with Clouds and Fields at Sunset.
Source: Shutterstock Stock vector ID: 114379009
Design: Mai

∞ The paper in this book meets the requirements for permanence of ISO 9706:1994.

GENDERED LANDSCAPES

*Short Fiction by
Modern and Contemporary
Korean Women Novelists*

Translated and with an Introduction by

Yung-Hee Kim

East Asia Program
Cornell University
Ithaca, New York 14853

Contents

vii

Preface

Gendered Landscapes showcases nine short stories and novellas by Korean women writers published between 1935 and 1998. These are signature pieces selected from the repertoire of a group of acclaimed authors who are vital constituents of modern Korean literary traditions, as well as key figures in the genealogy of Korea's female literary community. Following the publication of my book, *Questioning Minds: Short Stories by Modern Korean Women Writers* (Honolulu: University of Hawai'i Press, 2010), this volume advances my goal of making such works accessible to a wide English-language readership interested in the interrelationships among Korean, and even East-Asian, literature, women, culture, and society. The anthology is also a timely tribute to the achievements of these inspirational and virtuoso women writers in celebration of the centennial of the birth of modern Korean women's fiction writing in 1917.[1] As such, *Gendered Landscapes* will contribute to illuminating a century-old legacy of Korean women writers' literary engagement and bring to light the cumulative impact of their creative energy on the development of modern Korean literature at large.

The fictional narratives in *Gendered Landscapes* have been selected not simply because they are the products of women authors. Thoughtful and extensive research has been done to identify and locate stories that address or problematize issues related to Korean women as gendered beings in a Confucian-dominated patriarchal

---

1. In 1917, the first modern Korean woman writer, Kim Myŏng-sun (1896–ca.1951), published her debut short story, "Ŭisim ŭi sonyŏ" (A girl of mystery) in the magazine *Ch'ŏngch'un* (Youth; no. 11, November 1917). For an English translation of this story, its textual analysis, and information about the writer, see Yung-Hee Kim, *Questioning Minds*, 15-23.

society. Thematically interlinked, these stories bring into full view the vivid and colorful mosaic of Korean women's lives from the mid-1930s to the end of the twentieth century, engendered under the formidable sway of centuries-old Confucian patriarchal ideologies. They bear eloquent testimony to how deeply and irremovably entrenched Confucian gender principles and practices have been in Korean society—potently at work even at the end of the twentieth century. Each story challenges its reader to examine what patriarchal assumptions, prejudices, and customs operate to define, circumscribe, and even quell Korean women's dreams, opportunities, quality and meaning of life, and above all, self-identities.

These narratives deftly, and often forcefully, speak out on woman-focused private dramas and present an array of portraits of Korean women today, just as they offer a revealing window on the inner landscapes of Korean women over the last several decades. Invariably, these texts testify to their authors' ingenuity and imaginative vision in utilizing the power of storytelling, by drawing from their own lived experiences, challenging the social and gender expectations they were born into, documenting the truths of other's lives, or by imagining alternative realities in which they might hope to have lived. Such re-visional, oppositional, or alternative gender consciousness makes the texts in *Gendered Landscapes* counter-scripts to Confucian master narratives. They are powerful beacons not only for the personal voyages of their fictional characters, but also for the transformation of communities of readers at large. The magnetic and thought-provoking stories in *Gendered Landscapes* are literary gems that must be shared with audiences beyond the boundaries of languages, cultures, time, and disparate literary traditions.

Given the current conspicuous lack of English translations of the works of modern Korean women writers, *Gendered Landscapes* will provide much needed information and material for scholars, instructors, and students of Korean literature. The collection may also stimulate interest in specialists in various fields outside of Korean literature, such as women's studies, Asian studies, history, anthropology, comparative literature, and other East-Asian literatures. Even a far broader and larger English-speaking audience, including the general public, will find these stories enriching, instructive, and most of all, relatable. In light of the explosion of talents of young Korean women writers, who have dominated the Korean literary world since the mid-1990s, *Gendered Landscapes* will play a significant role in circulating new knowledge about modern and contemporary Korean women writers' artistic and intellectual accomplishments, enhance their international recognition, and in the end, promote informed and genuine appreciation of Korean literature and culture on the whole.

In the modern Korean literary world, short fiction is considered a testing ground for a writer's thematic originality and literary craftsmanship. It has long served—even today—as the springboard for a debut writer. In fact, the genre is so esteemed that it represents the ultimate form for an aspiring author to perfect. Consequently, many modern writers' reputations rest on their short stories, and some writers are best remembered for their well-known short fiction. Seven of the nine stories in this anthology are translated for the first time into English, while the remaining two were in urgent need of updated translations.[2] These short stories are arranged in chronological order by year of publication to display the historical development of Korean women's fiction-writing practices in terms of both thematic concerns and narrative strategies.

The McCune-Reischauer system has been used for the Romanization of Korean. Korean names follow the native practice, with surname first followed by given name. ଔ

---

2. These two short stories are: Ch'oe Chŏng-hŭi's "Mountain Rites" (Sanje; 1938) and Im Og-in's "Chronicle of a Third Wife" (Huch'ŏgi; 1940).

Acknowledgments

Gendered Landscapes is the final product of a long, winding, and eventful journey to create a venue for its audience to gain germane and satisfying reading experiences. The course of this venture called for continuous readjustment, modification, and alteration. From the outset, the selection of authors, short stories, and the introductory material to be included in the collection necessitated wide-ranging, systematic, and comprehensive research and judicious decisions. As expected, the translated texts themselves required frequent and repeated revisions to do justice to the originals and for their readability in English. Even the structure and presentational format of the anthology went through significant rearrangement and reorganization. The constantly fluctuating and often challenging voyage, however, has proved to be a meaningful and enriching time for me to reconfirm and appreciate the individual novelists' creative aspirations, their craftsmanship, and the excellence of the selected works.

Along the way, a number of individuals have played crucial roles in pushing the project forward and have been integral to bringing it to completion. First, I would like to thank the currently active authors for their permission for translation and publication of their works and for their encouragement: Ch'oe Yun, Kim In-suk, Ch'a Hyŏn-suk, and Yi Hye-gyŏng. My deep gratitude goes to the daughters of three late authors who have granted permission for translation and publication: Kim Ch'ae-wŏn for her mother, Ch'oe Chŏng-hŭi; Young-Key Kim-Renaud for Han Mu-suk; and Ho Won-sook for Pak Wan-sŏ. I am especially grateful to Ch'ae Chŏng-un, a novelist who went out of her way to obtain official information and documents to clarify the copyright of works by the late Im Og-in—

Ch'ae's mentor through her days as a Korean literature major at Ewha Womans University, Seoul, Korea.

My sincere gratitude is extended to Mai Shaikhanuar-Cota, managing editor, Cornell East Asia Series, who first recognized the merit of *Gendered Landscapes* and the necessity for publishing it. Ever since, her patience, multitasking commitments, and well-timed administrative orchestration have been driving forces for bringing the manuscript to publication. I would also like to offer thanks to the external reviewers whose insightful and pertinent observations and pointers contributed to refining my perspective on and approach to the manuscript and in the end consolidating its substance and framework. The copyediting done by Amy Odum was essential to raising the manuscript to a new level of clarity and uniformity.

At various stages of manuscript preparation, I benefitted from editorial assistance from Anjoli Roy and Daniel C. Kane, whose sharp, critical eyes and expertise helped upgrade the quality of my writing. I also remain indebted to Michael E. Macmillan, who, on innumerable occasions, has lent a helping hand, providing discerning suggestions, technical aid, and moral support.

An appreciative acknowledgment goes to the Literature Translation Institute of Korea for its generous translation and publication grant. The Institute's President Kim Seong-Kon has been an enthusiastic supporter, and Yum Sooyon, program officer of the Institute, has offered untiring guidance and cooperation. Additionally, the publication subvention fund from the Min Kwan-Shik Faculty Enhancement Award, Center for Korean Studies, University of Hawai'i at Mānoa, is gratefully acknowledged for its invaluable provision of incentive and momentum.

Gendered Landscapes will fulfill its purpose and function whenever it spurs its readers—in the general public as well as in academia—to embark on their own memorable and enlivening journeys in company with the stories and their creators. ∽

Introduction

"The short story is the most purely artistic form."[1]

—*Georg Lukács*

"I discovered again … that translation was the most intimate act of reading."[2]

—*Gayatri Chakravorty Spivak*

This introduction is formulated and organized with the needs of English-speaking audiences in mind, such as general readers and nonspecialists in Korean literature, who are likely to be unfamiliar with the women-specific ideological, cultural, and literary contexts in which the original stories were produced. Conceived thus, considerable space has been allocated to offering readers the historical backdrop, cultural milieu, and textual information pertinent to an informed and proper understanding of the stories. That is, the introductory material in *Gendered Landscapes* provides both the framework and explicatory tools to facilitate the audience's nuanced and cogent reading of the translated stories. These contextual elucidations are expected as well to serve already initiated readers, and even experts in Korean literature, as recaps or ready references, unavailable in currently existing anthologies of Korean women's fiction in English translation. I encourage adept readers to gloss this introduction for a refresher that might deepen their reading of these stories, jump to the textual readings of the stories, or dive right into the stories themselves, as they see fit.

---

1. Georg Lukács, *The Theory of the Novel* (Cambridge, MA: The MIT Press, 1978), 51.
2. Gayatri Chakravorty Spivak, "Translation as Culture," *Parallax* 6, no. 1 (2000): 20.

CONFUCIANISM AND GENDER: MAPPING THE BACKGROUND

This section provides an overview of the fundamentals in Confucian gender principles and praxis, which become focal points of conflict and tension in the stories in *Gendered Landscapes*. It primarily aims to uncover and decode how these ideas and customs are refracted through the authorial prisms and appear as targets of contesting voices in the fictional texts in the anthology. Therefore, the survey limits itself to providing the most prominent, orthodox, and widespread features of Confucian gender requirements and provisions, which the individual authors of the stories seize as their major points of contention.

As is generally known, the patriarchal gender ideologies and conventions in Korean society took root during the Chosŏn (or Yi) dynasty (1392–1910), which hoisted Neo-Confucianism as its central governing principle. In parallel with elaborating on and implementing rigidly stratified class systems[3] and ethical codes[4] for Chosŏn citizens, the dynastic rulers, administrators, and philosophers articulated fundamental ideas and principles regarding women members of the kingdom and laid out model womanly thought and behavioral patterns for them to conform to. These Confucian female canons were aimed at producing the "virtuous woman," ethically and morally exemplary for members of extended family systems and an accomplished manager of kinship bonds and clan networks—all deemed to contribute to the stability and harmony of Chosŏn patriarchal society.

In Chosŏn there were no formal, institutionalized schools for women outside the home, so informal home education became paramount in educating girls. Daughters were tutored in the basics of womanly virtues by their mothers, grandmothers, and other female relatives through their own personal examples and oral in-

---

3. Chosŏn society was divided into four classes: nobility, peasant, artisan, and merchant. Beneath these were outcasts, including slaves, butchers, morticians, itinerant performers, *kisaeng* (lower-class women entertainers), and others. Mobility between these classes was prohibited and impossible.

4. Called "Oryun" (five codes for moral conduct), these rules were fundamental principles governing social and interpersonal relationships among people in Chosŏn: righteousness between sovereign and subject; authority of father over son; separation of roles between husband and wife; hierarchical order between old and young; and faithfulness between senior and junior.

struction within the multigenerational, extended family environment. The home-based teaching "was focused entirely on filling the role of married women," and "to prepare girls for their future functions as moral guardians of the domestic sphere and providers for the physical needs of their families."[5] For *yangban* women, these instructional lessons were anchored in textbooks for women,[6] and their guidelines were most rigorously indoctrinated on and followed through by upper-class women.[7] Still, the fundamental Confucian female principles were filtered down to women of plebian classes and guided them just as surely as they did *yangban* women, providing them with a similar outlook on the gender order, familial relationships, and personal behavior.[8] Therefore, the following expositions are for the most part derived from information and studies on *yangban* women's gender requirements and customs.

---

5. See Martina Deuchler, "The Tradition: Women during the Yi Dynasty," in *Virtues in Conflict: Tradition and the Korean Woman Today*, ed. Sandra Mattielli (Seoul: The Royal Asiatic Society, Korea Branch, 1977), 6–7.

6. Of these, most prominent and influential was *Naehun* (Instructions for women; 1475) written in *han'gŭl* (Korean alphabet) by Queen-Consort Sohye (1437–1504) and based on Chinese classics. Queen-Consort Sohye was the mother of King Sŏngjong (r. 1469–1494), who contributed to solidifying the legal foundation of the Chosŏn dynasty by promulgating major law codes, *Kyŏngguk taejŏn* (A comprehensive code of laws for governing the country; 1485). Other standard primers in *han'gŭl* for female edification were translated from Chinese sources, including *Sohak* (Ch. *Xiaoxue*; Book of lesser learning), *Yŏllyŏ-jŏn* (Biographies of faithful women), *Yŏgye* (Moral teaching for women), and *Yŏch'ik* (Rules of conduct for women)—all published during the reign of King Chungjong (r. 1506–1544). See Yung-Chung Kim, ed. and trans., *Women of Korea: A History from Ancient Times to 1945* (Seoul: Ewha Womans University Press, 1979), 156. See also John Duncan, "The *Naehun* and the Politics of Gender in Fifteenth-Century Korea," in *Creative Women of Korea: The Fifteenth Through the Twentieth Centuries*, ed. Young-Key Kim-Renaud (Armonk, NY: M.E. Sharpe, 2004), 26–57.

7. Undoubtedly, compared with the women of the gentry, commoner women of peasant, artisan, and merchant classes were not as strictly and severely subjected to these rules. Their mode of livelihood, which required farming, fishing, commercial, or other physical work in close contact and in cooperation with men in and outside the home, afforded them more flexibility and freedom in terms of personal carriage, activity, and mobility.

8. See Martina Deuchler, "Propagating Female Virtues in Chosŏn Korea," in *Women and Confucian Cultures in Premodern China, Korea, and Japan*, ed. Dorothy Ko, JaHyun Kim Haboush, and Joan R. Piggott (Berkeley: University of California Press, 2003), 161–162.

Foremost and central in Confucian gender ideology were the concepts of "namjon yŏbi" (man superior, woman inferior) and "namnyŏ yubyŏl" (distinction between male and female). The former established an immutable gender hierarchy in Chosŏn society and culture, which placed women in a subordinate and secondary position vis-à-vis men, while the latter defined an inflexible gender role partition between man and woman. With these principles as two axes, numerous women-targeted stipulations and rituals were constructed and propagated throughout the Chosŏn period.

The command, "samjong chido" (three rules of obedience), prescribed that a woman should obey her father before marriage, her husband after marriage, and her son(s) after her husband's death. It decreed the position of women as underling in their relationship with men in their lives, regardless of age or marital status, enjoining women to respect and adhere to male authority, leadership, and supervision all their lives. No less mandatory was the decree of "naeoebŏp" (laws of distinction between inside [woman] and outside [man]). It drew stiff, polarizing lines between the domestic and public spheres, and between male and female gender roles. Wives were not supposed to be nosy about or interfere with their husbands' public and business matters outside the home, while husbands were not to meddle in their wives' domestic affairs. Elaborations on these rules included "puch'ang pusu" (husband speaks, wife concurs) and "yŏp'il chongbu" (wife must follow husband), which stipulated women's passivity, deference, and dependency upon their husbands. In fact, a *yangban* house was gender-marked and was spatially and structurally divided into the outer/front (male) quarters and the inner/sequestered (female) quarters. Free contact or interaction between the two spaces was forbidden. The division of gender roles and responsibilities made the world outside the home beyond women's ken and reach. [9]

Related to such gender segregation was the interdiction of "namnyŏ ch'ilse pudongsŏk" (male and female from age seven should not sit together). In the realm of Chosŏn morality, which put women's sexual purity on a pedestal as their supreme virtue, woman's sexual honor was equated with her very life, to be defended at

---

9. Martina Deuchler, *The Confucian Transformation of Korea: A Study of Society and Ideology* (Cambridge, MA: Council on East Asian Studies, Harvard University, 1992), 261.

all cost.[10] From such a gender perspective, the proscription on physical proximity or contact between males and females from their pre-puberty years would deter young girls from sexual misbehavior that would contaminate their premarital virginity and ruin their life for good.

Marriage was the sole profession and career track available and known to gentry Chosŏn women. Arranged marriage was the norm, and it was coordinated through negotiations by a third party, such as relatives or friends of the marital candidates' parents. Matrimony meant a contract between the two families, and it had to be honored—never to be revoked or terminated. Customarily, the wedding was held at the bride's home, where the marriage partners, who were total strangers, met for the first time. After elaborate procedures—particularly in the case of upper-class newlyweds—over an extended period, the bride finally left her home and went to live at her in-laws' residence.[11]

The custom of early marriage, especially for young girls, was one of the major factors making the life of a Chosŏn woman one of victimization.[12] Young children were married off even before they reached puberty to ensure the continuation of the patrilineal line by having male descendants as early as possible.[13] Economic consideration was another chief reason for early marriage, since bringing in a daughter-in-law meant adding more manpower to the husband's household in the predominantly agrarian Korean society.[14] A weighty rationale for the upper-classes to marry their daughters

---

10. For instance, during the Japanese invasions from 1592 to 1598, a great number of Korean women committed suicide to protect their chastity and their family's honor rather than submit themselves to sexual violation by enemy soldiers. See Yung-Chung Kim, *Women of Korea*, 104–106.

11. For the complex traditional wedding procedures, see Deuchler, *The Confucian Transformation of Korea*, 252–257.

12. See Deuchler, *The Confucian Transformation of Korea*, 241. The practice was already in place among commoners during the late Koryŏ period (918–1392), when parents of young daughters married them off to dodge the court's draft of virgins to be sent as part of the regular tribute to the Yuan dynasty (1273–1368). See also Yung-Chung Kim, *Women of Korea*, 93–94.

13. The legal age for marriage was fourteen for girls and fifteen for boys as calculated by the lunar calendar, which means they were actually a mere thirteen or fourteen by our modern understanding. See Yung-Chung Kim, *Women of Korea*, 92.

14. Yung-Chung Kim, *Women of Korea*, 94.

early was to avoid the unpredictable, nationwide ban on marriage, when the royal matrimonial processes of choosing consorts were underway.[15]

The dictum "ch'ilgŏ chiak" (seven vices for which wives were expelled) spelled out a set of women's personal traits and corporeal conditions as grounds for annulment of marriage—a one-sided prerogative given only to husbands. Listed in order of importance, these were disobedience to parents-in-law, barrenness, adultery, jealousy, larceny, talkativeness, and hereditary disease.[16]

"Disobedience to parents-in-law" underlined the absolute power of in-laws over a daughter-in-law's success or failure in marriage. The newly inducted daughter-in-law was most vulnerable in her husband's home. An outsider severed from her natal family and transplanted to the foreign culture and environment of her in-laws' household, the young bride (often in her teens) was situated in a liminal, defenseless condition. Particularly prickly and distressing for the daughter-in-law was the often demanding, hostile, and even abusive mother-in-law, who policed the younger charge with authority based on her own difficult experience in the stringent patriarchal regimen of her husband's household.[17] This politics of dominance and subordination among women, and the ensuing intergenerational tension and conflicts in the domestic realm,

---

15. A temporary marriage ban on *yangban* classes was announced when the court was selecting a consort for its royal males. To elude the draft into the onerous selection procedures, some noble families married their daughters early. See Yung-Chung Kim, *Women of Korea*, 92–93. See also Deuchler, *The Confucian Transformation of Korea*, 243; Kim Tu-hŏn, *Han'guk kajok chedo yŏn'gu* [Study on Korean family systems] (Seoul: Sŏul Taehakkyo Ch'ulp'anbu, 1969; 1989), 456; 459–468.

16. The "seven vices" was counterbalanced by the "sambulgŏ" (three conditions for disallowing divorce) provision. It specified the circumstances under which a husband could not send away his wife: when she completed a three-year mourning for his parents; when she contributed to the prosperity of her husband's household; and when she had no place to return. Although these principles seemingly upheld humanitarian and more civilized treatment of wives, they were fundamentally based on a woman's value in terms of her contribution to the maintenance of her husband's lineage.

17. See Deuchler, *The Confucian Transformation of Korea*, 261–262. The infamous animosity and adversarial relationship between mother-in-law and daughter-in-law was a pervasive phenomenon and Korean proverbs are legion in commenting on it. See Helen Rose Tieszen, "Korean Proverbs about Women," in *Virtues in Conflict*, 55–60.

produced a peculiar, psychological subculture within the women's insulated inner quarters.[18]

Woman's "barrenness" became an obsessive concern in Chosŏn, where the primary purpose of marriage was to produce male children for the unbroken preservation of patrilineage.[19] A wife had to produce male heir(s), and only when she bore a son(s) did a wife's position in her husband's household become secure,[20] and she could even wield influence and power through her son(s).[21] This in turn brought about preference for male progenies. In some cases, the infertile wife of the *yangban* classes was counseled to urge her husband to take a secondary wife and even went out of her way to find her own replacement.[22] In fact, "A woman who did not produce a son was considered a nonperson."[23] Essentially, a woman's body was considered a biological and material instrument to serve patrilineal interests. The adoption practice in traditional Korea, which allowed only sons to assume the headship of an heirless family within the same male clan, stems from this obligation to maintain the male line.[24]

Condemnation of "adultery" was applied to women only. A husband could have extramarital affairs with little censure, tangentially allowing male sexual license and concubinage. In such cases, the wife had to resign herself to the situation without exhibiting "jealousy" toward her rivals—all for the sake of maintaining her family's peace.[25] The restriction on "talkativeness" was a mechanism to silence women literally and figuratively. Women's verbal-

---

18. For a detailed study of this topic, see Yi Kwang-gyu, "Pugye kajok esŏ ŭi kobu kwan'gye" [Mother-in-law and daughter-in-law relationship in the patriarchal family], in his *Han'guk kajok ŭi sahoe illyuhak* [Social anthropology of the Korean family] (Seoul: Jimmundang, 1998), 97–114.

19. See Deuchler, *The Confucian Transformation of Korea*, 236–237.

20. Ibid., 263.

21. On this topic of "mother power," see Haejoang Cho, "Male Dominance and Mother Power: The Two Sides of Confucian Patriarchy in Korea," in *Confucianism and the Family*, ed. Walter H. Slote and George A. De Vos (Albany: State University of New York, 1998), 187–207.

22. See Deuchler, "Propagating Female Virtues in Chosŏn Korea," 155.

23. See Haejoang Cho, "Male Dominance and Mother Power," 193.

24. Yung-Chung Kim, *Women of Korea*, 101.

25. Both concubine and her offspring were looked down upon and suffered discrimination, alienation, and even hostility from the primary wife and other members of the household and community.

ization of their desires and thoughts would cause nothing but disruption of family orderliness and unity. Thus, women were made
to suppress themselves and, often, each other, and such self-
censorship curtailed women's development of critical thinking,
ability for self-expression, and confidence in their own thought
and emotions.

A married daughter was known as *ch'ulga oein* (once married, an
outsider) to her natal family, and her failure in marriage ending in
divorce meant unforgivable and often inconceivable disgrace and
humiliation to the woman's natal family. A divorced woman could
even be rejected by her own kinfolk.[26] Actual divorce was rare in
Chosŏn; however, the threat of divorce under these precepts puts
pressure on a married woman to make her marriage work to avoid
such a personal disaster.

Last but not least was the taboo of widow's remarriage; "yŏja
pulgyŏng ibu" (women do not serve two husbands) meant that marriage was a once-in-a-lifetime affair for women.[27] A widow's remarriage would presumably mix and therefore confuse different male
bloodlines, and the ban thus would safeguard the purity of her
dead husband's patrilineage.[28] During the Chosŏn period, as a strat-
agem to bolster this prohibition, sons of remarried widows were
denied the opportunity to take the government examination, robbing them of prospects for making a career in officialdom.[29] No
mother concerned about her son's future would dare violate this
injunction, and it effectively pressured widows to remain loyal to
their deceased husbands' lineage until their own death.[30] The remarriage ban was particularly bleak and punishing for young,

---

26. See Haejoang Cho, "Male Dominance and Mother Power," 196.

27. The prohibition of remarriage of widows was legally institutionalized
during the reign of King Sŏngjong with the official proclamation of the *Kyŏngguk
taejŏn*, the supreme legal canon of the Chosŏn dynasty, in 1485. This idea of woman's loyalty to her husband, either living or dead, was a transfer to the domestic-
gender realm of the ideal of a subject's (male) serving only one master in the
politico-public arena. See Deuchler, "Propagating Female Virtues in Chosŏn
Korea," 160.

28. Yi Pae-yong, "Chosŏn sidae yugyojŏk saenghwal munhwa wa yŏsŏng ŭi
chiwi" [Confucian life culture and women's status during the Chosŏn period],
Minjok kwa munhwa 9 (2000): 28.

29. Yung-Chung Kim, *Women of Korea*, 98.

30. Some flexibility was allowed for widows of commoner classes to remarry
without legal sanction. See Yung-Chung Kim, *Women of Korea*, 99.

childless widows, because it left them without maternal identity and the insurance of offspring's filial support later in life. What's more, there was a social stigma attached to widowhood, even though their husbands' passing was no fault of theirs. By contrast, widowers were never tied down by such rules, and in fact, they were encouraged and usually expected to remarry. Their male lines could thus continue, and the remarried men would enjoy their domestic stability and creature comforts without interruption.

It has been observed that during the Chosŏn period, women could exercise a measure of control over their sons as their backers and advisors in the domestic realm.[31] Some highborn women also garnered respect and solidified their familial position for their work behind the scenes (*naejo*; inside help) for the sake of their husbands' success as scholars or officials.[32] Yet "mother power" and "wife power" were acquired by women's self-sacrificial, instrumental support of their sons and husbands and through their proxy accessibility to the Confucian, male power sources. In this sense, both "mother power" and "wife power" were vicariously obtained female spheres of influence within the domestic boundaries, not a meritorious distinction for or acknowledgment of their personal achievements in the public arena through cultivation of their own intellectual and cultural capital. That is, such familial accolades were bestowed upon women as the result of mobilizing their personal assets for the maintenance and perpetuation of patrilineal familism. They did little to remove the fundamental structure of inner/outer gender bifurcation and role specifications and the concomitant women's subsidiary significance in Chosŏn Confucian culture and society.[33]

---

31. See Haejoang Cho, "Male Dominance and Mother Power," 187–207. Cho observed that "mother power may be the most secure source of power for women under the patriarchal system," but that women "have much more difficulty in achieving independence from their sons and establishing their identity as autonomous individuals." Cho also commented that maternal devotion to sons was the mother's "survival strategy" in a patriarchal society, and "seems to have been based on the self-help principle of the blood-related kinship unit rather than expanding the public sphere." See Cho, "Male Dominance and Mother Power," 200, 202.

32. See Deuchler, "Propagating Female Virtues in Chosŏn Korea," 152; Haejoang Cho, "Male Dominance and Mother Power," 197–198.

33. On this topic, see Hyaeweol Choi, *Gender and Mission Encounters in Korea: New Women, Old Ways* (Berkeley: University of California Press, 2009), 40–41.

It is true that a handful of *yangban* women of Chosŏn *did* diverge from Confucian gender parameters and were lauded for their artistic and literary accomplishments.[34] In addition, a number of Chosŏn elite women ventured into a wide range of genres and produced works in Chinese such as philosophical treatises, critical essays, letters, and poetry.[35] Even *kisaeng* (lower-class women entertainers) contributed their poems to the repertory of premodern Korean literature.[36] In the context of Chosŏn regular practice in the intellec-

---

34. The most celebrated were Sin Saimdang (1504–1551), Hŏ Nansŏrhŏn (1563–1589), and Hyegyŏnggung Hong Ssi (1735–1815). Sin Saimdang, the mother of the eminent Neo-Confucian scholar Yi I (1538–1584; pen name, Yulgok), is best known for her brush paintings. Hŏ Nansŏrhŏn wrote a large number of poems in both Korean and Chinese but before her death she burned most of them in fear of posterity's criticism that such creative activities were unbecoming of women. Her extant poems were collected by her younger brother, Hŏ Kyun (1569–1618), the author of *Hong Kil-dong chŏn* (Tale of Hong Kil-dong), and were first published in China. Hyegyŏnggung Hong Ssi (Lady Hyegyŏng), consort of the Crown Prince Changhŏn (1735–1762; also known as Crown Prince Sado), and the mother of King Chŏngjo (r. 1776–1800), wrote her autobiography, *Hanjungnok* (1795–1805), detailing court politics and the circumstances of her husband's death. See Kim Yong-suk, *Chosŏnjo yŏryu munhak yŏn'gu* [Study of women's literature during the Chosŏn dynasty], rev. and enlarged (Seoul: Yejin Sŏgwan, 1990), 158–253; 388–405. See also Yi Sŏng-mi, "Sin Saimdang: The Foremost Woman Painter of the Chosŏn Dynasty," in *Creative Women of Korea*, ed. Young-Key Kim-Renaud, 58–77; Kichung Kim, "Hŏ Nansŏrhŏn and 'Shakespeare's Sister,'" in *Creative Women of Korea*, 78–95; and JaHyun Kim Haboush, "Private Memory and Public History: The Memoirs of Lady Hyegyŏng and Testimonial Literature," in *Creative Women of Korea*, 122–141.

35. Im Yunjidang (1721–1793) was foremost among these women writers, especially noted for her tracts on Neo-Confucianism. See Deuchler, "Female Virtues in Chosŏn Korea," 163–164. On works by this group of women, see Kim Kyŏng-mi, "18segi yangban yŏsŏng ŭi kŭlssugi ŭi ch'ŭng'wi wa kŭ ŭimi" [Levels of writings by upper-class women of the 18th century and their significance], *Han'guk kojŏn munhak yŏn'gu* 11 (2005): 5–50; Mun Hŭi-sun, "Hosŏ chiyŏk yŏsŏng hanmunhak ŭi sajŏk chŏngae" [Historical development of literature in Chinese by women of Ch'ungch'ŏng province areas], *Han'guk hanmunhak yŏn'gu* 39 (2007): 85–116; Yi Hye-sun, *Chosŏnjo hugi yŏsŏng chisŏngsa* [Intellectual history of women in the late Chosŏn dynasty] (Seoul: Ihwa Yŏja Taehakkyo Ch'ulp'anbu, 2007). For Chosŏn women's work in the poetry genre, see Hye-sun Yi, *The Poetic World of Classic Korean Women Writer*, trans. Won-Jae Hur (Seoul: Ewha Womans University Press, 2005).

36. The most saluted is Hwang Chin-i (ca. 1520–1560). See Kim Yong-suk, *Chosŏnjo yŏryu munhak yŏn'gu*, 408–430. See also Kevin O'Rourke, "Demythologizing Hwang Chini," in *Creative Women of Korea*, ed. Young-Key Kim-Renaud, 96–121.

tual, literary, and academic realms, which discouraged and excluded women's participation, these select instances of women were truly outstanding and incomparable, and therefore, exceptional—not commonplace or large in number.[37]

All told, traditional Korean women, labeled and treated as the "Other" by Confucianism, faithfully internalized the cult of womanly respectability and prescribed to patriarchally ordained gender standards, values, roles—the very ways they were marginalized. Their lifelong goal was to become paragons of the "virtuous woman" and custodians of Confucian-idealized feminine qualities, and to ensure their female descendants followed in their footsteps. With all options outside the home practically closed off to them, the only viable means for women to validate their worth was success as daughters-in-law, wives, and mothers—possible only through their limitless patience, silence, self-negation, prudence, obedience, stoic fortitude, and fertility in producing male heirs. Some unidentified, high-born women took out their personal plights and agonies in poetic forms,[38] but the majority of Chosŏn women lived up to these high standards of personal integrity, inner strengths, even spiritual nobility, and such social gender expectations and conditions continued nearly unaltered up to the mid-nineteenth century.[39]

---

37. It is revealing that some of them made known the difficulties they faced in their venture into the male arena of cultured and scholarly enterprises by circumventing the gender boundaries and obstacles imposed on them by their society and culture. For instance, Hŏ Nansŏrhŏn is known to have expressed her three regrets: on being born in Chosŏn; being a woman; and being a wife of her husband. See Kim Yong-suk, *Chosŏnjo yŏryu munhak yŏn'gu*, 400. In the meantime, Im Yunjidang "is said to have regretted that she had not been born a man." See Deuchler, "Propagating Female Virtues in Chosŏn Korea," 164.

38. See Kichung Kim, *An Introduction to Classical Korean Literature: From 'Hyangga' to 'P'ansori'* (Armonk, NY: M.E. Sharpe, 1996), 127–136.

39. Confucian gender regulations and regimens on Chosŏn women are known to have become far stricter and more conservative during the seventeenth century in the wake of the Japanese invasions from 1592 to 1598. This development stemmed from the Chosŏn court's effort to cope with the devastating aftermath of the foreign aggression by restoring and stabilizing the social and moral order through reinforcement of *yangban* family institutions and values, including women's gender principles and precepts. Especially, the implementation of the primogeniture system during this period further diminished women's social status and standing. See Han'guk Yŏsŏng Yŏn'guso Yŏsŏngsa Yŏn'gusil, *Uri yŏsŏng ŭi yŏksa* [History of Korean women] (Seoul: Ch'ŏngnyŏnsa, 1999; 2006), 227–228.

CHALLENGES TO TRADITIONAL GENDER IDEOLOGIES

The Chosŏn Confucian gender order began to be seriously challenged and destabilized from the mid-1800s and went through wide-ranging, fundamental revisions, with enduring ramifications on Korean women's historically gendered existence. The forces that brought these changes were closely synchronized with international geopolitical developments. The Chosŏn government, facing increasing threats and encroachments from imperialistic, colonial ambitions of world superpowers—most ominously Japan—was compelled to reenvision and restructure itself through numerous paradigm shifts and through the construction of a new national identity, political directions, and administrative policies and strategies. In this national project of reinvention, the "woman question" figured notably, and some of its major watershed moments are illustrated in the following, with some generalization and simplification.

The first stirring of pro-woman ideas in Chosŏn was manifested in Tonghak (Eastern Learning; also called Ch'ŏndogyo, the Religon of Heavenly Way), founded by Ch'ŏe Ch-u (1824–1864).[40] Based on the principle of the equality of all human beings, the gist of the indigenous religion lay in its nationalistic proposal for sociopolitical reform of Chosŏn to strengthen itself and thereby to fend off foreign aggression. It proclaimed that such national goal could only be achieved through the eradication of Confucian dominance, its deleterious ideologies and discriminatory practices, and the government's corruption. The most ingenious, bold, and inciting aspect of the Tonghak agenda included demands for elimination of social classes, remarriage of widows, and egalitarian spousal relationships, among others.[41] Such liberating messages appealed to those at the lower rungs of Chosŏn society and grew into a widespread grassroots movement. And the Tonghak concept of women represented the earliest revision of and challenge to the Confucian oppressive definition of Korean women.

---

40. For brief summary of Tonghak, see Kyung Moon Hwang, *A History of Korea: An Episodic Narrative* (New York: Palgrave, 2010), 121-123.

41. See Yung-Hee Kim, "Under the Mandate of Nationalism: Development of Feminist Enterprises in Modern Korea, 1860–1910," *Journal of Women's History* 7 (1995): 121–122.

By the late nineteenth century, Chosŏn abandoned its age-old isolationism and China-centrism and opened diplomatic and trade relationships with Western industrialized nations and Japan.[42] To obtain new politico-social and cultural information useful for catching up with rapidly evolving world affairs and for national strengthening and progress, the court dispatched overseas missions comprised of young elites.[43] As the leaders of these missions upon their return home launched enlightenment movements in the 1880s, new gender ideas, along with knowledge about Western social customs, cultural activities, modes of thought, and world views, trickled into Chosŏn.[44]

The Kabo Reform (1894–1896), the direct outcome of the Tonghak revolt,[45] was intended to reorganize Chosŏn into a modern nation-state, and pronounced, among other measures, the prohibition of early marriage and the right of widows to remarry.[46] It marked the

---

42. Korea was forced to conclude a trade treaty with Japan in 1876, which was followed by a series of so-called amity treaties with Western countries: the United States (1882), Great Britain (1883), Germany (1884), Italy (1884), Russia (1884), and France (1886). See Carter J. Eckert et al., *Korea Old and New: A History* (Seoul: Ilchokak, 1990), 205–208. Korea most frequently sent missions to Japan: in 1876, 1880, 1881, and 1882; the first Korean envoy to the United States was dispatched in 1883.

43. They were the leaders of "Kaehwadang" (Progressive Party), which included Kim Ok-kyun (1851–1894), Yu Kil-chun (1856–1914), Pak Yŏng-hyo (1861–1939), Yun Ch'i-ho (1865–1945), and Sŏ Chae-p'il (1866–1951). See Yi Kwang-nin, *Han'guk kaehwa sasang yŏn'gu* [Study of Korean enlightenment thought] (Seoul: Ilchogak, 1979; 1981), 50–51; 100–101. After the Kaehwadang's failed coup in 1884, its members dispersed abroad.

44. One of the first Korean books introducing Western cultures was *Sŏyu kyŏnmun* (Records of a journey through the West) by Yu Kil-chun, a member of the first Korean diplomatic mission to the United States in 1883. The book documents the author's observations of America and then other Western countries during his tour of Europe prior to his return home in 1885. Among its many topics are the manners and customs of Western women. Yu called attention to the higher status women enjoyed in the West, attributing this to the education Western women received. *Sŏyu kyŏnmun* was published in Japan 1895. See Yi Kwang-nin, *Han'guk kaehwa sasang yŏn'gu*, 54–56.

45. For details of the interrelationship between the Kabo Reform and Tonghak, see Carter J. Eckert et al., *Korea Old and New*, 214–222.

46. The Reform was undertaken under pressure from Japan—the victor in the Sino-Japanese War (1894–1895). Major components of the Reform included the establishment of a constitutional monarchy, implementation of universal education to replace the traditional civil examination system available only to the sons of nobility, elimination of the class system, abolition of slavery, provision of oppor-

first official delegitimization and deregulation in Chosŏn history of Confucian gender rules, now deemed uncivilized remnants of an old order. Theoretically, women now could have matrimonial autonomy and freedom from patri-centered body politics.

The publication of Korea's first vernacular newspaper, *Tongnip sinmun* (The Independent Newspaper; 1896–1899),[47] was another landmark in Korean woman's gender history. The newspaper put as its central priority the eradication of the Confucian oppression of women, equating it with slavery,[48] and its pages consistently emphasized women's formal education at institutionalized schools as the best means of attaining this goal.[49] Such a pro-woman position was amplified in the following editorial:

> Women's education means a reinstatement of tens of thousands of women, half of our population, from the state of lost objects to human beings. From now on, women will no longer be mistreated, because they will recover their rights. Children will obtain loving teachers and men will acquire beautiful friends whose friendship will last over a hundred years. And Korea will naturally develop into a civilized country.[50]

Unmistakable in this vision is a seminal form of "hyŏnmo yangch'ŏ" (wise mother, good wife), which idealizes Korean woman as an ef-

---

tunities for commoners to participate in the legislative process, prohibition of early marriage, and permission for widows to remarry. Subsequently, in 1897, Chosŏn changed its name to "Taehan Cheguk" (Taehan or Korean Empire). For details on the Reform, see Young I. Lew, "Korean-Japanese Politics Behind the Kabo-Ŭlmi Reform Movement, 1894 to 1896," *Journal of Korean Studies* 3 (1981): 39–81.

47. Sŏ Chae-p'il (1864–1951), also known as Philip Jaisohn, was the newspaper's publisher and editor. Sŏ fled to Japan when the Kaehwadang coup failed in 1884. Thereafter, he went to the United States, where he earned a medical degree from Columbia Medical College in Washington, D.C. (now the Medical College of George Washington University) in 1893. He was the first Korean to obtain U.S. citizenship (1890). Urged by his former Kaehwadang colleagues who worked for the Kabo Reform, he returned to Korea in 1895. Sŏ returned to the United States in May 1898 under pressure from the Korean government due to his sharp criticism of its ineptitude. Thereafter, the editorship of *Tongnip sinmun* passed to Yun Ch'i-ho. See Yi Kwang-nin, *Han'guk kaehwa sasang yŏn'gu*, 103–108; 148; 158–159.

48. *Tongnip sinmun*, Sept. 13, 1898.

49. *Tongnip sinmun*, Sept. 5, 1896.

50. *Tongnip sinmun*, May 26, 1899.

fective educator of her children and as a congenial companion of her husband.[51] This projection of a modern-minted, nuclear home with newfangled democratic familial relations and ethos virtually deconstructed the Chosŏn extended family system—a far cry from traditional Confucian gender ideologies such as "namjon yŏbi" (man superior, woman inferior), "yŏp'il chongbu" (wife must follow husband), and "puch'ang pusu" (husband speaks, wife concurs).

In this educational pitch for women we also detect a strain of statism—a nation-centered ideology. It suggests that the ultimate objective of women's education is to produce state-serving citizens who uphold the national interest as their priority in life. In other words, women were co-opted into the communal, political identity of the nation. The nation-driven gender ideology was to be invoked and reiterated as an uppermost point of reference in woman-related discourses in the *Tongnip sinmun* and left an inerasable imprint on those that followed suit throughout the following colonial period.[52]

Chiming with the spirit of the Kabo Reform, the *Tongnip sinmun* never ceased to advocate the abolition of the custom of early, arranged marriage,[53] concubinage, and prostitution,[54] and the allowance of remarriage for widows.[55] The Independence Club, an organization closely associated with the *Tongnip sinmun*, shored up the reform propositions and feminist drive undertaken by the newspaper.[56] The combined initiatives by the *Tongnip sinmun* and the

---

51. This "hyŏnmo yangch'ŏ" concept is much in line with the Japanese "ryōsai kenbo" (good wife, wise mother in Japanese) ideal promoted by such Meiji Enlightenment leaders as Iwamoto Zenji (or Iwamoto Yoshiharu; 1863–1942). For the evolution of the notion in Japan, see Sharon L. Sievers, *Flowers in Salt: The Beginnings of Feminist Consciousness in Modern Japan* (Stanford, CA: Stanford University Press, 1983), 106–113.

52. See Yung-Hee Kim, "Under the Mandate of Nationalism," 126–127, 133.

53. *Tongnip sinmun*, Feb. 12, 1898; June 20, 1898; Oct. 7, 1899.

54. *Tongnip sinmun*, Feb. 12, 1898.

55. *Tongnip sinmun*, March 15, 1899.

56. The Independence Club was established on July 2, 1896, with Sŏ Chae-p'il as its advisor. Members included Yun Ch'i-ho, Namkung Ŏk (1863–1959), and Yi Sang-jae (1850–1927). The Club, essentially a social pressure group, often organized mass rallies for popular rights movements to awaken Korean citizens to their social responsibilities and civic duties. It also sponsored a public forum on wide-ranging topics, including gender questions, family reforms, and women's education. Korean women were frequently invited to participate in such meet-

Independence Club represented Korea's first public endeavor to enlist women as integral and indispensable constituents of their country in an impending political crisis by politicizing gender issues
and elevating them to national dimensions.

NEW FICTIONAL CONSTRUCTS OF GENDER AND WOMAN

In 1905, at the conclusion of the Russo-Japanese War (1904–1905),
Korea became a Japanese protectorate and lost diplomatic sovereignty vis-à-vis foreign countries with the concomitant diminution
and crippling of government authority in political, military, economic and other spheres.[57] This national calamity, however, gener-
ated unforeseen waves of patriotic zeal and activities on a national
scale from the elites to the grassroots. The range of such undertak-
ings included guerilla wars by Righteous Armies;[58] a national campaign to repay debts to Japan and to buy Korean-made products;
the formation of civil, educational, and cultural organizations to
stimulate Koreans' political and social consciousness; the establishment of modern schools for boys and girls; an intensification of
scholarly research on the Korean language and *han'gŭl*; and the proliferation of translations of histories of foreign countries or biographies of their leaders, to name but a few.[59]

---

ings. For a detailed study in English on the Independence Club, see Vipan Chandra, *Imperialism, Resistance, and Reform in Late Nineteenth-Century Korea: Enlightenment and the Independence Club* (Berkeley: University of California, Institute of East
Asian Studies, Center for Korean Studies, 1988).

57. The Treaty of Portsmouth, concluded after Japan's victory in the Russo-
Japanese War (1904–1905), forced Russia to vouchsafe Japan's uncontested control
over matters related to Korea. See Eckert et al., *Korea Old and New*, 236–239.

58. Righteous Armies is a common translation of the Korean word *ŭibyŏng*, a
kind of partisan militia active against the Japanese in Korea, Manchuria, and Si-
beria. Especially after the dissolution of the Korean army in 1907, hundreds of
these guerilla bands, made up largely of peasants and former soldiers, battled
with the Japanese army and police.

59. See Eckert et al., *Korea Old and New*, 241–253. Some of these translations
included short biographical accounts of legendary Western women such as Joan
of Arc (1412–1431) and Marie-Jeanne Roland (1754–1793), both published in 1907.
See Kim Pyŏng-ch'ŏl, *Han'guk kŭndae pŏnyŏk munhaksa yŏn'gu* [Historical study on
translations of literature in modern Korea] (Seoul: Ŭllyu Munhwasa, 1975), 231–
234, 245.

Amidst this whirlpool of popular movements, a modern literary genre called *sinsosŏl* (new novel) appeared.[60] A transitional genre between the classical novel and modern fiction, *sinsosŏl* began with the publication of *Hyŏl ŭi nu* (Tears of Blood; 1906) by Yi In-jik (1862–1916), the representative writer in the field, and flourished well into the mid-1910s.[61] The main themes of *sinsosŏl* encompassed critiques of the class system, abuse of power by the upper classes, traditional familial arrangements, the detrimental relationship between mother-in-law and daughter-in-law, the evils of concubinage, and harmful superstitious practices, while advocating the legitimacy of widows' remarriage.

The major distinction of *sinsosŏl* lies in its role as forerunner in promoting new views on gender questions, particularly women's education and roles in contemporary Korean society. The best-known *sinsosŏl*, such as *Hyŏl ŭi nu*, *Moranbyŏng* (The peony screen; 1911) by Yi Hae-jo (1869-1927), and *Ch'uwŏlsaek* (Color of the autumn moon; 1912) by Ch'oe Ch'an-sik (1881–1951) put young female characters at the center of the narrative drama. These women, after successfully overcoming a series of complicated and all but insurmountable trials and tribulations—often punctuated with coincidences arbitrarily constructed by the authors—become shining examples of contributory national citizens, usually by means of education abroad in Japan or the United States.[62] These female protagonists function as metaphors for the transformation of Chosŏn women by their transnational and transcultural education into ideal patriotic women—a radical deviation from traditional Korean images of women. In this sense, the role of *sinsosŏl* in constructing new gender concepts and prototypes of the "new woman," and bringing them into public view in sustained novelistic format and style, is unmistakable.

---

60. See Kwŏn Yŏng-min, "Sinsosŏl ŭi munhaksa chŏk sŏnggyŏk chaeron" [Review of the literary and historical character of the new novel], *Inmunhak yŏn'gu* 17 (2010): 5–40.

61. All written by male writers, *sinsosŏl* were at first serialized in newspapers and magazines, and some were later published in book form. On the *sinsosŏl* genre, see Ji-Eun Lee, *Women Pre-scripted: Forging Modern Roles Through Korean Print* (Honolulu: University of Hawai'i Press, 2015), 36–57.

62. See Chŏng Hye-yŏng, "Sinsosŏl kwa oeguk yuhak munje—Yi In-jik ŭi 'Hyŏl ŭi nu' rŭl chungsim ŭro" [New novel and the question of study abroad—focusing on Yi In-jik's *Hyŏl ŭi nu*], *Hyŏndae sosŏl yŏn'gu* 20 (2003): 193–213.

In 1910 the Taehan Cheguk (Great Korean Empire) was annexed by Japan and lost its political sovereignty. The subsequent semi-military rule by the Japanese Government-General implemented wide-ranging colonial policies to maintain tight control over its new colony: banning political organizations and the right of assembly; enforcing Japanese as the first language and Korean as the second; controlling Korean school curriculum and textbooks in public schools; reinforcing press and publication censorship (already in place since 1907); surveilling Korean intellectuals; discontinuing Korean newspapers and replacing them with the Korean-language *Maeil sinbo* (Daily newspaper; 1910–1945), the organ of the Government-General's office, to name a few.[63]

Under such dispiriting colonial conditions, feminist stirrings seminally manifested in the *sinsosŏl* genre received masterly elaboration in Yi Kwang-su's (1892–1950) *Mujŏng* (The heartless; 1917),[64] the first full-fledged modern Korean novel and an explosive best-seller among its young readers.[65] The group of characters in *Mujŏng*, entangled in complicated interpersonal and social relationships, represents Yi's in-depth and expansive exploration of the interwoven issues of individual subjectivity and decision-making, gender equity, ideal love and marriage, women's education, elites' social and communal obligations, and ultimately, the reconstruction of Korean society and citizenry through Western-inspired education and knowledge.

The authorial thematic objective is epitomized in the female protagonist's transformation from a Confucian-indoctrinated, filial young daughter and a sexually violated *kisaeng* to a modern woman awakened to a new self-identity, progressive gender relations, and novel purposes in life.[66] The conclusion of *Mujŏng* salutes with great fanfare the departure of all its principal characters for their studies

63. See Eckert, *Korea Old and New*, 254–264.

64. See Yi Tong-ha. "*Hyŏl ŭi nu wa Mujŏng ŭi pigyo koch'al*" [Comparative study of *Hyŏl ŭi nu* and *Mujŏng*], *Kwanak ŏmun yŏn'gu* 8 (1983): 357–370.

65. The novel was serialized in 126 installments from January 1 to June 14, 1917, in the *Maeil sinbo*. At the time, Yi Kwang-su was a philosophy major at Waseda University in Tokyo. See Ann Sung-hi Lee, *Yi Kwang-su and Modern Korean Literature* (Ithaca, NY: East Asia Program, Cornell University, 2005), 21.

66. See Yung-Hee Kim, "Re-visioning Gender and Womanhood in Colonial Korea: Yi Kwang-su's *Mujŏng* (The heartless)," *The Review of Korean Studies* 6, no. 1 (June 2003): 187–218.

abroad—to Japan and even Europe—to pursue their chosen fields of specialization, with the determination to dedicate themselves, upon their return home, to the enlightenment of the Korean masses. Taken as a whole, the fictional cast of *Mujŏng* is a mouthpiece for Yi's liberal gender views and nationalistic visions, which are enhanced by his literary dexterity in probing the psychological complexities of his characters, subsets of secondary characters from different social and educational backgrounds, narrative plot orchestration, use of travel motifs, and rendering of nature's symbolic bearing on human affairs, among other issues.

Yi Kwang-su furthered his challenge of Confucian conventions through his treatises critical of early marriage customs, asymmetrical gender relations, hierarchical arrangement in familial relationships, and abuse of parental authority over children.[67] Yi's pioneering revisionist writings struck a sympathetic chord in the hearts of his young contemporaries, and he soared as their cultural and social idol. Additionally, these contentious topics were reprocessed as thematic leitmotifs of fictional narratives by the first generation of modern women writers, who began their literary career from the late 1910s.

WOMEN IN THEIR OWN VOICE

The appearance of the first generation of modern Korean women writers, represented by Kim Myŏng-sun (1896–ca.1951), Na Hye-sŏk (1896–1948), and Kim Wŏn-ju (1896–1971), was a milestone in the Korean cultural, literary, and gender fields. For the first time in Korean history, women entered the public literary arena, traditionally off-limits to them, and there openly expressed their emotions and ideas, transgressing the Confucian injunction on female silence. Collectively, their major works challenged existing Confucian gen-

---

67. Yi Kwang-su's best-known tracts in these categories are: "Chohon ŭi aksŭp" (Evil practices of early marriage), *Maeil sinbo*, Nov. 23–26, 1916, in *Yi Kwang-su chŏnjip* [Collected works of Yi Kwang-su] 1: 499–503 (Seoul: Samjungdang, 1962); "Chosŏn kajŏng ŭi kaehyŏk" (Reforms of Korean family), *Maeil sinbo*, Dec. 14–22, 1916, in *Yi Kwang-su chŏnjip* 1:490–498; "Honin non" (On marriage), *Maeil sinbo*, Nov. 21–30, 1917, in *Yi Kwang-su chŏnjip* 17:138–148; "Chanyŏ chungsim non" (On children-centered ideas), *Ch'ŏngch'un* (no. 15; Sept. 1918), in *Yi Kwang-su chŏnjip* 17:40–47.

der ideologies and parameters, while offering fresh feminist visions and programs for their readers, both male and female, and their society at large caught in the competing claims of traditionalism, nationalism, and colonial modernity. The feminist pioneers were essentially dealing with the "woman question," in a broad sense, within the complex sociopolitical and cultural contexts of early twentieth-century Korea.

"Ŭisim ŭi sonyŏ" (A girl of mystery; 1917), the debut work of Kim Myŏng-sun, ushered in the modern Korean women's writing tradition.[68] This short story is a pointed critique of male-privileging sexual license and concubinage. The theme is conveyed through the suicide of a young *yangban* wife and mother in protest of her husband's chronic sexual escapades.[69] No less groundbreaking was Na Hye-sŏk's first novella, "Kyŏnghŭi" (March 1918).[70] The eponymous heroine Kyŏnghŭi, an art student in a Japanese college, is symbolic of the gender cultural wars between Confucian traditionalism and feminist individualism—a clash over women's identity politics. In the end, Kyŏnghŭi rejects her father's patriarchal command to marry in order to pursue her studies and possibly a professional career. She is a testament to the efficacy of women's modern education, which enables her to repudiate and subvert the patriarchally mandated "three rules of obedience" and the sanctioned feminine track of wife and mother. Her courage and determination to be herself and to follow the dictates of her heart makes her stand out as an original and uplifting paradigm of the modern Korean woman.

---

68. "Ŭisim ŭi sonyŏ" won second place in a literary competition held by the magazine *Ch'ŏngch'un* and was published in its issue no. 11 (November 1917). The contest's judge Yi Kwang-su gave the work his unstinted praise for its realistic approach and avoidance of moralizing. See Yi Kwang-su, "Hyŏnsang sosŏl kosŏn yŏŏn" [On selecting award-winning novels], *Ch'ŏngch'un* (no. 12; March 1918), 99–100.

69. Kim Myŏng-sun herself was the daughter of the concubine of a rich merchant. Kim's suffering and grievance over this haunted her life and her work. For Kim's biography and an English translation and analysis of the story, see Yung-Hee Kim, *Questioning Minds*, 15–23.

70. For Na Hye-sŏk's biography and an English translation and analysis of the story, see Yung-Hee Kim, "Creating New Paradigms of Womanhood in Modern Korean Literature: Na Hye-sŏk's 'Kyŏnghŭi,'" *Korean Studies* 26, no. 1 (2002): 1–86.

In a similar manner, Kim Wŏn-ju's debut short story, "Ŏnŭ sonyŏ ŭi sa" (Death of a girl; 1920),[71] stages a rebellious dissent against Confucian parental tyranny over the matter of the matrimony of children—especially the objectification of daughters as exchangeable goods in the marriage market. The message is communicated through the suicide of the heroine, a high-school graduate, in defiance of her parents' depraved plan to sell her off as a conqubine to a rich libertine in town. The end of the story shows the singular literary skill of the author, who grants the heroine a tool for protest: two suicide notes she leaves behind. One is addressed to her parents in condemnation of their immorality, the other to a newspaper to publicize her unjustifiable victimization. In this sense "Ŏnŭ sonyŏ ŭi sa" makes the personal the social/political, calling for systemic as well ideological changes for oppressed and helpless women. Kim Wŏn-ju's major work, "Chagak" (Awakening; 1926), is another affirmation of the power of modern education, which is exemplified in the transformation of a young, exemplary tradition-bound wife and mother of a toddler son into a self-determining modern woman, after the unexpected painful experience of divorce forced on her by her unfaithful husband.[72] "Awakening" is a heroic feat by a self-awakened woman, who refuses to be defined in terms of wife, mother, or divorcée and becomes the architect of her life with an open, positive, and confident outlook.

Essentially, these narratives by the first generation of modern Korean women writers are constructions of a "new woman" (sinyŏsŏng) who questions and undermines the Confucian-defined female ideals encapsulated in "virtuous woman." They offer a new cultural symbolism for woman as a person capable of subversive acts, including the demand for equitable gender morality, and courageous enough to pursue the risky, untrodden paths toward authentic, modern personhood. The three feminist forerunners wrote new rules of gender and followed their personal truths, while striving to undercut Confucian feminine mandates with an eye toward offering the agency Korean women had long been denied.

71. For Kim Wŏn-ju's biography and an English translation and analysis of the story, see Yung-Hee Kim, "A Critique on Traditional Korean Family Institutions: Kim Wŏnju's 'Death of a Girl,'" *Korean Studies* 23 (1999): 24–42.

72. For an English translation and analytical reading of the story, see Yung-Hee Kim, "From Subservience to Autonomy: Kim Wŏnju's 'Awakening,'" *Korean Studies* 21 (1997): 1–30.

Furthermore, Kim Wŏn-ju, Na Hye-sŏk, and their like-minded friends, who were the best-educated Korean women of their time, organized themselves and became prime movers of a feminist journal, *Sinyŏja* (New woman; March 1920), with Kim serving as its editor.[73] They quickly took advantage of the "cultural policy," implemented in 1920 by the Japanese colonial government in the wake of the nationwide anti-Japanese independence movement in March 1919.[74] One of the measures of the policy most welcomed by Koreans was the relaxation of press and publication laws and rights of assembly. It resulted in a proliferation of newspapers, magazines, journals, and literary circles.[75] The major newspapers, *Chosŏn ilbo* (Chosŏn daily; March 5, 1920) and *Tonga ilbo* (Tonga daily; April 1, 1920), and the leading general culture magazine, *Kaeyŏk* (Creation; June 1920–August 1926), were the products of this period of Korean "renaissance."[76] It is noteworthy that *Sinyŏja* even predated the publication of *Tonga ilbo* and *Kaeyŏk.*[77]

Capitalizing on the affective power of print, *Sinyŏja* provided a channel for circulating woman-centered ideas, information, and literary programs. The press for and by women, the journal helped promote gendered readings of modern women's views, culture, and experience. While constructing a discursive and interpretative community for women, *Sinyŏja* promoted the power of women as thinkers and authors of progressive gender discourse and stimu-

---

73. *Sinyŏja* was financed by Ewha Haktang (Ewha Girls' School), the first girls' school in Korea, which was founded in 1886 in Seoul by an American Methodist missionary, Mary Fitch Scranton (1832–1909). On the establishment of Ewha, see Chŏng Ch'ung-nyang, *Ihwa p'alsimnyŏn sa* [Eighty-year history of Ewha] (Seoul: Idae Ch'ulp'anbu, 1967), 600–608. See also Hyaeweol Choi, *Gender and Mission Encounters in Korea*, 104–107. The founding members of *Sinyŏja*, except for Na Hye-sŏk, were graduates of Ewha's college program: Kim Wŏn-ju (class of 1918); Pak In-dŏk (or Pahk Induk; 1897–1980; class of 1916); Sin Chul-lyŏ (1898–1980; also Syn Julia; class of 1917); and Kim Hwal-lan (1899–1970; also Helen Kim; class of 1918).

74. The policy was designed to appease the pervasive anticolonial sentiments of Koreans and amend the world's negative opinion of Japan's brutal crackdown on peaceful popular demonstrations, but most significantly, to make Japanese colonial administration more effective. See Eckert, *Korea Old and New*, 282.

75. See Michael E. Robinson, *Korea's Twentieth-century Odyssey: A Short History* (Honolulu: University of Hawai'i Press, 2007), 56–59.

76. Eckert, *Korea Old and New*, 283, 286–289.

77. For details on *Sinyŏja*, see Yung-Hee Kim, "In Quest of Modern Womanhood: *Sinyŏja*, A Feminist Journal in Colonial Korea," *Korean Studies* 37 (2013): 44–78.

lated their capacity and competence to express and display that power. It is noteworthy that the title of the journal, *Sinyŏja*, gave currency to the eponym and neologism "*sinyŏja*," new woman.[78]

Sinyŏja had an intercultural and transnational link to *Seitō* (1911–1916), the organ of the Japanese feminist group, Seitō (the Bluestockings), spearheaded by Hiratsuka Raichō (1886–1971).[79] The Sinyŏja group also called themselves "Ch'ŏngt'aphoe" (Korean for "Bluestockings")[80] and proclaimed that the objective of *Sinyŏja* was to provide a platform for Korean women's literary self-expression,[81] echoing the founding purpose of *Seitō*.[82] *Sinyŏja* even voiced its ambition to excavate many buried talents of Korean women and nurture them to become internationally recognized personages on a par with Western literary women luminaries.[83] To lead the way, the *Sinyŏja* group penned fiction (mainly short stories), poetry, essays, feminist tracts, translations, epigrams, proverbs, and even novel

---

78. Chŏn Tae-ung, "'Sinyŏsŏng kwa kŭ munjejŏm" [New women and their issues], *Yŏsŏng munje yŏn'gu* 5–6 (1976): 351.

79. In publishing *Seitō*, Raichō had support from Yosano Akiko (1878–1942), the renowned and innovative woman poet. Regarding an overview of *Seitō*, see Sharon L. Sievers, *Flowers in Salt*, 163–188. On Raichō's life and work, see Hiratsuaka Raichō, *In the Beginning, Woman Was the Sun: The Autobiography of a Japanese Feminist*, trans. with an introduction and notes by Teruko Craig (New York: Columbia University Press, 2006). On Akiko and her work, see Laurel Rasplica Rodd, "Yosano Akiko and the Taishō Debate over the 'New Woman,'" in *Recreating Japanese Women, 1600–1945*, ed. Gail Lee Bernstein (Berkeley: University of California Press, 1991), 175–198.

80. The term "the Bluestockings" originated from the famed British upper-class women's club organized around Mrs. Elizabeth Montagu (ca. 1720–1800). The group met at Mrs. Montagu's salon to promote female friendship and to discuss intellectual and religious matters, publication of literary works, and philanthropic projects. For more on the membership, programs, and activities of the group, see Sylvia Harcstark Myers, *The Bluestocking Circle: Women, Friendship, and the Life of the Mind in Eighteenth-Century England* (Oxford: Clarendon Press, 1990); Nicole Pohl and Betty A. Schellenberg, eds., *Reconsidering the Bluestockings* (San Marino, CA: Huntington Library, 2003).

81. See Yung-Hee Kim, "In Quest of Modern Womanhood," 50.

82. See Hiroko Tomida, *Hiratsuka Raichō and Early Japanese Feminism* (Leiden: Brill, 2004), 144.

83. See Yung-Hee Kim, "In Quest of Modern Womanhood," 50. The decisions on the part of the founders of *Sinyŏja* to strike out on their own, independent of the Japanese example, can be interpreted as their oblique posture of resistance—to disconnect *Sinyŏja* from *Seitō* which was deemed a Japanese colonial cultural product, and to establish its distinctiveness from it.

forms of cartoons (by Na Hye-sŏk), and fashioned a literary cultured communicative space of women's own.[84]

Equally reminiscent of *Seitō*'s various advocacies—gender equality, reform in marriage and family institutions, restoration of
women's human dignity, women's firm self-identity, and women's
professional career—as a means of self-support and economic
independence,[85] what pulses through *Sinyŏja* is its contributors'
deep sense of mission to hold out new feminist thought and suggestions for fellow Korean women and ameliorate their gender-
beleaguered realities. Kim Wŏn-ju's editorials are the journal's most
consistent and spirited propagation of feminist visions and zeal,
whose mantra was the sweeping "reformation" (*kaejo*) of women,
and thereby of Korean society. The key was education. Under her
leadership, *Sinyŏja* mapped out guidelines, strategies, and means for
Korean women to overhaul their lives and develop into authentic
and liberated modern women.

Essentially, *Sinyŏja* was a literary, cultural, and feminist
consciousness-raising, and at a higher level, a nationalistic, campaign. Its express emphasis was on advancing women's initiatives
for self-transformation into modern women equipped with a firm
sense of self and communal responsibility and commitment, and
repurposing them to contribute to the causes beyond the narrow
limits of home. Through publication of the journal, feminist literary
elites concretely exemplified women's capacity to rebuff patriarchal
discourses and deconstruct the traditional gender codes, standards,
and values of Chosŏn society as a whole.

Sinyŏja immediately attracted press recognition.[86] Leading newspapers, especially *Tonga ilbo*, published articles and essays on current gender and sociocultural issues by members of the *Sinyŏja*
group and helped raised their intellectual prestige and social visi-
bility.[87] Furthermore, these women pioneers worked side by side
with male literary and cultural pillars such as Ch'oe Nam-sŏn
(1890–1957) and Yi Kwang-su, and contributed to Korean literature's

---

84. See Yu Chin-wŏl, *Kim Iryŏp ŭi 'Sinyŏja' yŏn'gu* [Study of Kim Iryŏp's *Sinyŏja*]
(Seoul: P'urŭn Sasang, 2006), 29–49.

85. See Dina Lowry, *The Japanese "New Woman": Images of Gender and Modernity*
(New Brunswick, NJ: Rutgers University Press, 2007), 84–93.

86. *Tonga ilbo* (May 4, 1920) was the first to report that the inaugural issue of
Sinyŏja sold two thousand copies.

87. See Yung-Hee Kim, "In Quest of Modern Womanhood," 53; 75 n49–51.

unprecedented departure from premodern literary practices in both form and themes.[88] In this sense, Kim Myŏng-sun, Na Hye-sŏk, Kim Wŏn-ju, and their women colleagues were atypical and at the same time emblematic of their age in the throes of colonial modernity and feminist literary activism. In time, together with the *Sinyŏja* cohort, Kim Myŏng-sun, Na Hye-sŏk, and Kim Wŏn-ju, they became well-known social celebrities and icons of the "new woman." Despite the efforts by its founding members to avoid Japanese control, *Sinyŏja* fell victim to Japanese censorship on a trumped-up charge of "disrupting social order and morality," and folded in June 1920 after only four issues.[89]

"NEW WOMAN" POLEMICS

Such public esteem for Kim Myŏng-sun, Na Hye-sŏk, and Kim Wŏn-ju did not last long. These women writers, as well as *yŏhaksaeng* (girl students), became the target of *sinyŏsŏng* polemics that began to heat up among Korean intellectuals—mostly males—from the mid-1920s and lasted until the end of the colonial period.[90] To a large extent, these unremitting and often convoluted disputes were condemnatory backlashes against educated women. The Korean print media

---

88. Ch'oe Nam-sŏn is known as the first Korean modern poet with his poem, "Hae esŏ sonyŏn ege" (From the sea to the boy), published in the inaugural issue of his own magazine, *Sonyŏn* (Boy; 1908–1911). He dedicated himself to the systematization and preservation of Korean culture through his studies and publications, which ranged from history, folklore, geography, religion to the revival of Korean classical poetry. He founded his own publishing house, and was a trailblazer in the field of periodicals, publishing *Sonyŏn*, *Ch'ŏngch'un* (1914–1918), *Tongmyŏng* (Eastern light; 1922–1923), and others. Ch'oe drafted the text of the March 1919 Korean "Declaration of Independence."

89. Regarding the censorship of *Sinyŏja* and its discontinuation, see Yung-Hee Kim, "In Quest of Modern Womanhood," 53–55.

90. For a detailed study of discourses on this issue, see Jiyoung Suh, "The 'New Woman' and the Topography of Modernity in Colonial Korea," *Korean Studies* 37 (2013): 11–43. See also Kim Su-jin, *Sinyŏsŏng, kŭndae ŭi kwaing: singminji Chosŏn ŭi sinyŏsŏng tamnon kwa jendŏ chŏngch'i, 1920–1934* [New woman, excess of the modern: new woman discourse and gender politics in colonial Korea, 1920–1934] (Seoul: Somyŏng Ch'ulp'an), 450–471; Theodore Jun Yoo, "The 'New Woman' and the Politics of Love, Marriage and Divorce in Colonial Korea," *Gender and History* 17 (2005): 295–324; Hyaeweol Choi, *Gender and Mission Encounters in Korea*, 121–144.

had a field day, sensationalizing, trivializing, and ridiculing *sinyŏsŏng*, and embellished their coverage with mockery and disparagement.[91] It took delight in reporting, accompanied by lurid and salaciously detailed descriptions, on young women's physiques, hairstyles, demeanor and carriage, attire, accessories, and personal accoutrements as markers of their promiscuity, moral degeneration, vanity, and mindlessness.[92] The media's favorite topics were on exchanges of love letters and rendezvous among young students, and on marriage and divorce of the contemporary young Korean elites.[93] Occasionally, concerns over lesbianism among female students were also raised.[94] Especially in the cartoon and causerie sections of popular magazines and newspapers *sinyŏsŏng* were often oversexualized or eroticized as titillating, voyeuristic objects of the male gaze and entertaining spectacles.[95] Public opinion judged *sinyŏsŏng* to be a corrupting influence, scandalous creatures contaminated with unscrupulous flirtation with Western feminist ideas and culture, and

---

91. At the forefront of these controversial exchanges was the magazine *Sinyŏsŏng* (Modern woman; 1923–1934), run by male intellectuals and journalists of the time. *Sinyŏsŏng* was a sister magazine of *Kaebyŏk*, whose writers were mostly socialists. For details about the magazine *Sinyŏsŏng*, see Kim Su-jin, *Sinyŏsŏng, kŭndae ŭi kwaing*, 138–214. See also Ji-Eun Lee, *Women Pre-scripted*, 103–128.

92. *Sinyŏsŏng* (Aug. 1925: 34–53) dedicated a special section to a discussion of women's short hair styles.

93. See Kim Ki-jin, "Kyŏron kwa ihon e taehayŏ" [On marriage and divorce], *Sinyŏsŏng* (May 1924): 30–37. See also Kwŏn Podŭrae, *Yŏnae ŭi sidae: 1920-yŏndae ch'oban ŭi munhwa wa yuhaeng* [Age of love: culture and fad in the early 1920s] (Seoul: Hyŏnsil Munhwa Yŏn'gu, 2003), 123–147.

94. See Hyŏn Nu-yŏng (Hyŏn Ch'ŏl), "Yohaksaeng kwa tongsŏng yŏnae munje: tongsŏng ae esŏ isŏng ae ro chinjŏn hal ttae ŭi wihyŏm" [Girl students and the problem of lesbianism—the danger when their lesbian love advances to heterosexual love], *Sinyŏsŏng* (Dec. 1924): 20–25.

95. See Sŏ Chi-yŏng. *Kyŏngsŏng ŭi modŏn kŏl: sobi, nodong, chendŏ ro pon singminji kŭndae* [Modern girls in Seoul: colonial modernity seen through consumption, labor, gender] (Seoul: Tosŏ Ch'ulp'an Yŏiyŏn, 2013), 79–91. For illustrations and comic strips about new women and their culture, see Sin Myŏng-jik, *Modŏn ppoi kyŏngsŏng ŭl kŏnilda* [Modern boy strolls Seoul streets] (Seoul: Hyŏnsil Munhwa Yŏn'gu, 2003). The best-known illustrator/caricaturist was An Sŏk-chu (1901–1950). A similar phenomenon of media coverage under the rubric of "modan garu" (modern girl) was going on in 1920s Japan. See Barbara Sato, *The New Japanese Woman: Modernity, Media, and Women in Interwar Japan* (Durham, NC: Duke University Press, 2003): 49–77.

specimens of bourgeois decadence.[96] Through their willful violation of long-sanctioned Confucian female virtues and respectability, they were desecrating the nation's tradition and tearing its basic social fabric apart, in total disregard of Korea's woeful colonial reality. These *sinyŏsŏng* were not merely visually offensive but were threats to the preservation of Korean society's moral, cultural, and spiritual integrity under colonial rule. Altogether, "*sinyŏsŏng*" came to represent modern education gone awry, a useless and harmful burden on society that the country could ill afford.

These controversies exploded in conjunction with the debates about the "wise mother, good wife" doctrine, under which young women of the 1920s received their schooling.[97] The slogan was the Japanese official female educational motto, "ryōsai kenbo,"[98] forced on Korean schools by the colonial government.[99] The policy was an integral part of Japan's colonial strategies to mold Korean women into loyal subjects of the Japanese empire.[100] It commanded women to be home-bound, devoted to the roles of caretaker and nurturer of the home, while producing dutiful sons of the Japanese empire as the instruments for fulfilling its imperial ambitions and goals. Korean intellectuals tweaked this idea of "wise mother, good wife" and upheld it as a means of reining in the allegedly out-of-control *sinyŏsŏng* and reshaping them into sober, prudent, and patriotic citizens of Chosŏn, rather than vehicles for serving the Japanese empire.

---

96. Pak Tal-sŏng, "Yosai haksaeng kip'ung: namnyŏ haksaeng ŭi yŏnbyŏng kwa munjil" [Recent trends among students: love-sickness and literary diseases of male and female students], *Sinyŏsŏng* (July 1924): 54–57. See also Sŏ Chi-yŏng, *Kyŏngsŏng ŭi modŏn kŏl*, 100–107; Ŏm Mi-ok, *Yŏhaksaeng kŭndae rŭl mannada: Han'guk kŭndae sosŏl ŭi hyŏngsŏng kwa yŏhaksaeng* [Girl students meet the modern era: formation of modern Korean novel and girl students] (Seoul: Yŏngnak, 2011), 140–142.

97. See Hong Yang-hŭi, "Ilje sigi Chosŏn ŭi yŏsŏng kyoyuk—hyŏnmo yangch'ŏ kyoyuk ŭl chungsim ŭro" [Education of Chosŏn women during the period of Japanese rule—focusing on "wise mother, good wife" education], *Tong Asia munhwa yŏn'gu* 35 (2001): 219–257.

98. The concept of "ryōsai kenbo" was officially adopted as the guideline for women's education in Japan in 1899. See Sievers, *Flowers in Salt*, 112.

99. The first public girls' school in Korea, Hansŏng Girls High School (1908) in Seoul, upheld "wise mother, good wife" as its educational principle. See Pak Yong-ok, *Han'guk yŏsŏng kŭndaehwa ŭi yŏksajŏk maengnak* [Historical contexts of modernization of women in Korea] (Seoul: Chisik Sanŭpsa, 2001), 353.

100. See Suh, "The 'New Woman' and the Topography of Modernity in Colonial Korea," 17–19.

Through the power of public opinion reigning over *sinyŏsŏng*, Korean society would be able to achieve the goal of maintaining and safeguarding Korean national and cultural integrity and thwarting Japan's colonial pressure to collude with its grand, state-run aspirations. In the end, such attacks on *sinyŏsŏng* coerced educated women to retreat into domesticity and neo-familism—a regression to the traditional Confucian gender cast of "virtuous woman."[101]

Kim Myŏng-sun, Na Hye-sŏk, and Kim Wŏn-ju were also affected by this destructive storm of controversy. All of them experienced failed love relationships and some also went through divorce.[102] Largely due to their high social profiles as writers, their iconoclastic ideas, and the nonconforming patterns of their personal lives—unimaginable and extraordinary by any standards in contemporary Korea—the three women unsurprisingly attracted attention from the press and provoked by turns the public's fascination and condemnation.[103] They were regarded as cautionary tales against an unscrupulous bourgeois flirtation with imported Western feminism and individualism. The trio were branded as frivolous social rebels who propagated free love, sexual anarchy, and immorality, intent on un-

---

101. At one level, male Korean intellectuals—traumatized, feminized, and disempowered colonial subjects, who felt threatened by *sinyŏsŏng*—may have found in subjecting those educated women to public ridicule a release from their insecurity and fear of emasculation, and probably gained some measure of self-governing authority and power. See Ŏm Mi-ok, *Yŏhaksaeng kŭndae rŭl mannada*, 282–283, 286.

102. Kim Myŏng-sun, never married, was rumored to have had a number of affairs with male intellectuals during her stay in Korea and Japan. At the end of a series of complicated relationships, she went to Tokyo around 1937 and presumably died there some time in 1951, reduced to poverty and suffering mental illness. As for Kim Wŏn-ju, her first marriage ended in divorce, and her second marriage also failed; finally, she took tonsure and became a Buddhist nun in 1933. Na Hye-sŏk, mother of four young children, was divorced in 1930 on charges of adultery.

103. Some of the most withering and degrading personal attacks were led by the prominent journalist, critic, and frequent contributor to *Sinyŏsŏng*, Kim Ki-jin. See his two articles, "Kim Myŏng-sun ssi e taehan konggaechang" [An open letter to Miss Kim Myŏng-sun], *Sinyŏsŏng* (November 1924): 46–50; and "Kim Wŏn-ju ssi e taehan konggaechang" [An open letter to Miss Kim Wŏn-ju], *Sinyŏsŏng* (November 1924): 51–54. For an up-to-date and fact-based study of the life of Kim Myŏng-sun, which brings to light the prejudicial treatment of her by contemporary Korean intellectuals, see Kim Kyŏng-ae, *Kŭndae kabujangje sahoe ŭi kyunyŏl* [Cracks in modern patriarchal society] (Seoul: P'urŭn Sasang, 2014), 15–127.

dermining the fundamental moral fabric of their country under colonial rule. Even leading male writers such as Yŏm Sang-sŏp (1897–
1963) and Kim Tong-in (1900–1951), who were once these women's
literary associates, joined in the fray and published inflammatory
parodies and caricatures about them.[104] By the mid-1930s, the life stories of Kim Myŏng-sun, Na Hye-sŏk, and Kim Wŏn-ju had blighted
their literary works as well as their personal reputations and career
achievements. Over time, the first generation of Korean women
writers was erased from their society's literary conversation and
collective memory.[105]

PROLETARIAN STRIPES

Into this literary space vacated by the first generation of Korean
women writers entered a handful of women authors: Pak Hwa-sŏng
(1904–1988), Kang Kyŏng-ae (1907–1944), and Paek Sin-ae (1908–
1939). The dominant literary trend of the time was controlled by the
Marxist-oriented KAPF (Korean Artist Proletariat Federation; 1925–
1935) group and its activities, which, buttressed by the establishment of the Korean Communist Party in 1925, prevailed from the
mid-1920s to the mid-1930s.[106] This politically motivated literary

---

104. The best-known examples are: Yŏm Sang-sŏp's *Nŏhŭidŭl ŭn muŏt ŭl
ŏdŏnnŭnya* [What have you gained?], serialized in *Tonga ilbo* (Aug. 27, 1923–Feb. 5,
1924); Kim Tong-in's *Kim Yŏn-sil chŏn* [Biography of Kim Yŏn-sil], *Munjang* (Literary writing; serialized March 1939, May 1939, Feb. 1941). Regarding the ruinous
implications of these male writers' works, see Ch'oe Myŏng-p'yo, "Somun ŭro
kusŏngdoen Kim Myŏng-sun ŭi sam kwa munhak" [Life and literature of Kim
Myŏng-sun constructed on rumors], *Hyŏndae munhak iron yŏn'gu* 30 (2007): 221–245.

105. For research on the "modern woman" phenomon from global perspectives, see The Modern Girl Around the World Research Group, *The Modern Girl
Around the World: Consumption, Modernity, and Globalization* (Durham, NC: Duke
University Press, 2008). It will be an illuminating project to further pursue the
topic of Korean "new woman" issue in light of such research results.

106. On KAPF theories, programs, and movements, see Kimberly Chung,
"Proletarian Sensibilities: The Body Politics of New Tendency Literature (1924–
1927)," *Journal of Korean Studies* 19, no. 1 (Spring 2014): 37–57. See also Sunyoung
Park, *The Proletarian Wave: Literature and Leftist Culture in Colonial Korea, 1910–1945*
(Cambridge, MA: Harvard University Asian Center, 2015); Kwŏn Yŏng-min,
Han'guk kyegŭp munhak undongsa [History of Korean class-literature movement]
(Seoul: Munye Ch'ulp'ansa, 1998). The KAPF was disbanded by order of the Japa-
nese colonial government in 1935.

movement, organized by a cohort of male writers, journalists, and theorists, saw the primary obligation and function of the writer as speaking for the oppressed and disenfranchised and arousing in the reader a proletarian class-consciousness, sense of social justice, and zeal to fight for working-class revolution.[107] Rallying around the slogan of "art for life's sake," the socialist-inspired writers focused on exposing the predicament of the destitute and helpless peasantry and other lower classes, exploited by land-owning classes, capitalists, and even Japanese colonial industrialists.[108] This "poverty literature" was the idiosyncratic product of the period, replete with depictions of the grim realities of the poor and powerless and their struggle against their oppressors, which frequently involved violent and bloody confrontations, and in extreme cases ending in murder.

Pak Hwa-sŏng, Kang Kyŏng-ae, and Paek Sin-ae, known as proletarian sympathizers, produced works consistent with socialists' thematic preoccupations, often adding familial and gendered dimensions to their articulations, and came to be identified as experts in poverty literature. For instance, Pak Hwa-sŏng, at the forefront of the Korean woman's socialist literary movement, spoke up unequivocally for the have-nots and their suffering from her debut short story, "Ch'usŏk chŏnya" (The night before the fall harvest festival; 1925), to "Hasudo kongsa" (Sewage repair work; 1932), "Hongsu chŏnhu" (Before and after the flood; 1934), "Hanggwi" (Ghost of drought; 1935), and "Kohyang ŏmnŭn saramdŭl" (People who lost home; 1936). These works demonstrate the author's overarching effort to give voice to the downtrodden, with a subtextual denunciation of colonial exploitation and its injustice.

Similar thematic orientations and objectives stamp Kang Kyŏng-ae's literary corpus from her debut story, "P'agŭm" (Broken mandolin; 1931) to "Sogŭm" (Salt; 1934), In'gan munje (Human question; 1934), "Moja" (Mother and son; 1935), and "Chihach'on" (Underground village; 1936). Kang's masterpiece, In'gan munje, her longest full-length novel, is an all-encompassing repository of the author's key themes: the sufferings of the lower-classes at the hands of the

---

107. See Kwŏn Yŏng-min, *Han'guk kyegŭp munhak undongsa*, 48–84.

108. Major leaders of the KAPF included Kim Ki-jin (1903–1985), Pak Yŏng-hŭi (1901–1950), Cho Myŏng-hŭi (1894–1938), Yi Ki-yŏng (1895–1984), Han Sŏrya (1900–1976), and Im Hwa (1908–1953).

traditional landowning-class and Japanese capitalists alike; class-based sexual harassment and violence against women; the disintegration of family ties caused by poverty; the need to develop proletarian class-consciousness; the struggle for socialist economic revolution, and other socioeconomic issues.

In tune with Pak and Kang, Paek Sin-ae's narratives are studies of the same inhuman conditions of the poor at the bottom of Korean society. Her representative stories, "Kkŏraei" (Koreans; 1934), "Poksŏni" (Poksŏni; 1934), "Ch'aesaekkyo" (A colored bridge; 1934), "Chŏkpin" (Abject poverty; 1934), "Akpuja" (A long-jawed rich man; 1935) and "Sodokpu" (A small she-devil; 1938) are variations on the same themes, reciting the dire consequences of poverty on those who are most defenseless and incapacitated. Especially prominent in these stories are the author's attention to women's afflictions due to their young age, gender conventions (young brides as victims of early marriage), or even their own altruistic nature (mothers' overprotective sacrifices for their sons).

In terms of their attitude toward sinyŏsŏng, Pak Hwa-sŏng and Kang Kyŏng-ae share common features in that both put across revisionary and alternative views of educated women, much in line with contemporary socialist gender views on educated women. For instance, in "Hasudo kongsa" Pak presents a favorable image of a socially committed young woman, who admires her sweetheart's work for exploited and despondent lower classes and voluntarily follows his path. In "Pit'al" (The slope; 1933) Pak delivers a pronounced and negative message regarding a sinyŏsŏng, one of the major women of the story, who personifies bourgeois, materialistic mentality, egotism, and an over-romanticized idea of love, by making her fall down a steep slope to her death. In her place, Pak extols a Japan-educated college student, who, tutored by a male socialist friend, is enthusiastically committed to work for the needy farmers of her home village. Through this deliberate contrast, Pak shows her new ideal paradigm of sinyŏsŏng constructed from a socialist gender angle. At the same time, Pak reproduces the same Chosŏn gender hierarchical notion that women should follow male leadership, as they are in need of men's guidance and tutelage.[109]

---

109. See Ch'oe Ch'ang-gŭn, "Pak Hwa-sŏng sosŏl ŭi yŏsŏng insik yŏn'gu—'Sinhon yŏhaeng' kwa 'Pit'al' ŭl chungsim ŭro" [Study of Pak Hwa-sŏng's female

In the case of Kang Kyŏng-ae, her works show an evolving and shifting take on *sinyŏsŏng*. In her first novel, *Ŏmŏni wa ttal* (Mother and daughter; 1931–1932), Kang vouches for the positive transfiguration of a *kuyŏsŏng* (tradition-bound woman) into a self-reliant *sinyŏsŏng* through modern education and upholds *sinyŏsŏng's* female bonding and mutual support to counter male negative gender views and spiteful manners toward women. Simultaneously, the narrative scoffs at the frivolity and folly of the educated classes of men of the time, who chase after extramarital or love relationships with *sinyŏsŏng* with no clear understanding of the true meaning of love and its moral consequences.[110]

Kang's "Kŭ yŏja" (The woman; 1932), however, is the author's pejorative study of *sinyŏsŏng*, which, with sarcasm and derision, brings down the heroine—a writer and much sought-after public speaker. The female protagonist is depicted as a snobbish *sinyŏsŏng*, self-absorbed and disconnected from the brutal realities of the populace. She in the end invites her own public humiliation and downfall by the displaced and economically deprived male audiences unable to hold back their hostility and rage toward her. In Kang's *In'gan munje*, the same denunciatory stance is reflected in the example of an important *sinyŏsŏng* character, a supercilious, educated woman who flaunts bourgeois, materialistic attitudes and pursues egotistic comfort and self-serving love affairs in total disregard of the suffering of the underprivileged people around her. Thus seen, Kang's description of educated Korean women corresponds much to the dominant, uncomplimentary discourses on *sinyŏsŏng* of her times.

AT THE COLONIAL NADIR

The last phase of colonial period from the late 1930s to the mid-1940s was the lowest point for Korean writers, and for Koreans as a

consciousness—focusing on "Honeymoon" and "The slope"], *Honam munhwa yŏn'gu* 58 (2015): 376–378.

110. See Kim Yun-sŏn, "1930 nyŏndae Han'guk sosŏl e natanan sŏngdamnon yŏn'gu—Kang Kyŏng-ae ŭi *Ŏmŏni wa ttal* e nnoatanan yŏsŏng ŭisik ŭl chungsim ŭro" [Study of gender discourses in Korean novel of the 1930s—focusing on feminist consciousness in Kang Kyŏng-ae's *Mother and daughter*], *Hansŏng ŏmunhak* 22 (2003): 135–170.

whole. Upon the disbanding of KAPF in 1935 by the Japanese colonial government, major writers had to denounce their socialist literary pledges and produce conversion literature, resulting in tensions, splits, and desertions within the group.[111] What's more, Japanese colonial efforts to make Korea the strategic and material basis of Japan's expansionist ambitions intensified, while the Japanization of Koreans accelerated, with the objective of wiping out Korean national identity. The use of the Korean language was banned; Koreans were forced to change their names into Japanese-styled ones and to worship the Japanese emperor; young Korean women were drafted as sex slaves, "comfort women," to serve Japanese troops abroad; Korean male college students were conscripted into the Japanese armed forces; and two Korean dailies, *Tonga ilbo* and *Chosŏn ilbo*, were forced to close. A number of writers, both male and female, gave in under these pressures and turned pro-Japanese—the most notable cases being Yi Kwang-su and Ch'oe Nam-sŏn. Others simply stopped writing and remained silent.[112]

During this dark, demoralizing time in the last phase of the colonial period, key works by Im Og-in (1915–1995) and Ch'oe Chŏng-hŭi (1912–1990) appeared. They revisited from nonpoliticized perspectives the topic of the "new woman," with a focus on middle-class, educated women's private lives in the domestic realm away from the public domain. Im's "Huch'ŏgi" (Chronicle of a third wife; 1940) and "Chŏnch'ŏgi" (Chronicle of the former wife; 1941) are positive portraits of *sinyŏsŏng*, self-confident and capable, who become architects of their own life, disregarding other's Confucian-colored gender expectations. The *sinyŏsŏng* protagonists of Ch'oe Chŏng-hŭi's trademark trilogy, "Chimaek" (Earthly connections; 1939), "Inmaek" (Human connections; 1940), and "Ch'ŏnmaek" (Heavenly connections; 1941), all defied conventional marriage morality and gender norms. The novellas provide pictures of these women's extramarital adventures, illegitimate marriage with married men, single motherhood with children born out of wedlock, and remarriage with children from their previous marriage. These narratives

---

111. For details of the complicated process behind the dissolution of KAPF, see Kwŏn Yŏng-min, *Han'guk kyegŭp munhak undongsa*, 292–347.

112. A noted instance was the woman writer Pak Hwa-sŏng, whose short story "Hobak" (Pumpkins; 1937) was the last work she published during the colonial period.

by Im and Ch'oe kept the intractable *sinyŏsŏng* topic alive to the very end of the colonial period.

POLITICAL UPHEAVALS AND GENDER DISCOURSES
1950s-1960s

With the end of World War II came Korea's liberation from Japan in August 1945. Koreans' jubilation, however, was short-lived. The country was officially divided into ideologically and politically op-posing South (democratic) and North (communist) in 1948 and be-came a focal point of the Cold War geopolitical wrangling. During this post-liberation period, a number of eminent Korean writers—mostly of socialist leaning—defected to the North,[113] while a tribu-nal was convened to prosecute Japanese collaborators such as Yi Kwang-su and Ch'oe Nam-sŏn.[114] Two years after the establishment of separate governments in the North and South, the fratricidal conflict known as the Korean War (1950–1953) broke out.[115] This epic national catastrophe affected every area of Koreans' lives, bringing with it massive human casualties, economic crisis, and a pervading sense of hopelessness and nihilism. It also irrevocably damaged the literary world.[116] Koreans' first task was to survive and come to grips with the cataclysmic and pressing issues of the war and its aftermath.

In the South, this bleak spiritual and material wasteland was dominated by the government's rigid anticommunist political ide-ology, which reinforced conventional patriarchal gender morality and conservative sexual norms. The politico-social and cultural mi-lieu of the 1950s and 1960s, therefore, allowed little leisure of mind or room for women writers to speak about the "woman question," and in fact the period saw little literary production related to gen-der discourses. In fact, most of women writers' work produced dur-

---

113. Yi Ki-Yŏng, Han Sŏrya, and Im Hwa were the most notable literary defec-tors to North Korea.

114. Regarding the implicatons of activities by Yi Kwang-su and Ch'oe Nam-sŏn during the colonial period, see Kyung Moon Hwang, *A History of Korea*, 190-193.

115. The war began on June 25, 1950, and the armistice was concluded on July 27, 1953.

116. For instance, Yi Kwang-su was kidnapped and taken to North Korea, while Kim Tong-in died in Seoul.

ing the post-Korean War decades regressed to promoting romantic and escapist love and conjugal relationships without seriously addressing the "woman question" or Confucian gender oppression.[117] Pak Kyŏng-ni (1927–2008), who was to become one of the pillars of modern Korean literature, emerged during this period, and as a Korean War widow herself, she focused on the destructive aftermath of war. Her acclaimed story, "Pulsin sidae" (Age of distrust; 1957), decries the morally corrupt and mammonism-obsessed post-war Korean society, while her novel, *Sijang kwa chŏnjang* (The market place and battle field; 1964), revolves around the tragedies of young Koreans engulfed in the armed conflict.

Similarly, Kang Sin-jae's (1924–2001) *Imjingang ŭi mindŭlle* (Dandelions on the Imjin riverbanks; 1960) recaptures the war ordeal and economic deprivation of its women characters and their families. At around the same time, Han Mal-suk (b. 1931), through her short story, "Sinhwa ŭi tanae" (A cliff of myths; 1957), gained distinction as illustrator of the *après-guerre* syndrome among young, educated Korean women who indulge in amoral and fleeting sexual relationships with no concern for the future.

Seen in this light, "Wŏrun" (Halo around the moon; 1955) by Han Mu-suk (1918–1993) and "Kam i ingnŭn ohu" (An afternoon of ripening persimmons; 1956) by Son So-hŭi (1917–1987) are rare examples for the time that delve into Confucian-generated gender issues in search of the true meaning of women's lives and their authentic, integrated inner selves. One of Son So-hŭi's hallmark stories, "Kam i ingnŭn ohu" raises questions about how a woman's childbearing function factors into marriage in modern Korean society. The story recycles the trope of the barren wife, who, after silently enduring mortifications and indignity, plagued by a sense of shame and inferiority, announces her vow at long last to enter the Buddhist order, by leaving her marriage. Her declaration emblematizes a radical rejection of patriarchal authority to exploit the female body as an apparatus for perpetuating the male line. In other words, the heroine proclaims her self-exile and exodus from a Confucian-

---

117. See Kim Pok-sun, "Pundan ch'ogi yŏsŏng chakka ŭi chinjŏngsŏng ch'ugu yangsang: Im Og-in non" [Features of pursuit of sincerity in women writers of the early division period: On Im Og-in], in *Peminijŭm kwa sosŏl pip'yŏng: hyŏndae p'yŏn* [Feminism and criticism of novel: contempoary period], ed. Han'guk Munhak Yŏn'guhoe (Seoul: Han'gilsa, 1997), 28–31.

controlled conjugal relationship, obtaining in the end her transcendence from patriarchal gender culture itself.

Han Mu-suk in particular continued to scrutinize women's Confucian-repressed sexuality and their gender-trapped existence through her major works, which centered on female characters, such as "Kamjŏng i innŭn simyŏn" (Emotional abyss; 1957). It is noteworthy that during this period the socialist writer Pak Hwa-sŏng, who had come to prominence in the 1930s, joined Han Mu-suk and Son So-hŭi in rejecting Confucian gender ethos in her "Pudŏk" (Womanly virtue; 1955). The story critiques male sexual excess, concubinage, and the culture that allowed such lopsided gender practices. It dramatizes the sense of futility, disempowerment, and hollowness experienced by a respectable, traditional wife and mother in her mid-forties after the death of her rich, philandering husband, whose four concubines she had tolerated throughout her married life.

RESURGENCE OF LITERARY GENDER DIALOGUE
1970s-1980s

With hardly time to recover from the devastation of the Korean War, South Korean society experienced the April 1960 student revolution followed immediately thereafter by the military coup of May 1961. These national crises flung the country into a prolonged period of sociopolitical turmoil that stretched over three decades to the early 1990s, when a civilian government was finally reinstated. During these historically trying times, the "woman question" emerged as one of the central concerns in the works of Pak Wan-sŏ (1931–2011), who debuted in 1970 with her first novel, *Namok* (Naked tree).

A prolific and award-winning writer, Pak was known for her flair in capturing women's gender troubles played out within the family and society in the rapidly industrializing and consumerism-driven Korean society of her time. Best-known examples are her "Ŏttŏn nadŭri" (An outing; 1971), "Chirŏng'i urŭm sori" (The cry of an earthworm; 1973), and "Chippogi nŭn kŭrŏkke kkŭnnatta" (Thus ended my housekeeping; 1978). These narratives disclose the hidden, midlife identity crisis of their women protagonists, all of them middle-class, full-time housewives living in metropolitan

Seoul. Plagued by a sense of dissatisfaction and emptiness, they question the value and direction of their lives and long to be something more than model housewives and mothers upholding Confucian standards. But they find themselves stuck in a rut with no meaningful prospects. Thus, Pak Wan-sŏ from the early stage of her career contributed to reviving queries into the plights of the Korean woman's Confucian-subscribed actuality, questions that had been effectively placed on the back burner since the late 1950s.

The Korean sociopolitical environment of the 1980s was marred by the Kwangju Uprising (1980) of civilians by the military regime, which intensified nationwide antigovernment, democratization movements by college students and dissident intellectuals. Confrontations between police and students on and off campus, often turning bloody and with casualties, became almost a daily ritual. Activist students were placed under police surveillance and even imprisoned. Labor disputes and union strikes spotlighted economic injustice and disparity between capitalist firm owners and factory workers, and radicalized student sympathizers joined the fight for the rights of wage earners. Collectively called the "386 generation,"[118] these college populations developed a firm sense of sociopolitical mission and communal solidarity, convinced of their vital and history-making role in reforming their country.

Young women writers, who grew up and received their college education amidst this violent and terrorizing atmosphere, published works reflecting their own political and ideological leanings as well as the chaotic conditions of their society. These writers assumed the role of spokespersons and literary historians for their contemporaries and actively contributed to the grand narrative of their era. Their thematic preoccupation and directions were much reminiscent of their predecessors of the 1920s-1930s, committed to the Marxist-stirred social literary production.[119] Representative writers of this sociopolitically charged era included Ch'oe Yun (b. 1953), Yang Kwi-ja (b. 1955), Kim In-suk (b. 1963), Sin Kyŏng-suk (b. 1963), Kong Chi-yŏng (b. 1963), and Kong Sŏn-ok (b. 1963). Sin Kyŏng-suk's debut

---

118. The "386 generation" was a term coined in the early 1990s and refers to young Korean adults in their thirties, who attended university in the 1980s, and were born in the 1960s.

119. For a leading work on the literary development in Korea of the 1980s, see Paek Nak-ch'ŏng, *Minjok munhak kwa segye munhak II* [National literature and world literature II] (Seoul: Ch'angjak Kwa Pip'yŏngsa, 1985).

work, "Kyŏul uhwa" (A winter fable; 1985), elegizes the derailed love story of a pair of college students in the 1980s, both inadvertent victims of the senseless military rule. Ch'oe Yun's "Chŏgi sori ŏpsi hanjŏm kkonnip i chigo" (There, a petal silently falls; 1988) condemns the hideous savagery of the Kwangju carnage, while Kim In-suk's "Hamkke kŏnnŭn kil" (Walking together on the road; 1988) applauds young housewives' participation in labor strikes alongside their husbands.

During this time, Pak Wan-sŏ confronted the issue of divorce—then a taboo topic—in her major novels, *Sara innŭn nal ŭi sijak* (The beginning of living life; 1980) and *Sŏ innŭn yŏja* (A woman who is standing; 1985)—both related to the women protagonists' struggles during and after marital splits. In her "Haesan pagaji" (Gourds for a birthing mother; 1985), Pak also directed criticism at the age-old, anachronistic gender prejudice, popularly known as "boy preference," which woefully dominates the mindset of the urban, middle classes and educated professional elites. In step with Pak, her younger colleague, Yi Kyŏng-ja (b. 1948), came out with a piercing critique of Confucian gender and familial customs in her collection of short stories, *Chŏlban ŭi silp'ae* (Half failure; 1988). The wide range of its thematic canvas that depicts conflicts between mother-in-law and daughter-in-law, a womanizing husband, domestic violence, the life of a divorcée, and men's sexual seduction of women under false promises of marriage firmly established Yi's reputation as a realist feminist writer.

The establishment of women's studies as an academic discipline in Korean universities in the late 1970s was instrumental in systematically introducing theories and practices of Western feminism and developing scholars and specialists in the field.[120] Their first task was to reach back to the roots of modern Korean women's literary traditions in the late 1910s. Thanks to their research efforts in the 1980s, the first generation of Korean women writers—including Kim Myŏng-sun, Na Hye-sŏk, and Kim Wŏn-ju—and their works were excavated, resurrected, and restored to their rightful place in modern Korean literary, intellectual, and gender history. By the mid-1980s, the publication of the feminist journals *Tto hana ŭi munhwa* (Alternative culture; 1985) and *Yŏsŏng* (Woman; 1985) provided multidisciplinary discur-

---

120. The first women's studies program in Korea was established at Ewha Womans University in 1977.

sive venues aimed at exploring pressing issues related to women, family, and society in contemporary Korea.[121] These two journals provided a much-needed theoretically informed and vibrant forum for debates, not only for Korean feminist studies but also for the general public, including college-educated readers.

NEW VISTAS: THE 1990S

Decades-long, antimilitary democratization movements bore fruit in 1993, when a civilian government was reestablished. Freed from social and moral obligations to join in the fight for restoration of a bona fide democratic system in their country, Korean writers now enjoyed far greater opportunities and options for their creative aspirations and activities. This auspicious and celebratory turning point in modern Korean political history coincided with the dazzling rise of a group of new young women writers who, together with their predecessors of the 1980s mentioned above, formed a powerful sector in the Korean literary world. These included Ǔn Hǔi-gyǒng (b. 1959), Yi Hye-gyǒng (b. 1960), Kim Hyǒng-gyǒng (b. 1960), Sǒ Ha-jin (b. 1960), Chǒn Kyǒng-nin (b. 1962), Ch'a Hyǒn-suk (b. 1963), and Pae Su-a (b. 1965).

Many of these writers—recipients of prestigious literary awards—turned to the "woman question" and produced works reassessing or reimagining the gendered modes of living experienced by women of their generation. For instance, the female protagonist of Ǔn Hǔi-gyǒng's "Pinch'ǒ" (Poverty-stricken wife; 1992), expresses in her diary the galling sense of spiritual paucity, lethargy, and frustration over the lack of communication with her self-centered husband, who goes out drinking until late at night and returns home with no regard for his wife's distress or inner conflicts. Her husband, after accidentally reading her writing, comes to realize his insensitivity and selfishness, and the short story ends with the possibility of revitalization of their conjugal relationship based on mutual consideration and care.[122]

---

121. In 1990, *Yǒsǒng* changed its title to *Yǒsǒng kwa sahoe* (Woman and society). Regarding *Tto hana ǔi munhwa* and *Yǒsǒng*, see Yi Sang-gyǒng, *Han'guk kǔndae yǒsǒng munhaksa non* [On the history of modern Korean woman's literature] (Seoul: Somyǒng Ch'ulp'an, 2002), 21–30.

122. See Kim Mi-hyǒn. *Yǒsǒng munhak ǔl nǒmǒsǒ* [Beyond woman's literature] (Seoul: Minǔmsa, 2002), 109–113.

Kong Chi-yŏng's first full-length novel, *Muso ŭi ppul ch'ŏrŏm honjasŏ kara* (Go alone like a rhinoceros's horn; 1993), is a pungent denunciation of spousal abuse, domestic violence, and male womanizing. It dramatizes the wasted potential of three college-educated women trapped in dead-end marriages, their damaged self-identity, and their loss of purpose in life. In a similar, critical tone, the heroine of Chŏn Kyŏng-nin's "Yŏmso rŭl monŭn yŏja" (A woman herding a goat; 1996) defiantly rejects the wifely virtue of acquiescence and submission when she leaves home, fed up with her husband's habitual womanizing and the prisonlike family life that oppresses her individuality and destroys her innate human decency.

More gloomily, Kim Hyŏng-gyŏng exposes the problem of lethal domestic abuse and moral double standards in "Tambae p'iunŭn yŏja" (A woman who smokes; 1996), which uncovers the cruelty and hypocrisy of a husband—a smoker—who physically abuses his wife for smoking, and in the end drives her to her death. Kim's "Sesang ŭi tunggŭn chibung" (The world's round roof; 1996) examines the issues of domestic abuse, a wife's infertility, and its effect on marriage, while looking at the truthful meaning of parenthood and the possibility of surrogate motherhood.[123] Ch'a Hyŏn-suk's "Nabi ŭi kkum, 1995" (Dreams of butterflies, 1995; 1995) vents the frustration of college-educated housewives, whose neoliberal society denies them their dream and chance for self-fulfillment through putting their education into practice; it instead traps them in the mind-numbing daily routine of caring for all family members except themselves. The last story in *Gendered Landscapes*, Yi Hye-gyŏng's "Kŭ chip ap" (In front of the house; 1998), laments the issue of concubinage still practiced unchecked in modern-day Korea, but Yi anticipates that such an antiquated Confucian custom will not be operational in the heroine's generation and thereafter.

Over the past century, modern women writers' literary ability to challenge, remove, or even transcend Confucian gender barriers and divides and create imaginary spaces for women to connect with their unalloyed selves has ebbed and flowed. The fluctuation has been in-

---

123. See Kim Ye-rim, "Pulhwa ŭi hyŏnsil kwa hwahae ŭi tang'wi: Kim Hyŏng-gyŏng non" [The reality of discord and the mandate for reconciliation: on Kim Hyŏng-gyŏng] in *P'eminijŭm ŭn hyumŏnijŭm ida: 90-yŏndae munje chakka rŭl chindan handa* [Feminism is humanism: diagnosing problematic writers of the 1990s], ed. Han'guk Munhak Yŏn'guhoe (Seoul: Han'gilsa, 2000), 313–318.

tricately linked with the crucial moments in the historical narratives of modern Korea, and it has shown how history, politics, culture, woman, and gender issues are interconnected and mutually defining. At the same time, this survey has confirmed the tenacity of the Confucian grip on Korean women's existence and the difficulty of divesting Korean society of its established gender views and practices. It would be illuminating to continue this line of study on the "woman question" to see how these interlocked and often elusive social, cultural, and gender categories will develop in the narratives of the "new generation writers," Korean women writers of this fast-evolving global twenty-first century.[124]

PROFILES OF THE STORIES

The thematic cores and range of the stories in *Gendered Landscapes* can be classified into a number of categories, although several of them overlap, intersect, or merge in the same text. These interlocked tropes encompass disquieting questions that take issue with early and arranged marriage customs; moral double standards and male sexual license; concubinage; in-law relationships in extended family systems; taboo of widows' remarriage; commercialization of the female body as an object of economic transaction and exchange; woman as a biological instrument for patrilineal continuation; familial and domestic violence; the "new woman" question; modern, and contemporary educated women and the pursuit of professional work or careers, to name a few. All together, these intricately interwoven motifs form the backbone, configuration, and image of modern Korean women's gendered existence and actuality as envisaged in the stories translated here.

From the first story, "Manuscript Payment," to the last, "In Front of the House," these fictional texts cast women as primary actors in perennial female scenarios and familial dramas. The protagonists are members of closely knit family networks at different seasons in the Korean woman's life cycle—daughters, brides, wives, daughters-

---

124. For a critical look at the prospective activities of Korean women writers who represent the upcoming generation of the twenty-first century, see Kim Yang-sŏn, *Kyŏnggye e sŏn yŏsŏng munhak* [Woman's literature on the border] (Seoul: Yŏngnak, 2009), 33–48.

in-law, mothers, widows, aunts, and nieces. They appear in *Gendered Landscapes* from across widely differentiated socioeconomic, educational, familial, marital, and age backgrounds, and are separated from one another by wide temporal and political divides, from the colonial period to the end of the twentieth century. Yet all of them stand at the gender-triggered crossroads of life—personally overwhelming and often existentially perilous[125]—which exact from them tough, life-altering decisions and actions. In this sense, the stories in *Gendered Landscapes* are the loci of contention between the Confucian gender order and the fictional female characters.

Some of the stories dramatize the traumas and heartbreaking misfortunes of their heroines as defenseless victims of patriarchal oppression and impugn the injustices and wrongs inflicted upon them. Others depict in poignant strokes female figures who are keenly aware of their patriarchal entrapment but find themselves unable to cut loose. The majority of the women characters, however, enact valiant breakthroughs as they defy Confucian gender blueprints and embark in new directions and explore new avenues for their lives. Although such endeavors are only partially honored or grudgingly recognized by those around them or by their society at large, these plucky souls are determined to escape the existing gender-restricted cultural norms and traditions and achieve new modes of life fulfillment, integration with their true inner core, and pathways to healing—and all on their own terms.

As the female characters' journeys and actualities suggest, however, such personal forays or objectives are far from painless or trouble-free. In this sense, these narratives are pointed reminders of how deeply and unshakably Confucian indoctrination has been ingrained in the Korean mindset—both male and female. However, the complexion and trajectory of the vicissitudes of female protagonists' lives express—either obliquely or bluntly—their authors' critical stances and responses toward patriarchal power and its ramifications. The unfaltering and determined attention the women novelists pay to the roadblocks and difficulties on the life paths of their characters stress the authors' discontent with the prevalence of such misogynistic bigotry, with its power and influence undiminished from the colonial period to postmodern Korea

---

125. See F.K. Stanzel, *A Theory of Narrative*, trans. by Charlotte Goedsche with a preface by Paul Hernadi (New York: Cambridge University Press, 1984), 93.

at the threshold of the twenty-first century. Much of their arguments is of opposition, refutation, and rejection of male domination, offering woman-affirming counter-narratives and perspectives. Ultimately, they offer possibilities—through the transformative actions of their female protagonists in the theater of gender, marriage, and family—for altering such distorted and prejudicial ways of looking at women with an eye toward overhauling Korea's ingrained cultural and social systems negatively affecting its female members. Herein are found the merit, potency, and allure of these short stories, which thematically resonate with one another across the span of seven decades.

One important technical feature to keep in mind when reading the stories in *Gendered Landscapes* is that six of the nine stories are rendered in the first-person narrative format. These stories have the first-person "I" as narrators, who are both major participants in the fictional world (homodiegetic mode) of the story as well as its protagonists (autodiegetic mode).[126] The "I" character thus performs simultaneously the roles of actor and observer, and carries on "act(s) of self-disclosure"[127] throughout the discursive space and time provided in the story. These stories take a variety of narrative structures: a single-voiced, epistolary mode, "a univocal structure,"[128] condensed personal memoirs or autobiographical life stories,[129] or witness accounts and testimonies.[130] These different modes of first-person narrations are often intermixed or combined to add depth and complexity to the significance of the narrator's experience, thoughts, and views in his/her fictional world and culture. For instance, "An Episode at Dusk, 2," "A Mute's Chant," and "Love and Daggers" have a dual-narration arrangement in that these narra-

---

126. For the differences between the terms "homodiegetic" and "autodiegetic," see Susan Sniader Lanser, *Fictions of Authority: Women Writers and Narrative Voice* (Ithaca, NY: Cornell University Press, 1992), 19.

127. Susan David Bernstein, *Confessional Subjects: Revelations of Gender and Power in Victorian Literature and Culture* (Chapel Hill: The University of North Carolina Press, 1997), 33.

128. See Lanser, *Fictions of Authority*, 46–47. "Manuscript Payment" is such an example.

129. Examples are "Chronicle of a Third Wife," "Dreams of Butterflies, 1995," "In Front of the House."

130. Stories in these categories include "An Episode at Dusk, 2," "A Mute's Chant," "Love and Daggers."

tives are the protagonists' own autobiographical storytelling and at the same time, the records of their experiences as eyewitnesses of or participants in the unfolding events in the life of another important character.

Furthermore, it is illuminating that in this first-person narrative framing for the stories in *Gendered Landscapes*, six stories have women who are both protagonists and narrating in the first-person—the narating "I"—and they position themselves as confessional subjects.[131] Readers are given only what is observed, known, thought, felt, or argued by the female narrator-protagonist—unmediated by other voices. In an important sense, this woman-centered "I" narrative approach is a rhetorical strategy on the part of the authors, who strive to probe in depth and capture with authenticity the consciousness, experience, knowledge, and emotions of the narrators and enhance the authority of the female voice and the world it represents.[132] It seems women writers believe that women's stories are best understood when told and inscribed by women, especially when they touch upon the intricate and subtle pulses of the deep, hidden inner lives of women.

Another noteworthy point is that most of the characters in these stories are not given personal names. Instead, they are identified in familial terms, indicating their relational place within their family or kinship network. For instance, a number of characters are simply dubbed wife, mother, father, sister, husband, uncle, aunt, grandmother, mother-in-law, sister-in-law, brother-in-law, and so on. Even in cases where the first name of the character is known, it is usually left unused, and the characters refer to each other by their familial designations, even between husband and wife. Re-

---

131. In *Gendered Landscapes*, the only story with a male narrator is "A Mute's Chant."

132. The first-person narrative technique was widely explored and adopted by Korean writers, especially by male novelists, from the 1910s. See U Chŏng-gwŏn, *Han'guk kŭndae kobaek sosŏl ŭi hyŏngsŏng kwa sŏsa yangsik* [The formation of modern Korean confessional novel and its narrative modes] (Seoul: Somyŏng Ch'ulp'an, 2004). In fact, the first "I" narrative in letter-writing format by a modern Korean woman was by Na Hye-sŏk, titled "Chapkam—K ŏnni ege yŏham" (Miscellaneous thoughts to sister K), which was published in *Hakchigwang* [Light of knowledge] no. 7 (1917). See Yu Hong-ju, "Kobaekch'e wa yŏsŏngjŏk kŭlssŭgi—Na Hye-sŏk ŭl chungsim ŭro [Confessional style and female writing—focusing on Na Hye-sŏk], *Hyŏndae munhak iron yŏn'gu* 27 (2006): 197–216. Kim Wŏn-ju's "Chagak" was also written in first-person epistolary format.

lated to this custom of avoiding the use of personal names is the consciousness of age hierarchy in Korea, which still prevails today. In this hierarchical family system, older members can address younger ones by their given names, but never vice versa. What further complicates this situation is that when necessary, characters are identified by the specific terms differentiating their affiliation with either paternal or maternal sides, such as tagging them as "paternal" grandmother, "maternal" uncle or aunt, or "paternal" cousin, and so forth. These appellation conventions reflect the uppermost importance of family and kin connections as part of the foundation and source of Koreans' individual identity and personal standing.

The textual readings for each of the stories are presented following the author's biography, supplemented by occasional comments on the distinctive technical characteristics of the texts in question. It is hoped that these sketches will assist the reader in identifying core issues and deciphering major thematic thrusts of the individual stories. They are intended as prompters or springboards—not final or definitive analyses—for readers to explore other possible readings and construct new textual or subtextual meanings of their own. ଓ

Stories

Manuscript Payment

Kang Kyŏng-ae

My dear little sister K!

Thank you very much for your last letter. I am relieved to learn that your health has improved and that you feel somewhat better. As you know, whatever one may say, nothing is more important than health.

Dear K! You said that you feel more troubled than happy and more distressed than hopeful with graduation coming upon you soon. Yes, given your circumstances, I don't blame you for feeling so. But you must gain clear insights for yourself amidst this pain and discouragement and ought to find a new path full of joy and hope.

Dear K! I am aware that I still lack knowledge to put in a nutshell my views about love and marriage that you have asked me about. So I am going to jot down in a plain and unpolished manner my present life just as it is and all the emotions aroused by it. And I suggest that you, a judicious person, do what you like with them in any way you see fit.

Dear K! As you well know, I recently had my novel serialized in *D Newspaper* and got some two hundred wŏn as payment.[1] I've never had this much money in my life! All of a sudden, my mind

The title of the original is "Wŏngoryo ibaegwŏn" (Manuscript payment of two-hundred *wŏn*), first published in *Sin'gajŏng* (New family), February 1935. The present translation is based on the version included in *Kang Kyŏng-ae chŏnjip* [Collected works of Kang Kyŏng-ae], ed. Yi Sang-gyŏng (Seoul: Somyŏng Ch'ulp'an, 1999), 559–567.

1. The author's biography suggests that the novel in question may very well be her longest novel, *In'gan munje* (Human question), serialized in the *Tonga ilbo*

has become vibrant with life, and I've started indulging in all sorts of fantasies.

Dear K! I wonder if you know anything about my family background. I was brought up in needy circumstances that have continued well into my adulthood. Even my education, meager though it is, is thanks to my brother-in-law, the husband of my older sister. From my childhood, I never enjoyed colorful holiday clothes, and for food I had nothing but coarse millet. During my school days, I was always short of school supplies. At the beginning of each semester, I melted into tears because I couldn't buy textbooks, and then barely managed to get used books from others. I can't even remember how many times my small heart pounded with worry because I had neither paper nor pen.

Dear K! I still remember vividly an incident from my first-grade year. An exam was about to begin, but I had no paper or pen. Desperate, I stole from my classmate sitting next to me and got a good scolding from my teacher. You can't imagine how much my classmates jeered at me, yelling "Hey, you thief!" What's worse, my teacher, her big eyes glaring, punished me by keeping me from going out and playing during recess. While my friends were enjoying making a snowman, clapping their hands in joy, I could do nothing but stand vacantly by the classroom window. Even though I had to keep my arms stretched out as punishment, I couldn't help but giggle and cry by turns at the snowman's funny mouth and eyes.

Dear K! It was out of childish innocence that I even thought of stealing from someone else. But once I became a middle-school student such thoughts never again crossed my mind, no matter how hard-pressed I was. The money provided by my brother-in-law barely covered my room and board and tuition. At times, unable to pay tuition, I cowered in front of my teachers and dared not even ask them questions about the school subjects that I needed explained. So I became crestfallen and felt like a dimwit. In the end, I had not a single close friend. The loneliness pushed me to rely on God all the more, and I went to the dormitory auditorium every

---

newspaper from August 1 to December 22, 1934, while she resided in Manchuria. The present short story is also a product of her sojourn in Manchuria, and her experience in this foreign region provides the backdrop for the piece. Considering the average monthly salary for school teachers was around thirty *wŏn* at the time, the protagonist's payment was a handsome monetary compensation.

night and prayed while weeping bitterly. Instead of decreasing, my pain only grew.

All about me, my classmates were bustling—buying new parasols, dressing in serge blouses and skirts, knitting sweaters trimmed with woolen collars, wearing watches, and so on. Looking back, it seems silly, but at the time I felt so envious of them that I was near tears. When I watched my friend knit a collar with soft wool yarn, I touched it in spite of myself and melted into tears. Who'd understand the touch of wool yarn that can only be experienced by schoolgirls! Sometimes, when my husband looks at me and asks, "How come you don't even know how to knit a sweater?" I recall those school days and feel anew the thrill that passed through my body when I touched my friend's wool yarn.

Dear K! One summer, the time to go home for vacation was just around the corner, and my friends were busy preparing. At the time, rayon was not yet available. Everyone had linen blouses and skirts made for them and were dressed up as delicately as dragonfly wings, and they also bought white or black parasols. I was at a loss as to what to do. Most of all, I was dying to have a parasol. Nowadays, even ordinary housewives have parasols, but in those days, people thought they were just something for girl students. The parasol was considered the unspoken identification marker of girl students. As I was so immature, I didn't feel like going home unless I owned a parasol. So I kept crying. One of my roommates—I don't know whether she read my mind or was trying to make fun of me—gave me an old, broken parasol that she had picked up somewhere. I was overjoyed. Yet I felt embarrassed and couldn't accept it right away. As I sat primly showing no interest, the girl chuckled and left the room. Thereupon, I grabbed the parasol and opened it, but found that every single part of it was broken. I felt a surge of indescribable anger and sorrow choking my throat. Yet I couldn't throw it away.

Dear K! I seem to have rambled on. By now, I guess you've got some idea about my past. While trying to talk about my present life, I seem to have revealed what I'd rather have kept to myself.

But dear K! Before getting paid for the novel I couldn't fall asleep at night, distracted by thoughts of what I should do with the money. I am ashamed to tell you now, but I had all my plans figured out: "First of all, since it is winter, I need to get a wool coat, a stole, and a pair of shoes. There is a big gap between my two front teeth that needs fixing with a small, gold filling. I'd also like to have a thin gold ring, a watch, and … but, what if my husband objects to these plans? So what? It's my money that I earned myself and he's in no position to argue about what I should do with it. If I don't take any action now, I won't even be able to have a gold watch. I will go ahead with my plans, ignoring everything else. But I guess I should get my husband a new suit. The one he has now has seen better days!"

Finally, the day of payment arrived and I got the money. Dear K! Both my husband and I were ecstatic.

Looking at the lamplight, especially bright that night, I spoke to my husband to find out his opinion, "What do you think we should do with the money?"

He sat silent and then said as if talking to himself, "Oh well, people like us feel more comfortable when we don't have money. However, now that we've got money, I guess we should use it. The first thing we should do is hospitalize our comrade Ungho."

I was so stunned by my husband's unexpected remark that I was speechless. Suddenly, his face gazing at me looked like a dog's, and his eyes no different than a bull's.

My husband went on, "Next, there's Hongsik's wife. I think we have no choice but to take care of her this winter." I no longer wanted to listen listening to what he was saying so I turned my head and blankly stared across at the opposite wall. Of course, I *did* have sympathy for Ungho, my husband's comrade, and the wife of his friend, Hongsik. Therefore, I had been willing to help them as much as we could, until I got the payment. As soon as I held some two hundred *wŏn* in my hand, my earlier feelings vanished without a trace. I couldn't help but feel that way. Since I remained silent, my husband looked at me for a good while and then said in a rather rough voice, "Well, how would you like to use the money?"

This question set off a shower of tears that I had tried so desperately to hold back by biting my tongue. At that moment, my husband appeared to me as insensitive and hopeless as a rock statue. The first thing he should have remembered was the fact he hadn't even given me a ring when we married—something everyone does—to say nothing of a pair of shoes. It's not that I didn't understand his situation. I *did* know he didn't have any money at the time. But today when we had money—money that *I*, not he, earned— wouldn't it only be fair for him to say with good grace that I should go ahead and buy a ring or a pair of shoes, my lifelong desires? But it seemed this man—such a blockhead—had never given a thought to such things. This realization stirred up bitterness in me more than anything else.

Let me tell you the story behind the shoes I have now. A few years ago, when I went to Seoul to take care of my middle-ear infection, Kim Kyŏngho, a friend of my husband's, insisted that I take the old shoes his wife no longer needed.[2] Obviously, the pathetic look of my shoes at the time prompted his suggestion. I couldn't have felt more humiliated. As with anyone, why would I want to wear hand-me-downs? But after looking at my shoes, I couldn't bring myself to refuse his offer so I examined the woman's shoes and at least found no holes in them. I wanted to take them, but as I didn't know how my husband would react upon learning of the matter, I wrote to him. A few days later, I received his letter of approval. That's how I came to wear this pair of shoes. But, you see, I could never shake off that sense of humiliation whenever I looked at them.

That night, the same shame surged in my throat afresh, triggering uncontrollable sobs. In the end, I wept like a child, my mouth wide open. My husband sprang up and slapped me on the cheek so violently that my ears almost rang. Already weeping and racked with resentment against him, I was driven into a wild rage.

"Why did you hit me? Why!" I flew at him.

His tigerlike eyes glowering, my husband pounced on me again and grabbed a clump of my hair. During this tussle, the lamp got knocked off, breaking noisily into pieces. In a flash, whiffs of kerosene spread throughout the room.

"Kill me, kill me!" I screamed in a choking voice. I felt this was finally the end with him.

Gasping, my husband barked, "Hahh! The likes of you deserve death a hundred times! I know all too well what you're thinking. Now that you've got some money, you snub your husband, huh? Ugh, get out of here, you, shameless wench! Take all your money and get off to your home by tomorrow. I can't live with such a brash hussy. You, sly vixen! You too want to become one of those sluts, those so-called modern girls, don't you? Ah, as a first-rate woman

---

2. Kang Kyŏng-ae suffered from the same medical condition and had treatment in Seoul around June 1932.

writer, you should be like them too! Well, well, I don't have the qualifications to be a husband of such a famous writer! You mean you want to be the kind of woman writer who has her hair singed and frizzled, paints her mug thick with floury powder, wears gold watches, diamond rings, and wool coats, and declares sympathy for proletariats, paying nothing but a lip service to them, don't you? Get out of my sight, now!"

My husband grabbed my wrist and dragged me out.

I was kicked out of my home.

Dear K! The severity of the cold wind in this northern region is beyond words. It's been four years since I moved here, but I had never experienced anything like the cutting winds on that night. The whole world seemed to have turned into a lump of ice. The bright moon hanging in the middle of the sky was cold enough to freeze my gaze, and the snowflakes were whirling about, blown by piercing winds. The snowflakes striking my body stung like sharp knives stabbing my skin. I stood motionless in the snow with folded arms, while my head was about to burst, beset by countless thoughts.

Murmuring to myself, "What am I supposed to do?" I began to sort out these thoughts swirling around in my head in order to come up with some decisions. The first idea that came rushing to my mind was to leave that fellow—even pieces of gold couldn't make me live with him. Then what should I do? Should I go back to my home village? My home village … I cringed as I pictured the faces of the villagers snickering at me—"Did she split up again? I told you so! What a whore. How long did she think she'd last?"— and my mother's anguished face. Then how about going to Seoul and getting a job with a newspaper or magazine? Given the examples of women journalists in the past who ended up becoming the butt of gossip for their love affairs, I realized that I wouldn't turn out much different from them. Where then should I go and what should I do? Should I go to Tokyo and take up studies? Who'd pay for my education? It seemed that taking up studies for a person in my situation would only lead to moral degeneration, not to a genuine education. When I came to this conclusion, I felt abandoned by this world, with no one to welcome me no matter where I should turn. And yet, it seemed there was no one else to hold my hand except that man sitting back in that room, huffing and puffing like a tiger.

Dear K! Could this be love? If not, what was it?

Once again, I shed torrents of hot tears. At the same time, the ranting and raving by the tigerlike fellow came flooding back.

Then the images of Hongsik's wife and his shabbily clothed child, and Ungho's skeletal face—all too ghastly—entered my mind. Hongsik's wife and her son, trembling in fear after her husband was sent off to jail! Ungho, who groans with pain since his release from prison, where he was stricken with heart disease! The two hundred *wŏn* clutched in my hand ... With this I could save them. I am still healthy and in no want of clothes, either. Desire for more than this means vanity, doesn't it? Suddenly I came to a clear realization that I had been dreaming dangerous dreams.

Dear K! Who in my circumstance needs a gold watch, a gold ring, and a wool coat? If I could save the life of a comrade with the money for those things, how honorable would that be? How much more so, if he is my husband's comrade? No, isn't he my comrade as well? I ran straight back to the gate without delay.

"Dear, I am sorry," I called out.

In no time, the gate was flung open. I rushed in and hung onto my husband.

"I'm sorry, dear. I won't do it again," I sobbed, choking.

Dear K! Please understand that my crying this time was very different from before.

Letting out a deep sigh, my husband stroked my head and said, "I do understand how you feel because all you've got is this blouse and skirt! But you are not entirely hard-up for clothing; you do have something on you. You have nothing to worry about. But think about comrade Ungho and Hongsik's wife. How can we turn our faces away and hold onto the money in our hands when our comrades are dying of sickness and hunger? That's why we should live under the same conditions, you see. I mean it. Even I feel changed since we got the money." After smacking his lips, my husband fell silent. I realized that his remarks were the result of his mulling things over after he had kicked me out of the house and that his earlier outburst was not to vent his anger on me but to keep in check all the objectionable thoughts arising in his own mind. I was quite emboldened, and I felt a hot flame flaring up in my heart.

I said, "Dear, let's get a set of inexpensive clothes for each of us, buy a bushel of rice and a load of firewood, and then give the remainder to them. Don't you think we'll surely be able to make more money in the future?"

My husband flung his arms around me. "That's it!"

Dear K! I'm sorry for boring you with my long, tedious tale. I fully understand that, facing graduation, your mind is filled with all sorts of fanciful ideas. Needless to say, such fantasies are inevitable at some stages of life, and so I am not about to find fault with what you are thinking. But I urge you to leave your dream world and turn your attention to reality.

Let's take time to think about the disaster victims of the three southern provinces.[3] How about the masses fleeing in tens of thousands to this desolate Manchuria, leaving behind their beloved homeland? Even if they come here, who in Manchuria is going to clothe and feed them? They flock here to make a better life, but they end up wandering about these vast plains crying and wailing, having their wives and daughters taken away to slave in diner kitchens or to become rich men's concubines. The problem doesn't stop with the disaster victims from the three southern provinces. Sometime ago, masses of people from Ullŭng Island reportedly landed at Wŏnsan port as refugees.[4] Are you aware that the poverty-stricken masses all over Chosŏn—no, the proletariats the world over—are at this moment on the verge of starvation?

Dear K! Recently, bands of punitive forces have swarmed into this Manchuria, and the clamor of their guns and swords are making people tremble in fear. Farmers who can no longer till their fields or fell trees in the mountains are crowding into cities like Yongjŏng and Yŏn'gil,[5] which are relatively safe, in hopes of saving their lives. But what will guarantee their future livelihood? Here a human life isn't worth that of a dog!

Dear K! I wonder if you are losing heart now because you won't be able to go to college or are unable to marry and make a happy home. I would like you to close your eyes and take a moment to reflect on how pointless your pessimistic concerns are. You may by some chance have your dreams come true for a while. But they

---

3. This means Ch'ungch'ŏng, Chŏlla, and Kyŏngsang provinces in Korea.

4. Wŏnsan is a port city in South Hamgyŏng Province.

5. These are two major cities (Longjing and Yanji in Chinese) in northern Manchuria across the Yalu River from Korea that served as centers for Korean immigrants.

won't last long and you will find yourself again in the same misfortune as the masses. Would you then commit suicide?

Dear K! The education you have now is good enough. Now is the very moment for you to acquire true knowledge by putting it into practice. You should put all your effort into developing your social values. If you devote yourself to boosting the so-called exchange values devoid of these social values, you are a loser and a decadent. I am not telling you this because I regard you as merchandise or an object, but because I would like you to understand that these are the two different approaches to life that all human beings, depending on their inner character, must choose between.

CʒƐ

Kang Kyŏng-ae (1906-1944)

The daughter of an impoverished farmer, Kang Kyŏng-ae was born in Songhwa County in Hwanghae Province, North Korea. From childhood, Kang's life was plagued by poverty, personal adversities, and continuous uprootedness, beginning with the loss of her father when she was just four years old. Her mother had to remarry to support Kang and her family. Kang's stepsiblings mistreated her, and she was not given access to formal education until age ten. All of these factors contributed to her misery and suffering. Yet Kang's love of literature manifested itself at a very early age. As a seven-year-old, she taught herself the Korean alphabet, devoured Korean vernacular classics, and became a valued and sought-after storyteller among her village elders. The meandering course of Kang's life experiences thereafter—including being economically destitute and distressed—was to become the background, substance, and the repeated subject matter of her later literary works.

In 1921, at fifteen, Kang entered Sung'ŭi Girls' School in Pyongyang, with financial help from her brother-in-law (her older stepsister's husband). Just two years later, Kang fell in love with Yang Chu-dong (1903–1977), a native of her hometown and a divorcé who was an English major at Waseda University, Japan. In 1923 Kang's participation in the student strike against the school's rigid dormitory rules and overbearing interference with students' life resulted in her expulsion that same year. Thereupon she moved to Seoul with Yang Chu-dong and studied for a year at Tongdŏk Girls' School.

When Kang's romantic escapade with Yang eventually failed,[6] forcing her to return home, she became the talk of the town, to the dismay and anger of her kin.[7] Unable to withstand her community's criticism of her erratic romantic ventures and unconventional lifestyle, she moved to Yongjŏng in Manchuria, only to suffer job-

---

6. After his graduation from Waseda in 1928, Yang Chu-dong taught at Sung-sil College in Pyŏngyang. During the colonial period, he achieved reputation as critic, poet, and essay writer. In 1947, he became a professor at Tongguk University in Seoul and was widely commended for his pioneering research and publications on Korean classical poetry.

7. Her brother-in-law, her educational supporter, was so outraged that he struck her on the ear, although he meant to hit her cheek. This became the cause for her lifelong ear and hearing ailment. See *Kang Kyŏng-ae chŏnjip*, 816-817.

lessness, abject poverty, and ill health. In the end, after about a year and a half, she returned home, broken.

By 1929 Kang's Marxist inclination had emerged and she joined the local chapter of the Kŭnuhoe, a national women's organization founded to promote women's social advancement and that had begun to demonstrate socialist leanings since 1928.[8] Her first short story, "P'agŭm" (A broken mandolin; 1931), about a Korean male intellectual's tragic end as an anti-Japanese activist in Manchuria, became one of the earliest examples of Korean diasporic literature.

Around this time, Kang became romantically involved with Chang Ha-il (dates unknown), a married man and a boarder in her house. Chang had taken up the position of a county official in her hometown, and Kang eventually married him, though he had not divorced his wife. Having provoked the wrath of Chang's legal wife, the couple fled to the port city of Inch'ŏn near Seoul, and after eking out a meager living as day laborers, they moved to Manchuria. Kang's husband, who maintained connections with anti-Japanese resistance fighters in the region, proved to be a supportive backer of her creative writing, reading her manuscript drafts and providing advice. It was through his arrangements with one of his friends that Kang's first novel, *Ŏmŏni wa ttal* (Mother and daughter; serialized in the magazine *Hyesŏng* [Comet] from August 1931 to December 1932), was published. The novel contrasts an illiterate mother's life, fettered by traditional gender oppression, against that of her daughter, who overcomes her personal disadvantages and carves out her own future as an educated, modern woman.

Except for occasional visits to Korea in 1932, Kang stayed mostly in Manchuria, where her literary career flourished well into 1939. Most of her works focused on the predicaments and struggles of Korean immigrants in Manchuria. Kang's short story, "Kŭ yŏja" (The woman; 1932), also related the wretched conditions faced by Koreans in Manchuria, anticipated her ambivalence and skepticism about the *sinyŏsŏng* issue, which was to be reiterated in her "Wŏngoryo ibaegwŏn" (Manuscript payment; 1935). Kang's *In'gan munje* (Human question; serialized in *Tonga ilbo*, Aug. 1–Dec. 22,

---

8. Regarding the Kŭnuhoe, see Kenneth M. Wells, "The Price of Legitimacy: Women and the *Kŭnuhoe* Movement, 1927–1931," in *Colonial Modernity in Korea*, ed. Gi-Wook Shin and Michael Robinson (Cambridge, MA: Harvard University Asia Center, 1999), 191–220.

1934), a tragic story of a young heroine in a farming village who was sexually abused both by her landlord and the colonial overseer of a textile factory, is based largely on the author's experience as a wage laborer in Inch'ŏn in 1931. It is now recognized as the finest realistic novel of the Japanese colonial period.

Another tour de force by Kang, "Chihach'on" (Underground village; 1936), touches the depths of human misery and despair wrought by the destructive power of poverty. It portrays in graphic detail the realities of hellish hunger, ghastly images of neglected and diseased children living in subhuman filth and squalor, starving and overworked mothers' inability to perform their parental roles, and the ultimate breakdown of the family into dysfunctional and unfeeling individuals.[9] The short story sealed Kang's reputation as a naturalist virtuoso.

In 1939, after briefly working as the manager of the branch office of the *Chosŏn Daily* newspaper in Manchuria, Kang returned to her hometown due to failing health, and with this, her literary activities practically ceased. She died in 1944, by then completely deaf and blind. In 1949, Kang's husband published her *Ingan munje* as a monograph—his first public tribute to his wife's literary achievements. It was only in the 1970s that Kang's work and career began to be rediscovered in South Korea. In 1999 a stone monument was built in Yongjŏng, Manchuria, commemorate the 105th anniversary of her birth and her contributions to modern Korean literature. ଔ

TEXTUAL READINGS

Largely autobiographical[10] and presented in epistolary format addressed to the protagonist's silent recipient, "Manuscript Payment" depicts a complex and conflict-ridden conjugal relationship between the narrator, a *sinyŏsŏng* writer, and her Marxist husband.

---

9. For analysis of "Chihach'on," see Choi Kyeong-Hee, "Impaired Body as Colonial Trope: Kang Kyŏng'ae's 'Underground Village,'" *Public Culture* 13, no. 3 (2001): 431–458.

10. See Kang Kyŏng-ae, "Chasŏ sojŏn" [My short autobiography], in *Kang Kyŏng-ae chŏnjip*, 788–789.

Instead of rejoicing in the wife's literary success and the money she has earned, the jobless husband self-righteously assumes the role of mentor to his supposedly socially blind wife, snubs her, and coerces her into accepting his position in the household through physical abuse. The heroine's moments of self-assertion as an individual—not as a wife—with socially and economically recognized distinction is ruthlessly crushed by her husband, who perpetrates the traditional marital gender hierarchy. The narrative shows how a woman's creativity and intellectual accomplishment is belittled and easily usurped by a man when his opinions are garbed in politically idealistic terms. Her husband's crude harangue and his trivialization of her accomplishments eloquently convey the Korean "new men's" or general public's censure of and determination to put down the personal desires and lifestyle of the *sinyŏsŏng*.[11] In this sense, the story dramatizes the hegemonic contention between a woman's attempt at asserting individualistic agency and male-controlled socialist ideology, in which the former loses out.

The most grievous dilemma that the *sinyŏsŏng* faces, as revealed in the heroine's musings after she is kicked out her home by her husband, is that her options for life after divorce are nonexistent. For one, her disrepute as a divorcée will bring unforgivable shame upon her family, while at the same time there is little chance for her to pursue a professional career or further her education because of her lack of financial means. Facing the reality of her dead-end situation, the heroine renounces her rightful desires and abdicates her entitlement to her intellectual property. The heroine's change of heart to follow her husband's lead, notwithstanding that she is the victim of his mental cruelty and physical violence, is disconcerting, rendering her preaching stance arbitrary, strained, and unconvincing.[12] This also illustrates the divided subjectivity of the heroine as well as the author's ambivalence about her position on the tension between the private and the public. Kang's portrayal of the *sinyŏsŏng*

---

11. See Pak Hye-gyŏng, "Kang Kyŏng-ae chakp'um e natanan yŏsŏng insik ŭi munje" [The issue of women's awareness in Kang Kyŏng-ae's works], *Minjok munhaksa yŏn'gu* 23 (2003), 259–260.

12. Song In-hwa, "Hach'ŭngmin yŏsŏng ŭi pigŭk kwa chagi insik ŭi tojŏng: Kang Kyŏng-ae non" [Tragedy of lower-class women and their path to self-awareness: a study on Kang Kyŏng-ae], in *Peminijŭm kwa sosŏl pip'yŏng: kŭndae p'yŏn* [Feminism and criticism of novel: modern period], ed. Han'guk Yŏsŏng Sosŏl Yŏn'guhoe (Seoul: Han'gilsa, 1996), 282–283.

of her times, highlighted by the heroine's final and rushed conversion as her husband's impassioned, ideological proponent, in the end confirms that their status and position in colonial Korean society was much disputed and perilous, at best.

The jolting and unexpected conclusion of the narrative may have its base in the socialist-oriented author's politicized use of literature. Kang sees her work as a means of elevating socialist ideology to the highest principles for Korean intellectuals to live by and put into action—even to be practiced in marital relationships in the domestic sphere. In this way, Kang participates in the Korean leftist literary movements of the 1930s, which subordinated literature to Marxist ideological social service. "Manuscript Payment" can be read as one example of the author's allegiance to proletariat literary objectives.

"Manuscript Payment" also provides a first-rate, detailed picture of the lives and culture of the much-debated and maligned *sinyŏsŏng* group. The story documents their school regimen and rules, interpersonal and social interactions, female cultural values and priorities, materialistic fashion interests, consciousness of class division and prejudice, and so on. Much of this information is negatively colored by the poverty-stricken heroine's position as a bystander/outsider who, because of her (like the author's) destitute economic situation, is alienated and marginalized from her own educational environment. ∞

Mountain Rites

Ch'oe Chŏng-hŭi

[1]

"Ahhgh! Help!" Tchokkan kept screaming, unable to bear the suffocating and awful pain that seemed to be tearing her bowels apart.[1] Startled by her own scream, she woke up. As soon as she opened her eyes, she pushed her husband off her chest, who was pressing her down like a huge rock. She bolted up frantically, sprinted forward, and wildly began to bang, push, and shake whatever she could lay her hands on.

She thought she was facing a door. But what she thought was a door wouldn't budge, no matter how much she banged, pushed, shook, and kicked. Her two small fists began to hurt, as if they were striking a slab of iron. As the pain began to spread from her hands throughout her body, she stopped and, resting her fists where they were, stared for a while at the "thing" in front of her. She began to see the "thing" gradually change into something like a black wall. The wall stretched upward beyond the reach of her eye. Tchokkan tried to follow with her eyes the imposing wall as far up as she was able. It kept stretching up and up, forcing her to bend her neck all the way back. In this posture, Tchokkan asked herself, "What on earth is this place?"

The title of the original is "Sanje" (Mountain rites), first published in *Tonga ilbo*, April 8–15, 1938. The present translation is based on the version included in *Ch'oe Chŏng-hŭi sŏnjip* [Selected works of Ch'oe Chŏng-hŭi]. *Sin Han'guk munhak chŏnjip* [Complete works of new Korean literature] (Seoul: Ŏmungak, 1973), 12: 332–345.

---

1. The name Tchokkan is likely a diminutive form of the Korean adjective, "small" or "tiny" (*chogŭman*), with a folksy tone of endearment.

Then, as if suddenly coming to her senses, she lowered her neck slightly and stealthily looked over her shoulder; she felt as if she saw her husband lying sprawled like a hideous giant. But she soon realized that she was not in that horrifying room where her monster husband was lying stretched out. Instead, it was a jail cell, where her cellmates who, sharing the same fate as hers, were sleeping like corpses—their ashen faces sticking out of dark blue, cotton bedclothes. It finally dawned on Tchokkan that she had had a bad dream. Drawing a long breath of relief, she wiped the cold sweat from her forehead and looked around nervously.

She took a few steps back and carefully checked everything around her. Before her was the stretch of the immobile cement wall—darker now than during the day—which she had so frantically pounded, pushed, shaken, and kicked a moment ago. There was the small electric light bulb—shining dimly like the light in a far-off village—hanging down from the center of the ceiling that connected the wide and high walls. She dropped her gaze and saw the heavy door that was always kept locked, and next to it, the clear-cut, tiny, holelike square surveillance window. A shiny, dark-brown, glazed earthenware pot—a chamber pot—stood upright in the corner of the room. When she finished looking over these things, she was finally certain that she was in prison—safe and protected—and not in that horrible room, and once more let out a long sigh of relief. After muttering to herself, "It was just a dream," she tucked herself back in the bed out of which she had jumped earlier.

The night seemed deep, and Tchokkan's cellmates were still drowned in sleep. The rattling sound the warden made when she opened and shut the wood-burning stove door faded away beyond the high prison walls, swept by the rough, whistling winds. The unforgettable, frightening, and revolting image of her husband that had appeared in her dream, however, lingered on for some time as she lay in her bed. Tchokkan pulled the quilt over her head. When she heard at long last the sounds of the warden stirring about, Tchokkan straightened out her body, which had drawn up like a snail, and pushing her cold feet into the bosom of her cellmate lying crosswise, she gradually dropped off to sleep as if she now felt quite secure.

Usually, Tchokkan didn't find it painful or miserable to be shut up behind the rampartlike, red-brick prison, its heavy iron gates and sooty, high fences, and to be under the warden's constant watch in the cell behind the cement walls and the sturdy door. To the contrary, she felt those insurmountable obstacles entirely reassuring.

Three months ago, at dusk in late autumn, Tchokkan was sent to jail, and for a few days thereafter she trembled like a frightened rabbit at the sound of the warden's footsteps in the hallway. What's more, she soiled her clothes when she was too scared to use the chamber pot, which brought on harsh scolding from the warden. As time went by, however, she became friends with her jailmates and also learned the prison rules. When the female warden, a widow with a fourteen-year-old daughter—the same age as Tchokkan—began to show pity on her, the young female prisoner known as "troublemaker" also became very nice to her. This made Tchokkan happy to be in the prison, except for the warden's beatings and the senior prisoners' vulgar railings. So on the day the judge sentenced her to a six-year prison term, the emaciated Tchokkan said smiling, "I'd like to stay in prison a long time." The widow warden grieved for her, "Oh, dear! You'll be twenty when you're released," but Tchokkan meant what she had said.

Before Tchokkan received her sentence, her cellmates speculated about her upcoming prison term. Some said that, given her tender age, Tchokkan would be released on probation. Another predicted a three-year sentence, while others suggested one or two years. The young "troublemaker" said that, since Tchokkan was charged with the same offense as hers and because Tchokkan was of the same age she was at the time of her own incarceration, Tchokkan would surely get a six-year sentence. Each time Tchokkan heard the prisoners talk, she prayed that the prediction of the "troublemaker" would come true and her release on probation would never happen. One reason was her deep sense of shame; she didn't want to be released before people had forgotten about her crime. But more important, she knew that unless her family paid back the rice and barley received from her in-laws as dowry, she would have to return to her awful and horrible in-laws' house. What Tchokkan earnestly hoped for was that while she was serving her long prison term her own family would have good harvests to pay off the debt of her in-laws' rice and barley. That would make her able to return to Big Village on the day of her discharge from prison—to her beloved home with the tangerine tree, where her thrifty and hardworking parents were living together with her younger siblings.

[2]

Early in the morning, ten days after the rice and barley were delivered to her home, Tchokkan left her home in a palanquin. The day before the wedding ceremony, her father, Yi Chusa, abruptly broke the usual matrimonial custom that has the groom come to the bride's home and instead asked the groom's side to send the palanquin to his house. Thus, before dawn in Big Village and even before the arrival of his dear friend Yun Ch'ambong and his wife, he had the bride Tchokkan board the palanquin and the party slipped out of the village like an alley cat. Yi Chusa had told the neighbors, his wife, and even Tchokkan that he had to do without the ceremony to be held at his house because of his poverty. This was simply an excuse. The real reason was the story he had heard from Yun Ch'ambong a few days before on his way home from the market place, after he had done some shopping for the wedding.

Yun Ch'ambong called out to Yi Chusa, who was hurrying home at dusk, a mesh bag flung over his shoulder into which he had put dried pollack, eggs, candies, fruits, and other items.

"I've got something to tell you," said Yun Ch'ambong.

"What's it about?" asked Yi Chusa.

"As you know, nothing is perfect in this world, but …" Yun Ch'ambong trailed off after opening the conversation, as if he felt ill at ease. Then he began, "I didn't mean to deceive you, so please don't hold anything against me. As you know, when a husband lacks something, he takes good care of his wife."

Yi Chusa, who was walking ahead of Yun Ch'ambong, stopped and turned back to look at his friend who was following him briskly. Noticing the abrupt change in the color of Yi Chusa's face, Yun Ch'ambong also stopped and said in a much lower voice, "It's about the groom—they said he became so because of the darned measles."

Stunned by Yun's words, Yi Chusa felt as if the ground had sunk under his feet and the skies collapsed. Feeling dizzy, he couldn't even take a step forward.

"Including me, who'd want a cripple, you see? It's not that I didn't know about it. In fact, I went and saw him myself. Other than one of his eyes, everything else seemed fine with him," said Yun.

He went on, "As I told you before, he is diligent and trustworthy. He works on other people's farms besides his own and is well known in his village for his steady character. I should have told you from the start. ..." Yun babbled on as he walked in step with Yi Chusa, who had slowed his brisk pace and was now falling behind. As Yi Chusa, with a downcast look, began gasping for breath and grew silent, Yun Ch'ambong couldn't finish his words and peeped at Yi Chusa's face, cocking his head a little. Yi Chusa's eyes—hollow and spiritless—were filled with tears, and he remained silent as before. Clearly, he was crushed. After thinking over how to comfort Yi Chusa, Yun Ch'ambong repeated what he'd said when he first suggested the marriage to Yi Chusa, "Look here, isn't it better than keeping her starving at home? It's all for her good and it'll also help feed the rest of your family. Don't you agree?"

Yi Chusa remained silent. Crestfallen, he wobbled along the hilly road, often stumbling and tripping. He considered breaking off the engagement but remembered how difficult it was to undo a match. He would first have to return the rice and barley, but over the ten days since the arrival of the grains, his family had eaten most of it, and besides, more than half of the five sacks of rice and ten sacks of barley were gone to pay off his debts to others. He knew he had no way to make up for the missing amount, but even if it were possible, he couldn't break off the match because Yun Ch'ambong had arranged it as a go-between. Were it not for Yun Ch'ambong, he might have been able to find fault with the one-eyed groom and break off the affair. Yi Chusa knew full well that Yun Ch'ambong, his one and only chum, had taken up the matter out of genuine concern for his friend's family, and he couldn't make Yun Ch'ambong lose face by breaking off the betrothal.

Now that Yi Chusa had made up his mind, he realized that it was his daughter who was the most wronged. The day after Yun Ch'ambong had received consent from Yi Chusa, an ox-drawn carriage piled with sacks of rice and barley had arrived from the groom's house in Pangjuk Village.

Villagers thronged into the yard of Yi Chusa and exclaimed, "What a stroke of luck for Tchokkan's family!"

Some said enviously, "You won't have any worries about food until next spring's lean season."

Such fuss actually made Yi Chusa feel something like loathing surge within him. With sunken eyes, he silently looked at the dark mountains in front of his house as he sucked on his pipe stuffed with dried pumpkin leaves. Now that he heard the news of the groom's handicap, he couldn't help but feel dazed.

When Yi Chusa saw that Yun Ch'ambong was having a hard time walking, he managed to say, "You don't have to worry. What the hell if he's one-eyed! He isn't any less of a man for it." His voice was so shaky and unclear that Yi Chusa himself could hardly make any sense of his own words.

Yet Yun Ch'ambong was so delighted with his friend's answer that, after a long pause, he stopped again and shouted, "You're quite right! I'm very happy you take it that way."

Yi Chusa and Yun Ch'ambong had been friends for more than forty years, sharing the joys and sorrows of life like brothers. They were of the same age and their paths in life were also similar. Yi Chusa had become a helpless orphan, having lost both his parents at the age of eleven during a flu epidemic, and then entered as a cowherd in the Big Gate House. Yun Ch'ambong, however, had spent happier days. He lived with his two younger siblings under the care of his parents, who worked as servants at the same Big Gate House. Yi Chusa's real name was Ch'undŭk, while Yun Ch'ambong's was Ŭlsoe. Up to the age of thirteen, they were simply squabbling pals, partners in rice milling, and fellow cowherds. But the spring they turned fourteen, Ŭlsoe's father suddenly fell ill and died. His mother, who had had a hard life with her children for about half a year, disappeared one night leaving him behind alone. Since then, Ch'undŭk and Ŭlsoe lived together.

As the two grew older, they moved up from cowherd to servant status. They had remained loyal servants within the same Big Gate House until they were over thirty. Ŭlsoe married first, a year ahead of Ch'undŭk, to a daughter of a servant in the house next door and set up a separate home. In autumn the following year, thanks to Ŭlsoe's matchmaking, Ch'undŭk also married, got a house, and likewise set up his own separate household. Although they were still tenant farmers of the Big Gate House and worked as its servants, they felt their hearts—long desolate—gradually easing, softening, and warming like spring days as they relaxed into their own homes with their wives. First Ŭlsoe had a brawny son, and then the next year, a daughter as pretty as a cotton blossom was born to Ch'undŭk, as if he didn't want to fall behind his friend. The two men never felt tired, even though they worked their fingers to the bone. They didn't own any land and cows, but their yards were running out of space from season to season filled with piles of shimmering barley, strings of well-ripened soybeans and adzuki beans, and waving heads of rice.

[3]

The households of Ŭlsoe and Ch'undŭk had the glow of bounty and were filled with peace and harmony. As their children grew up steadily and healthy, Ŭlsoe and Ch'undŭk spruced themselves up to look gentlemanly, having gotten rid of their servants' mien, and villagers began to call Ŭlsoe by the name Yun Ch'ambong and Ch'undŭk, Yi Chusa,[2] although no one could tell who first named them such. For a few years thereafter, the two men continued enjoying their happiness, but as time passed and human hearts changed, they began, like so many other farmers, to be pressed down by newly imposed financial burdens unknown before. Because of these burdens, farmers went into debt, which led them to learn such bizarre expressions as "seizure of growing rice crop before the harvest." That is, even before the farmers had a chance to harvest them, the grains of their rice plants, which they had tended with all their sweat and blood, fell—still standing in the paddies—into creditors' clutches. Adding on to their misery, droughts and floods followed one after another, bringing their year's farming to ruin time and again. The result was nothing but baleful poverty.

As time passed, the joyous homes of Yi Chusa and Yun Ch'ambong grew cheerless. But amidst these changes, the true friendship between these two men remained firm. Even when they had to survive by eating plant roots, tree bark, or even dirt—having completely forgotten about the olden times when they enjoyed cooked rice—they sought each other out to help and talked about ways to survive. In this sense, Tchokkan's arranged marriage was the upshot of the true friendship between these two men, based on mutual trust and reliance. Notwithstanding his own troubles, Yun Ch'ambong found it unbearable to see Yi Chusa's family eating lumps of mud—desperate from hunger for days on end—and col-

---

2. *Ch'ambong* was the title for a low-ranking government official in the Chosŏn dynasty, while *chusa* was the title of the government official posted in large rural towns. These titles were given to Yun and Yi, respectively, as expressions of respect paid by the villagers to them.

lapsing on the floor, unable to relieve themselves and all swollen up like grimy earthworms. Then Yun Ch'ambong recalled the story of the one-eyed man—sincere, hard-working, and making a solid living—that he had once heard from his wife's older sister, who lived in Pangjuk Village and was a neighbor of the man. She had said that, although he was a good candidate for bridegroom, because of his handicap, all talk of marriage failed. Yun Ch'ambong paid a visit to his sister-in-law in person, got a look at the prospective groom, and then and there concluded the marriage proposal with a bridal dowry of five sacks of rice and ten sacks of barley.

Yi Chusa and his wife protested, "We would rather all die together before we let go of our little daughter."

But Yun Ch'ambong pleaded with them, "You know, in the old days, girls as young as fourteen could bear children. Instead of starving her to death at home, it's better to get her fed and to help keep your family alive too. More than anything else, you'd be able to feed your children and yourselves with five sacks of rice and ten sacks of barley."

Although Yi Chusa and his wife were not persuaded by Yun Ch'ambong, they found themselves helpless to reject his kindness. Simply trusting his word, they didn't even take a personal look at the young man in question or check up on his family, and accepted the rice and barley delivered to their house the very next day.

After Yi Chusa heard Yun Ch'ambong's story about the groom, he racked his brain over the matter and resolved to keep his family from meeting the groom by taking only Tchokkan to conclude the matrimony—no matter what the consequences might be. He thought this plan was better in that it would keep the groom from becoming the laughingstock of his village as well as prevent his wife and Tchokkan from disappointment in advance. So the morning before the wedding he sent word to the groom's family that it was not necessary for him to come because the bride's family was too poor to prepare for his reception, and on top of that, the travel back and forth over the long distance would take too long. Instead, he requested only a palanquin to be sent to his home at dawn to carry the bride to the groom's house.

Thereafter, Yi Chusa spent the whole day absentmindedly puffing at his pumpkin-leaf-packed pipe. In the late evening, when Yun Ch'ambong, his wife, and all the rest of the people returned home, he approached his wife, who was sitting in front of a large feast table she had set up for the groom. Tchokkan lay across her mother's knees and submitted to having her soft hair steadily removed with a linen thread rolling across her forehead under the dimly lit kerosene lamp.

Suddenly Yi Chusa blurted out, "Look here, I asked the groom not to come tomorrow," as if he had never hesitated about his words. His wife stopped what she was doing and stared at her husband, her eyes wide open, as she was completely lost.

"What are you talking about?" she asked.

Quite taken aback by the unexpected, strong reaction from his wife, Yi Chusa hesitated for a moment and then answered that he had done so because he felt very much ashamed of his shabby house.

His wife clucked her tongue, "We'll be on everybody's lips for sure."

"So what?" Yi Chusa said. "What's wrong with asking the groom not to come because we are poor?"

"Listen, have you ever heard of a wedding without a groom? It's so embarrassing," said his wife.

"Not to worry! Early in the morning, a palanquin will be coming from the groom's side, so you'd better get Tchokkan ready."

"I won't. Why can't we do what all others do? Even if our house is poky, they will go back the same day, and you worry so much …"

"Keep quiet!" Yi Chusa shouted angrily, even before his wife had finished. It was not because he couldn't stand his wife's grumbling but because he felt so fearful about the marriage, shuddering at the mere mention of it. His wife burst into tears like a child, not only because her husband's unusually blunt words upset her but because she had already been given to weeping more frequently as her daughter's wedding day approached. Tchokkan, lying on her mother's knees and with her hair plucked from her forehead, followed her mother in sobbing. Yi Chusa, who knew that he wouldn't feel better even if he cried his eyes out holding his wife and daughter in his arms, left the house without another word. As soon as Yi Chusa was gone, his wife wiped away her tears and soothed her wailing daughter.

"Don't cry, my dear. If the groom has to come all the way to our house and then go back, it will be dark before the wedding at his house. Besides, our house is so grubby that we really feel embarrassed about it. My dear, stop crying. Your eyes will swell up. They say that in the old days, many brides were taken to the in-laws without grooms, if they had to go a long way."

Tchokkan kept crying. She didn't cry because she hated being married without the groom, as her mother said. Since the evening when the rice and barley arrived, she began to feel empty without knowing why. Her heart pounded, she felt scared and often wanted to cry. So she slipped out to the backyard from time to time and cried her heart out, hiding it from her parents and siblings.

[4]

Tchokkan's mother had no way of knowing exactly how Tchokkan felt, even after her daughter stopped crying. Early the following morning before the crack of dawn in the village, Yi Chusa secretly helped Tchokkan into the palanquin sent from the groom's side and then sneaked out of Big Village, following the palanquin stealthily as an alley cat. Even then Tchokkan's mother thought her daughter's sadness was due to the groom's absence. After her daughter's departure, she said to the people who gathered around, "It's so awful! As we are so poor, we couldn't provide for her well. What's worse, my heart breaks when I think of her going away without the groom and crying all day along the way." She couldn't stop her tears from showering down. If the heart of the mother, who thought that her daughter cried because the groom was not there to accompany her due to her family's poverty, ached that much, how much more wrenching the pain of Yi Chusa, who was walking behind the palanquin hiding a dreadful secret!

By the time the sunlight spread as far as the deep valley, the palanquin had passed the wide fields and low hills of Big Village and climbed the Juniper Mountain trail. There were no traces of people in the fields, where the harvesting had already been finished. Only the squawks of magpies digging up the dark rubbish piled high like heaps of straw sounded noisily under autumn skies that were as clear as glass. The palanquin carriers, who were climbing the long, steep, and rugged Juniper Mountain Pass, broke into a sweat and gasped for breath. For nearly five miles Yi Chusa remained quiet, walking listlessly behind the palanquin, and often had to help shore up the back of the palanquin that kept falling backward. He had no idea how many times he had tripped on jagged rocks, or just how soaked with sweat he was as, panting breath-lessly, he tried to keep pace with the young palanquin carriers. All the while, his heart ached over his daughter, who must have been deep in thought.

He said loudly, "Tchokkan, dear, don't you feel dizzy?" His voice was one of plaintive appeal.

There was no response from Tchokkan to her father's mournful question, causing Yi Chusa to wonder.

Yi Chusa asked again in the same tone, "My dear, don't you feel dizzy?"

Still there was no reply.

Yi Chusa thought that his daughter was crying. No, he was not imagining—he seemed to hear Tchokkan sobbing and wanted to plop himself down on the ground and collapse wailing. His heart was heavy with pain, the ringing in his ears got louder, and the ground seemed to be shifting, and he had to hold on to the palan-quin poles to steady himself. From his sunken eyes, tears streamed down.

He wanted to talk to his daughter once more, but he couldn't, fearful that his voice would crack. He simply kept walking, holding on to the palanquin poles. He began to regret not having broken off the betrothal after he heard about the groom from Yun Ch'ambong. When the palanquin climbed over the Juniper Mountain Pass and came near Pangjuk Village, he wiped his tear-drenched, blurry eyes, pretending to wipe away the sweat on his face. Thinking he had to allow his daughter to relieve herself before reaching her in-laws' house, as well as to soothe her, he spoke again, "Look here, Tchokkan, don't you want to pee?"

Again, he heard nothing.

This time, Yi Chusa said in a tone of coaxing a small child, cran-ing his neck toward the palanquin door, "My dear! Listen! Let's go pee."

Yet there was no answer from Tchokkan.

When the palanquin carriers heard Yi Chusa keep mentioning "pee," they quickly put down the palanquin beside the road and disappeared beyond the hilly road they had just passed. They did so because, for one, they too felt nature's call but, more than that, they also thought it would be better to have the bride relieve herself before their arrival at her in-laws.

Taking advantage of the well-timed disappearance of the palanquin carriers, Yi Chusa flung the palanquin door open and shouted at the top of his voice, "Tchokkan!" Could he ever have imagined what he saw? His daughter, whom he had thought would be crying, was sound asleep! At first, his heart sank at the thought that she had passed out after too much crying. But when he saw her slowly open her dried eyes, awakened from sleep by the puff of late autumn wind passing through the open palanquin door, he was very much relieved. He said to her, full of joy, "Have you been sleeping?"

Instead of answering her father, Tchokkan nodded her head smiling.

Because Tchokkan had stayed up all night for a few nights, she fell asleep as soon as she settled in the palanquin. She smiled at her father because she felt good after such a sound sleep, but she also felt compelled to do so after seeing the worried look on her father's face when he flung open the palanquin door.

Recognizing that his daughter looked better than he had imagined, Yi Chusa lightened up a bit, and in a different tone than before, said, "You see, we'll soon be there, so you have to pee."

But Tchokkan shook her head.

"You know, over there you won't be able to do so all day," Yi Chusa said.

"Yes, I know," Tchokkan replied, displaying the same good mood.

Delighted that his daughter, whom he had thought to be a mere child, was smiling instead of crying, and seemed to grasp everything, he asked, "How is it you understand such things?"

"Mother told me," Tchokkan said.

"Did your mother teach you all other things too?"

Tchokkan nodded. Yi Chusa gave credit to his wife, who had seemed to do nothing but cry over her daughter's marriage, for having the sense to teach her daughter about such matters, but he was far prouder of young Tchokkan because she had kept her mother's words in mind.

Yi Chusa asked Tchokkan, "Are you happy to get married?" This question had been on his mind for a long time, but he couldn't bring himself to ask it; he dared not ask for fear of hearing her say "no."

Tchokkan tried to answer with a smile as before, but as hot tears quickly filled her eyes—almost making her snivel—she ended up dropping her head. Once more Yi Chusa felt heavy-hearted.

Suddenly, he recalled the incident involving the new bride of the stone mill owner a few months before. The bride from Chinan had married the lame, eldest son of the mill owner, but as she found him scary and hateful, she hanged herself from a pine tree on the mountain behind the house in the dark night three days after the wedding. After the bride's death, her mother came over, and when she saw the daughter's lolled-out tongue and her eyes turned all white, she cried her heart out, clinging to the dead body, and said, "We killed her because of damned poverty!"

[5]

The palanquin party reached the groom's house at noon, casting short shadows behind themselves under the midday sun. It was bustling with people just as a banqueting house should be. Tchokkan muddled through the day, playing the awkward role of a new bride amidst the hustle and bustle of people. Yet she never stopped wondering what the groom would look like and from time to time, with her head down, she would look around to see if she could spot him. The kind of groom Tchokkan had had in mind should have on a light-blue coat and black leather shoes, and he should be on the small side with a round, flat, and softly smiling face—someone like the new groom at the Big Gate House—and he'd always wear a smile. This image had always been in Tchokkan's head. She had nursed it at the back of her mind ever since the evening her family accepted the rice and barley, making her feel so sorrowful, lonely, terrified, and anxious.

When the afternoon had gone, and long after all the people in the bride's room had slipped out one after another, the groom finally opened the door and strode in.

He was not the type of groom Tchokkan had hoped for. He was as tall as the village guardian post—a broad-shouldered, flat-faced man. One of his eyes was hollow, dark, and sunken, conspicuous even at first glance—and his mouth was as large as that of a tiger. All of this was terrifying to Tchokkan. Far more horrifying was the way he handled her as soon as he stepped inside the room. Without a word, he pounced on her and began to take her clothes off, and when she moved back out of fear, he grabbed her with his rough hands and held her tightly in his arms and, panting noisily, stripped her as if he were skinning a chicken. He blew out the flickering light of the lamp standing in the corner of the room and brusquely took her to the bed. Like a mouse before a cat, Tchokkan couldn't budge and trembled like an aspen leaf, having fallen into a half-fainting state in the dark.

When the night passed and the windows were growing light, Tchokkan came back to her senses. She looked around and, finding her husband lying next to her, she frantically pushed away the bed-clothes and sprang to her feet. As she tried to put on her clothes, she found it impossible to move. Her back and hips seemed to have fallen out of place. Shocked, she burst into tears.

She thought she was about to die. Her sobbing and her frantic attempts to put on her clothes shook her husband out of a deep sleep. Looking at the way she was crying and getting dressed, he sensed something had gone wrong. He immediately got up and soothed her with nice words and cajoled her in every way he could think of. The more he tried, the harder Tchokkan wailed, fearful lest the groom touch her body. Her eyes bulging with disgust as if she were trying to avoid a disgusting worm, she shuddered spo-radically and turned her face away.

Tchokkan couldn't help herself because she had never had her first monthly period, and in that sense, she was not even a fully grown woman. Furthermore, after such a sudden and unexpected experience, it was only natural for her to be shocked and terrified. Never had she heard of such matters from anyone. Tchokkan's mother, worried about her daughter's young age, had admonished and instructed her about all sorts of things, even after seating her daughter in the palanquin. But she had never told Tchokkan about what would happen in the bridal room the first night. As such mat-ters were considered taboo for everyone, Chokkan's mother couldn't mention it to her daughter, although she had coached her on every-thing else.

The groom felt embarrassed as well as anxious, because his bride kept crying, her eyes growing bigger and bigger with fright. He gave her a mild scolding: "It's not worth crying, I say!" Yet over and over again he regretted his actions during the night.

He had had no such intentions before meeting his bride. Self-conscious about his eye handicap that had caused the rejection of every one of his marriage proposals, he had taken the time to se-cretly clean and scrape out the dirty-looking discharges and gummy matter always gathered in the corner of his impaired eye before stepping into the bride's room. As if on an adventure, he had felt edgy and had kept going in and out of the house. In fact, he had made up his mind that, upon entering the bride's room, he would pull the bedclothes over his head and go straight to sleep like a corpse. But the adorable little bride, soft as a cotton blossom, stole his heart and thirty years of uncontrollable sexual desire burst forth.

"Stop crying, I won't do it again," he pleaded. As all his cajoling and coaxing fell on deaf ears, he left the room at a loss, feeling help-less, uneasy, and wretched.

[6]

No sooner had the groom gone than the sliding door was opened and then shut a few times, and Tchokkan became aware of several people peeping into her room. Then a young woman, a stranger to her, came in with a bowl of water and told her to wash her face. Tchokkan bent her face over the washbowl placed in front of her and splashed the water over her face. She didn't want others to see her crying. Had it been her own home, she would have cried, kick-ing up a racket, and still wouldn't have felt satisfied. But as she now found herself among total strangers, she gulped down her sobs, and facing the earthen washbowl, she tried to blink her eyes from time to time. Then with her eyes closed, she splattered the water over her face with her hands. Her tears wouldn't stop. It was as though her effort to fight back her tears made her that much more sorrowful.

While Tchokkan kept crying, a portable breakfast table was brought in. She washed her eyes over and over again, pretending to clean her face, and forced herself to sit in front of the table. Yet the salted fish, pork, grilled dry pollack, and soybean sprout dishes had no taste, and the cooked rice felt like grains of sand in her mouth. After a few bites, she laid down her spoon, whereupon the young woman who had brought in the wash water slipped the spoon back into Tchokkan's hand, saying they would have break-fast together since sharing food should stimulate the appetite. So urged, Tchokkan held the spoon, but eating together didn't whet her appetite either. The tears in her eyes made the table appear to reel, and the sounds she made with her spoon sounded far away as if in a dream.

The young woman seemed to have taken pity on Tchokkan, who kept crying without taking any food, and she told her that she was the wife of the groom's cousin. The woman chattered on saying that all brides cry at first but they forget their own home once they become familiar with the in-laws, and so on, while now and then bragging about her own husband.

When the woman saw that she couldn't get through to Tchokkan, she stopped smiling and snapped at her, "I tell you, stop crying!"

The woman's irritation, however, had no effect on Tchokkan. Still holding the spoon, her tears fell in ceaseless drops.

Just then, Tchokkan heard someone outside shout, "The bride's father has left." Although no other noises had had any effect on Tchokkan, these words reached her ear as quickly as an arrow. She threw down the spoon and darted outside, making her way to the brushwood gate. By the time Tchokkan reached the road outside the gate, people who had seen her father off were returning. He had already entered upon the slope of Mount Kŭmbong, having passed the road in front of the wide field.

Her arms held by the cousin-in-law woman and by others who had chased after her, Tchokkan screamed, "Daddy, let me go with you, let me go with you!" stamping her feet desperately. Her cry at the top of her throat was heart-rending and pitiful.

As if unaware of his daughter's grief-stricken voice, Tchokkan's white-clad father disappeared under the morning light beyond the bend at the foot of mountain.

When the sight of her retreating father passed from view, Tchokkan felt like she was left all alone in the world. She kept sobbing, her head turned toward the mountain slope, even as she was dragged by her arms back to her room. She paid no attention to the words of the cousin-in-law woman, who told her, "Stop it! It's embarrassing," or to the village women, old and young folks, children and grownups, who tittle-tattled as they stole glances at her by looking over the hedge, peeping through the holes in the fence, or sneaking a quick look over the brushwood gate.

From that day on, the mountain slope became an object of sorrow for Tchokkan. It remained so, not only that day but for all the days that led up to the village's mountain rites. The slope would remain mournfully, abidingly etched in the corner of her heart, even after all her memories became dim with the long passage of time.

The village's mountain rites were to be held on the fourth night following Tchokkan's wedding. There were fewer than thirty families in small Pangjuk Village, and the villagers, ever since they had set up the rule for these mountain ceremonies, never failed to hold them annually under the P'ogi tree in Spring Valley.[3] The rites were performed after the villagers had paid off their rents in rice upon completing the harvest. Even if gripped with hunger and with belts tightened, they made sure to prepare offerings to the mountain gods for their future happiness. It became a fixed custom for them—regardless of age or sex—to be on their best behavior from a few days before the service. Not only tenant farmers but also landowners, who were as scary as tigers to the sharecroppers, conducted themselves discreetly for days to bring themselves good luck. On the service day, the villagers changed into new clothes, as if it were an important holiday, and spent the whole day in a far more pious manner. Each year, the families would take turns completing different tasks, such as making rice cakes, preparing cooked rice, providing a pig, or preparing fruits, fried cakes, and other such things. They all got busy with their given assignments.

This year Tchokkan's in-laws were given the task of offering a slaughtered pig to the mountain god during the rites. Tchokkan, along with her sister-in-law, went puffing up and down the hilly road beneath the P'ogi tree in the deep, faraway Spring Valley, where that morning her husband had put a large cattle-feed boiling pot, which needed to be filled with water. The Spring Valley, which was screened off by deep mountains, wouldn't allow Tchokkan the view of either the village houses or the hilly slope on which her father had disappeared. After filling the pot with six jars of water, Tchokkan stood looking around the mountains blankly and, pointing to a mountain to the west, said to her sister-in-law, "I'd like to go climb that mountain together with you." Tchokkan's sister-in-law, who was four years older than her, couldn't oppose the words—which were few and far between to begin with—of her older brother's wife.

---

3. The meaning of P'ogi tree is unclear.

"Ok, let's go, sis," she gladly agreed, although she knew that they had to cook rice in time for this special day.

The members of Tchokkan's in-law family were always kind to her. For one thing, they were good-hearted by nature, and for another, they had to be extra nice to Tchokkan in order to make her feel at home. After the first night, Tchokkan refused to go to her husband's room and tried to sleep in the cowshed, in the barley straw stack, or even near the kitchen furnace. But her mother-in-law never scolded her and instead coaxed and sweet-talked her into sleeping next to her. During the day, she had her own daughter, not Tchokkan, work on sewing or take care of all kinds of kitchen chores. Tchokkan's mother-in-law had no choice in the first place, because she—widowed at age forty—was totally devoted to her son and daughter and hoped to live happily after marrying each of her children to a good spouse. Luckily, her son, who was over thirty, got married, but she was troubled by Tchokkan, who cried every day, raising a ruckus and embarrassing her in the eyes of other people. More important, she was concerned about her son, who looked more pitiful after he got married, and on top of that, she had to arrange a marriage for her daughter who had passed her marriageable age because of her older brother's difficulties in getting married.

Tchokkan's sister-in-law was anxious about the possibility of Tchokkan running away from her house or going back to her own home never to return. For one thing, this would make her mother and brother miserable, but her own marriage prospects would also suffer if rumors of such incident spread widely. Nevertheless, the more Tchokkan loathed her husband, the more she detested her in-laws' kindness.

[7]

The moment she heard her sister-in-law answer, "Yes, let's," Tchokkan headed in the direction she had in mind and in no time was running halfway up the mountain, as if she had reached there by leaping or even by flying.

Frantically following behind Tchokkan, who was growing smaller and smaller amidst the pine forest, her sister-in-law panted with outstretched neck, "Sis, wait up!"

But Tchokkan, far from looking back at her sister-in-law, raced even faster ahead, her fists clenched because the woman's calling her "sis" sounded as repulsive and nauseating as a maggot. Tchokkan reached the ridge of the mountain far ahead of her sister-in-law. The dream Tchokkan had held before climbing the mountain, however, was dashed to pieces at the summit.

Tchokkan had thought that once she had climbed and stood on top of the mountain, she'd be able to see Big Village with its tangerine tree, where her dear mother, father, and siblings were living. But no Big Village appeared in her view—only countless, rugged mountain ridges just like the one she was standing on swam up and down in her tearful eyes. The wind blew noisily through the pine forests. Mountain birds cried plaintively.

By the time Tchokkan got back home with her sister-in-law, her mother-in-law had already finished cooking the rice, while her husband had been casting anxious looks toward Spring Valley, waiting for them. The moment he saw the pair enter the house, he stopped what he had been doing to get ready for the rite such as preparing ropes to tie the pig and an A-frame to carry it to the ceremonial site. Excited, he popped in and out between the kitchen and the yard like a child, holding the ropes in his hand. With no idea of just how much Tchokkan feared and loathed him, he kept staring at every inch of her lovely face and body. He was seized by an intense desire to take her in with all his sight, to speak to her, and to hold her tightly in his arms.

After dinner, Tchokkan's husband left ahead for the ceremonial site, carrying on the A-frame the pig and firewood. Following after him, his mother and sister and Tchokkan carried on their heads or held in their hands the utensils they would need—a huge wooden container to put the pig in, gourds, an earthen vessel to hold the pig's blood for sausage stuffing, a razor-sharp knife, a cutting board and the like.

At the site, the old man Ch'ambong, respected as the village elder, had young men put the altar in order, sweep the area under the P'ogi tree, stack the firewood, and place torches on each side of the altar. Standing far away from where her husband was boiling the water for scalding the pig, Tchokkan carefully examined every one of the young men who were going back and forth under the P'ogi tree at dusk and searched to see if there were any one-eyed men like her husband. She found, however, that everyone had two healthy eyes; no one was so tall, had such large face, and was as old as her husband. She compared them with her husband, who, seated with his buttocks a little bit raised, was keeping the firewood going—the man, whose large oily face glistened like a shiny copperplate, looked more revolting against the blazing flames. To Tchokkan, the other young men appeared like heavenly beings, while her husband looked like a demon.

The evening gradually darkened, and all the villagers, from the children to the elderly, thronged to the site of the ceremony. All the families, in charge by turns of the rice cake, cooked rice, fried cakes, and fruit, came up one after another. The torches standing at either side of the altar flared up and fluttered like the reddish tongues of animals, and the firewood piled on the ground was set on fire. On the altar, the rice cake, cooked rice, dried pollack, fried cakes, and fruit had been personally arranged by the old man Ch'ambong. The ceremony was set to begin once the pig was killed. The pig was supposed to be butchered with the villagers in absolute quiet and solemnity. The reason was that the final shrieks of the dying pig had to be heard by the mountain gods—an ancient custom of the village.

In the dead, solemn quiet, Tchokkan's husband mounted the pig, which, tied with ropes, was grunting and squealing beside the altar. After grabbing the pig's forehead firmly with one hand, Tchokkan's husband stepped lightly on the pig's four hooves bound with ropes and then thrust the sharp knife into its neck, letting out dark, thick streams of blood. The pig broke into shrieks that rang throughout the mountains, and after pouring out a brimful of its blood into the earthenware pot, it lay dead, its four legs outstretched. All the villagers were watching the slaughter of the pig with the same sense of tension and self-restraint, except for Tchokkan, who, in spite of herself, backed away from the scene, overpowered by fear, horror, and bewilderment.

The moment Tchokkan saw the blood, the memory of what had happened on her wedding night flashed before her eyes like lightning. She felt suffocated when she saw her husband mount the pig and release its blood in a steady stream after thrusting the sharp knife into its neck. She also felt choked when she caught sight of her husband's buttocks moving up and down each time the gasping pig floundered its limbs and wriggled its body. Tchokkan thought that one day she would also die like the pig, spilling her blood.

After her wedding night, no such incident had occurred again because she slept beside her mother-in-law or in the barley straw stacks piled up in the cowshed. Still, her entire body broke out in a cold sweat, terrified at the thought that she had lived in the same house with her husband for an entire four days. She made up her mind that, although the dark night was terrifying, she had to run away from that dreadful husband. So, when the villagers turned toward the altar in utter piety amidst the crimson flames of the torches and firewood—all flaring up with increasing intensity at the ceremony site—Tchokkan stole away without anybody noticing and came down to the entrance of Spring Valley.

In the sky, only the stars were out and the wind was chilly. Night in the village without the benefit of torches and firewood was frightening, and the houses with no trace of lights appeared to Tchokkan like creepy animals crawling slowly toward her. Yet Tchokkan did not stop and finally made it to the front of the brush-wood gate of her in-laws' house. Dogs howled wildly. Startled at each bark of the dogs, Tchokkan opened the gate and carefully stepped into the kitchen. When she tripped over the furnace poker and each time the dried beanstalks crackled under her feet, she drew back, terror-stricken. Still she groped for something with her hands. Under her fumbling hands, the gourds, aluminum pots, and earthenware bowls bumped against one another and made ghostly noises. Finally, the thing Tchokkan was looking for came into her grasp with a rattle. Instead of feeling thrilled, she felt a chill creep over her.

Night deepened. The skies remained as star-studded as ever and the wind as chilly as before. The dogs stopped barking. Tchokkan carried armfuls of barley straw a few times and dumped them in her husband's room and deftly scratched the thing in her hand—a match. The straw caught fire quickly. When the fire in the damned, horrible room grew as large as the width of her skirt, she felt greatly relieved. But once the fire stretched up to the ceiling and furiously burst into flames, she leaped down to the yard, utterly terrified, and then hollered, jumping up and down. The neighborhood dogs came over in packs again and barked, jumping wildly with Tchokkan.

In no time, the blaze shot out of the ceiling of the room and spread to the outside. The more intense the black smoke, ashes, red flames, crackling noises of the fire, and the sounds of the house collapsing became, the more Tchokkan screamed and cried. Her original intention before setting the fire was to run for the hilly road along which her father had gone, once she made sure that the hateful house had completely burned down. But overpowered by the blaze shooting toward the sky, Tchokkan fell senseless to the ground in the main road in front of the village before the fire had burned itself out.

After Tchokkan had passed out, the fire destroyed as many as three more houses. Just then, the villagers came down from the mountain rites. Her mother-in-law, sister-in-law, and their neighbors whose houses had burned down rushed at Tchokkan as if to kill her and bawled and yelled. Her husband tried to revive the unconscious Tchokkan before helping to put out the fire. Even the next day when the policeman tightly bound Tchokkan with a rope in front of the village, where the neighborhood people gathered together, and dragged her along behind his bicycle, her husband followed Tchokkan, who was just shivering—too terrified to cry and her eyes nearly popping out of her head—rubbing his hands repeatedly and begging the policeman to forgive her.

ೞ

Ch'oe Chŏng-hŭi (1912-1990)

A native of Sŏngjin County, North Hamgyŏng Province, North Korea, Ch'oe Chŏng-hŭi was the oldest of four children born of a Chinese herbal doctor father and a devout Christian mother. With her father's encouragement, Ch'oe began schooling at the age of five, but when he left the family for another woman, Ch'oe experienced the sorrow and pain of parental betrayal in addition to bitter, shameful poverty. During this time, her love of singing became a source of comfort and joy.[4]

In 1924, she ran away with a friend to Seoul but, thanks to her mother's support, she was able to study at Sukmyŏng Girls' School from 1925 to 1928. Upon graduation, she entered Chung-ang College, a two-year training school for kindergarten teachers so she could earn a living. After a brief stint at a countryside kindergarten in Haman, South Kyŏngsang Province, in 1930 she went to Tokyo, where she found a job as a kindergarten teacher and joined a Korean students' theater group. But because of financial difficulties, she returned to Seoul within a year.

In 1931, Ch'oe met a stage and film director, Kim Yu-yŏng (1907–1940). She worked for him, perhaps dreaming of becoming an actress but more likely to make a living, and eventually married him. Her marriage to Kim was an utter disappointment, complicated by their financial troubles and the birth of a son. Out of desperation, Ch'oe sought out work as a reporter at the popular magazine *Samch'ŏlli* (Korean peninsula; 1929–1941) and was hired. Its editor/publisher Kim Tong-hwan (1901–1958), known as the first modern epic poet, provided her with encouragement and opened a path to her writing career. Ch'oe's first short story, "Chŏngdanghan sŭp'ai" (A legitimate spy; 1931), was published in *Samch'ŏlli*. Soon Ch'oe separated from her husband and left their son with him.

Ch'oe's work in the early 1930s showed a socialist bent, and in 1934 she was arrested in the wake of the crackdown on members of the Marxist literary organization, KAPF (Korean Artist Proletariat Fed-

---

4. For a biography and the works of Ch'oe Chŏng-hŭi, see Sŏ Yŏng-ŭn, *Ch'oe Chŏng-hŭi chŏngi: kangmul ŭi kkŭt* [Biography of Ch'oe Chŏng-hŭi: the end of the river] (Seoul: Munhak Sasangsa, 1984). See also, Kim Pok-sun, *"Na nŭn yŏja ta": pangbŏp ŭrosŏŭi chendŏ* ["I am woman": gender as a method] (Seoul: Somyŏng Ch'ulp'an, 2012).

eration). Although she was not an official member of the group, she was imprisoned for eight months, the only Korean woman writer prosecuted in this particular roundup. After her release in 1935, Ch'oe served as a reporter for the newspaper *Chosŏn ilbo* and published her first widely acclaimed story in 1937, "Hyungga" (Haunted house). This first-person narrative depicts a financially strapped woman reporter who is stricken with tuberculosis and the difficulties of being a single mother and breadwinner. The work marked the author's shift toward dealing with personal and socioeconomic issues related to educated Korean women during the colonial period.

Ch'oe's most productive years followed with the publication of "Mountain Rites" (1938), and her trilogy, "Chimaek" (Earthly connections; 1939), "Inmaek" (Human connections; 1940), and "Ch'ŏn-maek" (Heavenly connections; 1941), which solidified her literary position. The trilogy is an exploration of the love life of new women and their complicated dilemma, torn between motherhood and individual identity—especially those entangled in unconventional and seemingly unacceptable marital relationships, including unmarried women with children out of wedlock. Collectively, these women defy existing gender norms and expectations while endorsing the need for accommodating women's nonconventional gender behavior and practices in contemporary Korea. This period was also a new phase in her life, marked by her husband's death and her subsequent marriage to Kim Tong-hwan.[5] Although it was later a source of regret, Ch'oe produced pro-Japanese works at the end of the colonial period, succumbing to the pressure to cooperate with colonial literary propaganda campaigns.

During the Korean War, Ch'oe participated in the programs and activities organized by South Korean writers to support the government's military campaign, having gone through the pain of Tong-hwan's abduction to the north. Her post-war novel, *In'gansa* (Human history; 1960–1964), was the recipient of the first Women Writers' Award. The novel chronicles the lives of Korean intellectuals—with a focus on female characters—during the tumultuous political environment from the latter part of the colonial period to the student revolution of April 1960. Until her death in 1990, Ch'oe continued to contribute to Korean literary and cultural arenas by serving as

---

5. Ch'oe had two daughters from this union: Kim Chi-wŏn (1942–2013) and Kim Ch'ae-wŏn (b. 1946). Both became well-known novelists.

president of the Association for Korean Women Writers, as a member of the prestigious Korean Academy of Arts, and an executive member of the Association of Korean Novelists. ❧

TEXTUAL READINGS

One of the early works by Ch'oe Chŏng-hŭi, "Mountain Rites" is a critique of the Confucian principles governing traditional Korean arranged marriage customs, the practice of child-bride barter,[6] the rigid interpersonal protocols among members of a closely knit rural community, and the economic exploitation of the lowest Korean classes by Japanese colonialists during the 1930s. Foregrounding the tragic victimization of protagonist Tchokkan, an innocent fourteen-year-old farmer's daughter, this short story looks obliquely into the causes for her misery along with the quandary her parents face. Meticulous in its detail, "Mountain Rites" reveals how these issues become entangled until they drive the pitiful heroine to a criminal act.

The wedding night is a nightmarish trauma for Tchokkan—essentially a rape—and her identification of the horrific, ritual sacrifice of the pig with herself during the mountain rites unhinges her and pushes her into a temporary insanity. Tchokkan's setting the room on fire is a symbolic annihilation of her husband and thereby freedom from her insufferable marriage. It is an action taken on her own initiative and on her own behalf for the first time in her life—a striking contrast to her usual passivity, submissiveness, and acquiescence to the external conditions and incidents up to that point. In a sense, her frenzied actions are symbolic subversion—albeit subliminal, negative, and even self-destructive. The young girl's innocence, utter ignorance about conjugal sexual matters, acute separation anxiety and homesickness, and complete inability to grasp the

---

6. This practice increased at an unparalleled rate in the mid-1930s and in direct proportion to Japanese colonial economic exploitation. It became an alarming social phenomenon, as young daughters of poor families were sold off to save their family from indigence and starvation. See Kim Kyŏng-il, "Ilje ha chohon munje e taehan yŏn'gu" [Study of the early marriage issue during Japanese colonial rule], *Tong Asia munhwa yŏn'gu* 41 (2007): 380–381.

implications of her offense, render the injustice of her personal calamity still more poignant. Most ironic and pitiable is that Tchokkan finds prison a place of security and liberation. Here the protagonist is given a narrative space for the cry of her heart and soul,
enabling her to assert herself and openly declare her desires for the
first time. This drastic makeover offers a captivatingly potent thematic edge to the story.

Indisputably, "Mountain Rites" takes issue with Koreans' unchanged adherence to detrimental Confucian ways of thinking and
practices related to social interactions, marriage customs, and gender. These conspire to reduce the heroine to helpless prey and, most
disastrously, reduce her into the absurd state of criminal, whose
destructive consequences affect not only the heroine but people directly related to her and others in her community.

Tchokkan's story can also be read as an implicit indictment of
the colonial economic exploitation of Koreans, disclosing the ex-
tremities of affliction and despondency of farmers, the majority of
Koreans. The fact that all the characters, including Tchokkan's father, his friend Yun Ch'ambong, Tchokkan's in-laws and even her
husband, are basically good people, makes the injustice and misfortune they faced doubly tragic and unjustifiable. Tchokkan's father is
himself a victim of his circumstances, and the depth of agony, self-
reproach, and grief he conceals, heightened by his painfully deep
love for his daughter, constitute the most gripping aspects of the
narrative.

The skilfully executed narrative strategy, which backtracks
Tchokkan's storyline from the present to the past and finally back
to the present—the reversal of the standard, linear temporal flow—
helps enhance the sense of suspense, urgency, and expectancy of
the unfolding story of the heroine's calamitous debacle. The apt
use of foreshadowing (the suicide of the new bride in the village)
and the symbolism involving the slaughtered pig and the ceremonial fire also add complexity and multilayered meaning to the
narrative. ○ঽ

Chronicle of a Third Wife

Im Og-in

It took more than eight hours to get from Seoul to S Village by train, but throughout this long journey, my husband remained sullen and had little to say to me, only gazing out the window or occasionally nodding off to sleep. He barely answered my questions, and this trip, taken three days after our wedding, turned out to be simply dismal.

I had already gathered from my first impression of him that he was an unsociable man of few words. This had the effect of making him appear trustworthy to me, helping me go through all the steps leading to the conclusion of my marriage. Yet, as I began to think about my life together with such a dull man all the way to old age, I felt a vague sense of anxiety rising in my mind. But I told myself, "No. To regret means weak-mindedness, and that is against my nature," and I continued sitting primly with my hands together and winking back the tears that often misted my eyes.

I smiled wryly to myself, recalling my good friend's remark: "It may be ok to marry a divorced man but never a widower." Come to think of it, my husband, who, sitting right across from me, kept gazing with a vague, blank expression out of the window into the far distance, appeared to me just like a person following a vanished shadow. It might have been my idle imagination. Suddenly I became worried, but scolded myself, "What's the good of having

The original title is "Huch'ŏgi," first published in *Munjang* (Literary writing) in November 1940. This translation is based on the version included in *Han'guk hyŏndae taep'yo sosŏlsŏn* [Selections from representative modern Korean fiction], comp. Im Hyŏng-taek et al. (Seoul: Ch'angjak Kwa Pip'yŏngsa, 1996), 6: 406–418.

doubts now about the person with whom I have to live for a very long time?" And I braced myself and sat up straight.

The train blew a long, shrill whistle. We were nearing S Village. Vast fields appeared, distant mountains capped by rising white clouds came into hazy sight, and a large river glistened into view. This was the famous N River. Even from afar it appeared clean and pure. I could hardly contain my curiosity about this new region.

"Ah, ah, the N River! Look at that river over there," I excitedly shook my husband's knees without realizing it. Startled, he stared at me. Placing the fan he was holding in his hand on the window-sill, he said bluntly, "Haven't you ever seen a river? What's the big deal?" Then, tuning his chin up, he lighted a cigarette between his lips. I wiped away the sweat on my back with a handkerchief and looked out the window dejectedly.

I knew that even when I got off the train at S Village I would recognize very few people. There would be my parents-in-law, who weren't at our wedding, my husband's younger siblings, and "those children." I was told that Yŏngsu was nine and Pokhŭi, seven. What kind of children would they be? Would they take after their father and be gruff just like him? Or, would they be gentle as their mother was rumored to be? Would they call me mother? What would I feel the moment I meet them?

Far more than these people, I was eager to see as soon as possible the things he had bought for me. A piano that cost five thousand *wŏn*, an organ that cost five hundred *wŏn*, a three-panel mirror that cost three hundred *wŏn*, a dresser, and so on. The first item I'd requested through the matchmaker, Dr. Sin, was the piano. I had never dreamed of my new home without a piano. No matter who my husband turned out to be, I had to have a piano in the house I moved into. And, indeed, I had my husband buy one for me. This matter was not simply related to my desire alone. Granted that I was a thirty-year-old bride, I was a girls' school teacher, and an accomplished woman with a junior college degree. So, when Yi Kyuch'ŏl, my husband, asked me, endowed with such qualifications, to be his "third" wife, I mustered my courage to make demands of him no matter how extreme and agreed to marry him. Reportedly, word got around that Yi Kyuch'ŏl, known as a penny-pincher, must have really fallen for his bride, because he'd spent thousands of *wŏn* on a piano to win her heart. He might have had some feelings for me, but I couldn't sense any tenderness or unreserved passion from him. All this might be better for me, I thought.

I am a woman who was jilted a few years ago by a man I loved. He was also a medical doctor, a young doctor not yet thirty. He ran off to Manchuria with a pretty nurse named Mina, spurning me—an old spinster eagerly anticipating her wedding day. This experience twisted my heart perversely, and my already innate testiness was hardened by this failure. I made up my mind that, if I ever married, my husband had to be a doctor—just like my former love. It didn't matter whether the man was marrying a third or fourth time, as long as he wore a white doctor's gown, carried a stethoscope, and could wear a solemn expression in front of people—just like my lost love. I wasn't quite sure if my husband's being a doctor was enough to make up for my past. Through my husband was I trying vicariously to feel the presence of the man who had walked out on me?

No matter how much I tried to picture my husband—a doctor, sitting across from me—in a doctor's white gown carrying a medical bag for house calls, there was nothing of the doctor about him. My image of a doctor (thanks to the man I stupidly had idolized) had to be a man with a fair face, a wide forehead, and a dark mustache—that is, a man of good bearing. But as I gazed at this man, my husband, with his rough physique, dark red face, and two reddened, narrow eyes rolling around menacingly behind his dull, black, Lloyd horn-rimmed spectacles,[1] I regretted the follies of my fantasies, fantasies that had brought me to this start of a truly joyless life. But I was determined to behave as a dignified doctor's wife from the moment I got off the train, and as the wife of a man of wealth, with tens of thousands of *wŏn* to boot. I would be an intellectual housewife standing above all women in S Village. I couldn't be happy out of joy, but I could find happiness enough out of my competitiveness.

I was shown to our house—a rather large one—located a little distance from my husband's clinic with a street running between

_____

1. . A type of eyeglasses, originally made of either horn or tortoise shell, these glasses were actually manufactured from plastics designed to imitate those materials. They became a popular fashion item after American comedian, film director and producer, screen writer, and stunt performer, Harold Lloyd (1893–1971) wore a round-rimmed pair in his short comedy silent movie, Over the Fence (1917).

them. Neither the exterior nor the interior of the house was to my liking. The same was true of the home furnishings. Although my own belongings, mailed long before, remained unpacked, the whole house was filled with an atmosphere and with household goods that suggested that his wife had been living there right up to an hour ago. But somehow or other, the house looked good enough for me to settle down in without unpacking my things.

A few people were gathered in the house. My father-in-law, although gray-bearded, was robust-looking with a shiny look on his blackish red face; my mother-in-law, a short woman, looked aged with hardships; and there were a few relatives from the countryside and people from the neighborhood. I didn't particularly feel like being respectful toward my husband's parents simply because they were my in-laws. The fact that they were old and were my parents-in-law should have been sufficient for me to be deferential toward them, but I couldn't feel any real respect for them. I went through the motions of paying my respects, and for their part, they didn't receive me with much pleasure either. This was obvious from the fact that they left for their home village immediately after my first greeting them, though they might have had some urgent business on hand.

In the drawing room decorated in Japanese-style, I found the piano, the organ, and the three-panel mirror my husband had bought for me. I opened the lids of the piano and the organ and, after examining the keyboards, felt satisfied. But it was very unpleasant to feel that there was in the room, besides me, the shadow of another woman—the woman who seemed to be closest to my husband—which filled the whole house.

After all the guests had gone, a woman in her fifties, who hadn't opened her room even once during the few hours we had been home, made an appearance, pouting and sticking out her thick lower lip.

"Are you the woman who came to replace my daughter? You've got your hands full with the kids!" Her attitude was arrogant and confrontational. I responded in kind and out of habit stuck out my thick lower lip. The woman lit a cigarette, put it in her mouth, and squinted her eyes slightly. Her posture triggered in me various thoughts about her younger days. She was tall and had a balanced body. Although she was dark-skinned, she had clear-cut facial features and a mellow, fine voice. I felt in her the "woman"—her daughter, that is, my husband's ex-wife—who had reportedly been the most beautiful woman in S Village. From the moment of our very first encounter, I was turned off by the old woman. The way her hand held the cigarette to her mouth, the manner in which she seated herself, and the look of her clothes were not those of an ordinary housewife. I intuitively sensed that this woman was my enemy—and a rather formidable one.

After my husband left for his clinic, having taken off his traveling outfit, I sat in front of the piano, suppressing unsettling feelings. Without sheet music, I struck the keyboard, and my fingers led me. The music was impromptu and symbolically expressed my feelings. I heard my husband's mother-in-law in the next room yell something, but I couldn't catch what she was saying.

When I stopped playing, she screamed, "Ah, Yŏngsu's dad surely picked up a lunatic somewhere and brought her in. My hard lot to meet with such a freak!" Sweeping my hair backward just as men do, I pretended not to have heard her.

At about half past three in the afternoon, the entrance hall door rattled open, and the cute voice of a boy called out, "Grandma!"

It's Yŏngsu, I figured, and watched him come in from the entrance hall carrying his knapsack. Upon spotting me, he suddenly stopped and smiled awkwardly, blinking his dark eyes.

Saying to myself, "Ok, I can win his heart," I went straight up to him and stroked his head.

"Yŏngsu, come over here! What are you doing there?" shouted his grandmother, and Yŏngsu rushed into her room.

A little after Yŏngsu's return from school, Pokhŭi came home. When she saw me, she said, "Who's that? I don't like her, Grandma." Then she picked up a broom from somewhere and hit me on the back with it. I was at a loss as to what to do.

"This young thing is going to be a pest," I murmured to myself. Though seven years old, Pokhŭi looked and talked saucily, just like an ill-natured adult. Compared to her, her older brother Yŏngsu looked rather innocent.

I heard that their maternal grandmother had taken care of the household with the help of a maid until my arrival. As my husband's ex-wife reportedly died three years before, the old woman seemed to have been in charge ever since.

Knowing that I couldn't bring myself to live under the same roof with her, after a discussion with my husband I had her live in another house. When she left, she demanded I give her all the household goods her daughter had used. I allowed her to take only an old sewing machine, a small chest of drawers, and a few kitchen utensils such as pots and dishes. I didn't allow her to touch anything else.

Granted this woman had money at her disposal, but I couldn't believe that in running this rustic household she spent all four hundred *wŏn* just feeding five family members, including the maid. Rumors had it that when she had money, she made free use of it, and when she ran out, she hadn't a grain of millet left. Determined not to care about what others might gossip about, I decided on things as I pleased and set about getting my hands on the two children. If they asked me to become a horse, I became one and crawled around on the floor. If they asked me to buy something, I met their demands even in the dead of night. In time, the brat Pokhŭi, who used to dub me "that thing, that thing," began to call me "mother." I absolutely forbade them to get in touch with their grandmother. I didn't know whether they snuck out to see her when I wasn't looking, but at least when I had an eye on them they didn't.

Also, I got rid of the maid, who was clueless about housekeeping and was dirty, sticky-fingered, and gluttonous. Now our family was made up of four: my husband, me, and the two children. My parents-in-law were living back in the village two-and-a-half miles away, and my younger brothers-in-law were studying abroad. Still, I was busy every day, hosting one visitor after another from far and near. I made all the purchases myself—not only groceries but also daily necessities such as laundry soap, toilet paper, and other items. As we had no well in our courtyard, I myself went to the communal well, drew up the water, and brought it home. Since the age of fourteen or fifteen I had been good at carrying the water jar on top of my head, but now when I tried it my arms trembled under the weight of the jar and I wobbled along, spilling the water. But in no time, I got used to this chore as well.

"Why don't you have someone do it for you? It's embarrassing to see you carry the jar on your head," my husband said.

"Ridiculous! What's so embarrassing about carrying a water jar on your head? You are not a Seoul snob, are you?"

My husband and I had such spats from time to time.

In the meantime, after having put my things in order, I got a look into the ex-wife's chest of drawers. The chest was jam-packed with countless expensive silk garments. According to what I had heard from others, she had brought nothing with her when she was married, but afterward when she observed other young women's indulgence in finery, she began to stock up on clothes. The drawers were filled with expensive silk dresses. Because I hated the dark-colored dresser, I intended either to chop it into firewood or give it away to her mother after removing all the clothes to my own wardrobe. But my husband seemed reluctant to part with traces of his ex-wife and said we should leave her household things intact. I stored away the clothes that I had brought with me deep in my drawers even though they were not as good as his ex-wife's, and put hers on when I was doing dirty work such as kitchen chores. I tore the seams of her Korean skirts and made them into the children's bedding and even into cushions. My intention was to get rid of the ex-wife's shadow by using up her belongings myself.

One day, while tidying up my husband's study, I found a thick photo album. It contained a few pictures that told the history of my husband and Oksuk, his ex. One picture taken at the Chuŭl Hot Springs[2] showed my beaming husband holding Oksuk's shoulders, who, in her new-bride outfit, looked much prettier than I had imagined. Another was their family photo, with each parent holding one of their two children. All these pictures galled me. I especially couldn't stand the enlarged, half-figure photograph, showing off the coquettish Oksuk. Almost in fits, I tore it to pieces, muttering something to myself, but I didn't even know what I was saying. Then I shredded the rest of the pictures, shoved them into the kitchen furnace, struck a match, and set them on fire. I felt my heart pounding furiously in my chest.

Naturally my husband found out about this matter. So did the children's grandmother. According to my friend Tŏksun, the old woman blew her top after learning what I had done with the pictures. Placated by Tŏksun, who pleaded with her, "Please hold your anger, for the sake of your son-in-law if no one else," the old woman avoided confronting me. But I was told that she had her only picture of her daughter enlarged and hung it in her room to look at.

My husband's love for his children, especially Pokhŭi, was extraordinary. From the night of my arrival at this house, even "in bed

---

2. The hot springs, one of the oldest hot springs in Korea and a popular resort, is located in Chuŭl Village in Kyŏngsŏng District, North Hamgyŏng Province.

with his bride"—so to speak—he slept holding Pokhŭi tightly in his arms. The more I looked at her, the more she appeared to be a copy of her mother. Her round face, high nose, slightly slanting eyes, and her lips etched with remarkably clear lines were identical to her mother's, as I had seen in those pictures.

"Pokhŭi is a carbon copy of her mother. She is getting prettier and prettier," said everyone who saw her. Whenever my husband heard such remarks, he patted her on the head, as if he couldn't help it, and looked at her face more attentively. It seemed as if she copied her dead mother's body and mind to torment me. Nonetheless, I never failed to help with the children's preparations for and review of their schoolwork and carefully fixed their lunches as well. I made sure to keep their underwear, outfits, and bedding clean. At first, I humored their whims but over time went on stamping out their bad habits one by one. I taught, corrected, and reasoned with them on how to be respectful of their elders, how to say thank you, and how to sit up straight. I regulated their snacks and avoided giving them allowances carelessly, and little by little the children's behavior improved. My husband seemed to be appreciative of me on this score, but if I went a bit overboard he would yell at me, eyes glaring, "Why are you so hard on them? How dare you?" At those moments, I would smile and let it go, but later, for days on end, I'd make snide remarks and carp. I even said, "Like mother, like daughter!" or screamed out, "That girl is fit to be a concubine!"

Pokhŭi put on a good show of obedience toward me, coolly calling me "mom, mom" in my presence, but I heard that, once out of my sight, she'd make cutting criticisms of me in a manner sharper than that of grown-ups. I became frightened of her growing up.

The children's grandmother started getting into financial trouble upon leaving our house. According to other people and based on my own observations, the woman didn't know how to save. When she was young, she had rich men opening their wallets for her, and afterward, thanks to her married daughter, she spent most lavishly. But once I was installed in the house, her life fell to a sorry state. Naturally, I was blamed for her plight, but my husband seemed to have realized, in view of the way I ran our household affairs, how irresponsible his mother-in-law had been. I heard that all that he supplied to her over the course of a year was a sack of rice. I felt victorious. I couldn't help hating that lazy woman, who always oiled her hair till it shined and, cigarette in mouth, would spend her days in idle chatter, gadding about from house to house.

Since I began living in the house, our living expenses were fully covered with one-third the amount spent by my husband's mother-in-law and ex-wife. That didn't mean we skipped the monthly treat of thick beef soup or seasoned steamed chicken. On market day, which came around every five days, I went shopping for a variety of food, but bought only nutritious and cheap items. I felt good only after I'd knocked down the price—even just one cent, and even when that meant haggling over unripe chili peppers, squash, cucumbers, or some such thing. My mannerisms, like clasping my hands behind my back and thrusting out my thick lower lip, and my bespectacled appearance, soon became well known throughout the marketplace.

They gossiped, "You know, she is Dr. Yi's new wife."

"Goodness gracious! How could you haggle with us? Far from bargaining, Dr. Yi's late wife used to give us more, no matter how small."

I countered, "Hmmph, that's nonsense! She acted after her kind, but some of us know the value of money, you see."

I would walk back home unconcernedly along the street, carrying a basketful of groceries. And I took an extremely hostile attitude toward people who, under the pretense of lending a helping hand, came to our house for no reason and tried to sponge off us, just as they had done before. These people demanded a lot of money for their puny help during the winter kimchi-making season, but I flatly refused their requests and paid only the minimum. Even when my parents-in-law visited us from their village, I treated them to ordinary meals, and if my father-in-law called for dinner before my husband's return from his clinic, I haughtily snapped at him, "Our house rule is to serve dinner after the return of the head of the family." Thereupon, he left for home, slamming the door behind him.

On one occasion, my mother-in-law sent us salted pollack roe—my husband's favorite—which she had tastily prepared and packed in a used kerosene barrel. We ate it throughout the winter either raw or cooked in bean-curd stew, but we still had a lot left. As I thought it was a waste to give it away to other people, I sold the roe off in the marketplace one day, having carried the barrel on top of my head. When I saw womenfolk I knew, I solicited them, "Look here! Won't you buy some roe from me?" I sold the roe until sunset, but still some was left. I took the remainder back home, and after sprinkling more salt over it, I packed it in tightly.

After this incident, my parents-in-law never sent anything to us again. I decided not to send them anything either. The gossip about Dr. Yi's wife selling the salted roe seemed to spread all over the small S Village.

"Oksuk, although a daughter of a *kisaeng*, was better mannered, come to think of it. She knew how to spend money and was generous. That's why her house was bustling with people when she was alive, I tell you."

"I'll say. She was worthy of being a gentleman's wife. Although Dr. Yi's first wife before Oksuk married him was uneducated, she was quite trustworthy, too, wasn't she? The present one is altogether ill-bred, and stingy to boot."

"Yet I hear she's good at taking care of the kids."

"She'd better be! If not, she'd be damned."

"But isn't it good enough for her to take good care of the kids?"

Criticisms of me seemed to be raging in this way. And no one except Tŏksun and the messenger from my husband's clinic dropped in at our house.

I busied myself daily. I polished furniture until it shined, tidied up every corner of the house, grew flowers and plants, did my wash, leaving nothing undone, and then ironed everything straightaway, set up the *changttokttae* sauce-jar deck nicely,[3] swept the courtyard clean, scrubbed the bathroom, and so on. I couldn't stand having no work to do. During the day, I even did sewing. I also did silk washings myself, smoothing the starched fabric by beating it on a fulling block. Once, when I was about to finish work on my husband's *myŏngju paji*, his traditional padded silk trousers, Pokhŭi spilled milk on them, forcing me to redo the whole wash. Even now, the recollection of this incident makes me grind my teeth.

I felt comfortable and even relieved at being left alone except for when Tŏksun would visit. Tŏksun was a friend—we were graduates from the same high school. She was the wife of a primary school teacher and mother of five children, and I was happy to see her running her needy household in an industrious and frugal manner.

---

3. The *changttokttae* sauce-jar deck is usually a raised cement deck in the yard on which different kinds of homemade soy sauce and soybean paste jars are placed for fermentation.

And I was delighted that she could carry on her work no less ably than old-fashioned women. In this sense, she and I were like-minded colleagues.

Once in a while, we talked to each other, unburdening ourselves. Through Tŏksun, I came to learn about my husband's past. Tŏksun, who was discreet, emphatically said, "I wonder if it's okay to talk about this kind of story." But goaded to tell everything without reserve, she told me several stories about my husband.

"Dr. Yi became a Buddhist monk after he lost Pokhŭi's mother."

"A monk?"

"What do you mean?" I asked again, as if I didn't fully understand her.

"Well, what I mean is that he lived like a monk—not that he actually entered the mountains and became a Buddhist priest."

"If he was living like a monk after losing his wife, why did he remarry?"

"You can say that again," Tŏksun clicked her tongue, and said, "but then, he is doing so well now. …"

She was referring to our conjugal relationship. But it seemed to me that my husband and I had no inner communication, as if there had been a wall between us from the beginning.

Tŏksun went on, "I heard that Dr. Yi married his first wife when he was very young. They separated because it was a loveless marriage. But he fell passionately in love with Pokhŭi's mother and married her. Ha! I can't believe Dr. Yi could even fall in love," Tŏksun laughed.

Tŏksun continued. My husband had lived happily with Pokhŭi's mother for five years before he split with his first wife. As Oksuk became pregnant during this period, it was incredibly difficult for him to get a divorce. While the divorce proceedings were going on, the first wife threw every wicked hurdle imaginable into the path of Pokhŭi's mother, like hiring a shaman to stick a knife into the roof or doing it herself.[4]

Although Pokhŭi's mother had long suffered from tuberculosis, people didn't know how serious her condition was, because she always sat straight up and never lay in bed, betraying no signs of her illness. She always smiled amiably to people, generously paid those

---

4. The act may have originated from a shaman's ritual performance to inflict harm on the enemy of her client.

who helped her, and was open-minded. As she had a way with her husband, he devoted all his heart to her—in his own tactless, honest way. As soon as he got home from work, this tight-lipped man was always all smiles and chattered away. Upon learning the gravity of his wife's illness, he quit going to his clinic and attended to her, staying by her bedside day and night.

The moment his wife breathed her last, he wailed, rolling his stocky body over and over, his laments ringing out across the neighborhood, "Oh good God, what am I going to do, what am I going to do?" After that he couldn't eat meat. Obviously, this was because of his lingering, vivid memories of his wife's bloody coughing and the sight of the baby she had given birth to moments before her death. "I'll remain single," he vowed to himself, and observed all the proprieties for the first and second anniversaries of the death of his wife.

After my husband married me, he sometimes went over to his clinic, carrying his bedding with him, and slept in the room next to the consultation room. I overheard him saying to his close friend that it was on those nights that he missed Pokhŭi's mother unbearably. Occasionally, he even cried because his marriage to me made him miss her all the more, or so they said. The woman who had possessed all those characteristics that attracted my husband's heart more than I did, the woman who monopolized her surly husband's susceptible heart, and the woman who still lived deep in his heart, even after her death! Her phantomlike image must be living in Pokhŭi, I reckoned. It seemed as if my husband felt the presence of his dead wife in his daughter Pokhŭi and took pleasure in doing so.

My husband had sent away his daughter from his first marriage along with her mom and reportedly hated the girl more than anyone else. Moreover, when he recalled after the death of Pokhŭi's mother how much his first wife, as she left him, raged against and maligned Oksuk with curses, he almost felt he could kill the woman if he ever ran into her, or so people said.

Tŏksun looked at me as if she shouldn't have relayed all these stories and as if she felt really sorry for me for having done so.

I remained expressionless and glum.

Pokhŭi's mother, who had never lifted a finger and lived a life of idleness, making others serve her, had totally controlled her husband's heart. Questions began to beset me: "Who am I to him, except someone serving as a maid in this house? Have I ever felt any warmth in his voice, look, or feelings toward me? No, never! Although I have buried my old love, who hurt me, in the duty called "marriage," my husband apparently misses his dead ex-wife all the more because of me. Due to my stubbornness, I have become unpopular and alienated from people. But haven't I kept busy, working ceaselessly and scrupulously? Why doesn't my husband recognize this pride I have in myself?"

I was sick and tired of thinking things over. I didn't care to listen to others or to talk to others. All this appeared meaningless to me. I completely broke off with Tŏksun after that day. Yet I didn't feel lonely. "Why should I feel lonely? That's a foolish indulgence," I said to myself, and I completely cut myself off from the outside world rather than making friends with it. I could take delight in my work, look down on people with the title of the wife of wealthy Dr. Yi, and spare myself the hassle of associating with people. I am deeply attached to my musical instruments, sewing machine, clothes, and other household furnishings. I polish them as shiny as mirrors, which puts a satisfied smile on my face. I am happy simply because I am alive, and I am proud that I have work to do. To my heart's content, I can laugh at everything but myself. I can show contempt for my husband's heart and all the people who criticize me.

Both Yŏngsu and Pokhŭi get good marks in their schoolwork. It tickles me to look at my husband, who is filled with satisfaction at their report cards.

"These kids did quite well," my husband says, never letting go of the report cards, which rank Yŏngsu third and Pokhŭi fifth in their respective classes.

I mumble to myself, "Doesn't he know it has nothing to do with them? They owe it all to me!" And I feel that the "one" moving inside me—the only thing belonging to me—would grow up well after its birth and do several times better than my husband's kids.

After I broke off with Tŏksun, no one, not even a puppy, hung around our house except our family members. Although I have completely detached myself from the outside world in this manner, I feel not one iota of loneliness or emptiness. The life growing inside me is my unique companion and is to me the most precious being. My heart almost bursts with joy when I simply think this is "mine."

While my surroundings grow increasingly limited, I feel like my heart expands infinitely. Within this world of mine, I beam with a smile, feeling the movements of my child growing inside me.

಄

Im Og-in (1911-1995)

The youngest of three siblings and the only daughter, Im Og-in was born in Tohwa Village in Kilju County, North Hamgyŏng Province, North Korea—a snowy and windswept region with long and severe winters.[5] She grew up in an extended farming family that included her great-grandparents and grandparents. Her father was an idealistic, enlightened man, whose zeal for learning made him enter middle school for a modern education after the births of all his children. From an early age, Im was frail but showed an exceptional enthusiasm for learning, like her father. Over her ultraconservative great-grandfather's objections, she took the initiative in receiving a primary school education, commuting a long distance on foot. Her school days were financially trying because of her father's failure in managing his dry goods store, but it was during this period that she vowed herself to become a teacher, a resolution reinforced by her embrace of Christianity.

In 1931 Im graduated first in her class from Yŏngsaeng Girls' School, a Presbyterian mission school in Hamhŭng, South Hamgyŏng Province. The following year, she had the exceptional distinction of receiving a scholarship from her alma mater and began her teacher's college education at Nara Women's Higher Normal School in Nara, Japan. Upon her return to Korea after graduation in spring 1935, she began teaching at her alma mater; it was her long-cherished dream come true. One summer, through her teacher's thoughtful arrangements, Im had a rare and invaluable opportunity to meet An Ch'ang-ho (1878–1938), Korea's most revered enlightenment pioneer and patriotic leader during the colonial period. She learned directly from him his life principle, "Seeking truth and striving to put it into practice." The same motto was to be the very backbone and basis of Im's life philosophy. During this time, she also had the benefit of encouragement from the contemporary literary giant Yi Kwang-su through written correspondence with him.

After some time off from teaching because of tuberculosis, Im taught at Lucy Girls' School in Wŏnsan from 1937 to 1940.[6] This

---

5. The year of Im's birth was verified and confirmed by her autobiography, *Na ŭi iryŏksŏ* [My personal history] (Seoul: Chŏng'u sa, 1985), 14. This book has been the main source of the biographical sketch of her in the following.

6. This school, founded in 1903, was named after an American woman Meth-

period saw the publication of her first short story, "Pongsŏnhwa" (Garden balsams; 1939), which depicted the pure romantic love of a woman who finds self-fulfillment in being the object of the love of her sweetheart. With the publication of "Koyŏng" (Lonely shadow) and "Huch'ŏgi" (Chronicle of a third wife) in 1940, Im officially made her debut. These stories were followed by another work of major significance to Im's literary repertoire, "Chŏnch'ŏgi"(Chronicle of a former wife; 1941), which highlighted the courage and self-confidence of an educated woman, who, forced into divorce by her husband because of her inability to bear children, begins a new life dedicated to women's education and finds her life purpose in it. The intensification of colonial oppression thereafter—especially the ban on the use of the Korean language in the early 1940s—drove Im to quit her teaching job and retreat to a remote rural area in South Hamgyŏng Province, where she established a night school for women to help eradicate illiteracy and improve their living conditions.

Following liberation in 1945, as North Korea increasingly fell to communism, Im fled alone to the South in 1946, in fear for her life at the hands of the communists. Before she had time to take root in the South, she had to go through the devastation of the Korean War and its aftereffects. Yet she did not slacken in her writing, and in 1957 succeeded in publishing her first full-length novel, *Wŏllam ch'onhu* (Before and after coming to the South). The work was an autobiographical account of her harrowing experience during the chaotic post-liberation period in the North that forced her to flee to the South. That same year, now forty years old, Im married the editor of a youth magazine, Pang Ki-hwan (1923–1993), who was twelve years her junior. Their marriage, based on Christian faith, was one of lasting, indisputable respect, understanding, and companionship, which served as the source of their strength in overcoming a number of crises stemming from Im's frequent ill health.

In 1955 Im started teaching at Ewha Womans University and Tŏksŏng Women's University in Seoul. The year 1957 turned out to be one of the most celebrated of her writing career: her novel, *Wŏllam ch'onhu*, received the esteemed Asian Freedom Literature Award and her major novels, such as *Tŭl e p'in paekhap'hwa rŭl poara*

---

odist missionary, Lucy Armfield Cuninggim (1838–1908), who provided funding for its construction.

(Look at the lilies on the field) and *Chŏlmŭn sŏlgyedo* (Young blue-prints), were published, in addition to over a dozen short stories. In 1959, Im began to lecture at Kŏnguk University, and the period thenceforward up to 1963 represented the peak of her creative productivity. The notable works published during this period included full-length novels such as *Changmi ŭi mun* (Rosy gate; 1960) and *Him ŭi sŏjŏng* (Lyricism of power; 1962) in addition to a number of short stories and essays. These novels—basically Christian-inspired—promoted images of ideal women who overcome their hard life through patience, love, and self-sacrifice.[7] Im Og-in's works reached a wider public beyond the print media, as radio stations aired the recitation of some of her major novels as series.

In 1966 she was promoted to associate professor at Kŏnguk University and in 1970 she was appointed that university's dean of the College of Home Economics. From the 1960s to the 1980s, her activities expanded to include a wide range of cultural and social services: she served as the president of Association of Korean Women Writers, first president of the Christian Writers Association, president of the YWCA Seoul branch, and a member of the Korean Academy of Arts. She had no children of her own but devoted herself to the care of orphans, many of whom became pastors, writers, and teachers. Im's autobiography, *Na ŭi iryŏksŏ*, is a testament to a life based on literature, education, and Christian faith in pursuit of integrity, genuine love, and the freedom of the human soul. ❧

TEXTUAL READINGS

A first-person, confessional biography of an educated woman, "Chronicle of a Third Wife" presents an exercise of personal power by another *sinyŏsŏng* in the domestic and conjugal battleground. The narrative shows the dogged and often amusing exploits by a strong-willed and unflappable female protagonist to install herself legitimately as her husband's third wife. Although thrown into a hostile and distressing familial and communal gender culture of a small provincial town, the heroine makes ingenious use of a variety

---

7. Kim Pok-sun, "Pundan ch'ogi yŏsŏng chakka," 64.

of tactics and maneuvers to accomplish her objectives and, in the process, undermines pigeonholed notions about wife, daughter-in-law, stepmother, and *sinyŏsŏng*. In the end, she flips the orthodox Confucian gender script and wins the war by transforming the household that she inherited from disarray to orderliness and respectability. "Chronicle of a Third Wife" is the success story of a *sinyŏsŏng*—equipped with mettle, ingenuity, and fierce drive—who comes off as the master of her life and circumstances with no need for the approval or validation by others.

Rather than dwelling on her past as a betrayed lover, the protagonist, a spinster (at least by contemporaneous Korean standards), enters her marriage as a proud and self-possessed woman and makes the most of her situation. Maximizing her husband's disadvantage of marrying a third time with two young children in tow, she extracts from him an extravagant, premarital dowry to prove her value to him and his family. From this strategic vantage point, she pushes her agenda item by item. First, as a new bride, she brazenly violates the paramount Confucian article of conduct for a daughter-in-law—obedience to parents-in-law through displays of respect and submissiveness. Impervious to her elders and unconcerned about the consequences of her offensive behavior, she drives the in-laws out of her life, making them nonfactors in her marriage. In one stroke, she thus clears away the most difficult obstacles on a new daughter-in-law's path, and, by extension, jettisons the revered hierarchy of the extended family system.

Although fully aware that her husband's heart is still possessed by the memory of his deceased wife, the heroine does not rush him to change nor seek to curry his affections. Instead, she pursues her own project of remaking a household in shambles. To reconstruct the household to her liking, she expels the specter of her husband's dead wife by wiping out the grating vestiges and mementoes that the woman left behind. The protagonist's most egregious assault was to burn her rival's photos and knowingly abuse her clothing and personal belongings. By expelling her husband's former mother-in-law, she seeks to sever the bonds between his children and their dead mother. As part of her housecleaning, the new wife also kicks out the maid—another legacy of the spendthrift dead wife and her household mismanagement and ineptitude.

The third wife utilizes more constructive and nuanced strategies in dealing with her young stepchildren, especially the step-daughter, who is the mirror image of her dead mother and the apple of her father's eye. The new wife's skillful use of both strict discipline and coaxing—probably drawn from her professional experience as a teacher—proves effective in removing the children's antagonism and resentment toward her as well as in improving their personal traits, behavior, and academic performance. Her reformative program helps win her husband's approval, if not his heart, and her exemplary role as caregiver and supervisor for her husband's children overcomes the proverbial acrimony between stepmother and stepchildren.

In sharp contrast to popular assumptions about *sinyŏsŏng* as conceited, flighty squanderers, the heroine turns out to be a thrifty, diligent, and down-to-earth housekeeper. She is a tightfisted wife who haggles over measly prices and even sells off the delicacies specially prepared for her husband by his mother in the village market for profit—all to his embarrassment and dismay. Without minding her less-than-glorious reputation circulating among the villagers, she takes pride in her pragmatic and economical household operation. In this manner, she also systematically destroys and demystifies the popular image of women as ornamental, dependent, and passive attachments to men or at the mercy of the men in their lives—the diametrical opposite of her dead rival.

In the end, the protagonist even cuts ties with her friend who represents the very historian and reminder of her husband's past, which she wants to banish for good. Her intentional isolation from the rest of the villagers highlights her insistence on self-sufficiency and independence rather than any personal misanthropic streaks. She is in secure possession of a world of her own making, not a hand-me-down from her husband's former wives, and is at peace with herself. Above all, she actively looks toward the future, having worked for a new beginning despite her own wounded past, whereas her husband goes on in nostalgic indulgence of his past.

The third wife's thorough and firmly realistic outlook on life, buttressed by her feistiness in navigating domestic turmoil and her total disregard of others' opinions, makes her one of the rare refreshing female characters in modern Korean fiction.[8] The heroine prefers authenticity over likability. She finally triumphs over her

---

8. See Kim Pok-sun, *P'eminijŭm mihak kwa pop'yŏnsŏng ŭi munje* [Problems of feminist aesthetics and universality] (Seoul: Somyŏng Ch'ulp'an, 2005), 197–198.

domestic adversity, as the author rewards her with the forthcoming birth of her own child and with it a chance to create a brand-new family stamped with her distinctive individuality and dreams. She may eventually savor victory over her ex-lover—a doctor no less— since, as the adage goes, success is sweet revenge. ❧

Halo around the Moon

Han Mu-suk

It was the night before the ownership of the orphanage was to be transferred to Lady Hong—something she had been anxiously hurrying along. For several months, she had put all her efforts into completing the process, but she didn't feel excited now as she sat in her room and thumbed through the documents. She felt ill at ease, as if she were sitting in a stranger's house. Lady Hong wondered whether her feelings were due to the mayflies that annoyingly rushed into the lamplight—probably because it was going to rain— and in no time dropped dead in a mass on the sundry documents she had spread out before her. That didn't seem to be the only reason, though. Normally, she would have lambasted her young maid, Kŭmsun, for not having closed the windows to prevent the insects from flying in, but tonight for some reason Lady Hong didn't feel like going that far and instead faltered over the fine print on the documents. Something invisible seemed to have invaded her home, pressing down on it oppressively, and she felt hesitant about recklessly kicking up dust.

When Lady Hong returned home toward evening, she found the cheeky attitude of the saucy Kŭmsun, who had left the house in such a mess, not so much insolent as ludicrous. Actually, from the time she'd turned into the alleyway to her house, Lady Hong had felt disturbed because she noticed that, even though the evening had already deepened with the moonrise, the main gate of her

The title of the original is "Wŏrun" and was first published in *Hyŏndae munhak* (Modern literature; August 1955). The present translation is based on the text published in *Han Mu-suk munhak chŏnjip* [Collected literary works of Han Mu-suk] (Seoul: Ŭllyu Munhwasa, 1992), 6: 228-240.

house remained wide open. When she rushed all the way from the alley to her house, she found no sign of people about but sensed some hustle and bustle going on. On the narrow porch in front of the room next to the gate rented out to Ongnye's family, the basket holding bean sprouts was left tossed about and the bean-sauce stew was boiling over wildly on the briquette stove. On the stone terrace steps, shoes were scattered every which way.

Lady Hong felt that some mishap must have occurred, but was not too concerned about it. Outraged that Kŭmsun had totally brushed off her mistress's orders, she roared, "Kŭmsun! Where are you?" in a voice befitting Lady Hong's nickname, "Tiger Grandma." Only then did Kŭmsun drawl out a "Y-e-s"—n a surprisingly inappropriate, cheerful tone—and pop out of the backyard. After casting Kŭmsun her usual withering glare, which the young maid always thought worse than being clubbed to death, Lady Hong brusquely opened the sliding door to her main room.

This room was also in a jumble, as if Kŭmsun were hoping for her own death at Lady Hong's hands. The bronze tripod brazier was left tumbled over upside down—just as it was when Lady Hong had left the house—and the middle drawer of her three-drawer dresser was left open, with rags and strings dangling untidily. She had given Ongnye's mother instructions to iron her new Korean dress—the one she had tailored expressly for the business-transfer ceremony the next day—but it was hanging there with its wrinkles intact.

Lady Hong couldn't tell when the portable dinner table had been brought in, but it was sitting all messy in the middle of the room, and judging from the way the spoon was stuck in the rice bowl, it seemed her nephew still hadn't finished dinner. At the foot of the dinner table there were traces of spilled rice water—the only spots in the room, shining under the moonlight that peeped through a piece of glass attached to the sliding door.

The eight-year-old Chinp'yo, Lady Hong's nephew, was sitting huddled up, his head toward the east-facing sliding door and his back toward the dinner table. Intensely absorbed in the pieces of paper scattered about the room, he didn't notice his aunt's return. As usual, he was up late playing a game of slap match. All at once Lady Hong felt her fatigue ebbing. Without thinking, she was about to seize young Chinp'yo by his skinny shoulder. Just at that moment, Kŭmsun, who, at times like this usually remained hidden in the kitchen like a mouse in its hole, came into the room, and said, "The lady in the backroom is going to have baby," as if she were in charge of a serious matter.

When Lady Hong finally realized that her house was in disarray because of this woman, she felt like blowing her top. She had no experience giving birth to a child, but she knew very well that delivering a baby was no easy task. Still, she thought it rather presumptuous for the young woman living as a tenant in the backroom to throw even her landlady's house into such utter confusion. It didn't mean the young woman incurred Lady Hong's ill will— never. On the contrary, she was neat and tidy at housekeeping, the kind of person any landlord would like to have as a boarder, just as the realtor—a bald, old man, whose office was located on the hilltop—had said. Lady Hong had no idea what the young woman's husband did for a living, but he was rarely home, and on the rare occasion he was around, he made not the slightest sound. Unprompted, the young woman, blushing, even volunteered the information that her husband makes frequent business trips to the countryside.

Aged about twenty-five or twenty-six, the woman had a fine forehead and eyebrows, and her snaggletooth, revealed when smiling, only added charm to her lovely face. At the end of each month, she'd come to pay her rent, her lovable, smiling face flushed. Given her punctuality in paying her rent, she could be more assertive, but she would keep to her room as if she had committed some crime. She couldn't talk without going red in the face, and her sentences were chopped by "uh, uh,"—jarring on Lady Hong's ear. Even when she came to pay the rent, she would hesitate before handing over the money, as if she were making a difficult request.

Giving knowing winks to Lady Hong, Ongnye's mom said that all these things meant something fishy. Ongnye's mom, the renter of the doorway room, was as good as her word. She was very amenable, going through fire and water and thick and thin without any fuss. Probably because she got along by doing odd jobs, she was in the know about what went on in the neighborhood. She tended to exaggerate, but she never gossiped. Even those stories of hers that needed to be taken with a grain of salt were never just wild talk. Such was Ongnye's mom, and she expressed her misgivings about the young woman, winking meaningfully at Lady Hong: No one had visited her—not even a fuzzy-headed puppy—over the seven months since she'd moved into the back room. Unless the woman was in hiding, and something like this was impossible, she must be feeling guilty about something. Otherwise she wouldn't offer without being asked that her husband often made business trips to the countryside. And who knows what she meant by the "countryside"—she could have very well meant a central part of Seoul. Ongnye's mom added that, for a mistress, the young woman was too quiet and courteous in her manner.

Lady Hong's negative feelings toward the young woman were partly due to what Ongnye's mom had told her, but they also stemmed from the incident that happened about a month after the young woman moved in. Lady Hong was about to pass by the woman's room on her way back from taking care of things in the storage in the backhouse, when she noticed the aluminum pot on the briquette stove in front of the woman's room hissing like a steam engine. Upon opening the lid, Lady Hong found that the bottom of the pot was burning and making sizzling sounds, though she couldn't tell for how long it had been doing so. Considering it would have taken quite a while for the water in the pot—even though it was only for the use of two people—to have boiled to nothing, she concluded that the woman wouldn't have let this happen if she had been in her room and checking the pot. Lady Hong first took it off the stove and then shouted, "Are you home?" There was no answer. Wondering if the woman had gone out without locking her room—something unusual nowadays—Lady Hong gently opened the door.

The next moment, Lady Hong was almost jolted out of her wits and panicked—more than the young woman who was adjusting her disheveled dress—and she slammed the door shut and ran off from the front of the woman's room. She had really no idea that the "husband" would be visiting the woman in broad daylight—long before the end of the workday. It seemed to Lady Hong that it was she, not the young woman, who was humiliated. She felt her heart pounding and her head spinning. She fled to her own room and, leaning against the wall, closed her eyes.

In the dark field of her vision, circle after circle swam in a bewildering manner. Gradually, the view inside her closed eyes brightened. It revealed masses of cherry blossoms in glorious bloom, almost bending the tree branches. Not a single bud was left unopened, and every delicate petal was perfectly preserved—it was nature at its peak. The fragrance of blossoms almost made her breathless.

Each time the bees buzzed in and out, the blossoms quivered ever so softly, and, as if it were too much for them, they gently let light yellow pollen flutter away. This had happened one mellow spring day, and while looking on these blossoms, Lady Hong felt her heart throbbing and her head giddy.

Now she felt the same dizziness she had experienced at that time. She thought it was a crazy mental association, but there was something in common between the blossoms and the scene she had just witnessed—they shared the same kind of disquiet and furtiveness.

From that time on, Lady Hong began to find dense masses of blossoms in full-bloom loathsome, and, to that extent, the young woman appeared to her to be lewd. Lady Hong had become a young widow around twenty and had kept the integrity of her womanly virtues intact. This might have contributed to the obsession with sexual purity that led her to regard the mating acts of animals or plants as something shameful—just the way she looked at life itself. At any rate, she held such an attitude, which ended up overturning her earlier impression about the young woman. Lady Hong had completely forgotten her horrible experiences with her previous young male boarders—workers in a carpenter's shop—who had rented her backroom before the young woman came along to occupy it. They were four yokels who, making excuses about their lack of work, half the time didn't pay their rent when it was due, and Lady Hong had a hard time getting rid of them. Compared with those louts, the young woman was just the right thing—a rare bit of luck—but Lady Hong began acting stuck-up about renting the room to the woman.

So it was not out of warm feelings for the woman that Lady Hong visited the birthing room. She was not at all alarmed by the woman's gasping moans, as they were to be expected. Rather, she felt a certain revulsion toward the woman—a young thing and in her present circumstances—all stretched out on the floor, straining with every bit of her strength. In fact, Lady Hong looked in the room partly because she felt a real need to kill her boredom, and she was about to tell the young woman that in olden days women in the middle of their toil of hulling barley with a mortar hurried to their room to give birth. This was a story she had heard from others, but she intended to tell it as if she had seen such things herself. But no sooner had she entered the room than she was struck dumb.

In the birthing room, a few candles were burning. One was on the small dining table, obviously used as a desk after meal times; another was at the head of the woman; and one close to her feet. The room was humid and stuffy without a trace of circulating air. Still, the flames of the candles, making scratching noises, kept flickering, sometimes shriveling to the point of extinction and then fluttering back to full life. Each time this happened, the shadows cast by the candlelight became entangled and flit across the ceiling, on the walls, and everywhere else.

The moment Lady Hong opened the door of the room, something got on her nerves. Was it the sight of the young woman and Ongnye's mom, whose multiple quivering shadows under the flickering candlelight struck her as extraordinary? The atmosphere of the room was not at all vulgar but it was fraught with something unsettling. When Lady Hong stepped into the room, the young woman didn't even give her a glance, and all Ongnye's mom did was draw back a bit toward the wall to make room for Lady Hong to sit down. What a meagre way to receive her.

As if that were not enough, Ongnye's mom said, "Ma'am, well, I wasn't able to iron your dress. You see, they told me that the waters broke before lunch and …" Her attitude was just like that of the cocky Kŭmsun. It seemed she was utterly disregarding Lady Hong. Nothing like this had ever happened. Lady Hong, thus snubbed upon entering the room, felt ill at ease, as if she had tagged along with someone to a stranger's house. Yet she could neither go on standing there nor leave right away now that she'd entered the room. So, though feeling awkward, she chose to sit down.

Her eyes closed, the young woman was letting out painful moans, lying face down on the rolled-up bedding. No sooner had she fallen asleep than her body writhed with a start, as if stung by something. Each time she did so, the knuckles of her milky white hands interlocked with those of Ongnye's mom, which looked like hooks made of crooked branches, made cracking noises. Still, Ongnye's mom was completely unfazed. Her hands were obviously hurting, but she let the young woman continue to grasp them, even while admonishing her "not to strain too hard." Lady Hong had no idea what such expressions as "the waters broke" or "not to strain too hard" meant. All that loomed ever larger in her tired head was the impression that something dreadful was going on beneath the flickering light.

"No wonder birthing mothers curse their husbands! Don't they say that the whole sky looks as small as a tiny penny to these women? But then, it's what everyone goes through, so …" said Ongnye's mom, while rubbing the young woman's back. Her tone was calm, apparently coming from her midwifery experiences more than ten years after having given birth to seven children herself. But the young woman didn't catch on to what Ongnye's mom was saying. She abruptly shifted her eyes sideways and then shut them tightly, but those eyes looked simply like gaping holes incapable of registering anything. Her usually gentle face had become totally strange, and her color had changed abruptly from hot red to an ashen pallor. She seemed on the verge of losing her mind. She showed neither shyness nor concern for keeping up outward appearances.

The birthing mother gave off a strong body odor, probably because of her profuse, cold sweat. Lady Hong felt suffocated. The northeast-facing room, with its bedding and clothes containers piled up in the corner, was so small that except for the space for the quilted bed-mat spread out for the woman to lie on, there was barely room for other people to sit down. But the size of the room was not the only reason Lady Hong felt suffocated. In fact, while watching the woman groaning, she felt more chill than sympathy creep over her. Especially when the young woman twisted her body in pain, her ashen lips— still more colorless against her flushed cheeks—curled up to bare her strong and straight teeth. At such times, it appeared to Lady Hong that the person moaning there in the room wasn't really a young woman but a kind of adult female animal. That is, the woman appeared to Lady Hong like one of those living creatures that are simply lumped together under the name of animal—not some specific animal such as a sheep or a fox. But the word "animal" in this case was different from the meaning of "beast," as in Lady Hong's pet phrase, "those beastly things," an expression always on her lips whenever she encountered indecent conduct.

The whole scene in the room caught Lady Hong off guard. There was nothing vulgar about it. To the contrary, a fiercely tense sense of awe, evocative of a religious ritual, was hovering over the creaturely fear associated with labor pains and giving birth.

Her multiple shadows dancing under the flickering light, Ongnye's mom looked solemn and dignified as she remained seated there—her hands so tightly clutched by the birthing mother that their knuckles seemed about to be put out of joint. It appeared as if Ongnye's mom was watching over not the young woman but something far more precious. Unable to stand it any longer, Lady Hong finally left the room.

*   *   *

Lady Hong removed her reading glasses, and after shaking the dead mayflies off the documents, turned off the light. It was about ten o'clock. The slightly waning moon was high in the sky with its halo spread widely. The moon was bright, but probably due to the moisture around it, its light was hazy as if sprinkled with fine silver dust. The jujube tree standing behind the well looked bejeweled with pearls, and beside it, mayflies were circling in a column. It seemed that those mayflies that earlier were annoyingly flinging themselves at the lamplight had flown in from there. The column grew bigger and bigger, as if the mayflies had flown back to it once the lamplight had been turned off.

Up until a while ago, the high roof of the house in front of Lady Hong's was casting its menacing shadow onto the roof of the front quarters of her own house. But as the moon rose higher, the shadow moved away from it. It was a night when even the howls of dogs from afar seemed to bring back memories.

Ongnye's mom must have come out of the room at some point, and now was calling out to Kŭmsun in a roaring voice. Sulky after being soundly scolded by Lady Hong, Kŭmsun was doing something in the kitchen and didn't answer. But Ongnye's mom kept hollering at her to draw water from the well and put it in the earthenware tub ahead of time so that they wouldn't be flustered later. There was an overbearing tone in the shouts of Ongnye's mom, as if Kŭmsun were her own maid.

Kŭmsun seemed to have dashed out immediately, because the noise of water being drawn with the well bucket was soon heard.

Ongnye's mom looked up at the moon and murmured, "It's her first, so …" It wasn't clear whether she meant that the young woman's birthing, as it was her first time, was difficult and took longer. But after shaking her head, Ongnye's mom returned to the backyard.

In the backroom, the young woman's moans grew louder.

The hen in the chicken coop flapped its wings as if it were being bitten by bugs. Kŭmsun was nowhere to be seen around the well, probably because she'd gone back to the kitchen and kept herself in there. Only the haloed moon was floating on the surface of the water she had just poured into the earthenware tub.

Lady Hong couldn't help feeling more and more baffled.

She was unable to fathom the incredibly brazen attitude of both Ongnye's mom and Kŭmsun, who acted so presumptuously. Was it because the young woman, who had been living under Lady Hong's thumb, completely ignored her? Or was it because Lady Hong herself had been on the run from morning till she was dead tired?

These things were not exactly what disturbed Lady Hong. Long after the shadow of the roof of the house in front of hers receded, she couldn't help but gaze at the roof of the front quarters of her own house, drenched in the hazy moonlight as if draped in a piece of white cloth. While the roof kept bringing certain memories to mind, the halo around the moon reflected on the water in the earthenware tub seemed to drag her against her will back to the past—it was all too much for her to bear.

*   *   *

The scene was the memorial service invoking the spirits of the dead that was performed after the clothes of the deceased were put on the roof. The light in the silk lantern was flickering. Lady Hong was lying prostrate on the straw mat, her face on a straw pillow, and someone pulled the decorative garnet hairpin out of her hair. The pin was never to be put back. She was nineteen at the time, and the year nineteen, which was considered unlucky, turned out to be true in her case. And it was in this manner that at her husband's funeral her hair fixed up in a chignon was undone and let down.

Fearful of the longstanding rules of a traditional upper-class family, the young bride, still in her crimson skirt, was exercising her utmost discretion in words and conduct. And there was no way for her to nurse her husband, who was gasping for breath in the small room in the outer quarters. All she could do was wait in the women's inner quarters for more than ten days for the news of his passing. Her young eighteen-year-old husband, one year her junior, had contracted tuberculosis less than half a year after their marriage, and the couple had been living separately in complete sexual abstinence for more than three years, not even able to see one another.[1] If her wet nurse, who had accompanied her as a maid at her marriage, had not hurriedly made arrangements upon hearing that his symptoms had taken a turn for the worse, Lady Hong would have missed the chance to see her husband's tall, slim body and hauntingly handsome looks that almost made her shudder. To her he remained a tall young groom whose slender face was clean and fair as beeswax.

When she got to see her husband, taking advantage of her stern father-in-law's absence to attend his clan's memorial service, it was almost like committing theft. His childlike appearance of three years before had vanished, and a thin shadow of facial hair was in place below his nose. Her heart raced. She felt shy and timid, but this was outweighed by her surging excitement.

Quietly, the young wife placed her trembling hand on the forehead of her ailing husband. It was burning with high fever. She pressed her hand down gently. Thereupon, her husband lifted his thin, feverish hand that was resting on his chest and put it on top of his wife's hand and pressed it down with a force unbelievably strong for such an emaciated invalid. It was almost as if he were trying to imprint the trace of his wife's hand on his forehead. In no time, held between the husband's fiery forehead and hand, the wife's hand became burningly hot. In the end, a feverish sensation ran through her whole body.

From that moment on, the wife prayed every night, ritually offering pure water. The moon waxed and waned on the bowl of pure water that she offered at midnight near the well. One evening in early summer when the haloed moon was up, the pure water, after mirroring the moon, was taken away. The ceremonial pure water, removed upon the young husband's passing, seemed to have been awaiting his death. Thenceforth, Lady Hong had to lead a long life as a widow. And for the nearly forty years up to the present she had never known another man.

With the passage of time, the hot sensation of the burning forehead and hand on that night cooled, and once in a while when the word "husband" flitted across her mind, Lady Hong couldn't even connect it with the eighteen-year-old youth with the fair, wax-white face. Although the name of her husband was Pak Uyang, it didn't

---

1. Obviously the wife's in-laws forbade the young couple's physical contact, especially sexual, to spare the sick husband from draining his energy.

matter to her whether a man was called Pak Uyang or Nam Uyang, since the womanly principle of "a chaste and virtuous wife who never serves two husbands" remained in her as an unchallenged, dignified rule.

She simply remembered her husband as a handsome youth, and even when she met his nephew, who was said to be an exact copy of his maternal uncle—her deceased husband—she was not particularly moved by past emotions. At such times, she smiled wryly at the thought that she had never really noticed her husband's facial features.

Someday, upon her eventual death, Lady Hong would be buried together with her dead husband in his grave in Yŏju.[2] But if the spirits of the dead truly exist, wouldn't the husband—a mere youth—and the aged wife with white hair, be very surprised and embarrassed at meeting each other after death? It seemed as if Lady Hong's life had already been absurdly entombed with her young, dead husband.

But up to the present (she was now sixty), such thoughts had never occurred to her. Just as a one-eyed person wouldn't fuss over a lost eye, so had she lived all the more unyieldingly, even capitalizing on her status as a widow.

When she set her mind to something, Lady Hong hurled herself upon it. The reason she returned to her natal home after having marked the third anniversary of her husband's death was to enter school, which others shunned as a place where a woman's virtues were ruined. After completing her studies to which she had abandoned herself, she obtained a position as a home economics teacher at a girls' school. She kept her seat for twenty years without interruption, and rumor spread that she had saved a handsome amount of money. Lady Hong put strict limits on her budget and dressed in a simple white calico Korean blouse or a gray serge blouse with a matching gray or black skirt. She went as far as to keep her eye on the food consumed by those working for her.

Lady Hong talked a lot about how happy she was to offer her matchmaking skills—she said she liked young people—but for

---

2. Yŏju is a city in Kyŏnggi Province, south of Seoul, along the Han River. The area is noted as the location of the tomb of King Sejong (1397–1450), in which he is buried together with his consort, Queen Sohŏn (1395–1446)—the first example of such a burial practice in the royal household.

some reason, none of her students had requested her intermediary role. Her adopted son and his wife, both quiet and meek, ran away before the outbreak of the Korean War without claiming anything from her, because they could no longer stand her. Ever since she'd taken in her maternal nephew, Chinp'yo, orphaned during the Korean War, her concern seemed to be to bring him up well, or as she often said, "I can't die until I make a decent human being out of him!" But Chinp'yo couldn't help but cringe in the presence of his aunt, burying his slender neck into his shoulders.

Just as a fortuneteller had predicted, Lady Hong's life had been rough, but she possessed a domineering power, as if destined to stand over others. After she quit teaching, she took up the role of representative of the neighborhood association. It consisted of nothing but running errands for others, but since she took the job it gave off the aura of a high-ranking official position. Her dedicated efforts as the so-called patriotic head of the neighborhood during the colonial period, which had kept her busy climbing up and down the steps of Korean Shinto shrines,[3] was altogether transferred after liberation to Christianity, and she was now known as a church deaconess.

It was also thanks to her church that she could take over the orphanage, but she had quite a hard time during the process of the transaction. Although throughout her life she had had to endure a great deal of waiting—both long and short—that tested her patience, this time, the matter was rather weighty and was hampered by various obstacles. So she thought that until she had the business of orphanage transfer concluded with the final seal firmly stamped she wouldn't be able to relax.

Aware that a restful sleep was out of question, Lady Hong thought the young woman's birthing labor might help her kill some time, but she had no idea her memories would drift in such a direction. Was it because tonight was an early summer night just like that haloed night in the past? Or, was it because the young woman's groans were reigning over everything else, amidst noiselessly agitating apprehension, just like that night? If not, then, is human life,

---

3. During the colonial period, especially from the early 1940s, Koreans were forced to pay homage to the Japanese emperor by making bows toward the east, the site of his throne, or by paying visits to a Shinto shrine. Obviously, Lady Hong was an eager follower of this colonial rule.

at its birth or at its death, not just the individual's own business, but a mystery that goes far beyond human speculation?

Without realizing it, Lady Hong shook her head. The old clock on the wall sleepily struck eleven.

Over her head, the outline of the moon tilted slightly toward the west and looked more diffused than before. The haloed moon was still mirrored on the water in the earthenware tub, but the mayfly column was gone.

She remembered the story told by her humorous natural history teacher when she was still a student about how a column of may-flies usually forms before it rains. He'd said that mayflies don't live for even one whole day. Forming such columns in the air, they fly around in a mass and mate. Then they fall to the ground, where males die immediately and females die soon after laying their eggs. Those stories now came crowding into her mind.

Does this mean, then, that the mayflies that until a while ago were frenziedly whirling about in the air had already died, having carried out their tasks? In a way, it meant that the mayflies that an-noyingly rushed into the light and burned to death and those that had died after forming a column and finishing their duties were alike in their plunge to death less than an hour apart. But for the species of insects themselves, wouldn't there be an enormous dif-ference between these two deaths? These words that she had heard long ago returned to her mind with a sharp poignancy.

Lady Hong felt that she could vaguely understand tonight's at-titudes on the part of Ongnye's mom and Kŭmsun. Weren't they participating in "life"? Wasn't this the reason they could be so au-dacious?

Lady Hong stood up as if she had received a sound whipping. It no longer mattered to her whether the young woman might be a mistress or that the baby's father was not even present at the birth. The moment carried a far greater urgency than such matters as morals or order. The woman was facing a most proper task that had to be undertaken: a task she had to carry out by descending to the level of an animal, the level Lady Hong had felt earlier, that is, by returning to nature itself.

Lady Hong stepped down from the main hall to the ground. Just at that moment, a rending shriek rang out from the back wing, fol-lowed by a feeble cry—as puny as that of a helpless animal.

Instantly, Lady Hong closed her eyes and imagined putting her palms together before the water in the earthenware tub, which was still mirroring the haloed moon, as if it were ritual, pure water.

For no apparent reason, Lady Hong felt something hot clouding her eyes. A thought flashed across her mind. Wasn't this what she had been waiting for all along, something that had passed her by while she was waiting?

Suddenly, an intense fatigue swooped down upon her. It was not a tiredness coming from the work that had kept her on the run from morning. Rather, it might well be the weariness she had been experiencing throughout her life.

CR

Han Mu-suk
(or Han Moo-Sook; 1918-1993)

Born and reared as the third of five children in an upper-class family in Seoul, Han Mu-suk enjoyed a privileged life from childhood. Her father, a highly educated government official known for his honesty and industriousness, held various official positions, including the governorship of Sach'ŏn County in South Kyŏngsang Province. Due to his repeated administrative relocations, the family had to move frequently to different parts of the country, forcing Han to transfer schools several times. Han's mother, a model *yangban* Seoulite, ran her household matters meticulously and with utmost propriety. She supervised the task of preparing traditional foods and clothing, observing traditional annual and seasonal rituals, and overseeing her children's upbringing to hand down properly the fine Korean customs and practices to the next generation.

Although Han was prone to illness from infancy, her parents' care and protection helped her through numerous medical emergencies; thanks to their unfaltering support, she obtained a high-quality education. Han's parents recognized and fostered their daughter's artistic gifts from early on. At age eight (1926), her painting placed in the Berlin international children's art exhibit and, from 1931 she began receiving private lessons from a Japanese painter. Han's aesthetic finesse, artistic perspectives, and stylistic refinement are detected in her literary texts, often in her descriptions of characters, background, and setting, and at times in her orchestration of key symbols and images.

Han attended Pusan Girls' School, a school for Japanese girls in Korea, and her plan after graduation was to major in painting in college. But her dreams were thwarted when she contracted tuberculosis in 1936, her senior year. Fortunately, she found respite from the long, distressing, and wearisome seclusion at home for convalescence by contributing illustrations to the novel *Millim* (The Jungle; part 2; 1937–1938; serialized in *Tonga ilbo*) by contemporary woman novelist Kim Mal-bong (1901–1962). This assignment was an honor and an exceptional public recognition of Han's talent. Han also voraciously consumed Western literary masterpieces (in Japanese translation) by novelists such as Anton Chekhov, Fyodor Dostoyevsky, André Gide, Nikolai Gogol, Maxim Gorky, Thomas Mann, and Leo Tolstoy, which were stocked in her home library and collected mostly by her older, Japan-educated brother. Han's literary visions and themes—notable for their emphasis on striking a balance between time-honored traditions and modernity, forming a harmony between East and West, and blurring the boundaries between life and death—may have been rooted in her education at home during those formative years.[4]

In 1940, when she had recovered from her illness, Han was married to the son of her father's friend, arranged by the two fathers without the marital partners' consent or knowledge of each other. The marriage was a momentous turn in Han's life, as she had to make a radical transition from the progressive, Westernized family environment to a Confucian-bound, formality-oriented in-law's multigenerational household. For the young bride, the daily routine was strenuous and draining—physically, emotionally, and mentally—often to a breaking point, which was compounded by the birth of her first daughter in 1941.

Chancing upon a newspaper advertisement about a literary competition held by the magazine *Sinsidae* (New Age), Han set out to write her first novel, *Tomoshibi o motsu hito* (The woman carrying a lamp), in Japanese, thanks to her training in the Japanese girls' school. Han wrote the work stealthily at night after she completed her household chores so no family members would notice, save for her caring and supportive husband. A desperate outlet for Han from the stress and frustration of her married life, the novel received first prize in 1942. Thenceforward, Han even ventured into the drama genre and won prizes for two plays, *Maŭm* (The heart; 1943) and *Sŏri kkot* (Flower of frost; 1944), but she was unable to attend the award ceremonies because of family duties.

Han's real entrance into the Korean literary world with five children in tow came with the publication of her post-liberation novel, *Yŏksa nŭn hŭrŭnda* (History flows; 1948), which won the competition sponsored by the newspaper *Kukche sinbo* (International news). A long-winding family saga, the novel traces the vicissitudes that *yangban* families and their servants underwent over three generations, from the most tumultuous closing years of the Chosŏn dynasty to the early post-liberation days. The novel reveals Han's view of time as an equalizer of power and class divides and history

---

4. See Yung-Hee Kim, "Dialectics of Life: Hahn Moo Sook and Her Literary World," in *Creative Women of Korea*, ed. Young-Key Kim-Renaud, 192–215.

as the ultimate judge of truth and justice. For a decade, from 1948 to 1958 (except for 1950 when the Korean War broke out), Han concentrated on writing short stories and published nearly thirty of them. "Wŏrun" and "Kamjŏng i innŭn simyŏn" (The abyss of emotion; 1957) are some of the acclaimed products of this period. The latter is noted for its delicate psychological probing into a young woman's guilt-ridden and conflicted views on sexuality and their negative impact on romantic love.

In the 1960s, Han resumed writing full-length novels and published *Pit ŭi kyedan* (Steps of light; 1960) and *Sŏngnyu namujip iyagi* (The tale of the house with pomegranate trees; 1964). The latter is another example of Han's interest in family history. It traces complicated developments of love triangles, treachery, hidden crimes, resentments, and other tainted interpersonal relationships of Korean intellectuals from the colonial period to modern times. Han also tried her hand at writing novellas and published the highly praised "Ch'ukche wa unmyŏng ŭi changso" (The site for festival and destiny; 1962) and "Yusuam" (The hermitage of flowing water; 1963), both of which question the meaning of the lives of women who are dependent upon men. The same period also saw another diversification in Han's career as she took up international travels to places like Japan, Yugoslavia, France, Israel, Sweden, Mexico, and the United States to participate in international literary conferences as a Korean representative and to deliver special lectures. Such activities continued well into the late 1980s.

In 1976, Han and her husband, a successful financier and accomplished painter in his own right, held their first joint art exhibition, displaying their paintings, calligraphy, and sketches; the couple's exhibit was held again in 1985 and 1990. These creative projects reconfirmed Han's lasting passion for art, her first love, and her artistic gifts. Han's last novel, *Mannam* (Encounter; 1989), represents the peak of her enduring fascination with the family chronicle. The text relates the complex and intricate life story of Chŏng Yag-yong (1762–1836), the eminent court official and the most erudite scholar of practical learning of the Chosŏn dynasty, by intertwining it with the heartbreaking life course of his nephew—both caught in the Chosŏn government's persecution of Catholics. After Han's death, the Han Moo-Sook Foundation was established by her family in 1995, which has since annually awarded the Han Moo-Sook Literature Award. ∝

TEXTUAL READINGS

Undergirded by the author's skillful deployment of natural images such as the moon and mayflies and the apt use of memory, "Halo around the Moon" unveils the damaging ramifications of the long-standing Confucian prohibition on widow's remarriage and its corollary, female sexual morality. Protagonist Lady Hong is a classic example of a traditional upper-class widow. Married at nineteen, she was a flawless bride for her ailing husband and a perfect daughter-in-law who impeccably followed the strict spousal protocols and ritual formalities set by her in-law's household. All her wifely devotion and ritualized performances having gone for nothing, she was widowed childless at twenty-two. Since then—her modern education and professional career notwithstanding—she kept her widowhood spotless, resolutely subscribing to the Confucian mandates required of her. Lady Hong appears to have a cynical view about her expected burial with the dead husband she barely knew, but she is aware that she cannot free herself from such a binding marriage custom even after her death. Thus, an exemplary specimen of widowhood, she maintains an attitude of moral superiority and is rigid, overbearing, and unforgiving in interpersonal relationships and social interactions. Most of all, she harbors a puritanical view of sex as something obscene, disorderly, and bestial—something beneath human dignity to be despised and shunned—never to be part of her life. Truth be told, Lady Hong's whole existence has been mortgaged and fossilized by the patriarchal gender codes she has embraced without question.

As the story reveals, the make-up of Lady Hong's character, her moral fiber, is far from perfect. She has opportunistic and dishonorable streaks, displayed in her pro-Japanese conduct during the colonial period and her chameleon-like change into a devout Christian after liberation. Her impending takeover of the orphanage is the very result of her obsequious affiliation with the Christian establishment that had a powerful influence in Korea following the Korean War. Lady Hong is an indomitable, shrewd, and even underhanded self-seeker and survivor in the public domain. Her treatment of people of lesser social standing and the underprivileged and needy in her private realm, such as her young, war-orphaned nephew and the maid Kŭmsun, is abrasive and domineering. People familiar with Lady Hong's personal traits would rather avoid her despite her professed kindness and concern for them. It is ironic that such a woman with a hardened heart, frosty, and inflexible and dubbed "Tiger Grandma," is about to take possession of an orphanage. Her sexual consciousness and energy, suppressed and warped by her adherence to the correct ways of widowhood, may have sought expression in the form of her dictatorial and harsh dealings with others.[5]

Lady Hong's frigid views on gender and sex, however, meet a startling challenge in her encounter with the seemingly young, unmarried female boarder who gives birth. Witnessing the young woman's birthing process throws Lady Hong's disdain off balance and concurrently grants her an epiphany. Lady Hong finds herself in awe of procreation and its sacredness and realizes a reverence for life no matter who has brought it into the world. It represents the suspension of her moral judgment and the purge of her self-righteousness—analogous to a religious conversion—with the young woman serving as the key catalyst. It serves as an enactment of her own spiritual rebirth in the wake of the death of her old self, occasioned by her symbolic partaking in the woman's birthing effort.

As Lady Hong catches sight of the haloed moon reflected on the water in the coarse pottery bowl prepared for the birthing mother and listens to the woman's moaning, she is struck by uncanny similarities between the woman's giving birth and her husband's death, the same haloed moon of early summer connecting them. Simultaneously, the death of the mayflies, which moments ago formed a thick mating column in the garden, awakens in Lady Hong a profound sense of mystery of how life and death are enmeshed. In such an epiphanic moment, she perceives the absolute truth in disposing her exacting moral/sexual categorization and judgmental arrogance toward other human beings. This marks a turning point wherein Lady Hong, who has been forced to forego motherhood, confronts her own self-deception expressed through her mixed feelings of jealousy and aversion of the young woman and so recognizes her own hypocrisy.[6]

---

5. See Song In-hwa, "Sŏng'ae ŭi sŭng'in kwa ch'egwan ŭi sisŏn" [Endorsement of sexual love and visions of resignation] in Ku Myŏng-suk et al., *Han Mu-suk munhak ŭi chip'yŏng* [The horizon of Han Mu-suk's literary world] (Seoul: Yerim Kihoek, 2008), 194–196.

6. See Ch'oe Ki-suk, "Chungch'ŏp toen sam ŭl ŭngsihanŭn tugae ŭi kŏul"

In the end, Lady Hong feels overwhelmed by fatigue, "the weariness of lifetime," suggestive of the exhaustion from her long, arbitrary performance as the custodian of unadulterated widowhood as exacted by her society. She has been sexually "othering" herself, which has fixed her in the ideologically frozen realm of Confucian widowhood, draining some forty years of her life of vitality and naturalness. The well-timed references to mating mayflies and cherry blossoms help accentuate the necessity for Lady Hong to embrace the universal law governing sexual and reproductive activities of all created beings, including humans, as natural and normal. Above all, the image of the moon—the symbol of enlightenment—heightens Lady Hong's gender awakening and suggests her liberation from her own cultural and moral prejudices. As such, "Halo around the Moon" represents a subtly crafted critique of gender and sexual imprisonment set up by the Confucian principle against widows and underscores the urgency of releasing women from such wasteful and dehumanizing shackles. ଔ

[Two mirrors intensely looking at the layers of life], in Yi Ho-gyu et al., *Han Mu-suk munhak segye* [Han Mu-suk's literary world] (Seoul: Saemi, 2000), 217–218.

An Episode at Dusk, 2

Pak Wan-sŏ

Though the sun was out, the playground in the apartment compound was empty. All the units in my apartment building had put their begonia pots on the flower stands outside their windows, which made it feel like spring. The residents of our apartment building communally bought these rectangular flower pots, recommended—not mandated—by the management office. Each one of these pots contained three plants, as cute as branchy young pines, which looked like merchandise just shipped in from a factory. Imagining that within a month these plants would dry up and die, wither and rot, become leafy only, or bloom beautifully—all depending on the owner's care, I felt a self-satisfied smile on my lips. It was because my apartment was the only unit with flowers blooming late into autumn.

In the apartment building I had lived in until the year prior the residents collectively purchased petunia pots every year. The colors and shapes of the petunias after the cold weather set in were especially delicate, and the young neighborhood women would ask me about the plant's name and admire the flowers, probably because they didn't realize they'd killed the same plants through their neglect. Not only flowers and plants but also animals such as dogs, cats, and birds that we raised at home thrived under my care, so I have heard since I was young that I have a nurturing hand.

The title of the original is "Chŏmun nal ŭi saphwa 2," and was first published in *Tto hana ŭi munhwa* (Alternative culture) in April 1987. The present translation is based on the text included in Pak Wan-sŏ, *Chŏmun nal ŭi saphwa: Pak Wan-sŏ sosŏlchip* (Episodes at dusk: collection of Pak Wan-sŏ's short stories) (Seoul: Munhak kwa Chisŏngsa, 1991), 88–106.

I felt a burning sense of frustration at the gap between my sure belief in my special power for nurturing life and my inability to put that power to good use for the things that really needed it. I opened the glass veranda door, beset by a premonition that fever-ish flames of emotion might blaze up within me. The weather was much colder than I'd expected. The wind thrashed like a wild ani-mal and made my blouse-sleeves swell up like footballs. Atop the roof of the neighborhood administrative building across from the pavilion for the elderly, the national flag, the New Village flag,[1] and the blue flag marked with the city seal fluttered violently, like a merciless whipping.

The sanitarium was on a hill overlooking a river to the south, but its main gate faced the north, along the road leading to the na-tional highway. This meant that the sanitarium sat with its murky-gray back toward the main gate. As the road from the main gate to the sanitarium was a long and winding incline, the building's un-sightly back was the only view visitors had all the way up the hill, and it weighed down every one of them—already anxiety-ridden—with an ominous foreboding. However, once they reached the sani-tarium, after having struggled up the slope, visitors were struck by its dazzlingly bright interior, as if they had been transported to an-other world. Probably because of such a surreal sensation, visitors often shook off the sinister premonitions that had been plaguing them up to that point, buoyed up by new illusions that everything was just fine.

My son looked carefree, and when he emerged alongside a white-robed doctor of his own age, both clapping each other on the shoulders, he looked more like the doctor's colleague than his pa-tient. "Everything is fine!" I exclaimed to myself, and with my heart ready to break, I hugged my son. When my son lifted me up and then set me down I felt elated, though only very briefly.

"You look great! Really! By the way, who is that doctor? I never saw him before," I asked. Regrettably, the doctor who had come out with my son left before I had the chance to say hello.

---

1. Begun in the early 1970s, the New Village Movement was a government-sponsored campaign for the modernization of the countryside, which had been left behind in the central government's overemphasis on the industrialization of major cities and urban centers. It grew into nationwide grassroots movements and resulted in the improvement of rural incomes, living standards, and overall morale among South Korea's farming populations.

"You mean that fellow? He comes here once or twice a month as a volunteer."

"Listen, you don't call your doctor 'fellow!'" I said in a shaky voice, my heart sinking anew.

My son answered with a soft laugh, "He's an upperclassman from my high school, Mom. We were very close, like friends."

"Really? You must have felt uncomfortable meeting him in a place like this," I said to my son, only stroking the back of his hand, unable to look him in the eyes.

Except for that small incident, my visit with my son on that day was no different from other visits. When I had lunch with him at the self-service cafeteria in the sanitarium, his health, good appetite, full and ruddy cheeks, and bright expression dissipated my hunger. I simply went through the motions of eating. As the other patients looked just as normal as my son, I couldn't believe this was a sanitarium for psychiatric treatment, and every now and then felt despair. After lunch, I held my son's hand and took a leisurely walk around the compound. Still, when the barred door that shut in patients like my son came into my view at some distance, I quickly turned my eyes away and pretended not to have seen it, as if I'd catch something infectious from it.

My son dragged me to the garden with the same innocent expression as when he'd entered primary school. He suggested we go find out how much the bud at the tip of the highest branch of the purple magnolia tree had grown since a few days ago, when he'd seen it swollen as big as a baby's hand.

"Look, Mom, it's grown as big as your fist," my son pointed to the top of the magnolia tree, bending my fingers one after another into a fist. I couldn't tell which one he meant, because at the tip of each straggling branch there were buds about to burst into blossom. The sky was dazzlingly bright in the broad daylight, making me feel dizzy.

"It sure has," I answered halfheartedly, and looked out at the river winding around the gently sloping hills. As if the river marked the limits of the land owned by the sanitarium, there was neither fence nor gate to the south, and I could spot nothing else that might serve as boundary marker for the sanitarium. The building looked completely different from the northern view. It was painted a bright, clean, and pale yellow, and its large windows were framed with red bricks. Overall, it looked more like a residential condominium than a sanitarium.

The garden was nicely landscaped with lawns and ornamental trees and gradually sloped into a hill, and birds flapped away from time to time at the approach of people. My son turned back from our walk, saying that I'd catch cold, although I didn't feel cold at all. Following my son, who was walking hurriedly as if being pursued, I asked him, panting, "When do you think you can leave here?"

"I really don't know."

"What do you mean?"

"I'm not interested in leaving."

I felt totally drained, the way water slips through a strainer. My son no longer held my arm for support. Even after reaching the sanitarium, I didn't dare say anything to him. Still unable to give up, I blurted out the same question to his doctor.

"Please don't be overanxious."

This was not the first time I'd heard this answer. Since I'd heard the same answer over and over before, I must have implored with the same question then. At the risk of disappointment and embarrassment, I ended up adding one more plea this time around, "My son is going to be thirty soon. I want him to return to society and find his share of work."

"This is also a society here, and Mr. Yun is doing a fine job, having found his share of work."

"Do you mean his playing the role of a patient?"

"No. Mr. Yun is not a patient here at all. He is helping with the work of treating the patients. The drama he wrote and produced went very well. Mr. Yun himself must have felt it rewarding, but I've never seen patients so happy before."

"Does this mean you plan to keep him here indefinitely to make him—a perfectly normal person—do such things?" Unable to control myself, I raised my voice but quickly dropped my head. I had had the bitter experience of having fought to take my son home in just this manner, only to have to bring him back later.

As I prepared to go home, my son was eager to see me off. At dusk, the wind was harsh on the hilly back road, already gloomy. Each time, when the wind against my chest suddenly blasted against my whole body like a stinging whip, I stopped and waved to my son, who was following me, to go back at once. He ignored me with a grin and kept following. He seemed to be enjoying the sharp winds. I liked his longish hair fluttering in the wind. As I looked back at him, his fresh, youthful countenance, incompatible with the gloomy back side of the sanitarium, stirred up in me a strong but hopeless motherly desire. While I kept gesturing to my son to go back, waving my hand, in truth, I wanted to take him along with me.

My son followed me precisely up to the main gate, then stopped there and said goodbye. His leave-taking was usually quite long. Besides saying the word "goodbye," he would become suddenly talkative, telling me not to miss my meals and morning walks, worrying about the health of his father, and expressing concerns for his older sisters and their husbands, and so on.

Growing exasperated, I cut him short. "Listen, won't you come along with me a little farther? I mean up to the bus stop just right over there."

My son shook his head and looked away. I was aware how ugly my face had turned in my desperate effort to manipulate him. My son stood stiff with fright, clutching the iron bar of the small entrance door attached to the tightly closed main gate, although no one was going to drag him out of there by force.

My son was free and healthy only within the enclosure of the sanitarium. He hadn't been fully healed. At one point in the past, he had aspired to bet his life on ideals incomprehensible to me, and how brilliantly his youthfulness glowed then! The present shabby appearance of my son, gripped by fear in place of his former idealism, pierced my heart.

"Hurry and go back! Hurry, you might catch cold." Leaving behind these words, which were shredded by the gusts of rising wind, I walked hurriedly in the direction of the bus stop. All the while, the spring wind kept kicking up wildly, and as soon as I got on the bus, I felt not just my cheeks but my entire body smart as if I'd just been flogged.

Just before closing the window, I stretched out my neck and looked up at the veranda above my unit. The light of the sky was so bright it stung my eyes, like when I'd looked up at the top of the purple magnolia tree with my son. The flower stand on the upstairs unit was empty. It was true that not every resident had to buy begonia pots or place them outside. Still, I couldn't let go of the fact that only the flower stand at Kayŏn's unit upstairs remained empty. I began to worry about one thing after another. My incurable, inborn habit of worrying made me apprehensive about Kayŏn's situation. I wondered if she had conjugal problems, financial troubles, despair, spiritual destitution, and so on. None of these concerns was confirmed, but they were not far off the mark, either.

Among the many students who had passed through the high school—my alma mater, where I taught Korean language for nearly twenty years—Kayŏn was not one of those students who left lasting impressions. Even after I learned she was living in the unit right above me, I couldn't recall her from her high school days.

It was only a few days after my move into the new apartment that I heard my doorbell ring. Before opening the door, I asked who was there, and the person outside feebly replied that she was from upstairs.

"Okay, is that you, the baby's mother?" I asked.

As soon as I opened the door, the woman stepped back a little, her eyes wide open, and said, as if suppressing a shriek, "Oh my goodness! Aren't you our teacher, Mrs. Kim Ch'ang-hŭi? I had no idea you were living in this apartment."

"Whoever you are, it's good to meet you," I said in a relaxed manner, because I often had such encounters.

"I am Min Kayŏn, the class of twenty-nine."

"Right, right, I remember. Come in. Well, what brings you here?"

"Ah … my stuff, no, my laundry seems to have fallen down on your flower stand."

"Is that right? Come in and check it out. I wonder if it's still there, since I don't know when it dropped down. You see, it's so windy in the flower stand area."

"It should be there because I just saw it."

It was summertime and Kayŏn had on sleeveless, baggy overalls, and her bare arms and legs appeared especially white and smooth. She was rather plump-looking and not sickly, but my heart went out to her, as she didn't appear up to the task of dealing with little rascals like her children. It should have been none of my business, but it was out of my motherly concern—a mother with a daughter her age. Sure enough, when I saw Kayŏn reenter the room after picking up things piece by piece from my flower stand on the veranda, I noticed that they were not laundry but a jumble of trivial things. Clearly, it had been her children's prank. Kayŏn cradled in her arms socks, a seasoning container, a pot mat, a comb, a shoe brush, and so on, as if to hide them from me, and hurriedly made to leave with no intention of sitting down.

"Why don't you have something cold to drink before you go? It's good timing, because I happen to be all by myself too."

"No, thank you, ma'am."

"What do you mean by 'no'? People say that female students are of no use,[2] but you shouldn't be so curt. I've given you credit for recognizing me first, but I guess you're no different from those who snub me."

I put a bottle of Coke and two glasses on the tea table, but Kayŏn remained standing, uneasy and hesitant, as if she were trying to think of a way to escape.

"Are you worried about your children? Let me tell you, they know how to find you. They must be very smart. I know how hard it is to raise kids without help. But it serves you young people right, who clamor for nuclear families. When you need to go out, you can leave your children with me from time to time," I said kindly, thinking about my married daughters.

"Ma'am, I don't have children yet." With these words behind her, Kayŏn left as if fleeing from me.

Alone, I felt rather embarrassed. Why did I make such a mistake? Even before I identified who Kayŏn was, upon learning she'd come from upstairs, I almost immediately treated her as a mother of young children. I'd jumped to the conclusion that she had two mischievous boys born within a year of each other, without even asking whether they were boys or girls or how old they were. If she had been hoping to have children, Kayŏn might have been hurt.

On the first or second day after our move into our new apartment, I heard noises from upstairs throughout the day. They sounded like noises made by children jumping repeatedly from something high or chasing after each other, playing a game of hide and seek. When they became unruly, the noises even shook the shade on our ceiling light. Sometimes I heard an adult shouting, unable to bear them any longer. It was a male voice, low but audible

---

2. This statement refers to the Korean general perception that female students, unlike male students, do not usually continue their relationship with their former teachers after their graduation either from high school or college, and especially after their marriage. In contrast, male students are presumably more inclined to keep up their teacher-student relationship, as they value the importance of such connections for their social and professional advancement.

from afar. I guessed that the gentle mother, driven to her wit's end by the mischief of her rascals, was seeking the help of her husband. My assumption seemed almost certain. However, I must have confused the floor on which Kayŏn's apartment was located with someone else's.

Upon reflection, I recalled that I had made a similar mistake when we moved into our previous apartment. At that time, I couldn't sleep well because of the sound of nails being hammered into a piece of hard wood in the middle of the night. The noise came from right above the ceiling of my inner room, where I was lying down to sleep. It was unbearable to be awakened by the same noise night after night—not just one or two nights. At first, I thought that a carpenter was living in that apartment, but there was no reason for anyone to work at night, unless carpentry work was illegal—secretly to be done after dark.

When we had an apartment association meeting, I discreetly inquired about who lived in apartment 806 and found out that a married couple, both schoolteachers, were living there with the husband's mother. The mother-in-law, who attended the meeting, lamented her life, as she was forced to live like a mute with no one to talk to day in, day out. She said that she could take it during the day at least, because the couple had to go to work. But it was unbearable for her not to see even their shadows from early evening to the following morning, once they disappeared into their room under the pretext of being tired. I was the only one there in the group old enough to listen to her complain about how the worst misery in the world was not having anyone to talk to. But instead of chiming in, I was absorbed with other thoughts.

Where was the hammering noise really coming from then? That night without fail I heard the same noise, and the unresolved mystery turned into a dark and sinister illusion to me. Now that I couldn't trust my sense of direction, the noise coming from upstairs sank below my pillow and then reverberated long into the distant future, snaking through my sweet and shallow sleep. Lying in an immobile trance state, I was listening to the noise of nails being driven into my coffin. Although I wasn't dead yet, none of my blood-related children, for whom I had worked my fingers to the bone, would leave home in search of medicinal herbs. Instead, they wailed wildly in tune with the nailing sounds. They were trying to make sure I died. It was a nightmare.

One night the nightmarish sounds of those nails peaked. A few days later I saw a three-storied chest made of pagoda tree, supposedly to be put on show at an arts and crafts exhibition, being carried out of the apartment building. The noises of nail hammering finally stopped. I discovered that the craftsman's apartment was located upstairs, diagonally opposite from ours. While I acknowledged that there was some problem with my sense of direction regarding the sound, still I went so far as to suspect that the walls of apartments had, instead of soundproofing, bizarre features designed to confuse the direction of the sound. Be that as it may, how could I make the same mistake again?

I heard nothing from Kayŏn, in spite of my expectation that she would come back soon to introduce herself formally. Accepting that was the way with young people these days, I decided to overlook the slight.

As good luck would have it, I received some melons sent from my daughter's farm. Since they were fresh and sweet, I selected a basketful of them. Carrying the basket, I took the initiative and paid a visit to Kayŏn. My visit was also colored with a curiosity to catch a glimpse of how she, still childless, exquisitely arranged her household furnishings and enjoyed her life. As for me, although I'd lived in different apartments over the past few years, I couldn't throw away my long-outdated household goods and dragged them along from one place to another. So when I saw apartments decorated with ever more fashionable and attractive furniture, I felt envious, while at the same time enjoying them as a feast for my eyes.

Kayŏn's apartment was unexpectedly uninviting and in disarray, as if they hadn't unpacked their belongings at all or had stopped in the middle of packing. There was not a picture frame or mirror to speak of. Moreover, the kitchenware was extremely simple and frugal, making it appear all the more novel and unfamiliar to me. I couldn't believe that there were people these days who still cooked rice in aluminum pots and used aluminum soup bowls! It was a fad among young brides in my neighborhood—as well as my daughters—to indulge in luxury kitchen items. I too maintained an admiration for this craze, sometimes imitating it or keeping my eye on certain items, with an intention of buying them someday in the future.

"Ah, ah, it's already melon season! I hadn't noticed," Kayŏn said in a surprisingly lively voice, but her facial expressions remained altogether lackluster. Melons were available all year round, but particularly these days they could be found at every turn. Even the fruit vendors on the street in front of the main gate of our apartment building were enjoying the busiest peak summer season, to the extent of disrupting passing traffic. Imagine Kayŏn is now seeing such commonplace melons for the first time! Even now, she was not paying any attention to the melons. While dumping the melons on the kitchen countertop, I looked out of the corner of my eye at the battered aluminum pot, a spoon stuck in it. The dried-up streaks of boiled-over rice water stuck on the pot seemed as obdurate as the crusts of the wife's resentment and boredom. I was at a loss what to do next.

"You can't leave before you taste some melon yourself, ma'am! Let me pick a sweet one for you. I guess the saying that girls who pick good melons pick good husbands is just idle talk." Kayŏn's voice was animated and urgent, showing no connection to the meaning of the adage. She sounded as if she were struggling to divert my scrutiny by any means.

"Are you good at picking out melons?"

"No, absolutely not."

"Well, that means you met a good husband."

"Ah, I really don't know, ma'am. I hate complicated things."

"If you find something like that so complicated, how are you going to adjust to modern life?" I said in an open and informal tone that I had used in the olden days when I had to set at ease girl students who brought mere trifles to the school counseling office and sobbed.

But Kayŏn wouldn't let her cunning guard down, like an unloved child who had mastered such tactics at an early age.

"Ma'am, you are curious about what sort of work my husband does for a living, aren't you? You'd find it insufferable if you went home without finding out anything about him, right? I know all too well," said Kayŏn.

"What a naughty girl! You act as if you had read someone else's mind! It's out of line for you to make me feel embarrassed—me, your teacher after all." My voice was trembling, unbecoming of my age. But the look in Kayŏn's eyes grew yet more perverse.

"I know well enough that no matter how refined people may look on the outside, they are not that refined when it comes down to curiosity. Besides, I know you're ready to find fault with me if you learn that my husband makes good money but my house-keeping is this dreadful. By the same token, I'm sure you are pre-pared to pity me if you find out that my husband is a penniless, good-for-nothing. But, neither is true."

Kayŏn seemed to overflow with vitality, entirely different from when I first saw her—probably stemming from her fierce willful-ness, which I hadn't noticed before. Using a crude-looking kitchen knife—I wondered if she had no fruit knife—she quickly pared the skin of the melon into thick strips, and after cutting the melon in two, she pushed one toward me and put the other into her mouth. As I stared at her chomping away at the melon, sloppily dripping its juice, words failed me and my lips dried up in dis-may. Just as Kayŏn had guessed, my shallow curiosity about what her husband did for a living had turned into a poisonous tension, robbing me of words. When Kayŏn glanced at me as I kept my si-lence, a faint scornful smile hovered around her lips. Such a sar-castic smirk was becoming to her, as if it were the only way she knew how to laugh, it seemed to me. At that moment, I felt a lump in my throat, as all manner of life's hardships that Kayŏn had had to witness and bear with such a cynical jeer began to float through my mind.

"If neither is true, what is your husband like?" I asked Kayŏn, having given up on concealing my curiosity.

"Although he doesn't make money, he's not an incompetent person. If we give credit to salarymen for their contribution to economic development, we may likewise say that my husband is contributing to the development of history. Just as ordinary men can't stand their family starving, my husband can't stand the fact that there are in our society people who are unable to live de-cently, like human beings, despite their hard work. He sides with them wholeheartedly. He is dreaming very beautiful dreams, but people won't leave his dreams alone. There were times when he was chased after, and at other times we had to vacate our house for the muddy boots to ransack and trample all over the wooden floor and the inner room. Sometimes it's even better to live with-out a telephone—now so commonplace they're found in shacks deep in the mountains …"

Kayŏn's grin became much clearer. But she wasn't looking at me. Her eyes were vacant, fixed on empty space, directed inward.

"Is your husband also involved in the 'movement' by any chance? I mean, not the sports kind …"[3]

"Why do you say 'also'? Those types are not to be met with every day."

"Because my son was also one of them."

"He isn't any more, right?"

"Right. It's a story long past."

"I guess he has turned into an ordinary salaryman, correct?"

"No. The moment he couldn't carry on work for the movement, his life ended."

"You mean he died?" Kayŏn said in a sudden and high-strung voice.

"No. He's living in a psychiatric sanitarium now. At one point, he was taken to a police station and was released horribly wrecked. At first, we thought it was only his body that had suffered, but we found out later that it was his mind that had really been damaged.

"Please stop, that's enough! Oh, it's horrible!" Kayŏn cried out in a shrill voice, shaking her head as if trying to wipe away a gruesome illusion. I also had no more to say.

Since last summer, when I learned about Kayŏn and her husband in this manner, my life suddenly began to take on vitality. As soon as my kimchi had fermented just right, I scooped up a bowlful and scurried up to Kayŏn's upstairs apartment, and sometimes I even fixed a special dish that required elaborate work just to have an excuse to visit her. Whenever I was preparing a delicious dish or healthy and highly nutritious food, I devoted my tender thoughts more to Kayŏn's husband than to her and felt my heart warming for no reason. From then on, the meaning of my life seemed to be wholly related to Kayŏn upstairs.

Eventually, I had the chance to meet her husband too, and he impressed me as unaffected, although a bit brusque. Somewhat to my disappointment, he never showed any interest in me beyond his curt, formal greetings, but my gaze toward him was filled with trust.

----

3. The "movement" refers to the popular antigovernment movement carried out by students, intellectuals, and labor groups against the military government's tyranny by means of street demonstrations, underground, subversive group activities, and strikes, which lasted from the 1970s to the early 1990s.

Sometimes, out of a blind, earnest desire to show the sense of trust I felt in him, I waited anxiously for him near the entrance of the apartment building, deliberately targeting the hours of his leaving or returning home. My timing seldom matched his irregular schedule. I was overjoyed when on those rare occasions I did run into him, and even tried to figure out with a highly sharpened sensibility whether he took notice of my heartfelt trust in him, just as teenagers try to fathom the effect of their first flirtatious glance.

Our apartment building had a rule in place for the elevator to make stops at even or odd numbered floors, alternating every three months. During the period when it stopped on my floor, I learned to recognize the sounds of his footsteps—so cautious as to disappear noiselessly. He's home! With a dreamy smile, I strained my ears to the sounds of his footsteps exiting the elevator on our floor and then slowly climbing the stairs that connected our floor to his. Just like the days when my son used to go in and out, I waited for the footsteps of Kayŏn's husband, took delight in them, and even tried to detect how tired he was or whether he was feeling good or bad.

Without my realizing it, my daily heightening interest in him began to slowly interfere with Kayŏn's family life. Kayŏn was completely defenseless against my intrusions. She might have already given up on her life even before my appearance in it. Otherwise, she couldn't have lived in that way, exposing her desolate life all over the place, granted that she was not so well off. This was the very point that annoyed me most about her. I naturally felt sorry for her husband, just like a mother-in-law who gets peeved by a daughter-in-law incapable of waiting on her son. I even lamented that Kayŏn's husband, having married the wrong woman, had long lost his chance to realize his lofty dreams. But I couldn't say this to Kayŏn.

It was thanks purely to Kayŏn's parents that her husband could subsist, even though for the past five or six years he'd been preoccupied with the so-called movement without earning a penny. Not only had he not starved during this period, but he was also able to bring his comrades home whenever he felt like it, offer them room and board, and even give them the shirt off his back. Kayŏn owed her large apartment, a luxury that was far beyond their means, judged by the dismal way they were now living, to her family's support. But it didn't mean that her parents had given away the apartment to their son-in-law, as they themselves were not that well off. In fact, they had bought the apartment with the intention of giving it to their married first son when he set up an independent household of his own, living apart from his parents. Since Kayŏn's parents were lending it to Kayŏn and her husband for free, as well as defraying the apartment association fees, her family seemed to be paying a heavy price for having a daughter.

Each time Kayŏn complained to me, "For all that, my husband shows no appreciation to my parents at all," I said in his defense, "Tsk, tsk! That can't be true. Don't you see? It's all because of his pride, unwilling to own up to his awkward situation."

"No, you don't understand. If he'd keep quiet, I would have taken it that way, too. But whenever he has a chance, he badmouths my parents, calling them stingy. He doesn't even want to acknowledge how much they have sacrificed for us. After all, my father's income from running an electronic goods retail store isn't that great. Nowadays, sales at such agencies have gone steeply downhill, as there is so much merchandise that is forcefully assigned to company employees and is sold at cut rates. In order to support us, my parents have tightened their belts and put off setting up a separate household for my brother and his wife, while trying to read how those two feel about the situation. I can more than feel for my parents' difficulty."

"Even so, your husband is a lucky guy. Do you know how priceless your parents' money is, as it is given to you from their understanding of the value of your husband's activities? The money from their penny-pinching to help you out is far more valuable than any spare money that is liberally handed out like alms."

"Did you say that my parents understand his activity? Oh, no! You don't know how much they hate him! My parents were against our marriage from the beginning. They didn't like him because it was plain to them that he'd bring me trouble. So just imagine how much they hated their daughter, who fell for and wanted to marry such a guy! You can't even begin to imagine how difficult it is for my parents to maintain relations with a hateful disgrace as us, to whom they have to provide living expenses. It's difficult for both sides."

"I see what you mean. It's too much to expect ordinary people to understand what your husband is doing. No doubt about that! But as long as your parents love you, they will feel good about providing for you, and I suppose you young folks should accept it with good cheer. Don't force your husband too much to thank your parents, do you hear?"

"Do you think my parents keep providing for us out of love for me? Oh, no, not at all! They do so because of the Molotov cocktail."

"Because of the Molotov cocktail?"

"All my parents know about the activist movement is the Molotov cocktail. They think every member of the movement carries in their bosom a Molotov cocktail like an identification card, and when provoked, will throw it anywhere they wish. My father has forbidden my mother or sister-in-law to complain about our living expenses. He says, 'We have no choice. If our whole family wants to live out their natural lives rather than be tossed together into a fiery pool …' Then he heaves a deep sigh in utter helplessness, so I hear."

Although it was as horrible a story as I'd ever heard, I wasn't surprised. It even occurred to me that I might have liked her husband because of the Molotov cocktail. I too was living my life burying deep in my bosom a Molotov cocktail that I wanted to hurl at the merciless forces that had driven my son to his wretched condition, and I wondered whether I was pulled toward Kayŏn's husband because I believed he was holding the same thing in his bosom. This fact was far from being horrible to me; indeed, it was even thrilling.

My son had been living in the sanitarium for more than four years and was briefly released a couple of times. Had it not been for his short releases, could I have endured those long, long, torturous, cruel hours? Ever since my son had ended up in that miserable state, my husband and I had not slept together. Of course, our sexual appetite had dwindled with our age, but we came to the same unspoken agreement that it was shameless for us to crave anything called "pleasure" in the face of our son's ordeal. But I was aware of my husband's occasional fondling of his withered sexual organ, with an extremely sorrowful expression on his face.

"Kayŏn, I think there is only one choice left for you. Why don't you get a job? You see, you don't have children yet, and besides, you have already completed the course requirements for teaching. Would you like me to look into it? It may be difficult for you to get an official appointment as a regular teacher right away, but you may be able to get a part-time lecturer position without much difficulty. You need to make a start on a job this way, without expecting too much at first. You should have done so a long time ago, silly!" I went on babbling, as if I'd hit on a grand scheme, but Kayŏn remained unexcited as before.

"Do you think I haven't thought about it myself? You see, I was offered jobs three or four times through my parents' connections. But my husband hates me working outside of home. He says he can't stand me making money, but more important, he says that, if I get a job, there won't be anyone to look after him or his comrades. In fact, it's not easy to take care of those guys."

"Seriously? Does he mean that he wants to keep depending on his wife's family because he can't handle that much inconvenience? He's got a lot of nerve, I'll say!" Utterly scandalized, I raised my voice.

"You see, he's made that way, so please don't side with him at every turn," said Kayŏn.

"Listen to this, girl! Tell me when I sided with him? In any event, there is no other way but for you to bear with him, right? You see, it's thanks to his guts that he's still working for the movement. As you know, the world has now changed, and not everyone can get involved in the movement."

"Do you think we need such a movement?" asked Kayŏn.

"Yes, we *do*. The Molotov cocktails held by many people have to be changed into a movement. Unless these bombs find their outlet in this way, they will explode into a crazy deluge of fire. Your family's not the only one that is dreading this crazy fire."

"There you go again, taking his side! Please let me tell you how cheeky my husband is. He questions why a participant in the movement should bend over backward to express his gratitude to his wife's family for their help, while judges, prosecutors, or medical doctors take it as a matter of course. By his logic he deserves the favors of his in-laws far more openly and squarely than those guys because he is working for a greater cause."

"Well, I don't know whether I should go so far as to accept that kind of nerve. Tell me, is he the sort of man who looks down on women all together?"

"I can't describe him exactly in those terms, but he surely has a set idea about how to deal with women. Believe me, this stresses me more than his disregard for my family or our financial problems."

"Tell me about his idea."

"I can't explain it in detail because it's simply my feeling. But, it seems to be a way of thinking, which is, 'the more forceful the domination the better.' He shouts with joy when he applies to women precisely the same logic of control used by the corrupt authority he resists."

Just as I learned later that my first encounter with Kayŏn was made possible by the things Kayŏn's husband had thrown out, I also learned that he often vented his anger from outside by smashing and throwing their scanty home furnishings. This was partly why Kayŏn's home had such a chilly atmosphere. Although I had been telling her to put up with it no matter what, I couldn't say so this time. I didn't want to lose the object of my hope—Kayŏn's husband.

False relationships are bound to come out in the open. For one, the relationship of Kayŏn's husband with her family was about to end. Her father's business went bankrupt, freeing him from being financially exploited due to his hatred and fear of his son-in-law. Because of a bad check Kayŏn's father wrote, she and her husband were soon going to be kicked out of the apartment that was in his name. It was just a few days ago that I was told this story by Kayŏn, who had become somewhat pale but still managed to be calm and collected. When I saw Kayŏn's flower stand still empty, I felt sick at heart, unable to ignore it. This was not simply because of my innate penchant for worry.

At the end of her talk, Kayŏn added, with a troubled smile, "Would you believe the first word he said after hearing his in-laws' family went under? 'It seems I need to get remarried.' He said it was only fair for him to have a countermeasure in place for his livelihood and that there was nothing to regret, either. He's really good at cracking jokes, isn't he?"

"That's enough! What a real son-of-a-bitch!" I burst into anger.

"I told you it was just a joke." This time Kayŏn tried to defend her husband.

That day, I let it go at that, but I was anxious to know what had been going on with Kayŏn since then. It was about the time of day when her husband was still at home, and I felt reluctant to go over to her apartment without any specific business, as my visit might be misunderstood as an attempt to snoop. Besides, I had nothing special at hand to take with me. As I was hanging around the house, uncertain what to do, the phone rang. It was from a friend—a principal of a high school attached to a business company—who asked me to recommend a home economics teacher.

What a stroke of luck! Kayŏn majored in home economics and even had a teaching certificate. Barely controlling my voice from bursting into a giddy tone, I inquired of my friend about the pay item by item. My friend said that she could guarantee a better salary than other public or private middle or high schools. That sounded quite satisfactory. It was pure luck. Reciting the saying, "Necessity is the mother of invention," and "There is always a way out," I felt excited about Kayŏn's sudden lucky break and I swaggered to her apartment upstairs. Kayŏn was by herself. The corners of her eyes were wet with tears.

"You've been crying, huh? What a crybaby!"

"I can't stop crying."

"You don't need to cry. I brought you some good news."

Kayŏn thanked me after hearing me out, but she wasn't as excited as I had expected.

"I don't know whether my husband would approve of it. It's a job I couldn't ever hope for, though."

"I won't let him say no. Don't worry! If I must do it, I am ready to wring an approval out of him."

"He is more weak-minded than he appears."

"Then it will be easier to get his approval, right?"

"No. Please look at this." Tucking up her skirt, Kayŏn knelt on the floor. I saw her exceptionally fair thighs lined up straight with her pretty round knees. On her fair-skinned thighs, I noticed vividly swollen spots, which looked as if plum blossoms had showered down all at once.

"He seared them with his cigarette. He often does it. This time it was especially painful … He said it was a reminder for me to stay put. He told me that since he needs my wifely help at home, I should hang back and remain behind. Then he began sobbing all choked up, you know."

"Son-of-a-bitch! Tears? A dime a dozen!" I spat out and rushed out of Kayŏn's apartment, without a second thought to her feelings. I even hated her crying. But I couldn't shake from my mind the sight of the burns on her thighs and felt as if one by one they were searing into my own flesh. I grieved for Kayŏn—a new feeling for me. I thought this new feeling might be friendship. Until then, I had been trying to tame rather than love her, and as a result, I had been on her husband's side, not hers. As she had told me, I wasn't on her side, not only when I defended him but also when I didn't. Just as a mother-in-law is fundamentally on her son's side!

My feelings of friendship for Kayŏn opened my eyes to see Kayŏn, her husband, and even their relationship exactly as they were. Inevitably, the hour to look at things squarely had arrived, and it was best for me to face up to reality, painful as it might be. First of all, I phoned the friend who had asked me to recommend a home economics teacher and told her I would bring a candidate for the job the next day. Then I went back up to Kayŏn's apartment.

"We are scheduled to visit the school for your job tomorrow, you understand? You'd better get your resumé and other documents ready."

"How could you do that, when you know perfectly well I can't go ahead without my husband's approval? He'll raise hell."

"First, you need to get on your own feet mentally and then tell him your intention to rely on yourself. Everything will then turn out ok. Nobody dares to hit a free person who is able to stand on her own."

"He said that he needs my wifely help … he said so while crying."

"For what great work does he think he is doing to need a wife's help?" I unburdened my mind without taking the trouble to hide my contempt for him.

"My goodness, ma'am! How come you change your mind so quickly now that you've helped find me a trifle like that job? Don't you remember you have always stood by him?"

"Me, changing my mind? It's because I have discovered that he is bogus. Listen, girl. How can I trust a guy who proclaims he is fighting for the people but can't recognize the large group of women, who have long been oppressed and exploited so ingeniously, as part of that populace? He's nothing but a sham when he demands the established power relinquish its vested interests, while he won't give up his vested male rights. How can I trust a guy who declares that he loves the populace while he treats his wife like a servant and has not a tinge of sympathy for her? Wifely help all sounds good, but doesn't it hurt your pride to offer your wifely help to a phony?"

"You've gone too far, ma'am! Please don't brand him a fraud. All the way to now he has lived only as a troublemaker, driven into a corner."

"I see. Then, it's up to you to decide whether he's a phony or not, by looking at him correctly. To see him correctly, you need to be able to stand on your own. I say, you should get up on your own feet not to feed him but to see him accurately and on an equal footing. Then it won't be too late to examine whether he's genuine or fake. But you can't put off your independence any longer." I pleaded with Kayŏn with all my heart, hoping my friendship would reach out and touch her.

CR

Pak Wan-sŏ (1931-2011)

One of the most prolific writers in modern Korean literature with a huge popular following, Pak Wan-sŏ was legendary for her unflagging productivity and dedication to her work to the end of her life. Debuting in 1970 at the age of thirty-nine, Pak, who wanted to remain "a writer on active duty," published some eighty short stories, more than a dozen novels, a number of essay collections, and even a few children's stories. An uncontested leader in the Korean women's literary world from the 1970s, Pak was protean in terms of thematic scope and variety, which ranged from the contemporary sociocultural unfolding, to gender issues, to political affairs. In her knack for capturing the most up-to-date happenings, trends, and social preoccupations, she was second to none. Her works speak to these topics garbed in her characteristic wit, acerbic humor, irony, exaggeration, and deliberate wordiness. Pak's passing in 2011 was mourned as an irreplaceable loss to modern Korean literature.

Pak was a native of a village in Kaep'ung District near Kaesŏng in Kyŏnggi Province, where she was born the second child (she had a ten-year-older brother) of a well-established family. At age three Pak lost her father; her widowed mother, passionate about and committed to her children's education, moved the family to Seoul, supporting their schooling and livelihood by her sewing. Known as a responsible and bright student during her high school days, Pak began to develop literary interests under the special guidance and encouragement of her teacher and entered Seoul National University in 1950 to major in Korean literature. However, the outbreak of the Korean War in June 1950 cut her college life short—never to be resumed—and destroyed her dreams of pursuing her literary studies. Worst of all, her brother, the idol of her mother and the mainstay of her family, was killed during the war, caught in the crossfire between two Koreas, democratic South and communist North. As the sole breadwinner for the bereaved family, including her brother's, Pak took a job at the U.S. military PX in Seoul from 1951 until her marriage in 1953.[4] For the next seventeen years, Pak focused on

---

4. PX is an acronym for Post Exchange, a type of department store operated on United States military bases to provide consumer goods and services for military personnel and their families.

raising her five children with no professional work or involvement outside of her family life.

Her debut novel, *Namok* (Naked tree; 1970), was winner of a fiction contest sponsored by the woman's magazine *Yŏsŏng tonga*, and is an autobiographical narrative closely based on her family tragedy and trauma during the Korean War. This public disclosure of the author's horrendous war experience, which had haunted her like a specter over two decades, was the first of its kind in modern Korean literature. The painful but necessary revisit to the war and its lasting ramifications was to become the central leitmotif of her works—short stories, novellas, and novels—throughout her career, as can be seen in "Puch'ŏnim kŭnch'ŏ (Nearby the buddha; 1973), "Kamera wa wŏk'ŏ" (Camera and boots; 1975), *Mongmarŭn kyejŏl* (Thirsty season; 1978), "Ŏmma ŭi malttuk" (Mother's stake, 1, 2, 3; 1980, 1981, 1991), and *Kŭ hae kyŏul ŭn tattŭt haenne* (That winter was warm; 1983), to name a few.

Another subject area Pak paid much attention to was hypocrisy, pretension, competitiveness, injustice, and corruption pervading various levels of modern-day Korean society. She found their most frequent and flagrant manifestations in the consumer rage, fixation with fads, vulgar materialism, and family egotism paraded by appearance-conscious, urban middle-class housewives. Pak's short stories, "Chumal nongjang" (The weekend farm; 1973), "Pukkŭrŏum ŭl karŭch'imnida" (Teaching a sense of shame; 1974), and "Toduk majŭn kanan" (The stolen poverty; 1975), belong to this category. The epitome of this theme, however, is her novel, *Hwich'ŏng kŏrinŭn ohu* (The tottering afternoon; 1978), a disastrous story of a materialistic, supercilious middle-class housewife whose blind ambition for her daughters to "marry up" for social prestige and wealth drags her whole family into ruin.

Scrutinizing the interrelationships between women, gender relations, and family dynamics, including conjugal and in-law relationships, was Pak's famed specialty. In some of her best-known stories, these topics are examined as inseparably interrelated issues. "Chippogi nŭn kŭrŏkke kkŭnnatta" (Thus ended my housekeeping; 1978), is a seminal piece, pointing out the crucial importance for a woman to reject gender inequality and prejudices perpetuated in patriarchal extended family systems, especially by her husband, and to rechart her life as wife, mother, and daughter-in-law on her own terms. Pak also targets her scathing criticism at "boy-preference" in favor over daughters from birth, a deep-rooted and undying, patriarchal obsession to continue the male line. One thought-provoking and memorable story is "Haesan pagaji" (Gourds for a birthing mother; 1985), which laments such gender bias flaunted by today's upper-classes and educated, elite young generations—the future leaders of the nation. Most ironic is the fact that a feminist scholar is part of this group. These two stories also offer vivid pictures of the intricate and testing relationships between mother-in-law and daughter-in-law. They highlight the daughter-in-law's formidable responsibilities and self-sacrifice to meet the needs of the mother-in-law who sees herself as the mother of the heir and head of the household, entitled to receive her daughter-in-law's whole-hearted filial piety.

Furthermore, a matter of great concern to Pak was the malaise of women's midlife-crisis syndrome, mostly as it pertained to financially secure, full-time housewives. Pak's middle-aged female characters feel disconnected from their spouses, see no special fulfillment in their children, and find their lives empty and boring. But their attempts to break this impasse by seeking outlets outside of the home prove to be of no avail, and these frustrated housewives remain in a rut, as illustrated in "Ŏttŏn nadŭri" (An outing; 1971) and "Chirŏng'i urŭm sori" (The cry of an earthworm; 1973). Pak was also at the forefront of dealing with the issue of divorce from a woman's perspective, and her two full-length novels, *Sara innŭn nal ŭi sijak* (The beginning of living days; 1980) and *Sŏ innŭn yŏja* (A woman who is standing; 1985), are extended expositions on young divorced women's struggles with the challenges of new personal realities.

Pak's interest in the elderly, whose problematic status and presence in extended families in today's Korea was longstanding from the 1970s, is eloquently related in "Chippogi nŭn kŭrŏkke kkŭnnatta" and "Haesan pagaji," mentioned above. A series of her stories published in the 1990s, including "Odong ŭi sumŭn sori yŏ" (Ah, the hidden sound of the paulownia; 1992), "Hwangak ŭi nabi" (A butterfly of illusion; 1995), and "Marŭn kkot" (Dried flowers; 1995), alerts the urgency of properly dealing with the rapidly growing problems of elder care in Korea. At the same time, Pak increasingly began to direct her eye to recapturing her past life from early childhood in autobiographical accounts, and *Kŭ mant'ŏn sing'a nŭn nuga ta mŏgŏssŭlkka* (Who ate up all those *sing'a* plants?; 1992) and *Kŭ san i chŏngmal kŏgi issŏssŭlkka* (Was that mountain really there?; 1995) are her masterworks. Her short autobiographical account, "Sŏgyang ŭl tŭng e chigo kŭrimja rŭl papta" (Stepping on the shadow with the sunset on my back; 2010), became Pak's last summary of her own cherished, eventful life.

As the most awarded Korean woman writer in modern times, Pak's achievements and contributions were recognized by Seoul National University in 2006 when it conferred on her an honorary doctorate. All said, Pak will be remembered as a sociocultural critic of unsurpassed insight, a living witness to and memoirist of contemporary Korea history, as well as a superb storyteller and vigilant, imaginative thinker. In commemoration of the first anniversary of Pak's death, a 22-volume collection of her works was published in 2012 (Seoul: Segesa). ⌀

TEXTUAL READINGS

Set against the highly violent and volatile political milieu of late-1980s Korea, "An Episode at Dusk, 2" offers an unvarnished and telling exposé of lopsided husband–wife relationships, the viciousness of spousal abuse, and most of all, the hypocrisy of the husband—an egotistic, self-promoting antigovernment activist, who, in his treatment of his wife, duplicates the very violence of the military regime he opposes. It is a first-person narrative by a middle-aged woman who has undergone frustrating experiences as the mother of a son who has been maimed mentally and psychologically by the military government's brutality inflicted on idealistic college populations. Once fired up by moral indignation after witnessing the appalling marital situation of her female former student, Kayŏn, the narrator willingly takes up the interceding role. Thus, "An Episode at Dusk, 2" is as much about disclosing Kayŏn's gender-based oppression as it is about the humane, compassionate, and gutsy stance of the narrator-protagonist, who dares take a stand against a hideous domestic crime.

Structurally, "An Episode at Dusk, 2" has a dual-storyline format. The first part relates the reprehensible and tragic story of the narrator's son, a casualty of the brutal military regime and a public justice system gone awry. Once an active, principled, and politically committed college student, he is now reduced to a socially dysfunctional patient confined to a psychiatric sanatorium. Given his artistic gifts and potential, his victimhood is doubly troubling and absurd. The second part of the narrative revolves around the gruesome domestic victimization of a young housewife, Kayŏn, at the hands of her husband. Kayŏn's situation is a variation on the same theme of horror, violence, and evil seen in the victimization of the narrator's son in the public domain now transported to and reenacted in the private realm of Kayŏn's home. These two seemingly separate but thematically related stories are brought together by the mediation of the narrator. Thus connected, the stories double up and reinforce the narrative's central message, a call for exposing the horrors of violence in both public and domestic domains in 1980s Korea and the urgency of rectifying the senseless and unjustifiable suffering of the victimized. The narrator's initiatives to salvage the young woman signal the first step to that end.

As the story progresses, the narrator's one-sided attention and partiality to Kayŏn's husband develops into her virtual identification of him with her own son and Kayŏn as her daughter-in-law. It is as if the narrator's frustrated and unutilized maternal energy and love for her son has been transferred to Kayŏn's husband, and her care for him in turn infuses in her a new vitality and life purpose. When the husband's duplicity, parasitic lifestyle, and especially his horrifying acts of physical violence, which have eluded the narrator for so long, are finally brought to light, "I" is awakened to her own illusions and misunderstanding of Kayŏn's spousal relationship. In this sense, "An Episode at Dusk, 2" can be read as a counsel against the injudicious, sentimental over-idealization or adulation of the student activists of the 1980s.

Pak Wan-sŏ's pro-woman position is unequivocally put into words in the narrator's advice to Kayŏn at the end of the narrative. The narrator's inborn ability to foster and nurture life, be it in plants or animals, as stated in her brief self-reflection at the beginning of the story, becomes the source of her mentoring and sponsorship of Kayŏn. "I" feels a transgenerational friendship for Kayŏn and demonstrates the need for exercising women's sisterly power to make a difference in the lives of other women in distress, especially those isolated in the complex of urban high rises.

As a surrogate mother figure and instructor of real-life matters, the protagonist drives a lesson into the mind of her protégé that financial independence and self-reliance is a prerequisite for a truly liberated woman to be on equal footing with a man. This makes "An Episode at Dusk, 2" one of Pak Wan-sŏ's most clear-cut, explicit fictional pieces in the feminist vein.[5] At the same time, the story functions as a scathing denunciation of the rampant, toxic sociopolitical culture of violence of 1980s Korea that even penetrated to the depths of the intimate husband-wife relationships of the younger generations. ∞

---

5. Kim Yun-jŏng, *Pak Wan-sŏ sosŏl ŭi chendŏ ŭisik yŏn'gu* [Study of gender consciousness in Pak Wan-sŏ's novel] (Seoul: Yŏngnak, 2013), 155.

A Mute's Chant

Ch'oe Yun

"I am a man who dreams of swimming against the ocean's current. I am also a person who has a special love for salmon, among other creatures living in that vast world of liquid. Do you know what commonality exists between the salmon, the fish, and me, a human being?"

I hurriedly tore out the sheet of the letter I was writing, which was starting to sound like a game of twenty questions or an absurd riddle.

I'd received a draft notice, informing me of the date I was to enlist in the army—the last thing I wanted to do—on a charge of having produced subversive recordings. With little else to do, I was spending my time fiddling with a few tapes I had already made when I witnessed an extremely weird scene. At the same time, I learned some secrets about my auntie—my mother's younger sister—about which probably I alone among my family had been left in the dark.

It was in front of a public phone booth a week ago when I met a mute woman for the first time … no, it was her voice that I heard for the first time. That day too I was aimlessly wandering about, tape recorder at my side, and feeling exhausted and lonely in the heart of the city, which was growing dusky at around five in the afternoon. Spurred by an urge to call someone to come meet me, I walked toward a nearby public phone.

The title of the original is "Pŏng'ŏri ch'ang," first published in *Munhak kwa sahoe* (Literaure and society) 2, no. 4 (1989). The present translation is based on the text published in *Chŏgi sori ŏpsi hanjŏm kkonnip i chigo: Ch'oe Yun sosŏlchip* [There, a petal silently falls: collection of Ch'oe Yun's short stories] (Seoul: Munhak Kwa Chisŏngsa, 1992; 1999), 147–177.

A woman was standing in front of the phone booth, talking over the telephone. But I realized that none of the phone conversation was audible. Moreover, the woman, standing motionless, holding the phone receiver to her ear, was not uttering even the minimum amount of words one expects to hear interspersed in a phone conversation, even when that person is simply listening to the other party talking.

My habit of taping other people's conversations, which I often did in front of public phones, at times even led to feelings of regret when they ended their conversations. As I had no specific person in mind to call, I was neither in a hurry nor feeling inconvenienced as I waited. So I was idly watching the woman's back from behind when I recognized that she remained silent in the phone booth. But the woman turned around and looked at me with a panicked expression and signaled me to wait a little bit longer, using the strange hand motions called sign language and letting out low moans. Needless to say, the woman in the phone booth was a mute.

But the next moment something very bizarre happened. The very woman whom I had concluded to be a mute suddenly uttered into the receiver a series of high-pitched sounds—as if perfected by practice—that I had never heard before. They were not what people might generally characterize as beautiful melodies or song tunes. The sounds were high and fine, but they momentarily blotted out the noises of the street. They seemed to have risen from the depths of her bowels or to have been drawn out from the bottom of an abyss. I felt as if some mythical monster had appeared inside the public phone booth in front of me and roared out, having miscalculated the time and the place. I was so taken aback that I even forgot to push the button of my mini tape recorder at my side.

The woman continued performing these dizzying vocal acrobatics for about a minute. Then, silence. In the end, she turned around and came out of the phone booth, her face wearing an expression of exhaustion, and set off down the road as if running away. She disappeared into a house—most likely a boarding house—not far from the street.

A week had passed since the incident, but the woman's sounds increasingly whipped up my curiosity, and finally goaded me to write a letter to the mute woman whose name, age, and address were not at all known to me.

"No matter who the partner of your phone conversation was, I'd make bold to say that the content of the message that you could deliver only through sounds was a desperate courting for love."

As I tore out yet another piece of stationery to start this letter over, yet again, I heard a familiar voice coming from the gate. It seemed my auntie had sought shelter in our house, having been beaten half to death by her husband. I looked at the clock. It was nearly eleven at night, about the time my older sister went to bed. Ordinarily, it was also about the time she was finishing her nightly cucumber facial.

In addition to the drama going on around me, I had been sponging off my older sister, who hadn't been able to marry even after reaching her mid-thirties. As payment to her, I offered, once in a while, to place on her face slices of cucumbers dipped in whipped eggs. I didn't complain about this, but I felt it was old-fashioned and pathetic of her to cover her face with a gauze towel soaked with raw eggs and cucumber in the hopes of reversing her aging. My sister, who was working at a pharmaceutical company, should be aware of all kinds of chemical treatments to keep her skin from aging, so why use such primitive method?

Each time I looked at my sister lying under the florescent light on the floor covered with a white gauze towel, a cold shiver ran through me as if I had become a mortician preparing a dead body for burial. It might be for this reason that I tried to entertain her— for fifteen minutes until I cleared away the cucumber slices—with smutty stories or wild rumors that I had picked up from people around me.

However, my sister's will to transcend the ineluctability of age was so strong that her facial muscles never registered any response strong enough to mess up her treatment. I had once been engrossed in inventing specious aphorisms, and at least one of them was totally inspired by my sister, and it drew quite a response from my silly audience at the time. It went like this: "A corpse never laughs."

Come to think of it, however, we'd be surprised to find out how many people in the world lead their lives preoccupied with matters as strange as "the laughter of a corpse" or as impossible as "making a corpse laugh." If I told people that I saw a mute talking on the phone or was impressed by the mute's voice, every one of them would laugh it off, saying, "Another one of his auditory hallucinations." But I positively heard the mute talking over the phone and heard her shouts of courtship as if gushing up from the depths of an abyss. To me it was no less real than the noises my auntie was making outside the gate now.

Auntie was awaiting our signal with perseverance, a perseverance I could never admire enough. Her knocking alternated between loud and timid, and it was marked with a familiar rhythm and intensity typical of her. It revealed that she had been driven to such a measure, and that it was not a natural thing for her to do so, drained of strength as she was. Ordinarily, when she dropped by on business, she always rang the doorbell. But on an occasion like tonight, she never failed to rap our iron gate with her knuckles, and in so doing, differentiated the objectives of her visits—either taking care of business or seeking shelter. Ever since we two siblings had settled in Seoul, Auntie made our place her haven and made free use of it in the dead of night. And my sister and I also accepted her frequent flights as natural, feeling as if we were giving alms to her—the black sheep of our household. As time passed, we lost even the minimum amount of curiosity about what areas of her body were bruised this time, what parts were broken and to what extent, or whether her hair, which she treasured like the crock enshrining the ancestral tablet, was all right. My sister said this phenomenon of gradual decline in concern was a result of the repeated application of shock.

Approaching sixty, Auntie was shunned by all the members of our family and for no specific reason. Except for the fact that she had no offspring to side with her, that she was a boozer second to none in town, and that she had a husband who belonged to the category of so-called crooks with unknown past records, she had no reason to be subjected to such treatment by our family. Yet Auntie seemed to take their abuse and cold treatment cavalierly as if it was natural. When something bad happened in the family, Auntie was indisputably blamed for it, and moreover, for the most part she was never notified of the family's important events. Sorry to say, among her nieces and nephews, Auntie favored me unconditionally simply because I was a student of music, and even this incurred the displeasure of her other family members. So, almost without exception, all the unsavory things that happened to me were imputed to Auntie. Occasionally, in order to escape her husband's beatings, and at other times, grieving over her family's mistreatment, but most of the time with no excuse at all, Auntie—dead drunk—would pound on our gate or shout out my or my sister's name at the top of her lungs.

I remained stock-still, even though I recognized that the rhythm of Auntie's pounding had changed from *adagio* to *allegro*. As I listened quietly, I became aware that she was not simply banging on the gate but was somehow keeping time to some music and moving her fingers following the rhyme of a certain song. It didn't take a long imaginative excursion for me to discern that the rhythm was a bar from an outdated popular song, "You Wouldn't Know," which had become part of my pet repertoire ever since Auntie, when she was quite tipsy, had taught it to me in my childhood. It was clear that Auntie was motivated by the bright idea of playing upon my heartstrings.

As there was no response from my room, located near the gate, Auntie proceeded to the next more effective stage, one most detested by my sister. At the fence facing my sister's window, Auntie began to shout out her full name in a high pitch, having abandoned the caution with which she had been knocking on the gate. Even before Auntie had finished screaming my sister's name for the third time, the door of my sister's room was flung open, accompanied by my sister's infuriated huffing and puffing, and I heard her rushed footsteps scurry past my door. In light of the fact that all our neighbors knew my sister was an unwilling practitioner of singlehood, it was no big deal to have her tabooed full name ring out in the midnight air. But Auntie was doubly calculating that her own action would serve as an insufferable insult to the person involved—my sister. Few people could outdo my auntie's determination, which had little regard for the thoughts of others. Soon I heard my sister screaming, "Auntie, get a divorce, I mean divorce," which was followed by Auntie's guffaw and her affectedly innocent reply, as if to get on my sister's nerves, "Why, what has that poor guy done to deserve it?"

There followed the noise of the bolt of the gate being unbarred, its closing, and then a loud bumping against something, and sighs. Then sound of footsteps stopped in front of my room. I held my breath as if I had committed a crime.

"Ch'angsu seems to be out late 'collecting,' isn't he?" Far from her customary, exaggerated blubbering, Auntie's tipsy, satisfied, and lively voice had an irresistible force in it. It possessed a force ready to throw open my room door if I—her usual accomplice—gave away even the slightest clue that I was in the room. No response from my sister. Again, noises of shoes being dragged and the sound of opening and closing the room door. Silence. And, after a while, Auntie's uninhibited wailing rang out as if aimed at my ears.

"Well, it's about time," with a smile floating across my lips, I felt an urge to collect Auntie's primeval cry once again—Auntie, who was also my authentic drinking instructor. But I already had as many as six recordings of Auntie's cries at such times, all of them full of an extraordinary vitality. What Auntie called "collecting" was a reference to my activities, carrying around a low-quality recorder with which I indiscriminatingly recorded noises as concrete as fights in the marketplace, all sorts of street demonstrations, secret conversations between a man and woman seated at a table adjoining mine in a tearoom, the hopelessly banal words of a well-known bigwig's speech, vague noises heard on buses, the sounds of wind blowing over boats at night, and the noises I made while sleeping. Although I met with countless mishaps because of this hobby, I also occasionally earned pocket money by supplying background sounds to my upperclassman who worked at a radio station.

*   *   *

"These tapes, which fill more than half the wall of my small room, would really be the only property I could carry with me when I one day leave this earth.[1] Someday—if only I owned a studio—they will be fixed up and edited, and in the end will certainly contribute to revolutionizing something, something not yet definite ..."

---

1. The following sections starting at the beginning of this paragraph from the sentence "These tapes," and ending with the sentence "But these tapes are to become important data ..." on p. 162 are jumbled recollections of the narrator, Pak Ch'ang-su. They are related to Pak's encounters with four different personages—his college professor, two police interrogators, and his college upperclassman. And their differing reactions and responses to Pak's tapes constitute the content of these separate segments. In the Korean original, Pak's remembered conversations with his interlocutors are presented in a single, long paragraph and in an extremely cryptic manner with no conventional writing markers and symbols to separate one segment from another. To make these complex parts more comprensible, I have divided them into more easily readable sections and put together the sentences that are separated or disrupted by unrelated conversations and Pak's own interjected thoughts and remarks.

"Look here, Mr. Kim! Is this a joke? Just what and how are you going to revolutionize? Your gibberish is nauseating. How dare you think this is a presentation?"

"Professor, sir, the very physical reaction you feel to the sounds I just had you listen to, um, I'm sorry, is evidence of the genuine features of the sounds ..."

Ah! I've no time to play on words with you. Send in the next student!"

*   *   *

"Hey, Ch'angsu, this is awesome! Very cool. These are really the breathing sounds of the guy XXX jogging in the morning, right? Play the tape again. What are these noises mixed in the middle? What? You mean they're sounds from the portable public toilet that you transmuted? Man, you're really something. But do you think it's ok to call even something like this music? By the way, let me borrow these to use as sound effects in a drama we're broadcasting tomorrow about a guy who dies twice. Sorry but the credit will be mine. But don't get discouraged and keep up the good work! You've got some future. Take this upperclassman's word for it!"

*   *   *

"Damn it! What are you doing, dude? You think you're a policeman or something? Look, what have you just been doing? Recording? Are you fanning a house on fire or what? You want some screwing up, huh? Hey, you're a spy, aren't you? Who's behind you? You think your tape is worth submitting to the police as data, huh? Look at you, jerk, still wet behind the ears! Sure, go ahead and submit the recording, you creep. Look here, you coming at me? Come on, talk, or I'll beat you up! Who ordered it? How much were you paid? Spit it out, damn you. Oh, now look at this jerk, clenching his teeth!"

(Even at that moment, my tape recorder at my side went on recording, but in the end, the tape was confiscated.)

*   *   *

"Now come on, you student, it's better to come clean, when I'm being reasonable with you. Why'd you make this recording? Who ordered it? And what do these fabricated sounds mean? Maybe there's a secret order encoded in these recorded rallying slogans. Is this some kind of joke? What do these noises have to do with music? Do you think I'm an idiot? Are you trying to play innocent, even with evidence like this?"

(The guy raised the plastic bag containing some dozen tapes that he had ferreted out in my room and violently shook it midair like a banner.)

"You see, we have no interest in small fry like you. Out with it! Unless you own up to whose order this is and its specific purpose, you're history. You punk, who do you think I am? Trying to avoid the question? You think you're some kind of professional reporter, sneaking around all sorts of street demonstrations like a rat and recording them, huh? Listen up, you can either be taught a lesson or spit it out without making a fuss. You scum, there's plenty of material here to lock you up there in a second."

*   *   *

How should I put it? But these tapes are to become important data, announcing the advent of a new world of sounds.

*   *   *

Auntie's cry was going on unexpectedly long. Her cry always provoked intense thirst in me. She probably knew this, I thought, and so was deliberately raising her voice to attract my attention. I gathered up the pieces of paper scattered around me and dumped them all into the wastebasket. It always turned out like this. No one would be able to match Auntie except her husband. I hastily put on my trousers and went over to my sister's room.

"Auntie, come on out! Let's go for a drink."

Auntie hurriedly opened the door and came out, her hands on her forehead. I didn't know whether my sister was sleeping with the quilt pulled over her head or was just feigning sleep, but we left her behind. As Auntie and I passed through the gate, we laughed our heads off in the dead of night for no reason at all.

We went to the covered street-food cart, called Ch'unch'ŏn Station, our favorite hangout, where we always dropped in on such nights as this. The owner of the joint—a middle-aged auntie—never failed, despite my unpaid tab, to receive me warmly. And now, her tired arms wide open, she placed *soju*, distilled spirits, in front of us before we even asked for it. Since we entered the lighted eatery, Auntie gave up covering up the black-and-blue, swollen bruise on her forehead, baring it all.

Looking at it, I asked, "What's it all about this time?"

"Well, this is ... never mind. Why don't you pour me some *soju*?"

In silence, we finished off half the bottle. Looking absentmind-edly at the screen of a small black-and-white TV in front of the Ch'unch'ŏn Station auntie, we made short work of the second half. Then Auntie sprang to her feet, the sign that she was moving from sobriety to a state of intoxication.

"I need to croon a tune."

Regardless of time and place, when Auntie wanted to sing, she would spring to her feet and grab the edge of whatever she could get her hand on. This was Auntie's ancient ritual, a habit no one could break, which dated from her younger years when she had dreamed of becoming a singer. At such moments, her face, that of a woman about to turn sixty, became most beautiful. I picked up a chopstick to beat time to the tune. Nodding her head to my chop-stick prelude, Auntie sang in an amazing voice and finished effort-lessly up to the second stanza of the song, "You Wouldn't Know." It was a song a young composer had reportedly written for her during her maiden days, the very jingle that had become part of my favor-ite repertoire. Although she cleared her voice with more than her usual care in such intoxicated states, it sounded gratingly broken, probably the effect of the liquor or her overeagerness. Still, it com-pletely cleared away my pent-up, brooding feelings over the past gloomy week.

Even after finishing the song, Auntie remained standing for some time, her eyes tightly closed, as if she were a real singer await-ing applause. When I gave her my customary enthusiastic hand, she finally took a deep breath, came to her seat and sat down.

"Hey, Ch'angsu, would you like me to tell you why I had a fight with Uncle?" Auntie lowered her voice furtively, as if there were new, hidden reasons for her row with her husband.

"No, thanks, Auntie. I suppose you tumbled down the stairs or bumped into a post, right?" Quoting Auntie's usual lame excuse, I tried to avoid hearing again about the same humdrum drama be-tween her and her husband. That evening I was oddly conscious of the Ch'unch'ŏn Station auntie, but she was dozing off on a grungy armchair she had picked up somewhere. After trying to read my face, Auntie changed the subject.

"To tell you the truth, I dropped by to discuss something with you. Well, it's ..." Auntie's face was completely flushed, but it didn't seem just from the *soju*, and, listening to her carefully, I could detect a distinct whimpering tone in her voice. Fearful she might burst into weeping hysterics over her drink while sitting at the snack-wagon in the middle of the night, I closely studied Auntie's wrinkled face. She suddenly changed her demeanor and, laughing loudly, patted me fondly on the cheek like she couldn't resist it.

"What are you up to, Ch'angsu? I'm not at all drunk. You're so spoiled!" But soon, she asked me with a serious look, "You sometimes have suggested that I become a singer, haven't you?"

I remained silent.

"Tell me whether that's true or not," asked Auntie.

"Yes, that's true, I have."

"You see, I've decided to become a singer. I'm telling you this— only you—because you're into the arts." Auntie put infinite emphasis on the word *arts*.

Judging from Uncle's frank response to Auntie's resolution, a response that had left its mark on her forehead, I knew I was not the first person to hear this confession from her.

She added, as if she had read my mind, "Your Uncle doesn't know anything about this. It's only between you and me. Got it? He really doesn't know anything. You don't know anything, either. No one knows how I feel, absolutely nobody!"

After a deep sigh and the flitting of a light smile over her lips, Auntie pushed her cup toward me. I poured a cupful of *soju* and waited for her next words. But, instead, she seemed to be waiting for me to speak.

I began cautiously, mindful not to spoil her tipsiness, "But, listen, Auntie! You can't get started as a singer on one song, 'You Wouldn't Know,' can you?"

"I tell you, from now on I'm not going to sing that song," Auntie said, shutting her eyes tightly.

I remained silent.

"Consider tonight my farewell performance. From now on, I'm into chanting," Auntie said without hesitation, as if she had already given it much thought.

"What do you mean chanting? You mean something like *p'ansori*?"

"Listen to you! How can you be so ignorant for a music student?" Auntie scolded me. "Why, do you think *p'ansori* is the only chanting

there is? Even though you know all too well, you're faking ignorance and are trying to get to me," said Auntie.

"Look, Auntie! You have no training whatsoever in chanting,
and now you say you've decided to go into it?"

"Don't you see? That's why I said I'm going to study it from now
on."

"Come on, at your age, Auntie?" I ended up putting my foot in
my mouth.

"Why, what's wrong with my age? Don't upset me with such
stuffy notions like your uncle does. Isn't it good enough if I study
starting now? Within a couple of years, I will become a famous
singer appearing on radio and television. I'll bet you."

There was something sincere in Auntie that night—something
that didn't go well with her usual self, and strangely, this made me
feel an unbounded sadness. To imagine she had resolved to learn
chanting at her age to be on radio or television! It seemed clear to
me that Auntie was trying to compensate in the wrong way for the
maltreatment that had been unduly doled out to her for far too long.
Though she wore thick makeup, Auntie's face—far more wretched-
looking than ever before—appeared to be ten years older than it
was. I had heard that until recently Auntie's husband had borrowed
money from people here and there for his fantasy of reaping wind-
fall profits by traveling from one resort area to another on the eastern or southern coasts. But he fled creditors who had stormed his
rented room, and he had since been holing up with his younger
sister, a gambler—his only blood relation and an owner of a saloon
somewhere in Chongno Street.[2] I considered Auntie's dreams of becoming a singer as just like his.

I ordered another bottle of *soju* and a side dish to go with it, and
then looked at Auntie. She was absentmindedly looking at the
black-and-white television that the Ch'unch'ŏn Station auntie was
watching.

Auntie seemed to be hesitating a little, but, without taking her
eyes from the television, asked me as if in passing, "I wonder
whether the television or radio programs from this side reach the
other side."

"What do you mean, 'this side' reach 'the other side'?"

---

2. Chongno is a main thoroughfare in downtown Seoul.

"I mean whether this side's radio or television broadcasts reach North Korea."

I remained silent.

I looked at Auntie blankly; she seemed to be talking to herself. "The world has changed so much, you see. Oh yes, no doubt, radio and television programs must have reached there. Unlike telephone, these can reach anywhere without lines, isn't that so?"

"Look, Auntie, why do you need to know something like that?"

"If I want to become a singer, I have to know."

"What does it have to do with your becoming a singer? I bet you'd have enough fans on this side crowding around you, and you want to have fans in the North too? You're so greedy, Auntie!" I teasingly said, since Auntie often hurled these sorts of outrageous questions at me.

"Why, does my greed strike you as strange? Oh well, Ch'angsu, just fill my cup!"

Thereafter, we drank until we became dead drunk, talking about silly stuff. I couldn't remember how long I stayed at Ch'unch'ŏn Station with Auntie, except for the following vague recollections: that evening, as I was wont to do when I got tipsy while drinking with Auntie, I pestered her to tell me about the composer of "You Wouldn't Know," whom she knew when she was young. Just as she had done at other such times, Auntie flatly denied she had ever known such a man, but I badgered her to talk about him, and we repeated this silly wrangling back and forth. On our way home, we staged a touching duet together for Auntie's last performance of "You Wouldn't Know," almost rocking our whole neighborhood. It seemed by now the light sleepers in our neighborhood must have completely mastered this song's lyrics.

*   *   *

In the deep ocean, I became a salmon during the spawning season—the salmon of my dream—and was struggling to swim up a waterfall dozens of meters high. The chill of the autumn ocean seeped into my bones. Watching most of my fellow salmon disappear in the end, having been snatched away by anglers' float-fastened hooks, I made every possible effort to leap up against the torrents of the waterfall. Several times, I almost made it to the top of the falls. In the midst of leaping as best I could by maneuvering my fins and tail with the last ounce of my strength, I woke up.

Though I had drunk my fill of water in the dream, I was parched with thirst and my arms and legs felt stiff and sore. I had been thrashing around so much my whole body, especially my backbone and belly—where the fins had been—ached severely. It took more than a full hour for me to retransform from a salmon back to Pak Ch'angsu. I must have drunk an awful lot the night before. I had a sour taste in my mouth, as if I had spoken lies all night long.

The moment I opened my eyes, out of habit, I picked up the blank manuscript paper and pencils scattered around my bedding, and then put them down. I noticed the clumsy wording of my letter to the mute woman, which had been interrupted by Auntie's sudden appearance. The memory of the woman's voice that had been stirring up my curiosity until yesterday—just as the botched wording of my letter showed—vaguely returned to me like a vexing reality. After folding the unfinished letter and putting it in an envelope, I stood up.

Did I really hear the mute woman talking on the phone, I wondered? Was she really shouting her desperate message to an unknown party on the other end of the line in a high-pitched language she had devised? Replacing these questions, Auntie's voice came back to me, asking suddenly whether the South's broadcasts were carried to the North. What if I asked Auntie to deliver this letter to the mute woman? With this crazy idea in my head, I went to my sister's room.

It was already approaching eleven in the morning, but Auntie was sitting vacantly, her disheveled head leaning against my sister's prized chest of drawers. The sour smell of booze stank in my nostrils. Normally, Auntie would have been applying makeup to her all-too-tearful eyes, after having taken off the lid of my rice bowl into which my sister scooped the cooked rice and dipped her black mascara in the vapor steamed up there. It wasn't pleasant at all, however, to discover Auntie in such a grannylike, shabby condition. In the past, no matter how rough Auntie's midnight jaunt had been, it never went beyond one night. As soon as morning came around, she'd neatly spruce herself up—in a way almost unbecoming her age—and after helping my sister get ready for work, she'd leave our house.

As I hesitated in the doorway with a surprised and questioning look on my face, Auntie looked at me blankly and, turning her back toward me, said as if talking to herself, "Looks like I'm getting old

… even the booze doesn't work on me. Before I get any older, I need to hurry and get my work done." And then as if she had recovered her senses, she abruptly sat up and said, mimicking the manner of speech of a spirit-possessed shaman delivering predictions of natural calamity, "In a few days your household will be turned upside down."

I was dumbfounded.

"Sure it will! What's meant to be overturned should be overturned. Shouldn't it be so?"

Auntie showed no interest whatsoever in my response, and and her monologue drifted more and more bewilderingly.

"Sure, there's no way for you to know the inside story of this Yi Chŏngbun. However, now that you're fully grown, you need to judge for yourself. Why, think about it—when the raw flesh is slashed, it's bound to bleed, and even if the rooster's neck is wrung, dawn is bound to break. Don't they say that even a mute squeals, when pushed against the wall? I, Yi Chŏngbun, have lived up to now without so much as a peep. But just wait and see. In a few days, your household will be turned upside down."

Repeating the same refrain, Auntie finished this weird combination of prophesy and gibberish. Thereafter, she remained silent for quite awhile, not even looking at me, the target of her talk. An inexplicable feverishness was raging in her eyes; gone was the usual, natural smile at the corners of her eyes touched with eye makeup. It seemed to me that something truly serious had happened to Auntie.

Because I didn't know what else to do, I stepped out of the room, leaving Auntie behind, her eyes staring straight ahead of her with hot anger.

When I was about to close the door, Auntie thundered out, "Hey, Ch'angsu, before you go away, give me some money if you've got any. I've got to go somewhere but I left my purse at home."

Of course, her excuses were lies. Most probably, having woken up late in the morning, she'd forgotten to ask for money from my sister on her way to work. I took out all the paper bills I had on me and handed them over to Auntie. Auntie stood up immediately and opened my sister's wardrobe. Auntie's bizarre mood just awhile ago was completely gone.

Auntie began to rummage through my sister's clothes with the same familiar movement she used when she went through her own wardrobe. Unfortunately, because my sister and Auntie were similar sizes, my sister's clothes, a handful, disappeared from time to time only to reappear with Auntie's next visit to our house. Auntie took out a dress my sister had recently bought and shouted in her usual cheerful voice, "Why, look at this naughty girl! She even left me a note on this, lest I should go out in it. What does she mean by saying this is the only clothing I shouldn't take, because it's for her marriage interviews? You've certainly got an out-and-out cheap-skate for a sister. Don't we all know she's got no desire to go to such interviews? If she goes out in this dress, it's sure to ruin her chance of success, I bet you."

Auntie nonchalantly removed my sister's note, and, winking at me, put on the dress. We broke out in laughter, just like the night before. But this time there was something awkward in Auntie's mischievous act. I detected an air of arbitrariness in it, as if she were trying to put me at ease or cover something up. Suddenly, Auntie looked like a stranger.

Might it be similar to the disillusionment one feels when one glimpses the real face of a person through that chink between his face and the comical mask he always wears while acting the fool? Come to think of it, neither my sister nor I knew Auntie very well. It occurred to me—oddly enough—that in this manner Auntie might have been deliberately asking for her family's mistreatment all along.

*   *   *

In the afternoon, I wandered for half an hour around the neigh-borhood of the boardinghouse into which the mute woman had disappeared. I jotted down in my pocket notebook the address of the house written on its gate plate. Upon returning home, I put in order my old recorded tapes covered with dust. Among them, I found a tape I'd been vaguely looking for. The tape was labeled "Unsan Falls." I could neither remember the location of the falls nor the date the tape was made. I put it into the tape recorder. The re-corded sounds of the falls, whose volume was raised to the maxi-mum, rang out like rough sea waves or the roar of a crowd. By using two tape recorders, I cut the recorded sounds of the falls and edited them—at first turning the volume low, and then gradually increas-ing it to a high-pitched tone until the tapes let out metallic sounds. Closing my eyes, I listened to the edited tapes from beginning to end. The high metallic sounds continued, howling on for about another minute.

Immediately I erased all the recorded sounds. Then I listened to the empty sounds from the deleted tapes, as if my whole body had soaked up all those erased sounds. I longed for live, human voices.

*   *   *

On her return home, my sister jumped out of her skin with anger, red hot as a heated iron. It was not only that Auntie had left in my sister's new outfit but she had also made off with my sister's emergency savings that she had tucked away in her wardrobe. My sister snatched up the telephone receiver, ready to pounce on Auntie that very moment. A smile stole over my face, because my sister had no way of knowing how to contact Auntie's folks as they changed their domicile almost every other day. But with that my sister's anger melted away. The moment she spotted the dishes Auntie had fixed without our noticing, my sister shook her head as if she couldn't help herself. My sister and I let Auntie slip from our minds, and sitting in front of the TV, where we had placed the portable dinner table as many people do in the evening hours, we finished our dinner, savoring the simple pleasure of chewing the grains of cooked rice.

Vaguely thinking of how Auntie aspired to be a singer on the radio or television, I gazed at the lips of the TV anchor sitting stiffly upright, as if her spine were stricken with a disk problem, and broadcasting the news. A hesitant look on her face, the anchor pursed her lips, as though she were picking out mud mixed in with cooked rice, but as her lips opened wider, they were for a moment overlapped by the big lips of Auntie—thickly made up and belting out a tune.

"Hey, Ch'angsu! Snap out of it and grate this cucumber. You might as well enjoy this job now, because once in the army you won't be able to do it even if you wanted to."

In a few seconds, my sister put an egg and a cucumber in front of me and flung herself into a resting posture on the floor. I grated the cucumber, whipped the egg, covered my sister's face with a gauze kerchief, and thickly spread the prepared slushy liquid over it. Just like a mortician preparing a real corpse for a funeral, with adept and skillful moves I began my sister's evening massage.

Even though the cucumber juice mixed with egg trickled down the back of her ears, my sister remained motionless without budging an inch, offered no complaint, and even wore a soft smile. Although I put twice the usual amount of cucumber juice on her face, from the start my sister relaxed herself completely and even seemed to have stopped breathing, as if she really intended to mimic a dead person. I was eagerly awaiting something, without knowing exactly what.

Suddenly, I put my hands on my sister's slender neck, and pressing them against the area of her windpipe, I blurted out, "Sis, you aren't a virgin, are you?"

My sister bolted up, as if to prove that she was totally alive, slapped me on the cheek without hesitation, and said, "Are you trying to take after your hoodlum Uncle? Don't you know, whenever he has a fit, he throttles Auntie's neck, using her childlessness as an excuse?"

At my sister's words, a cold shiver ran down my spine. My sister lay down again, spread the gauze kerchief on her face, and began to cover it herself with small amounts of the juice remaining in the container. Lying on the floor, she kept silent, responding no further to my wicked teasing. For a long time, I looked at my sister's face covered with the gauze kerchief, hoping she'd laugh.

The phone rang. What was I thinking, I wonder? I put the receiver against my ear with my heart pounding, as if the call were from the mute woman I saw a week ago. But that was out of the question. Even today, I hadn't delivered my letter to the woman. Why would that woman, who doesn't even know I exist, call me? As if trying to prolong my outlandish fantasy, instead of a human voice, indistinguishable noises came through from the other end of the line. Holding my breath, I listened to the noises.

After a while, I heard a faint voice say, "Is that Ch'angsu or is it Ch'angsun?"

"This is Ch'angsu," I answered in a voice as low as Auntie's.

"This is Yi Chŏngbun, and I'm in a very faraway place." Before I asked her where she was, Auntie told me the name of the place in an emotionless voice, as if she were reciting a secret code.

"Do you hear me? This is a place called Kŏjin in the middle of the east coast."[3]

_____

3. Kŏjin is a port in Kangwŏn Province on the east coast of Korea, and is very

I said nothing.

Auntie remained silent for quite a while. Then she said in a measured tone, as if making an important announcement, "You know this is a place absolutely forbidden to me … but what the heck, I came anyway. Call my family in the countryside for me and tell them your troublemaker auntie has now gone to Kŏjin. I bet the whole family will be turned upside down. Tell them slowly so that the weak-hearted old folks won't pass away in the same breath."

Then Auntie became silent again. I couldn't figure out what she was talking about. I sensed something serious had really happened to her, but in my mind, only the image of the back of the mute woman remaining silent in front of the phone box flickered. There was no hint of tipsiness in Auntie's voice.

"Ch'angsu, you still have a few days left before reporting to the army, right? Come here, because I have a story I've got to tell you."

"What kind of story?" I muttered hesitatingly.

"It's about the composer you've always pestered me to tell you about. No one except you has ever asked me to tell the story. It's a story I've never dared get off my chest, not even to you, lest all hell break loose."

By then, I began to worry whether Auntie, all alone in a place called Kŏjin, might by chance cause trouble.

"Auntie, please drop it and come back to Seoul. Why don't you stay with us here for a few days and tell me about it?"

"No. The story has to be told here. Just come here before you enter the army, and for a change of air as well. When you arrive in Kŏjin, look for a local lodging house." Then Auntie hung up.

"Auntie called me from a place called Kŏjin on the east coast. Do you have any idea why she went there?" I asked my sister, but she didn't answer.

"Shouldn't we ask around for Uncle's whereabouts and let him know what's going on?" I said, but my sister still didn't answer me.

I murmured, almost talking to myself, "What on earth is this story between Auntie and the composer she had known in her younger days all about?"

---

close to the demilitarized zone (DMZ), facing North Korea.

I got ready to go to my room, leaving my sister, who might have fallen asleep.

Still lying on the floor, my sister moved her lips under the gauze kerchief, saying, "I heard from Mom in passing that Kŏjin is a place where Auntie stayed for awhile toward the end of the Korean War. I don't know the details, but our Auntie is a really pitiful person. Go and bring her back. Be nice to her."

I came back to my room and checked the calendar. I had about ten days to spare before joining the army. I took my letter out of my pocket and read it once aloud.

                        *   *   *

Dear Ms. Han Miji,[4]

If your real name is not Han Miji, please accept my sincere apologies. I promise you that as soon as I learn your real name, I will revise the salutation at the beginning of this letter.

I am a person who dreams of becoming an ocean. I am also a person who has a special love for salmon among other creatures living in that vast liquid country. Do you know what commonality exists between the salmon and me?

A week ago, about five o'clock in the afternoon on May the first, I saw you for the first time in the public phone booth located near the bus stop on Ch'angch'ŏn Street. No, I heard your voice for the first time. I am not trying to insult you—a mute for sure—in this manner. Neither am I a medical student interested in finding out how a mute like you could continuously make such moving sounds. Nor am I writing to you out of curiosity to learn the content of the message you tried to communicate through a series of high-pitched sounds to the person on the other end of your phone line. Of course, I confess that the shock I received is not unrelated to the fact that you are a mute. I am merely a music student who wants to listen to your voice even just once and, if possible, record it in order to pass on the shock I received. If it is impossible for me to see you face to face, I sincerely request that you give me your permission to do so even through the phone. Attached please find my address and telephone number. Hoping as much as possible that there won't be any misunderstanding,

Sincerely yours,
Pak Ch'angsu

---

4. Italics added.

I put the letter in an envelope and wrote my name and address in the space for the sender. In the addressee's space, I wrote, "To the person who was making a phone call about five o'clock in the afternoon on May the first at the public phone booth located near the bus stop on Ch'angch'ŏn Street." I entered the address I had taken down from the gate plate of the house into which the woman had disappeared. I looked at my watch. It was close to eleven at night. I barely had time to put the letter into the letterbox of the house and return home.

*　　*　　*

Kŏjin. One of the tiniest estuaries on the east coast, barely noted on the map. A plain estuary that people are bound to miss or have difficulties finding, even if they know its general location. A rocky village, small like a speck, that looks about to be swept away by the waves that on occasion strike fiercely against it.

In Kŏjin, as in most of the small fishing villages near the demilitarized zone, the barbed-wire fences, lined up densely along the beach or along the pine forests, cut off the view of the blue sea indifferently. There were neither decent *hoe,* raw fish, eateries for visitors nor fishing boats worthy of note. Only small, cement-plastered houses were clustered together, lying flat on the ground as if they had collapsed in a faint. At the entrance to the village stood a public phone booth, planted defiantly like an empty sentry post as if it were a rare artifact. Its phone receiver had most likely been seized upon by Auntie like a drowning person clutching at straw. Although more than half a day had passed since my arrival in this village, I still had not seen anyone going into the phone booth.

I tried to picture this small fishing village some thirty years before. Perhaps the estuary would have been completely empty without a human trace. Besides a few stone-walled houses, which look like objects thrown away by mistake, only the groups of black sea rocks—blocking the estuary and sitting in a meditative posture on the changeless, blindingly white beach—would have been there, indifferently swallowing all the secrets the rough sea spewed out. Exactly thirty-seven years before. Undoubtedly, the color of the sea rocks would have been darker at that time and they wouldn't have had as many holes as they did now, the result of the rocks' exhaustion in trying to swallow since then all those commonplace stories that had affected every Korean citizen in one way or another. Most probably, in those days, neither the lonely lines of barbed-wire fences set up behind the sea rocks nor the long-distance, public phone booth, facing the North and always empty, existed in the village.

A few small fishing boats, looking spent, were moored among the black sea rocks. I wondered whether Kang Ujin, the up-and-coming composer, and his infant son, Hŭisŏk, born of him and Yi Chŏngbun and barely seven months old, had left for the North aboard a small boat just about the size of one of these fishing vessels.

True! Exactly thirty-six years ago, the twenty-five-year-old, promising composer Kang Ujin and the twenty-year-old Yi Chŏngbun arrived in Kŏjin on a winter's night. They had left their hometown, Sunch'ŏn,[5] separately and met at the home of Kang Ujin's acquaintance in Kangnŭng,[6] where Yi Chŏngbun, whose time was near, was barely able to give birth. At the end of Kang Ujin's two-month stay in Kangnŭng, waiting for certain important communications, they traveled to Kŏjin, which took nearly two weeks.

Following the success of "You Wouldn't Know," Kang Ujin worked actively in Seoul as a rising composer, but upon the outbreak of the Korean War he transformed himself into a member of the Southern Communist Party[7] and, after returning to his hometown, he began to take part in Party activities. Yi Chŏngbun's family began to regard her close relationship with Kang Ujin as a curse visited upon the Yi household. It could very well be said that Yi Chŏngbun's hardships began just from that point. Though her family locked her up, she'd slip out of the house for meetings and so on and wouldn't leave Kang Ujin, whom she had idolized since she was young. Neither beatings nor threats proved useless. Yi Chŏngbun ran away from home several times and each time was caught and returned to her hometown. Besides, it was pointless to run away to places where Kang Ujin was not. Before the baby growing inside her became large enough to be noticed, her family

---

5. Sunch'ŏn is a city in South Chŏlla Province.

6. Kangnŭng is a major city in Kangwŏn Province, south of Kŏjin.

7. Called "The Workers' Party of South Korea" (Namnodang), it was a communist party that thrived from 1946 to 1949 in the south. The party was outlawed by American occupation authorities in the south after Korea's liberation from Japan, but it was successful in organizing a network of clandestine cells and was able to obtain a considerable following. As the persecution of the party intensified, large numbers of the party leadership and members defected to the north.

sent her to a place far away from her village to root out even the seeds of the rumor that she was carrying a communist's child. What's more, Kang Ujin had conveniently vanished from the village some time before, as if he had completely changed the area of his activities.

While Yi Chŏngbun was spending day after day in a remote village unknown to her, suppressing her noticeably bulging belly with an almost primeval fear, Kang Ujin miraculously appeared there like a knight coming to her rescue. He had dropped from the ranks in search of her. That night, the two decided to stay awhile in the east coast area and then to defect to the North after Kang completed his assignment in Kangnŭng.

That period was a time for Yi Chŏngbun to sleep off her long-accumulated fatigue. In the meantime, Kang Ujin would be gone from their one-room stone-walled house for a week and sometimes for ten days. Once in a while, one or two men came to see Kang Ujin and they would steal away at night by boat. They never visited Yi Chŏngbun when she was alone, and they rarely stayed more than a day.

And one day, three people came to see Yi Chŏngbun in this nearly deserted village. It was a few days after Kang Ujin had left for somewhere. These members of her family tried to persuade her, explained the situation, scared and threatened her. The next day, the same tactics were repeated in the dark room in the same manner, and her uncle, whose life had barely been spared by the communists, beat her mercilessly, unable to control his anger. Before the eyes of Yi Chŏngbun, who had collapsed, thoroughly spent, the grisly scenes her uncle and cousins described flitted back and forth. That was the beginning of the threats that were to be repeated throughout Yi Chŏngbun's life.

Her family members had come thoroughly prepared. After waiting until she was completely worn out, someone lifted her up and carried her on his back. Even amidst this turmoil, Yi Chŏngbun heard her uncle's voice suggesting that the child who just turned seven months be entrusted to a fisherman living in the inward side of the estuary until the return of Kang Ujin. She also heard the frantic cries of the child separated from her fading away as if in a nightmare. In such a manner Yi Chŏngbun left Kŏjin.

That was all. For more than a year, Yi Chŏngbun lived like a prisoner under the pretext that she had contracted a dangerous disease, and the following year, she was sent to Seoul, where she jumped into a marriage with the first guy who came along. Her past involvement with a communist had to be completely deleted, because its revelation would mean the ruin of her family. As much as possible, she had to cut off contact with her natal family, and she had to gladly accept all her hardships—considered of her own making—as repayment to her family who had helped preserve her life. She had to forget not only everything about Kang Ujin but also all about the infant Hŭisŏk. She had to forget Kŏjin. To repay them, Auntie gave up on her own life by herself, mortgaging it to them.

How could this village, so laid back and even mellow at two in the afternoon, be the very site of Auntie's horrid nightmare! I stepped into one of the small boats on the beach and sat with my back to the sea. Under the stinging sunlight, the small fishing village, which quickly came into view, revealed its every corner like fresh scars. I couldn't suppress the fits of laughter that were welling up inside and sweeping over my entire body. I plopped down onto the wet boat bed and rolled about laughing my head off. Just what phantoms had produced this absurd drama, making Auntie their victim? She was a foolhardy actor who, having lived wearing a mask, had in the end become the face of the mask itself! Our actress, Ms. Yi Chŏngbun, who had tried to change the tragedy into a comedy! For a moment, I intensely hated Auntie's lifelong performance.

A few villagers came out of their gates and watched me through the barbed-wire fences, as if they had been awakened by my shrieking laughter. I sat up and perched on the prow of the boat again.

In what stone-walled house had Auntie stayed for five months? What was the location of the house in which Hŭisŏk, who'd be my older cousin, cried while waiting for his father, Kang Ujin, a member of the Southern Communist Party? But then, had they really left Kŏjin aboard a boat?

"Yes, of course. Kang Ujin must have become a famous composer. Hŭisŏk also should have made it. You could tell right away simply listening to the baby's cry. You see, nothing escapes my sharp ear. You listen to me carefully. Those who are meant to meet and live together are bound to meet again! No one can begin to understand the stubbornness that has been fermenting in an enraged heart for forty years. Sure! I will certainly end up meeting with them! Even if I can't, you, Ch'angsu, should meet your older cousin and tell my story by becoming a fine musician without fail." These were Auntie's answers.

I headed toward the only private lodging house in Kŏjin, where Auntie and I were staying. The owner said that Auntie had left for a valley in the mountains around the area. As I was walking toward the valley, inexplicably, I began thinking about the mute woman, who might have been sitting in a completely deserted valley in the depths of mountains, waiting for someone. What if I went straight on this mountain path … I vainly searched for Auntie deep down in the valley, while walking on the narrow mountain road that barely allowed a car to pass. After about thirty minutes, I noticed the unpaved dirt road narrowing into a trail. Still, Auntie was nowhere to be seen. Thinking that the owner of the lodging had given me wrong directions, I was about to turn around and backtrack along the road when I heard thin moans. I walked in the direction of the sounds but couldn't see any person there. After a long walk, I became aware of the moan changing into a high-pitched voice, and when I finally spotted Auntie, I realized that it was her voice.

Auntie was seated at a small cascade formed by the valley's waters, which was blocked by the rocks and then slipping through them. With her feet dipped in the water, she sang her lungs out in that eerie, high-pitched tune I had just heard. Seemingly unaware that a person was approaching her from the slope, she repeated the same vocal exercises: first, she dragged out her high screech—with neither lyrics nor pitches—until she was out of breath, when she stopped briefly to inhale. Then, she drew up the same throat-rending high-pitched sounds, as if breaking into a fit of screaming. Just like chanters who train their voices in front of waterfalls to master their vocalizing technique, Auntie endlessly repeated the vocal drill of "ŏ-ŏ-i" and "ŏ-ŏ-i" in the same monotonous rhythm, going all out, as if competing against the waterfall itself. Each time, her upper body trembled as if she had had a fit of spasm, and she even clenched her fists tight as if her practice was strenuous.

Just then, for the first time, it occurred to me that I was carrying my mini tape recorder at my side. I pushed the record button, hoping Auntie's roars would go on for a long time. In the valley surrounded by rocks, like panels of a folding screen, Auntie's chant that verged on screams created endless echoes. I too sat upright on a rock, not far from her, and with eyes closed, listened to her roars being recorded on my recorder, to the sounds of the falling waters, and to the echoes of their mixed sounds spreading.

*   *   *

The night before I left Kŏjin, I again had a dream in which I became a salmon. As before, my body was flailing in its attempt to swim up against the rough current coming down from the top of the more than ten-meter waterfall. Anglers thronged there and, with their hats cocked, were sparing no effort to cast their lines out far. Countless fishing lines became entangled at the bottom of the falls, and then, after they were disentangled, were cast again into the water. In no time, an untold number of salmon swarmed around, each of them flip-flapping to jump against the waterfall, while splashing their tails, bodies, and fins against the rough currents and trying to avoid the fishing lines. How much time had passed? As I felt myself getting more and more exhausted, I realized that my body was floating up higher and higher against the current of the falls, levitating as if by a miracle. As I soared up and up, I almost had a glimpse of the top of the waterfall right before my eyes. Then I felt my body being flung onto the flat surface at the top of the falls and my tail and fins swam freely there. Quickly I cast my glance in the direction of the precipitous falls from where I had just leapt. I saw numerous salmon at the bottom of the falls standing in a line under the steep currents and forming a kind of a long ladder. At that moment, I realized that I had scaled the falls by climbing this very ladder created by myriad other salmon. Before long, another salmon leapt up to the top of the falls and splashed its body. Soon after, another one, and then finally, scores of salmon came up in row upon row. I could see anglers way below, stunned and with mouths agape, watching the ladder the salmon were forming.

*   *   *

The following morning, Auntie and I left the lodging after walking around the village. Exactly as on the day of my arrival, the aluminum frame of the public phone booth, still empty under a bright and disinterested sunlight, shone sharply. We passed the village without looking back. I saw the rural public bus stop and in front of it, the sunburned faces of the villagers who, under the scorching sunlight, were waiting for the bus. Auntie stopped walking. She winked at me. As if we had already agreed, we walked toward the public phone.

I saw Auntie's rough finger dialing 114 for an operator.

Soon I heard her low and gentle voice—a tone she used when making an unreasonable demand of someone—as she said, "Hello,

I am going to make a difficult request, but would you please look for the phone number of a person named Kang Hŭisŏk in the North? I can wait as long as it takes."

I tried to picture the face of the telephone operator, who'd probably hang up the phone without even answering, treating Auntie like an utter lunatic. How many times a day would the operator get this kind of prank call? Though the other side had obviously already hung up, Auntie tenaciously waited in the heated, glass-paneled phone booth holding the receiver—undoubtedly ringing with noises only—closely against her ear.

I snatched the telephone receiver from Auntie. Then, arm in arm with our Auntie—a short but solidly built woman decked out in my sister's best clothes was watching me with a disappointed look while floating an enigmatic smile—I called my sister at her office. She answered that there was neither a letter nor a phone call for me. She told me that she'd be waiting, a *hoe* dish specially prepared for Auntie and me. Although my sister could have no inkling of the contents of my dream, I shuddered all over and said, "No thank you."

On the bus for Seoul, I gradually began to forget about the mute woman. Suppose one day a mute woman suddenly got to sing, why should it be considered such an anomaly anyway?

After the bus left the coastal area, Auntie pointed to my tape recorder and, blinking her eyes, said proudly, "What do you say? Don't you think Auntie is as good as a real chant-singer? By the time you come home on leave, I bet this Yi Chŏngbun's talent for chanting will be known everywhere."

☙

Ch'oe Yun (b. 1953)

The second of four daughters of a middle-class family, Ch'oe Yun was born in Seoul in July 1953 as the Korean War was about to end in a truce. From a young age, her politically concerned parents, whose secretive, nighttime conversations on Korean society she overheard, awakened in her curiosity and interest in such public, social matters, which would last through her life and literary career.[8] Adolescent Ch'oe loved to roam about her neighborhoods until late at night—a source of worry for her parents—taking in impressions of different classes of people, bustling marketplace scenes, young gang members in back alleys, and even the slum areas of the nearby hills. As a first-grader, she personally witnessed the bloody student demonstrations in Seoul streets—the Student Revolution in April 1960 that toppled the autocratic government of President Syngman Rhee (1875–1965). At around this time, Ch'oe, with a mania for comic books, created volumes of her own comics with a dream of becoming a cartoonist, much to her mother's disapproval. During her middle-school days, she began to hone her literary talents and published a collection of stories with a group of her friends. Ch'oe used to give her stories as birthday gifts to her friends, many of whom came from disadvantaged backgrounds. It was to major in Korean literature that Ch'oe entered Sogang University in Seoul.

The deeply politicized college culture of the 1970s quickly made Ch'oe its eager member. Her editorship of the university's student magazine subjected her to police surveillance, home searches, and investigation. Yet she obtained her BA (1976) without disruption, and in 1978, she earned her MA and made her debut as a literary critic with an article on modern Korean novels. The same year, Ch'oe left for France to undertake graduate work at the University of Provence in Aix-en-Provence, and in 1983, earned her PhD by writing on the French novelist Marguerite Duras (1914–1996).[9] On

---

8. The biographical information about Ch'oe Yun is largely based on her book, *Sujubŭn autsaidŏ ŭi kobaek: Ch'oe Yun sanmumjip* [Confessions of a shy outsider: collection of Ch'oe Yun's essays] (Seoul: Munhak Tongne, 1994).

9. Besides being a novelist in the French *nouveau roman* literary movement, Marguerite Duras was also a playwright, scriptwriter, essayist, and experimental filmmaker. See also footnote 23 on Marguerite Duras in "Dreams of Butterflies, 1995," p. 260.

returning to Korea in 1984, she began teaching at her alma mater in the Department of French.

In 1988, Ch'oe made her first appearance as novelist with her novella, "Chŏgi sori ŏpsi hanjŏm kkonnip i chigo" (There, a petal silently falls), a powerful but subtle denunciation of the butchery of innocent citizens by the Korean military government during the civilian Kwangju Uprising of May 1980. The author's censuring stance is conveyed through the heartrending, helpless suffering of a young girl deranged by the shock of her mother's horrifying death in the carnage. This narrative anticipated Ch'oe's trademark literary style, characterized by avant-garde experimentation, unconventional narrative points of view and structures, the deployment of mystifying images and symbols, and intellectually challenging and thought-provoking content. Thus began Ch'oe Yun's career as an academic, literary critic, and novelist.

The group of four short stories published subsequently, "Pŏng'ori ch'ang" (A Mute's chant; 1989), "Abŏji kamsi" (Keeping an eye on father; 1990), "Tangsin ŭi mulchebi" (Stone in your heart; 1992), and "Soksagim, soksagim" (Whisper, whisper; 1993), are in-depth and multifaceted explorations of the monstrosity, violence, and even incomprehensibility of the Cold War ideologies and their impact and long-lasting consequences in the lives of its Korean War–ravaged characters. These works belong to the "division literature" subgenre dealing with the problematic and often tragic reverberations of the fratricidal Korean War, which polarized the Korean nation geopolitically and ideologically. Ch'oe's lauded short story, "Hoesaek nun saram" (The gray snowman; 1992), winner of the Tong-in Literature Award, is another example of Ch'oe's persistent historico-political consciousness. It reassesses antigovernment covert activities by student dissidents in the 1980s and their true significance to those directly involved in them, even while it bemoans the mysterious disappearance and death of a young female college student, a member of such a subversive group.

In her "Hanak'o nŭn ŏpta" (There's no Hanak'o; 1994), recipient of the Yi Sang Literature Award, Ch'oe freshly adopted feminist, critical perspectives on the male-dominant ethos of a coeducational contemporary college campus, where female students are undervalued and even cheapened. The clinching end of the narrative, which spotlights the international reputation enjoyed by the female characters in their professional fields, forms a sharp contrast to the dull, desiccated, and uninspiring lives of their male friends in their post-college years. It succeeds in puncturing the empty, pompous charades of male superiority and misogyny, often flaunted in the underestimation and objectification of women as mere and perpetual men-pleasers. During these productive years, Ch'oe also published a collection of essays, *Sujubŭn autsaidŏ ŭi kobaek* (Confessions of a shy outsider; 1994), which offers its readers an intimate and informative window to her life from childhood, personal reflections, and adroit observations and viewpoints about her society.

Ch'oe's first full-length novel, *Kyŏul, At'ŭllant'isŭ* (Winter, Atlantis; 1997), amplifies her ideas about the epistemological impossibility of fathoming or deciphering the mysterious turns of human life by foregrounding parallel stories of two women characters, who try to trace the baffling, mysterious disappearance of their respective lovers to no avail. The author maintains that through the loss and absence of those they cherish, human beings become more keenly and intensely aware of their presence. This very loss paradoxically becomes the source of strength for people to endure their disconnectedness and suffering, just as the mythical continent Atlantis asserts its presence by its vanishing into the Indian Ocean. The novel also communicates the ubiquitousness of incomprehensible accidents and unexpected, sudden calamities that ambush human beings' ordinary daily routine and tragically wreak havoc on it, often shocking people into an acute existential awakening to the frailty and vulnerability of life—the real nature of life itself.

Ch'oe's second novel, *Maneking* (Mannequin; 2003), is an allegorical commentary on the immorality, evil, and destructiveness of materialism and greed that permeates human interrelationships among Koreans today. These unsavory trends are personified in the novel in a group of family members who financially exploit the body of the youngest daughter by making her a model for commercial advertising. The novel delivers its message by drawing a clear distinction between the selfish older members of the family (they are named after subhuman marine animals, such as starfish, agar, and conch, etc.) and the purity and beauty of the elflike young girl (with a human name, Chini), who, after escaping from the grip of her mercenary elders, exhausts her short life to give love and care to those in dire need of it.

The most recent novel by Ch'oe, *Orikmansti* (2011),[10] recaps the theme of exposing the hidden immorality and pathology of the materialistic value system and pleasure-driven Korean culture of the 1980s, exemplified by the main characters: a petit-bourgeois, young married couple. They nonchalantly carry on clandestine extramarital affairs, abortions, corrupt business transactions, public embezzlement, reckless real estate speculation, and indulgence in shopping sprees, taking this as perfectly normal behavior. The couple's sudden death, swept away by a mountain flash flood during a summer camping trip as they desperately try to save their belongings, dramatically reveals the triviality and inconsequentiality of their totally unexamined outlook on and way of life and brings to light their moral amnesia and derailment. The narrative also taps into the author's abiding thematic preoccupation about the unpredictability, randomness, and inscrutability of human existence and its meaning. The sudden, unforeseen deaths of the principal characters defy explanation through human language, and the author symbolically notes the fact by the cryptic and baffling title of the novel.

In addition to creative writing, Ch'oe has translated major novels by contemporary Korean writers into French and has also been actively engaged in promoting cultural relationships between France and Korea, both on campus and for the general public. In recognition of her achievements, the French government awarded Ch'oe "Chevalier dans l'Ordre des Arts et Lettres" in 2007. ∞

TEXTUAL READINGS

Playing on the oxymoron of its title, "A Mute's Chant" makes public a long-silenced and heart-rending trauma of one woman, a victim of Cold War ideologies, and brings into relief her pointless suffering and the need to set it right. Yi Chŏngbun, the protagonist, has buried her personal secret in the depths of her being for thirty-seven years. The only crime she ever committed was to fall in love with a musician, a communist activist, and having a son from her union with him. She has been unable to utter a single word about her

---

10. It is a nonsense word coined by Ch'oe Yun.

painful past, forbidden by an extended family in its desperate need to protect itself from guilt by association and potential persecution as a result of the South Korean government's inflexible anticommunist policies.[11] She has been made a pariah—denigrated, muted, and expelled by her own blood relations—and even deleted from her family history, ending up sealed in her current marital quagmire.

Approaching sixty, however, Yi Chŏngbun refuses to remain voiceless, and she confesses her unutterable truths.[12] Her vehicle for rebellion is the art of *ch'ang* singing, into which she throws her heart and soul.[13] *Ch'ang*, the traditional, plebian-rooted performing art, anteceded Cold War geopolitics and therefore was untainted by North-South rivalry and national polarization in 1948. Consequently, Yi Chŏngbun's musical venture takes on a profound meaning in that it is a depoliticized cultural act that reaches back to Korea's original unity. On the one hand, her grueling, ritual-like *ch'ang* training works as an exorcism and catharsis of her long-suppressed storied past (*han* in Korean). On the other, her undertaking is one of connectivity, restitution, and healing, which has a symbolic linkage with the homecoming instinct of the salmon and its effort to make a successful return to the source of its birth. Having shed herself of the ignominy of political and marital victimhood, Yi Chŏngbun is now reborn with an artistic identity and voice and open future, no longer a political and social mute. "A Mute's Chant" thus puts on public view a woman in revolt against dominant, mainstream po-

---

11. Yi In-yŏng et al., "Chŏnjaeng, kiŏk, yŏsŏng chŏngch'esŏng: Ch'oe Yun ŭi 'Pŏng'ŏri ch'ang' kwa 'Krista Polp'ŭ ŭi 'Krista T. e taehan ch'unyŏm' pigyo" [War, memory, women's identity: a comparative study of memorial writings by Ch'oe Yun's "A Mute's Chant" and Christa Wolf's "The Quest for Christa T"], *Kap'ŭka yŏn'gu* 12 (2004), 279.

12. Derived from Chinese astrology, the sixtieth birthday in Korea has traditionally been considered an important milestone in a person's life, as it means the individual, man or woman, has completed a full life cycle and is poised to begin a new life.

13. *Ch'ang*, interchangeably called *p'ansori*, is a genre of traditional one-person opera. The vocalist's singing and narration is accompanied by a drummer who beats rhythm on a drum called *changgo*. It is considered to have developed from shamanistic songs and enjoyed wide popularity among both the upperclasses and general populace of Chosŏn Korea during the mid-nineteenth century. For more on this art, see Chan E. Park, *Voices from the Straw Mat: Toward an Ethnography of Korean Story Singing* (Honolulu: University of Hawai'i Press, 2003).

litical narratives, mocking the violent logic of power and sociopolitical and familial censorship.

Yi Chŏngbun's willful insistence on returning to Kŏjin, where her original tragedy played out, boils down to her determination to physically revisit, relive, and confront her past wrong, root it out, and begin anew. Her return journey serves as a curative purging of her hurtful personal history and a point of departure for a new life. Her act echoes the homecoming instinct of salmon, a heroic endeavor to overcome physical limits and reach the destination for the sake of the next generation. Here, Ch'angsu's dream of himself reincarnated as a salmon and his arduous corporeal exertion to reach the top of the waterfall connote his figurative identification with his aunt and exemplifies his metaphorical reenactment of her strenuous rite of passage from victim to victor.

What makes "A Mute's Chant" a winsome story is the author's creation and use of its narrator, Pak Ch'angsu, Yi Chŏngbun's young nephew, a music-major college student. Ch'angsu's readiness to carry out the role of a confidant and facilitator for his aunt to pour out her secrets are prefigured and prescripted by his interest in the mute woman, an absolute stranger and the symbolic double of his aunt, who captures his attention. In addition, Ch'angsu, with his oddball interest in sounds, shares his aunt's quirky streak and is also her drinking buddy and partner in her zany music recital. He is misunderstood by his music professor, who thinks he is eccentric and even calls him by the wrong surname, "Mr. Kim." Pak's upperclassman usurps his creative work without giving him the rightful credit in his greed for commercial profit. As such, the narrator is an unappreciated and misjudged outsider—just like his aunt. Above all, Ch'angsu's own experience as a political scapegoat by the absurdity of the police, who punish him with a draft notice, eminently qualifies him as catalyst for his aunt's coming-out act. The narrator and his older sister genuinely embrace their aunt's ghastly legacy. Unlike their older kin, who annihilated Yi Chŏngbun's life, the pair represents a new, post-division generation and form a figurative correspondence with the school of salmon, whose kindred, mutual support enables them to reach their home together. ❧

Love and Daggers

Kim In-suk

[1]

Every human being is destined to die, though they seem to go on living for thousands of years. My paternal grandma's death is a case in point. Paralyzed by a stroke, she was unable to go to the toilet by herself for nearly three years. Despite her difficulty in eating, she still held on for three years. During this period, Mom's hardships were almost indescribable. Grandma kept on whining to everyone who called on her that her daughter-in-law, that is, my mom, didn't give her food so she wouldn't have to clean up her mother-in-law's bodily waste.

"Give me food," she would say. "If I die like this, I'll become a hungry ghost!"

I heard that Grandma's last words at her death were a plea for food. When I hurried to Kyŏngju at the news of Grandma's death, Mom was sitting vacantly with her mourning clothes all undone.[1] No one was wailing. Given the fact that Grandma passed away at the age of more than eighty and after three years of serious illness, her death was not unexpected; so mourning for her was to be accompanied by a sense of release.

The title of the original is "K'allal kwa sarang," and was first published in the journal *Changjak kwa pip'yŏng*, no. 80 (Summer 1993). The present translation is based on the text included in Kim In-suk, *K'allal kwa sarang: Kim In-suk sosŏlchip* [Love and daggers: collection of Kim In-suk's short stories] (Seoul: Changjak Kwa Pip'yŏngsa, 1993), 5–62.

---

1. Kyŏngju is a city in North Kyŏngsang Province in the southeastern part of Korea. It was once the capital of the Silla kingdom (57 BCE–935 CE).

187

As the saying goes, "the longer the illness, the less filial children become." Even my paternal aunts, who had always behaved selfishly, now seemed to be relieved at the death of their mother, as if a heavy load had been lifted from their shoulders. Mom was the only one who looked lost. Only later, when I learned of Grandma's dying words, did I finally realize that they had deeply hurt Mom's feelings.

"Oh, dear, I thought your grandmother would live on forever," said Auntie, Mom's younger sister—a slightly bitter look on her face—who had accompanied me to Kyŏngju on the same train. Auntie was gazing at Grandma's photograph. In the picture, probably taken some ten years before, Grandma still looked nice and healthy. I smiled wryly at her photo.

"Your mom looks as if she hasn't eaten anything. Go help her eat something," said Auntie. Auntie Chonghŭi, the youngest of Mom's siblings, knew better than anyone else how Mom was feeling. My mom cared for Auntie Chonghŭi after the death of their parents when Auntie was young. For a long time, Auntie had eaten my dead Grandma's salt and had often cried because of Grandma's irritable temperament. I still remember Auntie sniffling, crouched under the eaves. When I ran into the kitchen, shouting, "Mom, Auntie is crying," as if something terrible had happened, I found that Auntie wasn't the only one who was crying. At such times, Mom, sitting near the kitchen furnace, was also rubbing tears from her eyes.

The reason Auntie Chonghŭi rushed all the way down to Kyŏngju at the news of Grandma's death was not simply because she was related to Grandma through my mom. No matter how difficult it was for Auntie to be dependent on Grandma for support, studying her smile or frown, she had after all grown up in Grandma's household for more than ten years, and it was also Grandma who had helped with Auntie's bridal trousseau, even though it was filled with trifling objects.

"My goodness, what am I doing!" Auntie belatedly opened her handbag and took out an envelope containing her condolence money—she seemed to have forgotten about it, carried away by her emotions. I also brought with me some money that I had hurriedly scraped together but was looking for the chance to give it to Mom directly. I was curious about how much condolence money we were going to receive. I thought the total amount wouldn't be much because my father had already passed away and the oldest son in our family—my older brother—didn't even have a decent job. I even asked my husband to think about ways to secure a loan, just in case. He told me that he couldn't make it down to Kyŏngju until the afternoon due to some urgent company business.

"Thank goodness, how kind of you to come," said my uncle—the husband of my paternal aunt, who was in charge of receiving the condolence money—as he recognized Auntie.

"I'm sorry I've come by myself. My husband is on a business trip," said Auntie, awkwardly using the regional dialect, and presented him her envelope. Uncle received it politely.

"Hello," said my second paternal aunt, who had snuck up on us. Obviously, she was curious to know how much money Auntie had given. This was not only because Auntie wasn't the kind of person who would remain indifferent to Grandma's death, but also because my paternal aunt probably knew from rumors that Auntie's husband's business was enjoying increasing prosperity recently.

"Good heavens! You've given so much," exclaimed my uncle.

"It's only proper for me," said Auntie, blushing. Though Auntie was never the sort of person who would express her sincere feelings through something like money, the amount of her condolence money was enormous, even to me. I gave her a surprised look. I couldn't help it, especially because I knew she was not the kind of person whose sincerity would simply end with that condolence money. I was almost certain that she had prepared a separate envelope for Mom.

Auntie stayed up all night at Mom's side. Even Mom eventually fell asleep—in a crouching posture—most probably from exhaustion. But Auntie looked unable to sleep a wink. For my part, I couldn't fall asleep either, because I was irritated at my husband who, after having arrived late, joined in a card game, oblivious of his place as a grandson-in-law.

Many thoughts drifted into my mind. In truth, when I was notified of Grandma's passing, I felt nothing but relief. I had little affection for her, although she was extremely devoted to her grandchildren in contrast to her nastiness toward Mom. Grandma was the kind of woman who, if Mom tried to take a small piece off the fish dish at the table to eat, would quickly snatch the plate from her and push it toward her grandchildren.

While Mom's chopsticks were still suspended embarrassingly midair, Grandma would narrow the corner of her eyes and raise her voice cheerfully, "Go on, my dears, eat up. Eat up and grow taller and taller."

I wasn't interested in the fish or meat dishes placed in front of me. I was angry at the shame Mom was suffering, and at the insensitivity of my older brother and younger siblings, who stuffed themselves with the side dishes until their mouths almost burst.

Auntie Chonghŭi was the only person in my family I felt close to. There was an eleven-year difference between us. To me, the oldest daughter in my family, Auntie was more like an older sister than an aunt. When I was young, I felt sorry for her and commiserated with her, comparing her to Cinderella or K'ongjwi.[2]

Even now when I think of Auntie in those days, my heart aches for her.

It was about the time when she was preparing for her marriage. Uncle, who fell in love with Auntie's beauty at first sight while visiting his relatives in Kyŏngju, was the oldest son of a wealthy family in Seoul, which also owned a considerable amount of land in Kyŏngju. Naturally, the preparation of the required articles for the marriage greatly worried Mom and Auntie. Mom couldn't sleep at all, calculating the expenses, while Auntie would just hang around the kitchen hearth, a demoralized look always on her face.

When I asked her if she was happy to get married, she said, "I don't care a thing about marriage. I wish I could just die."

It was clear that she thought it was no longer possible for her to continue living as a burden on our family. Without a doubt, the last few days she spent with us were strained. Grandma would raise her shrill voice, continually bemoaning what a hard fate she had to suffer, having to marry off her in-law's daughter, while Mom wiped away her tears, standing with her back to Grandma.

As a young girl barely ten, I began to feel another kind of pity for Auntie when I noticed something in Mom's attitude. In those days, my family owned an American-made blender, although I had no idea how we'd gotten it. It was a very rare item, and Mom never used it, having hidden it deep in her chest of drawers. It might have been a present from Mom's cousin. About the time when preparations for Auntie's marriage were underway, I saw Mom taking the

---

2. K'ongjwi is the heroine of a Korean folktale, "K'ongjwi P'atchwi," a counterpart to the Western Cinderella story. K'ongjwi was also much maligned and mistreated by her stepmother.

blender in and out of her chest, repeating the same action three or four times in the middle of the night. I couldn't understand at all why she was behaving so strangely, but the reason finally became clear around the time I got married, when I found the blender among the jumble of household goods that Mom had brought over to our newlywed apartment. The blender, still new but by then miserably out of date, was enough to make me burst out laughing.

"My goodness, Mom, have you been keeping this thing all these years?"

"Why of course! I've kept it like a treasure for your wedding gift."

That was why! Now I understood that when Mom was getting ready to marry Auntie off she'd tortured herself over whether to give the blender to her poor younger sister, who was marrying into a wealthy Seoul family, or to keep it for her own eldest daughter, who would be married more than ten years later! And Mom went through the agony again and again, as she took the blender out and then put it back more than three or four times during the night.

It then occurred to me that those tears Mom had shed for her sister were not so pure, after all. Although Mom had felt so much for her youngest sister, there existed a measure of calculation even in her concern for Auntie. Of course, I couldn't blame Mom. If I had had a child and had to choose between her and my sister, I would have inevitably taken my child's side. I felt grateful that I didn't have to face such a dilemma. I believed that the agony and shame Mom had no doubt felt at the time was enough to atone for the greater part of her small sin.

Nevertheless, I felt sorry for Auntie. It was because she repaid me twice—no, more than ten, twenty times—for her trying life in our home over some ten years. I started living in her house since my high school days. I stayed on there through college, and it was also at Auntie's home that I received the traditional wedding gift chest from my in-laws.[3] All those years Auntie had probably shouldered more than half of my tuition. No, she might have borne all of it, although she insisted that she was pitching in just *a little* for Mom's sake.

Yet for all that she had done for us, Auntie still behaved as if she owed a large debt to my family, forever wearing apologetic expres-

---

3. As part of traditional Korean marriage customs, a gift box called a *"ham"* is sent from the groom's family to the bride's house the night before the wedding.

sions on her face. Although I loved her dearly, I couldn't help wondering whether Auntie's scrupulousness was something of a chronic illness.

The next day at the funeral it was very windy. The early spring wind was so piercing that I didn't feel like getting out of the hearse at all. I was also put out by the fact that Grandma's burial site was in a Christian garden cemetery. Grandma had been relentlessly superstitious all her life but converted to Christianity only after she had a stroke. Her conversion might have had something to do with her dogged desire that compelled her to turn to the Western god in hopes of prolonging her life, now that the twelve spirits she had believed in for so long were about to snatch it away. In fact, Grandma had never attended church. People from the church came over to our house to have worship services for her, but I heard that even on those occasions Grandma clung to the minister or the deacon, begging them to sneak in food for her because her daughter-in-law was starving her to death.

Mom looked confused about the Christian funeral procedures. This was hardly surprising, because she didn't know even a single line of a Christian hymn. It seemed that Mom wanted to count on Auntie, who, she thought, was more "modern" than herself. Mom must also have remembered that Auntie had attended church when she was a newlywed. Yet, each time Mom showed signs of asking for help from Auntie, Auntie expressed her unwillingness, waving her hands and stepping backward. In fact, as far as I know, Auntie had attended church for just about two or three years. It was during the time when her husband was raising hell, acting like a beast in human disguise. He heaped indescribable wrongs upon Auntie—drinking, gambling, womanizing, and physical abuse—and God was probably the only one she could turn to at the time. Nevertheless, one day, for some unknown reason, Auntie abruptly cut herself off from the church. She also got rid of all the sacred icons of Jesus, the Bible, and the hymnal from her home. In fact, it hadn't been very easy for her to go to church openly because Uncle used to burst into fits of rage at her church attendance. It was probably around the time when I was a high school junior. One Sunday morning, Auntie slept in soundly, having totally given up on attending the church to which she used to steal out at any cost. That was the end of it. Since then, I never saw Auntie displaying any nostalgia for faith.

"Does this mean that anyone who just believes can go to heaven?" I asked Auntie, while watching from afar the preparations to lower Grandma's coffin into the grave. Fatigue was written all over Auntie's face, probably because she hadn't slept at all last night. But I became curious. I wasn't necessarily thinking of Grandma. I began to wonder, suppose there was a villain, the worst kind imaginable. He committed all sorts of offenses while alive, but if he repented and entered the bosom of God just before death, would heaven open to him? Could there be anything more unfair than that?

"Well, I doubt anything like that would happen," Auntie answered in a gloomy voice.

Sensing something strange in her voice, I turned around and saw tears rimming her eyes. I turned away. It wouldn't be easy for me to understand Auntie's tears.

Auntie decided to marry Uncle, whose insincere streak she spotted at first glance, because she thought she had to leave our house for our family's sake. It probably had nothing to do with the fact that Uncle was the son of a rich family. At that time, even if a wild roving peddler had come up to her and proposed, Auntie might have accepted.

Auntie's married life had long been one of misery. Although Uncle's evildoing had gradually tapered off—he seemed like a changed man, the penitent prodigal son—for at least ten years Auntie led a life without human dignity. No less than three times, Uncle wrecked what he called the business he'd started, and as far as I know, he tormented Auntie with his extramarital affairs on two occasions. He lost ownership of his house once because of his gambling debts, and on another occasion he beat up Auntie until her shoulder bones broke. It was just five years ago that he repented for his wrongdoings. The trigger was his stomach cancer. He had to have an operation, and most of his stomach was removed. That brush with death seemed to have made him into a God-fearing man. Just before he was taken into the operating room, he held Auntie's hands and said, "I am sorry," and requested that if he died she at least remember his apology.

I remember Auntie's sobs. All the way through the long operation, she kept crying. Her tears seemed never-ending. I don't know whether it was because of her tears or not, but Uncle was spared death, recovered his health, rebuilt his business, and became a really changed man. Although his business had been wiped out so many times, he still had sufficient capital. Isn't this after all a world where money breeds money? The moment he repented, he became a stable, rich man, and thereupon, all of Auntie's hardships seemed to have ended. Her two sons had been good students, always maintaining either the top or second place in their classes, and never caused any trouble. Now, Uncle faithfully celebrated all sorts of anniversaries and presented Auntie with gifts like mink coats or diamond rings. Sometimes he even went so far as to buy her travel tickets.

Everyone who knew about Auntie's early hardships praised her virtue of patience. They said, "Who could have possibly endured it? She wouldn't have known that these blessings would finally come all at once in her middle age. It proves that one should first and foremost be a good person." Especially those close relatives, who knew Auntie's adversities like their own, were not at all jealous of the affluence Auntie was now enjoying, at least not outwardly. Likewise, no one openly spoke ill of Uncle any longer. Once when a waggish person pointedly quipped that, in view of Auntie's past heartache, Uncle still had to repay Auntie tens of thousands of times over, Uncle simply responded with a smile.

I was one of those who knew Auntie's personal history best. I lived at Auntie's when she was going through such hard times. Of course, I was still young and couldn't have comprehended every detail. But I saw Uncle hitting Auntie right in front of me, and I also witnessed his vulgar young women—stretched out on the floor of the inner room. Every time, I felt an extremely strong indignation toward Uncle. One might say that the material comfort Auntie was now enjoying was happiness, but I couldn't believe that her present happiness would be great enough to make up for all her past suffering.

Likewise, I still found it very difficult to accept Auntie's hardship lasting more than ten years and the patience that carried her through it all. I was convinced that if I had been in her shoes, I would never have tolerated it. Even if a prophet appeared suddenly and told me a trustworthy prophesy that, if I held on tooth and nail just for ten years, I'd thereafter be showered with happiness, I'd have no intention of sacrificing ten years of my life for that delayed blessing. What about for the children's sake? That couldn't be the reason either. I loathed the absurd notion of maternal responsibility promoted by all the women in the world, who say that they have no choice but to bear with fortitude for their children's sake. Seen this way, Auntie's suffering might have been of her own making. Now and then it seemed to me that her entire life since her birth in this world was nothing but a lesson in patience.

"When is Uncle coming?" I asked abruptly, thinking it unwise to leave her alone with her thoughts for too long.

"What day is it today? Okay, he'll be back in a week or so."

"Are you going to the airport?"

"Well …"

"You two look like newlyweds these days."

"How about you two? Is it the same for you as before?"

"Never mind."

I found it better for me not to talk to Auntie about my married life. No matter how I explained my problems to her, she would just smile and take them as something trivial. For a while, soon after my marriage, I used to visit Auntie's house quite frequently. I told her all my problems. An unusually patient person, Auntie never showed any sign of annoyance, even though I went on talking for more than two or three hours. Yet I soon sensed that my stories were no more than idle talk to her. Come to think of it, my stories regarding the newlywed spats between my husband and me wouldn't even qualify as a conversation piece for Auntie, who had led such a difficult life. It was futile to insist to Auntie that my problems went beyond simple quarrels.

"If the dead really have souls, then it's good for them to be buried in a public cemetery. There's nothing but graves here, is there?" I said.

"That's right. Absolutely right," said Auntie.

Surrounded by graves and tombstones in all directions, we looked down at the foot of the mountain for a while. There was another hearse climbing up the mountain.

"Auntie, look here. This person seems to have died quite young," I said, pointing to the tombstone of the grave in front of me. According to the dates engraved on it, the person in the grave had lived barely thirty years. Still, his child's name was recorded. How would the wife of this dead person be living now? Would she be raising her only child and living a lonely life as a widow?

"This one is the same. He lived only to forty," said Auntie.

"That's not so bad. Isn't forty a little better?" I said.

"Listen, I am already forty-five. If you say forty is good enough, what about me then? It looks as if I have lived five more useless years."

"Auntie, I never meant it that way."

A sad smile spread over Auntie's face, an expression that had almost become her habit after years of hardship.

"Don't you think you need to go and see what's going on? You are the granddaughter after all, and it doesn't seem right for you to stand over here and just look on."

"I might get punished for saying it, but I don't feel like going."

"Get going, you!" Auntie hit me on my back. I had no choice. Even if I didn't shovel the dirt on the lowered coffin, I was supposed to at least be on hand to take part in the ceremony. Leaving Auntie where she was, I took steps toward Mom. As I was walking down, I looked back briefly at Auntie. She seemed to be looking vacantly from one grave to another. Doesn't she know that there are better things to do than look at graves, I wondered. At any rate, the cemetery on the windy, cold day created an infinitely desolate scene.

Auntie's silhouette standing alone in that bleak landscape appeared poignantly beautiful to me. Just like a figure of a sorrowful, elegant gazelle!

[2]

Uncle returned from his business trip to the United States on Sunday, some three days after Auntie's return from Kyŏngju, where she had stayed on until Grandma's *samuje* rite.[4] During those few days, Auntie became more dead than alive. She already looked completely exhausted by the time we returned from Grandma's burial ceremony, and when we reached home, she ended up taking to her bed. It was out of character for her to behave this way unless she was really feeling tired. Amid the whirlpool of distractions, Mom told Auntie to get some medicine from the drugstore, but Auntie tried to nurse herself by simply lying down. It seems her condition persisted after my early departure to Seoul from Kyŏngju to return to my job. According to Mom, Auntie—whatever ailed her—didn't even go to the mountain on the day of *samuje*, although she must have stayed on in Kyŏngju for that express purpose. But when the day came around, she wouldn't even stir from her bed.

---

4. "Samuje" refers to the memorial service held on the third day after a funeral, when the family of the deceased visits the grave site.

In her own way, Mom interpreted Auntie's symptoms as: "She must be feeling great pain—really deeply hurt. Why wouldn't she be, when I feel this bad? I just don't understand how Grandma could live her life hurting others so much, given her life wouldn't go on forever!"

Mom meant that Grandma's death must have rekindled old sorrows in Auntie.

Mom said, "I may be damned for badmouthing the dead, but I have some suspicion. You too know how much your grandma wanted to cling to life. As she was reluctant to leave this world, she has now possessed the body of a living person. That's why your Auntie is acting like this, no energy to live on, as if she would bite her tongue and die on the spot. You see, we can't blame the living person but the ghost."

I agreed with Mom, although I had no way of completely fathoming Auntie's deep-rooted regrets, as Mom did. No matter how much Auntie tried to keep her composure, it seemed her sorrows, pouring out from the depths of her heart, proved too much for her.

Auntie's symptoms were more serious than Mom had thought, although no one knew whether it was because of her sorrow or because of Grandma's ghost. Even after her return to Seoul, she probably showed no sign of improvement. On the day Uncle was to return from abroad, Auntie phoned and asked me to go to the airport in her place. Her explanation was that she couldn't ask their chauffeur to do so, since it was Sunday. I knew it was not simply a matter of transportation, because Uncle, since his reform, had gotten into the habit of having Auntie meet him every time he returned from his business trips. Even so, I felt somewhat uncomfortable at her insistence that I meet him in her place, for it surely wasn't just a game she was playing, like a teenager. Especially so, I thought, because it was uncharacteristic of Auntie to impose a request on me for such a matter, granted that Uncle detested taking a taxi by himself.

I went to the airport to meet Uncle, as Auntie requested. Uncle's airplane arrived on time, and I had no problem meeting him. But I found out that a car from his company had been waiting for him, and it turned out that there was no need for me to have taken the trouble of going to the airport. Uncle looked very surprised to see me. He told me that when he had called home from Tokyo, Auntie told him she couldn't make it to the airport because she wasn't feeling well, so he'd made arrangements to have a company car stand by.

Noticing a sorry look on Uncle's face when he realized that I had no choice but to drive back again alone, I cheerfully said, "I guess Auntie felt bad about not coming to greet you." Although I felt I was not at all ready to like Uncle yet, I was courteous to him for Auntie's sake. Besides, Uncle seemed to be concerned about me, a young niece, more than anyone else in his wife's family. This may have been because of the fact that I had witnessed his former inhuman, brutish violence. His past was clearly a kind of burden on him. It was obvious that he was doing his best to atone for his sins, but the more he tried, the more his dark past seemed to be lurking somewhere within him.

"Hey, wait, Migyŏng!" I heard Uncle's voice along with his car horn, as I was looking for my car in the parking lot. His company car, a new Grandeur, had stopped near me.[5] "What's up, Uncle?"

"I almost forgot. I've brought something for you. Now that we've met, why don't I give it to you?"

"What is it, Uncle?"

The small package Uncle thrust out of his car window looked like a jewelry box. I looked at Uncle, wondering what it could be. He was beaming, unable to hide his feelings of satisfaction.

"I bought a bracelet for you. At first, I picked it out for your aunt, but the more I looked at it, the more it seemed too young for her. So I bought her something else. Unwrap it and see if you like it."

Uncle's smile appeared almost like that of a boy. I was baffled. Is this man really the old uncle of the past? I wondered.

"Thanks, but I'll open it after I get home." I took the other cars backed up behind Uncle's as a good excuse and was able to send him away ahead of me with those words. After making sure his car was gone, I got in my car and finally opened Uncle's package.

"What on earth!" As I had no eye for jewelry whatsoever, it was difficult to tell whether it was genuine or imitation but it was a dazzlingly beautiful bracelet. On occasions such as this, I couldn't help but be a woman. I felt my heart pounding, and even slightly trem-

---

5. The "Grandeur," a product of the Hyundai Motor Company from 1992, was a great success in the Korean domestic market since its appearance as the flagship sedan model. The car became a status symbol favored by business executives and high-level politicians.

bling. I tried the bracelet on my wrist. Although I'd kept my job as a working wife for a long time and had no children, I had little of my own that could be called accessories. Was it because in the monotonous flow of time I simply hadn't developed an interest in prettying myself up?

I really liked the bracelet. I even felt quite excited and drove all the way home. My husband, who had been taking a nap, opened the door for me and quickly noticed the bracelet on my wrist.

"What's that?"

"A present from Uncle." I raised my wrist proudly.

Holding my wrist, my husband carefully examined the bracelet and asked abruptly, "Is it real?"

"Does it look real?" I asked back.

Up until then, I had no idea how my husband would feel. So I just asked him back in the same excited tone, but on second thought, I realized—an almost chilly sensation running through me—how grossly insensitive I was to my husband's feelings at the moment.

"Lucky, you have such a rich uncle! That looks pretty darned expensive!"

In fact, the problem was that I hadn't realized how easily my husband could be offended by such trifles. I was dumbstruck. Could something like this stir up a feeling of inferiority in him? What kind of inferiority complex would it be?

My original plan to call Auntie as soon as I got home was completely waylaid due to this unexpected war of nerves between my husband and me. I got really disgusted with men when they displayed their pride over such trivialities, while they shamelessly turned away from those moments when they had to be truly manly. Since I had come this far, I wanted to press him to answer why he still hadn't registered at the infertility clinic, but I decided to hold back. I quickly calculated that, if I squabbled with him over that matter now, I wouldn't be able to wear the bracelet for some time to come.

Yet I felt utterly depressed. I had yet to get pregnant in the nearly six years since our wedding. Of course, I had never thought that I was solely responsible for my childlessness. Three years into my marriage, I had a physical checkup, and there was no decisive factor on my part to cause the infertility. Rather, the problem seemed to rest with my husband. Even though the doctor told my husband to go for a more thorough examination, he put it off time and again, and recently he had stopped mentioning it at all.

Still, it is appalling that, whenever our childlessness became the topic of conversation among people, I was the one who had to take all the blame. No matter who they were, they asked *only* me about the cause of the infertility. And then, they never hesitated to remark on how admirable my husband was, saying how he could keep going with no children. On every such occasion, I felt insufferable resentment writhing within me. If he had to put up with it, it was the same with me. If the childlessness made people unbearably lonely, I could have been suffering more severely than my husband. And yet, my husband was a victim, whereas I was the victimizer. By sheer force of convention, these people automatically came to these conclusions.

The reason I took such an aggressive attitude toward my husband during our minor quarrels might have something to do with my personality, but the more decisive factor might have been my desire to fight back against those prejudices. I'd been seized by a feeling that, if I were ever caught off-guard, even for a moment, I would fall into an unbearable pit. So I never held myself back or compromised. After having made up my mind not to squabble with my husband over such a trifle as a bracelet, I became very angry at myself—not at my husband. It seemed I wasn't cut out for being patient.

Mom phoned me from Kyŏngju that night. She usually phoned me about twice a month just to say hello, but unlike before, she asked after Auntie in detail.

"Your Auntie usually doesn't act like this, so I wonder if something's going on with her. Do you know of anything?"

"What's wrong, Mom?"

"No, nothing. I don't know why but something keeps bugging me. I wonder if I should arrange for a round of shaman ritual or something. I feel this strange unease in my heart, you know."

"Don't even mention exorcism, Mom!"

"I don't know what's with me. But whenever I think of her, I feel heavy in my chest. Good Lord, I hope there's nothing wrong with her."

"If there's anything wrong with Auntie, I'd be the first to know, Mom. If anything happens, I'll call you, so don't worry too much."

After I hung up the phone, I realized that Auntie had started behaving really strangely since the day of the funeral on the mountain. After mulling it over, I came to see that it began in the hearse on our way home from the mountain that day. Although Auntie said she was out of sorts because of her overexposure to the cold wind, she looked too down for me to think she was simply feeling physically ill. After we reached home, she took to her bed, the only person among so many others—something incongruous with her character—and I heard later that she stayed in bed not only all that day, but through the next few days.

Had something happened to Auntie, as Mom thought? Even if something did happen, I doubted my tight-lipped Auntie would ever have told me about it. Late that night, I was finally able to call Auntie. But it was Uncle who answered the phone. He asked me to call her back the next day because she'd already gone to bed feeling tired. I noticed something gloomy in Uncle's voice also.

The next day, I planned to go straight to Auntie's house after work. But before the closing hour, my husband called me at the office, saying that my mother-in-law had come to our home. My husband wasn't given to taking the trouble to call me at the office unless it was something important. And these important matters to him generally related to my in-laws only. Probably because my plan to visit Auntie was foiled, I felt somewhat miffed. As my mother-in-law had a separate key to our apartment, she could barge in any time she felt like it. Even though I had an extra key made for her so she would have free access to our home, when she took me at my word and dropped in abruptly, I got really annoyed.

If only she remained quietly resting whenever she visited our home, the matter would have been different. Instead, my mother-in-law would pop into my empty apartment about twice a month and then return to her own home after having done a complete makeover of my entire household. The last time this happened, I had a big fight with my husband. At that time, she had so thoroughly changed my housekeeping routine while I was at work that I could hardly find what I needed to start dinner after I got back home from the office. The refrigerator, the kitchen, and its cupboard, the bathroom, even the inside of my dresser in the inner room had been completely rearranged. When I said to her, "Mother, you didn't have to do all this," she replied, "I cleaned up a little. Don't worry. Working wives can't help themselves—they're all the same."

My mother-in-law was never the type of person who craved compliments for her hard work. One day, when she had washed all the bed sheets, she still took her toil lightly, repeating the same words, "Working wives can't help themselves—they are all the same." Yet the situation would change when my husband got home after work. As soon as he stepped inside, he was bound to notice the conspicuous changes and recognize his mother's touch every-where as well. He would tirelessly repeat praises for his mother's needless hard work, sometimes rebuking her for such work, and other times, he would massage her shoulders, behaving like a spoiled child. What dismayed me most was that, on such occasions, my mother-in-law would never refuse my husband's rubdown. With a supremely satisfied look on her face, she would leave her shoulders in the care of her son.

I really hated the way my mother-in-law willfully took care of my household affairs without talking to me. I wanted to have my seasoning containers on the counter within easy reach, but each time my mother-in-law came, she lined them up neatly in the cup-board. I wanted to keep the frying pans I used most often on the counter for easy use as well, but she always stacked them away in a neat pile inside the cabinet next to the sink. It was the same with hanging the laundry. All the wash I hung out in a slapdash manner would be rearranged and hung differently. While I appreciated her moving underwear out of view, which I'd thoughtlessly hung on the outer side, she always hung my husband's dress shirts and socks on the sunny side, while hanging my clothes on the damp, dark inner side. She would never leave my underwear on the drying rack on the veranda—they were removed and rehung in different places in the laundry room.

For a while after my marriage, I agreed that I should learn from my mother-in-law's neat and tidy personal traits—just the way my husband insisted. Since I kept my job at the company even after my marriage, I had never paid close attention to the household work. Over time, I started to suspect that I was by nature easygoing. It was next to impossible for me to mimic the tidiness of my mother-in-law.

Still, as time went by, I couldn't help but think that my mother-in-law went too far, overstepping her boundaries. Now that I had been married for more than five years, my home was no longer an inept newlywed's but my own household that I enjoyed and took care of by myself. Even though it's true that because of my office work I couldn't devote myself to housekeeping, I figured that if these circumstances and conditions were of my choice, my household ought to be structured to match this situation. It was impossible to perfectly take care of both office work and household chores. So shouldn't the concept of "perfection" itself be changed under these circumstances? For instance, perfection in this case would mean that you could get by without boiling your underwear each time you washed them, and that you didn't have to clean the inside of the sink every day with your wet dishrag. Moreover, you shouldn't be blamed for having missed perfection if there were a few strands of hair left in the bathroom drain.

It began to dawn on me that my mother-in-law's visits about twice a month and her work to completely overhaul my home were no longer done in the spirit of service for her working daughter-in-law but represented her unspoken demands and silent reproach of me. All my feelings of mortification were turned into anger and vented on my husband. If he believed that our home should always be kept in the same condition his mother put it in, he had no right whatsoever to remain idle either.

My firm belief in my husband as a progressive man, who at the time of our marriage had said that women who carried on activities outside the home were beautiful, was shattered to pieces. Of course, it was not that he didn't help at all with household chores. Occasionally, he did the dishes, and on Sundays, when I did a general home cleaning, he also pitched in and did his share of work without my having to grumble. Yet his work was perfunctory. He precisely marked out his share of work, and once he finished it, he thought I should wrap up the rest—that was his style. In fact, for a while after our marriage, I believed I should be grateful for the extent of work he did for me. I believed that there were far more husbands who wouldn't even go that far. It was especially so because my husband was better in helping with household chores than my friends' or my coworkers' husbands. In those days, I was so green as to brag to my friends about my husband for his washing my sanitary panties, whereupon my friends endlessly spoke ill of their husbands. But the incident of my husband's washing my sanitary underwear was never repeated. Through that meager once-in-a-lifetime gesture, my husband succeeded in making a great show of himself and in moving me deeply. I was so carried away, mistaking my husband for a man who would go to any length to take care of such work for his wife that, even when he did a perfunctory job, I wasn't able to critique him.

That day, after my mother-in-law left, I rearranged all my household items the way I liked, as my husband looked on. He seemed to interpret my action as a sign of revolt against his mom. I didn't care. Although I was not entirely so motivated, I couldn't say that my action was totally innocent of such feelings either.

"Why are you getting shallower and more narrow-minded as you get older?" my husband snapped, after glaring at me for a while. "You can't thank elderly Mom for her hard work cleaning for us, and must you carry on like this?"

"Thanks, but no thanks," I said, pushing the sock drawer toward him. His socks were neatly folded and put away in the front part of the drawer. Of course, mine were pushed so far back in the drawer that I almost had to pull the drawer all the way out to find them. "No, let me repeat. Actually, I don't even feel like thanking her."

I was becoming more and more of a veteran in domestic squabbles as the years of our marriage increased. I was no longer afraid of my husband or steeped in self-indulgent sentimentalism. It became my unshakable principle of life never to compromise over something worth fighting for. This was why my husband's attitude toward me verged on disgust. Oddly enough, though, as I grew stronger and more spiteful, my husband became less willing to confront my challenges. The most he did was to glare at me and then fall silent. No matter how hard I tried, he wouldn't talk. Silence was his greatest weapon. Then there was the "five minutes to midnight" tactic. By setting his time for returning home at five minutes to midnight, he intended to suggest the extent of his annoyance at me. Even though I had no idea whether this was my husband's real intention or not, this scheme made me feel far more insulted than when we had a real rough-and-tumble fight. He was not like that in the early days of our marriage, when we fought so fiercely as to make our next-door neighbor call us through the interphone to protest. But, after those fights, we had no problem in making up, because we had no energy left in us to brood over the other's motives.

Since my husband began to use the silent treatment, however, the situation changed. I started to have a lot of niggling thoughts about him. I couldn't figure out what kind of criticism he was heaping on me in his heart, veiled behind his silence, and had no way of knowing what his claims, which he believed valid, actually were. At any rate, it seemed as if the more time passed, the duller and drier our married life was becoming. We still had no child, and on top of that, we no longer had physical passion for each other. Once in a while, I asked myself why I continued living with my husband, but the most correct answer was that I had no reason to break up with him. Good heavens! I was simply staying with him for that reason.

[3]

Before I had a chance to call on Auntie, she phoned me just before my lunch hour. She said that she was in front of my office building and asked me to come down to meet her. Auntie was such a home-body, she rarely went out unless she had some special business to take care of. Her life was limited to the inside of her house. If her apartment hadn't been facing the sunny south, her face would have been as colorless as a mummy's. Grocery shopping was the only oc-casion Auntie left her home, but even that outing seemed to have stopped since Uncle had her hire a part-time helper.

"Auntie, what makes you happy?" I asked her once.

"Knowing nothing serious happens," she said, smiling softly. I could take her answer lightly if I wanted to, but my heart ached as I realized that it reflected her long difficult years. Could Auntie still be apprehensive about her present peace?

Suddenly, I recalled Uncle's face, smiling like a boy's, as he abruptly thrust the present toward me. Could a reformed man be-come like that? I wondered. I once heard that the affection of a man who mends his ways later in life is fierce. But I was still skeptical about the possibility of a new, budding love, with all the pain of the past forgotten. That's not love, but compromise. Of course, seen from Auntie's point of view, whether it is love or compromise, it was far better than nothing. As Auntie could never be me, and vice versa, it was important for me to make efforts to understand Auntie from her perspective.

Auntie was sitting in a corner of the restaurant on the basement floor of my office building. I was happy to see her, but when I ap-proached her, I noticed her face looked off-color. She was also dressed terribly—that's how I felt. As her outings were so infre-quent, she used to give the utmost care to her personal appearance when she did go out. She didn't dress up to impress others. Rather, on such occasions, she looked flustered, like a young schoolgirl leaving her dormitory on her first excursion. Now though, it seemed Auntie had come out in her everyday housedress with a jacket flung over it. I sat across from her without saying anything, an ominous feeling sweeping over me.

"I have something to ask you," Auntie blurted out. She sounded very agitated. I looked at her, worried.

"About what?"

"About your Uncle."

"What about him?"

"Your Uncle …" Auntie faltered a bit, in contrast to her flustered look. I was at a loss to figure out what this was all about. All I could do was looking at her in silence. The more I watched her face, the more pale and unwell it appeared, probably because of her long illness.

"What I mean is … at the airport."

As if she had made up her mind during the interval, Auntie continued, "Nothing happened at the airport, right?"

"What do you mean?"

Auntie baffled me. If she had not been a person who had long believed that patience is the only virtue, I might have easily guessed what she was trying to say. Yet Auntie had never even in roundabout ways tried to track down her husband's affairs throughout all those riotous years of his life. Even when he didn't come home for a month or two, she waited for him stoically, while I, who really had nothing to do with any of it—if I might say so—felt like going crazy. We knew all too well where he was staying during those months. He was definitely living with another woman, having set up a new home. Still, Auntie would simply wait. When Uncle abruptly crawled back after two or three months, Auntie prepared his dinner without one word of complaint.

"What's this all about?" I asked, almost dying of impatience.

Whereupon, Auntie almost shouted at me, her face flushing, "Didn't you notice anything strange about him? Like he had brought another woman along?"

"Auntie!"

"Didn't you see anything?"

"Auntie, what's the matter with you?"

"Come on, answer my question!"

"No, nothing happened. Uncle came out alone, that's all … that's all that I saw. What on earth is going on, Auntie? Has Uncle fallen back into his old ways again?"

"Are you sure nothing happened?"

"What's going on, Auntie?"

Auntie glared at me for a long time. Her eyes were flashing fire, as if she was trying to pry out secrets from an accomplice who was hiding Uncle's secrets. I was flabbergasted, but more than that, I was even forced to feel a kind of apprehension. As far as I knew, Auntie was not this kind of woman at all. Even if Uncle had really done something wrong, Auntie was not the type of person who would seek out her young niece to find out about it. Moreover, it was so unlike her to cast such a vulgar look and talk in such a crude manner.

Just at that moment, Auntie's long fierce look at me, which was about to explode into sparks, suddenly eased, and her body unsteadily sank back into her chair, as if she felt dizzy.

"Auntie!" The moment I cried out, Auntie was already wiping her eyes with the handkerchief she had taken from her handbag.

"Auntieee …"

"I don't know. I really don't know. I don't understand why I am acting this way …" Auntie broke into sobs—it was a cry of deep sorrow. I felt surreptitious glances from my section coworkers who had come in for tea. Bewildered, I just kept looking at Auntie. To comfort her in any other way was simply beyond me.

No, that was not entirely true. Just a drop of Auntie's tears was enough for me to figure out why she had to cry. It undoubtedly meant that Uncle had fallen back into his old ways. Now Auntie's sense of betrayal would be entirely different from that of the past. It was because back in those days she could have just given up on him as a hopeless case from the beginning.

I felt very strange that day. It was true that I came in contact with a very human side of Auntie as she abandoned her patent virtue of patience. But I didn't feel happy or relieved at this development. To be frank, while I watched Auntie dissolve wildly into tears in front of me, I wondered for a moment why she carried on in such an unsightly manner. Ah, undeniably, I was getting old, too! Perhaps I had fallen prey to run-of-the-mill conservative norms: I felt her tears were ugly.

That night, my husband and I had a fight, the fiercest in some time. In fact, we didn't have to fight that ferociously, since the day following my mother-in-law's visit we invariably had quarrels and sank into a cold war. Apparently, I was under the influence of Auntie. I took an extremely touchy and aggressive attitude, if for no other reason than a refusal to be mired in the consciousness that I too was helplessly growing old. I doggedly went after my husband, who fled from room to room, wielding silence as his weapon, and egged him on to a quarrel. The cause of our fight was the Chinese herbal medicine that my mother-in-law had left for me. The total amount of Chinese medicine I had taken until then came to more than ten packs.[6] I took them all by myself. I had no longer had any intention to fill every corner of my body with those bitter dregs of Chinese medicine, so I relentlessly bawled at my husband. If the medicine had to be consumed, I demanded we take it equally—fifty-fifty.

My husband said to me, "You are really something else. Why not ask me to share half the work of giving birth to a child? Tell me if you know a way to that. Why on earth are we living together anyway? Why do you live with me?"

After all, it was a wasteful quarrel. It drove me crazy to think that, as time went by, our fights became increasingly unproductive. Is nothing allowed between husband and wife except such vocabulary as "adjustment," "patience," and "compromise"? I wondered. What is love? Every time the word came to my mind, I felt a sort of cynicism like an itch in the small of my back. It seemed that for some time now I had become blasé about love.

When I went to bed a little early, I got to think again about Auntie's matter. I was also worried whether I should let Mom in Kyŏngju know how Auntie had behaved in my presence. I felt helpless, as there was absolutely nothing for me to do, even if it turned out to be true that Uncle was causing trouble again. How could I help with someone else's marital problems when I was powerless to handle my own?

If I were single, I might have tried to demand an explanation from Uncle, staring at him straight, with the kind of bravado and undisguised anger allowed to youngsters. In fact, it wasn't as if I had never done so before. I was perhaps a sophomore or junior in

---

6. Chinese herbal medicine is usually a mixed assortment of different medicinal herbs, which is packed in a paper wrapper and brewed over an extended period of time. One pack could include several smaller packages of herbal mixtures.

college when Uncle didn't come home for three nights, wrapped up in playing mahjong, utterly unconcerned about my sick auntie, who was unable to take even a spoonful of thin rice gruel. On the morning of the fourth day, when Uncle walked into the house with a face as perfectly clean as if he had just come out of a sauna, I screamed at him, forgetting my young age, "You are not even a human being. Why have you come back? Do you think Auntie can't live without you? I will take care of her! Do you hear me? I will take care of her!"

Even on that morning, Auntie sluggishly raised her body from the bed and tried to prepare Uncle's breakfast, in spite of my violent outrage and riotous commotion. In my own anger, I shut myself up in the room, and when I heard the noises Auntie made preparing breakfast for Uncle, dragging her sick body along, I thought Uncle wasn't the only one I couldn't forgive. Auntie was no more a human being than Uncle. It occurred to me that Auntie herself played a role in making Uncle indulge in inhuman, scandalous behavior, and at that time, I think I even went so far as to tell myself that I would never live like that. If I couldn't divorce my husband, I'd rather kill him. But I wouldn't live like that.

Come to think of it, I guess Auntie exerted influence on my life. But it was not only Auntie who influenced me. I grew up watching my widowed Mom subjected to all sorts of humiliation by my old, widowed, grouchy Grandma. Maybe patience ran in the blood of Mom's siblings. I got utterly sick and tired of the limitless patience of these women. Before they asked this sort of patience of me as well, I'd bare my fangs. Otherwise I might also have been stricken with a serious victim mentality.

It was some three days after Auntie's visit to my office that Uncle called asking me to meet with him. He phoned me at my office, as Auntie had done, and I could immediately sense that it was something to do with the tears Auntie had shed in front of me. That day, of all days, I had heaps of unfinished work on hand, but I passed it all off onto my junior coworker and left the office early. When I came out of my office building, I saw Uncle's car waiting for me. Uncle wasn't in the car. His chauffeur, who had been waiting, drove me to a Japanese restaurant on Yangjaedong Street.[7]

---

7. Located in Sŏch'o Ward, an upscale subsection in South Seoul, Yangjaedong Street is known for its numerous art galleries, performing arts centers, music halls, high-end restaurants, and department stores.

To my surprise, when I entered the restaurant Uncle was there with his two sons. The older, Chongsik, a freshman just admitted to college, and the younger, Chonggil, who had gone on to and boarded at a science high school,[8] were sitting together with Uncle. As soon as the boys saw me, they rose from their seats and bowed to me, although our relationship didn't require that kind of formality. I detected a strange mood circulating among the three of them, and the reason soon became clear. It was the birthday of the younger son, Chonggil, and Uncle had taken the trouble of bringing him up to Seoul from his dormitory. Auntie was the only one absent from this important gathering. Clearly, all of them were feeling uncomfortable about her absence.

Auntie's absence from Chonggil's birthday party combined with the family outing was something that couldn't be casually ignored. Auntie wasn't overly indulgent with her children, but she would never forget or neglect her son's birthday. Every time I saw Chongsik, who had made it into a top-ranking university, or Chonggil, who'd entered a competitive high school, I was reminded that the only fruit of Auntie's virtue of patience was her success in raising her children. If Auntie hadn't clung steadfastly to her capacity to endure and hadn't dodged each of her domestic troubles, her children, no matter how smart they were, could not have grown up in a normal manner. In all likelihood, neither Chongsik nor Chonggil had any idea what a scumbag their father had been. To that extent, Auntie had succeeded in keeping her suffering buried in her heart.

As soon as I joined the group, Chonggil stood up, saying that he had to return to his dormitory, and Chongsik immediately followed suit. Apparently, they had already finished their dinner. Chonggil was even holding a department store shopping bag—most likely containing his birthday gifts. Awkwardly, I apologized that I hadn't prepared a present for Chonggil. I was getting uneasy, because I felt that Uncle's real intention had not been to invite me to Chonggil's birthday table. The boys also seemed to have a hunch about the general drift of the situation. No longer welcome, they quietly left.

"Where's Auntie?" I hurriedly asked, as soon as the boys left.

---

8. Beginning in 1983, science high schools were founded to train bright young students in cutting-edge science and technology to develop them into leaders in their fields.

Uncle was pouring wine into a glass in front of him, with no thought of drinking it. He simply fumbled with the glass a few times and then looked gloomily at me.

"I wanted to see you because I have something to ask you."

"Please go ahead."

"It's about what happened when I was gone on my business trip."

"Okay."

"Did something happen to your auntie?"

"No."

"Think carefully."

"Why, Uncle?" I couldn't help but look at Uncle, feeling far more baffled than when Auntie had come to ask me whether something suspicious had happened at the airport on Uncle's return. Wasn't the word "something" always to do with Uncle? And Uncle had never even tried to hide his "somethings."

"Are you positive nothing happened?"

"I don't understand what you are asking. Nothing happened besides Grandma dying in Kyŏngju."

Could there really be something besides that? I wasn't thinking seriously about how I should answer Uncle's question. I was biding my time, waiting to ask Uncle whether "something" hadn't really happened to him instead. What prevented me from making such a move was the serious expression on Uncle's face.

"Of course, I know of your grandmother's passing. At that time, your auntie phoned to let me know. I noticed nothing unusual in her voice then, though. Since your grandmother was like a mother to your auntie, I guess her death means something special to her."

"Can't you tell me what's going on?" I asked.

"I don't know what it is either," said Uncle.

Although Uncle meant he didn't know what was going on, I knew that, even if there were some inside stories, he wasn't the kind of man who would tell me about them in detail. I felt panicky at the thought that I could end my meeting with Uncle without really finding out anything at all.

"Is anything wrong with you, Uncle?"

"Well, nothing particularly," he said at first casually, but in an instant, a flash of doubt crossed his face. "Did your Auntie say something to you?"

"Has something happened, Uncle?"

"Well now … !"

Uncle grabbed his wineglass. He gulped the wine and looked at me, but his eyes were no longer looking at me as a young niece, but flashed with a desperate effort to make a plea against a false charge aimed at him. He began to talk to me in a tone that seemed to match his feelings.

"I feel embarrassed about telling you like this, but since you know your auntie best, well … I'll tell you that she has suddenly been acting strange."

"What do you mean?"

"She seems to believe that I've got another woman."

"Do you mean she's totally wrong?"

Uncle looked shocked, and then embarrassed. After refilling the empty wineglass, he gulped it down. He looked at me with a shame-stricken face.

"Yes, I really have nothing to say against what you've said. I deserve it. I guess you could very well say so. But your auntie is different. Even if, by some chance, I did do something terrible again, she is not the sort of person to accuse me."

"Isn't Auntie a human being?" I said rather sarcastically, because, whatever was really going on, Uncle's attitude of blaming Auntie for it irritated me. I sensed that Uncle, too, quickly realized that he'd made a mistake in saying that about her.

"I don't mean I've done nothing wrong in the past. I know I can't apologize enough for my past, no matter how hard I try. But given the fact that she didn't ever behave this way even then, I just don't understand why she's now grossly misjudging me and carrying on this way—so unlike her."

"What's going on with her?"

"Look! Today is Chonggil's birthday, but she said she didn't even want to bother with it."

"Auntie said that?"

"Yes … " Uncle's face darkened further. Then he looked as if he had made some sort of decision. But what he said thereafter was really shocking to me, too.

"Your auntie said … that she can't stand living with me any longer."

"What?"

"I just don't understand. It seems to me she is not at all in her right mind. If this were a punishment I deserve, I'd accept it, but …

poor woman, now that I am trying to behave like a real human being … "

At that moment, I saw tears well up in Uncle's eyes. If he were lying to me, he would have to be a flawless con man, with this masterly performance. In that instant, I believed he was being earnest.

[4]

I curbed my impulse to go see Auntie right away that day, because Uncle told me that he was heading straight home after our meeting. But I made up my mind to visit her the next day, even if I had to skip work. When I got home, my husband, who had returned from work earlier than I had, told me that several phone calls had come from Mom in Kyŏngju. Sensing a strange foreboding, I called Mom right away. She answered the phone, saying that Auntie was down there. It seemed Mom also had a hunch that something was amiss. Mom told me that upon Auntie's arrival she'd been trying to reach me without Auntie's knowledge.

If my husband had not been home, I would have roughly told Mom what I had heard from Uncle, but I simply said that I would come down to Kyŏngju on the weekend and hung up. My husband, who was listening to the phone conversation nearby, grumbled about my making another trip to Kyŏngju so soon after my last one. The more cold-hearted I grew toward my in-laws, the more my husband responded in kind toward my family. My husband and I acted like two people who were measuring their heights, wrangling over every inch, not to be outdone. Still, I ignored my husband's provocation, as Auntie's affair was weighing on my mind.

It seemed Auntie was staying on in Kyŏngju for two more days until Saturday afternoon. After confirming she was still there, I finished my weekend work at the office and headed for the Kangnam Express Bus Terminal. During the considerable time it took to reach Kyŏngju by bus, I enjoyed no peace of mind, sunken as I was in one thought after another.

It was some time after I began to live at Auntie's house that a young woman, claiming to be Uncle's mistress, barged into the house. She appeared to be in her late twenties and wore thick makeup. As soon as she entered the house, she asked where the inner room was, and once inside she stretched herself out on the floor. I was just back from school and was stunned by the outrageous scene. I recalled Auntie turning around and looking at me, a smile on the corners of her lips. How could she smile at such a time?

At any rate, Auntie shoved a ten-thousand *wŏn* bill at me, asking me to take Chonggil and Chongsik outside. By the time I returned home, after spending the entire sum with the kids, the young woman was gone. As if nothing had happened, Auntie told us to have dinner together, as we must be very hungry.

I glared at Auntie with anger blazing in my eyes and said, "Auntie, you are a fool! You are an idiot, Auntie!"

I was so infuriated that I didn't touch any food that night. Auntie had dinner with Chonggil and Chongsik, who were still young. When I peered in on them through an opening in the door, Auntie was swallowing her rice, dishing it up in spoonfuls much larger than was her custom.

When I went down to Kyŏngju that year during the vacation, I finally learned that the woman who had invaded Auntie's house was pregnant with Uncle's child. Grandma brought the matter up almost deliberately, after asking me this and that about Auntie. It seemed Grandma was very displeased with my living at Auntie's. Grandma was worried about my future, exposed as I was to such horrid scenes. And, after my marriage—as it happened—I once ran away to Kyŏngju after a quarrel with my husband. At that time, too, Grandma declared that I could dare carry out such a nonsensical stunt because I had grown up witnessing shameful scenes at Auntie's house, and she got angrier at Auntie than at me.

According to the story that Grandma and Mom exchanged at the time, it was Auntie herself that had made all the arrangements for the young woman pregnant with Uncle's child to have an abortion. I wondered if Auntie really had any pride to speak of. Her stoic forbearance was a virtue of patience at best, and at worst, an example of totally deplorable and inane behavior. As I never directly asked Auntie about the matter, there's no way for me to know the whole story, but my guess was that Auntie had helped the woman with an abortion not simply out of her fear of having a stepchild. Of course, no matter how idiotic a woman might be, such concerns would have been greater than other reasons. Even so, Auntie undoubtedly thought that such a matter was a burden she had to carry alone. Auntie was such a woman, a woman who had never refused unfair oppression—no matter what it was—that weighed down on her shoulders and at times suffocated her. She was simply submission incarnate. Auntie seemed like a woman who firmly believed that her misfortune and hardships were her fate.

It was difficult for me to imagine that a woman like Auntie could exhibit such a sudden change in character at this late date. Granted that the peace bestowed on her over the past few years had been unexpectedly comfortable and surprisingly seductive, I could never believe that she could change her entire nature in order to keep it. I kept replaying in my mind the scene of Auntie's visit to my workplace, when she pressed me, bursting into tears, to tell her what had happened when I went to meet Uncle at the airport. All the same, I was totally lost about what was going on with her, and I couldn't even begin to guess what it was all about. All the way to Kyŏngju, I was on edge.

In the midst of this uneasiness, I tried to consider how fortunate it was that I had grown older—at least to some extent—since now I'd no longer look at Auntie's problem with youthful bravado or childishness. My age could as easily be a shortcoming as a strength, but I wanted to see it in a positive light. At any rate, I intended to tell Auntie never to hold back again. Even though I wasn't quite sure whether I could muster up the courage to tell her so when that moment arrived, my intention to do so was clear. I understand now that the conjugal relationship is such that, once one begins to give in, one must continuously do so, but it is also a relationship in which one shouldn't ever hold back, more so than in any other relationship.

For some reason, I felt like I was looking at Auntie's affair as a cross-sectional view of my future life. Of course I believe, as every woman in this world does, that at least my husband wouldn't stoop to womanizing. No matter how wretched my husband may turn out to be, I don't believe he would sink to the appalling level of depravity my uncle sank to. Yet I sense that my husband is also trying to make me live a life of patience. I don't know what level of patience or what level of acquiescence he might ask of me, but the problem would not be of that "level." I do not expect the most idealistic union with my husband, but at least up to now I haven't felt so dispirited in my relationship with him as to desire a perfunctory compromise. That's what I want to believe.

I reached Kyŏngju at night. I took a taxi and headed for Mom's house on the outskirts of the city, looking out of the window at the

Pomun Resort Development,[9] wrapped in darkness. The scenery of Kyŏngju had changed so much since I was growing up that it was difficult for me to feel even the slightest bit of nostalgia for it. The only thing that made me think of the words "hometown" or "nostalgia" was Auntie.

I arrived at my house around eight o'clock in the evening. By that time, it was already dusk in my village, and no sooner had I entered the alley than I heard screams coming from the direction of Mom's house. The voice was so strained that it wasn't easy to tell right away whose it was, but I concluded that it was Auntie's. When I rushed into the house, I saw, to my surprise, Uncle coming out of the wooden-floored room and stepping down into the courtyard.

"Uncle!" I cried out. Uncle—shaky on his legs, his face ghastly pale, and with his facial muscles twitching—didn't seem to be himself. From behind his back, cries, which were definitely Auntie's, were ringing out hideously.

"What's the matter? What happened?" I asked breathlessly and ran toward Uncle, but he looked as if his soul had completely left him.

"Your … your auntie's gone mad. She is beside herself." Uncle spat out the words and fled from the yard. I did not follow him. When I hurriedly stepped up onto the wooden floored-room and flung open the door from behind which the cries were coming, I found Auntie—a fine mess of tears—being held tightly in Mom's arms and sobbing wildly.

"Good heavens! She must have gone crazy! She's never done anything like this her entire life, and now I have no idea what's got into her!" Mom turned around and looked at me, her face looking bewildered.

"Auntiee …!" I called out, as if moaning. I could hardly believe that the person broken down into wailing before me was my youngest auntie, the very Auntie Chonghŭi I had known. As I watched Auntie, who was drowned in sobbing, I could find no trace of the patience that was her singular virtue, or anything like womanly prudence. Her face might be called human, stripped of all trappings. No, it looked more like that of an animal. She looked ugly.

---

9. The Pomun Resort Development is a tourist complex that includes hotels, golf courses, parks, leisure facilities, and an outdoor performance theatre, developed around the artificial Pomun Lake in Kyŏngju.

Still standing there, I asked Mom, "What on earth is the matter with her?"

"She says that your Uncle has started to play around again. But to my eyes, he seems innocent. He may have been bad tens and hundreds of times before, but this time I think he's innocent. I really don't know why she has to carry on this way."

"How do you know, Sis?" Auntie screamed at that very moment. Her voice was so piercing that I wondered where in her slender frame such a loud sound had been lurking.

Mom shouted as she grabbed Auntie's shoulders again, "What on earth is the matter with you? Whatever the matter is, why don't you try to control yourself?"

"You mean I have to put up with it? You're telling me to just swallow it? Telling me to tough it out again! No! I am not going to take it anymore!" Auntie pushed Mom away with amazing force. I finally understood the stunned expression on Uncle's face I'd encountered in the yard, because I, too, had no choice but to watch Auntie with my mouth agape.

It took nearly two hours for Auntie, who had been lying alone on the floor facing the wall and sunken in deep silence, to find her way out of the torrents of raging emotions. When she finally sat up, fixing her hair carelessly, the first thing she asked me was about Uncle. But I had nothing to answer her. Auntie took a look at the yard absently. There was no hint of craziness in those eyes any more.

"Auntie, can you tell me what this is all about?" I asked her cautiously.

Auntie merely raised the corners of her lips into a smile and told me that she wanted to go out for some fresh air. It was already late at night, after ten, but I felt compelled to accept her wishes. I knew all too well that Mom would be worried about us, but we went out together anyway. It was difficult to catch a taxi, and by the time we entered the tourist hotel in the Pomun Housing Development, it was close to eleven o'clock. The coffee shop was already closed. Auntie and I went up to the lounge and each of us ordered a cocktail.

"This place has changed too much, hasn't it?" Auntie said feebly, looking out of the window. But I didn't look outside—I was only studying Auntie's face. I wished Auntie would tell me anything, no matter what that was. But I knew it wouldn't be easy for her to do so. I decided that I would go ahead and talk first.

"Auntie," I said.

At that very moment, I was stopped by her smile—a very weird smile floating on her face. Then, in an instant, a sort of sparkle shone in her eyes. With the same shining eyes, Auntie looked at me and began to talk.

"Fifteen years ago ... I met a man here. No, this is not the same place. There was a hotel on this very site, although it's gone now. I came all the way down to Kyŏngju but I had no nerve to go home, so I came here for a cup of coffee. I felt utterly lost. Well, you know, a human being's fate is strange. Here, I met a man and fell in love."

The end of her sentence—"fell in love"—was delivered in a high tone, as if Auntie were lightheartedly relating one of her past memories. If it happened fifteen years ago, it was after Auntie had been married, of course. Her second son, Chonggil, might have been about two years old at the time. At any rate, Auntie was saying that she had met another man and had fallen in love.

So, why was it that I felt tickled, in spite of the fact that things were taking a very serious turn at that moment? Frankly, I thought, "My goodness, Auntie must have gone crazy, otherwise, how could she talk about her love affair under these circumstances? Falling in love, of all things? What nonsense!" That was the way I was feeling at the time. If I were a little worried at that moment, it was probably because I was concerned whether Auntie's mental state had become extremely unbalanced.

"You don't believe me, do you?" Auntie asked with the same intriguing smile on her face.

I shook my head—a little embarrassed—because I felt that my reaction would hurt Auntie's pride. As I was shaking my head, Auntie also shook hers.

"So, you won't believe me. Who would possibly believe me if I say I had an extramarital affair? Besides, it happened fifteen years ago, and the man in question is no longer in this world. Try as I might to prove it, there's no way to do so now. Good gracious! Now that things have turned out this way, I am not even sure if I really committed such a blunder or not. I wonder if I were dreaming, all by myself, you know. If it were so, oh dear, what could be more hopeless than that?"

"Auntie!" While listening to Auntie's talk, which sounded like a lament, I recalled the confounded look on Uncle's face and his muttering that Auntie seemed to have gone crazy. Auntie certainly didn't look normal. "Auntie, tell me straight. I am over thirty now—thirty-four means that I am in my mid-thirties. I am no longer a child. So it's okay for you to tell me anything you'd like. Auntie, if you keep things you want to say buried in your heart like you used to, you will really get sick. It's enough that you've lived like that up to now, but there's no need for you to do so any longer, isn't that right?"

"What do you want me to talk about?"

"Is Uncle at it again?"

"He swore on his life that he wasn't." A positively twisted, cynical smile flashed across her face and disappeared.

I began to fire questions at Auntie. "Isn't this feeling based on a hunch? Uncle himself denied it when he met me. But no one would own up to something like that easily. Besides, when it comes to Uncle … "

"Right, your uncle is a professional in that area."

"No, I didn't mean that exactly … in fact, Uncle has changed, hasn't he?"

"That's true."

"Well, then?"

"Do you think changes end everything? Does that mean the past never existed, and that's okay? Is that what you think?"

"Auntie, what on earth do you mean?"

"I tell you, I can't forgive him. Never, never! I can't forgive the things that jerk has done to me!"

Auntie was almost screaming. The gazes of those enjoying cocktails in the pleasant atmosphere of the lounge turned toward us. I felt so embarrassed that I just looked blankly at Auntie. It didn't matter to me, no matter how hysterically Auntie acted. What was utterly shocking to me was her scream that she could never forgive Uncle. I could hardly believe that had come from someone like her. Unable to control my shock, or rather because of the shock, I indiscreetly added, "Yes, you're right. Forgiveness isn't everything. That says it all, doesn't it? Then what's the matter with you, Auntie, really?"

[5]

"When your uncle was deeply given to gambling and left home with the house title deed, I felt I'd reached a breaking point. When I told him that he must never touch the deed, he kicked me and stormed out of the house. The kids were raising a ruckus, crying themselves into fits. Less than an hour after he left, my mother-in-law came over.

"Seeing the kids crying wildly and me sitting there with disheveled hair, she said, 'No matter what, the husband is the husband, and the family head is the family head. Why are you making such a big deal about a man and the household head for having some flings? What a shame. Just look at you. Aren't you a woman? Are you raising this hell because you're worried he'll starve you three to death? Stop crying! How could you, a woman, dare to let your cries be heard from outside?'

"I felt a chill all over me. I wanted to kill her. How could she, another woman, treat me like that? So I came down to Kyŏngju, even leaving the kids behind. Once in Kyŏngju, I couldn't bring myself to go home, because it was too obvious to me that I'd be lectured repeatedly to just put up with it, and that, at the end of it all, I'd be blessed, and that I'd done so well up to then in holding back!

"That night I met the guy. As I was sitting alone, he approached me. He asked me if I'd had a quarrel with my husband. I told him yes, and that I wanted to kill my husband. And he said there was a way to kill him. When I asked him what it was, he answered that I should have an affair with him. I seemed to have had a lot to drink. Was it because of the drinks? No, I don't think it was simply because I was under the influence of liquor. I really wanted to kill my husband, the jerk. So, I said okay. That night I slept with the guy in the hotel.

"You probably won't be able to understand, but it was the best night I had ever had. I felt like a real victor. The next morning, I suddenly came to my senses and realized what I had done. The guy was still sleeping, and for some unknown reason, I felt compelled to go through his pockets. I hoped to find a resident registration card, but to my surprise, I fished out a copy of his family census register. Imagine! That guy was also married! He had two kids. At that moment, the guy opened his eyes, and what do you think he told me? 'Forget about it. In fact, I wanted to kill my wife, too!'

"I might have felt a sort of jubilation at my action, if that guy hadn't talked down to me so brazenly that morning. You see, he couldn't help being a man, either. The guy talked to me in outright informal terms, saying brusquely 'Forget about it'—just like that. But I soon forgot my loathing for him. That very morning I hurried back to Seoul. But as usual, that jerk, my husband, hadn't returned home, and my mother-in-law had taken the kids away with her.

"When I phoned her, she berated me: 'A wench like you deserves a divorce a dozen times over. How dare a wife try to copy her husband's behavior? Do you think men and women are the same? You should be eternally grateful that we took you in, a parentless hussy, as daughter-in-law! And what's this impudence all about? Even if a slut like you disappeared, we could remarry the kids' father to a virgin.'

"After I hung up the phone, I thought, 'All of you, you filthy creatures, I have already killed you with my own hands. All of you are dead.' Yes, I killed them off and have lived on for fifteen years."

It would be difficult to explain in a word why Auntie confessed to me her affair from fifteen years before. No, Auntie was not in her right mind! For whatever the reason, Auntie was definitely becoming schizophrenic. Or was she falling into an expansive delusionary state?

I couldn't believe that Auntie had an affair fifteen years ago. It was too horrible to believe. If what Auntie told me was true, it meant that she had lived all these years concealing a secret dagger in her bosom. That's how she could put up with everything so well. No, she hadn't put up with it. Instead, her affair must have turned into a vitriolic revenge on her husband and mother-in-law carried out in her heart every minute since.

Auntie told me that she found out about the death of that man in the Christian garden cemetery where Grandma was buried. She first noticed that the name on one tombstone was the same as his and then found out that the age of the person and the names of the children he had left behind—which were engraved on the tombstone—agreed with those in his family census register, which she had kept memorized in the back of her mind.

Auntie didn't realize from the beginning that his death would bring such subtle changes to her. At first, she simply felt empty and very sentimental. But after returning to Seoul, and while waiting for Uncle's return from abroad, she realized that her heart began to swell with an overwhelming sense of anger and misgivings. Auntie became worried. She began to lose confidence in her patience, because if Uncle were ever to resume his old habits of womanizing or violence, she wouldn't know with what weapon to endure them.

Besides, Auntie's present life was not filled with such sufferings as it was in the past—the kind of sufferings she would relinquish, in the worst case—and then think that's that. Now, she didn't want to lose her own peace, and the more desperately she clung to it, the more the flame of her apprehension that her husband might betray her again flared up. Auntie finally reached the point where she began to suspect that Uncle's trip was not simply for business, but a secret tryst with a young woman. In fact, if Uncle had been his old self, his trip definitely would have been for an affair. What at first was just a suspicion on Auntie's part soon turned into a firm belief, and Auntie didn't know what to do with her anger. She told me that she felt as if she had plummeted into a pit with no outlet.

As I mentioned earlier, I couldn't believe everything Auntie had to tell me. I even suspected that a considerable portion of her account was embellished. For example, the part of her story where she told the man she wanted to kill Uncle sounded so dramatic that it didn't strike me as true. Besides, it was out of Auntie's character to utter such words.

I still felt I had to play along with what she was saying, though. So, as soon as her lengthy story ended, all that I asked of her was whether she had told Uncle the story. Clearly, Auntie was very much disappointed with my response. In fact, Auntie had sunken into an extremely sentimental state, and may have felt disappointed that her niece's response was so meager—at best.

Strangely enough though, at that moment I couldn't let my own sense of reality slip away. Whether Auntie's story was true or not, it was a very serious matter if she confessed it to Uncle. I had to wonder if Auntie was walking alone into a trap, a trap too enormous for such a frail woman to handle.

She surprised me when she answered so nonchalantly, "Sure I did, though I didn't tell him everything."

I pinned my hopes on her words that she hadn't told him everything. At that moment, I wondered what "everything" could mean. The fact that she didn't tell everything could mean that she had told him nothing.

But the next moment, Auntie said, "But I'm looking for a chance to."

"Why?"

"What do you mean 'why'? Do you think I must keep living with that fact buried in my bosom? Even taking it to my grave?"

"There's no reason for you to trouble with bringing it out, Auntie. As you said, it happened fifteen long years ago. Why do you have to get if off your chest now? If what you said is true, what's done is done, and there's nothing more to it. What's so different now that the guy is dead? Isn't it true that you might never have found out throughout your life whether the guy was dead or alive? Why don't you look at it that way?"

"You are so clever. I wonder if it's because you are young."

"Okay, I'm clever. But if I were you, I'd rather get a divorce than dream up such an absurd scheme of revenge."

"Are you disgusted with me?"

"Disgusted? Auntie, I love you more than anybody. That's why I am telling you—you're digging your own grave. Please consider the consequences if, by any chance, Uncle were to discover your affair. What move do you think he'd make?"

"Sure, I might lose everything! That jerk wouldn't accept me, I know. He might try to take everything from me. He would even snatch the kids away. You won't be able to understand what I am saying now—you see, I have everything to lose."

"That's what I mean. There's no reason for you to submit to such sacrifice by bringing the story out."

"Reason? Did you say reason? Reason? What about it? That jerk cheated on me more than a dozen times. I myself arranged abortions to get rid of his child at least three times. Who knows, he might even have children growing up somewhere I know nothing about! So how can you say that jerk is still entitled to get angry, while I have everything to lose?"

I felt a stabbing pain in my heart when I recalled Auntie's screams. Yet what I felt was directed more at myself than Auntie, an eerie feeling lurking in me at this uncertain age of thirty-four, neither old nor young.

The next morning, I returned to Seoul. True, I had to go back to work, but more than that, I realized there was no need for me to stay on in Kyŏngju. That morning, Uncle had phoned saying that he was still in Kyŏngju. It was obvious that there remained nothing more for me to do for them. I took the express bus bound for Seoul, leaving Auntie behind.

As soon as the bus geared up to move, I broke out laughing. The male passenger next to me cast an uneasy glance at me, but I couldn't stop laughing. I felt like crying, but at the same time, I felt myself getting truly angry, too. It seemed to me that up to that moment I had been unable to comprehend what Auntie had told me.

For a while, after my return from Kyŏngju, I looked like a person stricken with a sickness—loss of enthusiasm. I was terrified to look at my husband. The night after I returned from Kyŏngju I even had a dream in which I myself appeared, transformed into Auntie, as the protagonist in her dramatic tale.

I was drinking alone in a strange hotel lounge when a good-looking man approached me and suggested we have a drink to-gether.

"Why are you drinking alone?" he asked.

"Because I want to kill my husband," I answered.

"Why?"

"Because he's a mean egoist. He believes he has the innate right to totally possess his family and wife."

"What do you mean?"

"He sleeps in while I get up at sunrise to make his toast and clean the house. The little he does in the morning is to merely talk about his plans to earn lots of money as quickly as possible so that he can make his wife stay at home."

"Isn't it for your sake?"

"No. Actually, what he wants is to have a wife who both makes a lot of money and serves him on hands and knees. Yet, he tries to read my feelings—to a disgusting degree—as he is afraid of hurting his pride, should he ever show his desire openly. He holds back nicely until he finds some justification to get mad. Then he blows his top. It always has something to do with my in-laws, and nothing seems to give him a more Messianic justification than the so-called conflict between mother-in-law and daughter-in-law. Besides … I'm childless. He tells me that I should quit my job as soon as I have a child. But I don't know whether he really wants children or not. Sometimes he appears to be afraid of having children. It's because he has no guts to take back his words and knows that he won't be able to keep me from quitting my job if I insist. The prospect of one day having to suddenly provide for his wife and children all by himself is frightening to him, I guess."

"You seem to have misunderstood him. Maybe this is just your wild conjecture."

"Not at all! Once, in the past, I was almost moved to tears by the fact that he'd washed my sanitary panties. But it was a scam! I have evidence. You see, he still hasn't visited the infertility clinic for a checkup, even though it's been almost six years since we got married. He doesn't even make an effort, but throws all the blame on me for the loneliness and the sense of guilt stemming from our childlessness. It's clear that you too can't escape being a male. Otherwise, how could you tell me I'm making a wild conjecture? Do you think he has even once sincerely done dishes or cleaned the house?"

"Those are the squabbles of a young couple."

"No they're not! Such daily routines are at the heart of a marital relationship. My husband only takes the initiative now and then when he feels guilty. He does it to save face, and it's always like that! I don't know—I really don't understand why I am living with my husband."

"I am married, too."

"Then please tell me why you are living with your wife."

"I want to kill my wife, too."

"Ah! Good heavens! Well, you probably have your own reason for feeling that way. You must feel wronged too."

"I don't know why I go on living."

"Indeed, why do we go on living at all?"

[6]

I didn't phone Auntie. She didn't call me, either. It was only through Mom that I learned that Auntie had returned from Kyŏngju to Seoul. Around that time, Mom frequently called me, if only to talk about Auntie, as she was very much concerned about her. But I satisfied myself with the news Mom volunteered to tell me and didn't ask anything about Auntie first.

The only thing I did was to picture such things as the affair Auntie had committed fifteen years before, or the circumstances under which Auntie would decisively end up divorcing Uncle, without forgiving him anymore. Of course, from the bottom of my heart this was not what I wished. No matter how things ended up, I wanted Auntie to be happy.

I thought if Auntie were to bring divorce upon herself, it should be regarded as the means to pursue her own happiness. Yet, just as Auntie's desperate scream made clear, she had too little to fend for herself. What does it mean for a forty-five-year-old married woman, who all her life has done nothing but hold back and has never gotten her fair share, suddenly to find herself single? It means nothing but losing everything, just as Auntie had said.

Ah, poor Auntie! I was ready to shed tears for her sake. Of course, I would never cast a stone at her for her affair. It pained me to think that her sole means of revenge wasn't more than an affair, but considering the enormous obstacles of the so-called customs and prejudices of the world we live in, it could very well be the most scathing revenge imaginable. If Auntie were a bit tougher, I could have paid her my compliments. But the problem was that Auntie was too weak-hearted a woman. It was difficult to imagine how a fragile woman like Auntie could have lived with such a dagger hidden away in her heart over the past fifteen years. I wondered, could this mean that each of us had a hidden dagger that no one else knew about?

If so, what is my dagger? I never held anything in or compromised over anything. These were my ironclad principles regarding husband-wife relationships. On the one hand, I took pride in my sharp, alert behavior at every given moment, but at the same time, I couldn't help feeling that my whole life had turned out completely dull. Just as Auntie had gained nothing by living in her way, I wondered if my life weren't the same. I couldn't figure out what on earth I was living for.

My husband seemed to be totally baffled, as I remained in this gloomy state for some time without saying what I was upset about. Unusually short-tempered by nature, I had no capacity for mulling matters over or being patient, no matter how trivial the issue might be. It was probably the first time in our six years of marriage that I'd taken such a dispirited attitude. At first, my husband rattled on that the change in my attitude was a momentous event, worthy of recording in our family history, but as time went on he began to panic. He tried to read my face, did household chores on his own, and even took as much pains as possible not to irritate me.

But he ended by shouting at me, "Hey you, it'd be better if we just fought! After all, your natural charm comes alive when you're screaming and hurling things. Stop being someone else!"

But my depression continued. One night, I sat up alone and melted into tears. I was seized by a feeling that life was only meaningless and sorrowful.

Nearly a month passed. Uncle called me at my office. He wanted our families to get together for dinner, since we hadn't seen each other for a long time. For a while after Uncle's phone call, I couldn't focus on my work. What did Uncle's calm voice mean? Feeling anxious and agitated, I eagerly awaited the appointed date for the dinner.

Luckily it was Saturday and I was able to reach Auntie's house a little early. Probably because of my restlessness, I couldn't wait until the appointed time. Auntie opened the entrance hall door of her apartment. I noticed the part-time housekeeper working in the kitchen. Besides the familiar helper, there was another woman— probably a catering cook. The smell of cooking oil pervaded the whole house.

"Hi, Migyŏng … " Auntie acted flustered, as if she hadn't known of my coming at all. I quickly glanced over her shoulder to survey the interior landscape of her house. Everything was in its proper place—her house looked normal. At that moment, I felt an incomprehensible revulsion surging up, as if I was about to throw up. Nothing had happened? I couldn't stand that everything looked settled inside her house, as if all was well!

I sat silently on the sofa and killed time by watching a television sportscast. Although Auntie didn't betray her feelings, she seemed very nervous around me. She was probably dying of regret. She might have been thinking that it had been a fatal mistake to confess such a secret to her young niece. When I saw that Auntie—all jittery—couldn't occupy herself with work between the part-time housekeeper and the cook, I felt pity for her. When I finally saw her break a dish, I lost my nerve and couldn't stay put in her living room any longer. I made up my mind that I had to leave under any pretext and stood up from the sofa.

"Why are you leaving?" Auntie asked in an awkward voice, while sweeping up the broken pieces of the dish.

I forced a smile. "I'm bored. There's nothing much for me to help with here, so I'll go out, hang around a bit, and come back."

"Hang around and come back?"

"You know, I have a friend who lives nearby. I haven't seen her for quite a while, so I want to drop by her house."

"Really?"

"Uh-huh. There's nothing to watch on the television, either."

"Okay. Then do as you like." Auntie didn't stop me.

Feeling slightly bitter, I picked up my purse and headed toward the entrance hall. While putting my shoes on, I glanced at Auntie and thought I saw her trembling. I felt an urge to tell her not to worry about me, but I forced it back, realizing that it might be un- wise to say something like that. I feigned a smile by slightly moving the corners of my mouth.

But the moment I was about to step into the elevator, I saw Aun- tie's entrance door fling open and Auntie dash out. I saw her flushed face. By that time, I was already in the elevator but I pushed the "open" button to keep the doors from closing. Auntie blocked the elevator doors with her hands.

"What's the matter?" I asked.

Auntie seemed to be biting her lip.

I smiled halfheartedly again. If I were a little older, I could have smiled calmly at a moment like this, but all I could do was to smile a wry smile. Then I said to her, "Auntie, don't worry about me. I don't believe what you told me was true, you know."

It seemed to me that Auntie's face was turning ghastly pale. But I just stood watching her, the expression on my face saying that we were finished and she could let the elevator doors go now. Auntie held onto the doors for a long time. Suddenly, a teardrop rolled down her cheek. With that tear, Auntie's hands dropped from the elevator doors, which quickly began to close. Through the narrowing gap between the doors Auntie's pale face grew nar- rower, too.

Two hours later, Uncle, Auntie, my husband and I sat around the dinner table set for us. The food looked lavish for a mere four peo- ple. I lost my appetite because this splendid meal seemed to be a showy whitewash—enclosing the four of us. I was worried whether I could even eat. Still, I thought I at least had to go through the mo- tions of eating, because I noticed Auntie, seated next to me, looked noticeably uneasy.

As I was about pick up my spoon, Uncle said in a warm voice, "Would you wait for a moment?"

With the same warm look in his eyes, Uncle turned to Auntie.

Auntie looked startled, as if her hidden crime had been discovered. Yet that look lasted just a moment and in no time an incredible scene transpired between Uncle and Auntie. They said grace with their two hands joined together and with their heads bowed. Dumbfounded, my husband and I looked at each other with spoons in our hands. In the meantime, their short grace ended, and Uncle's gentle face came into view again.

"Now, let's eat."

"Do you go to church?" my husband asked Uncle.

"That's what I have decided to do. As I've committed many sins, it's now time that I repented. How about you? It would be nice if Migyŏng and all of us went to church together."

My husband said, "Who, me? I'll go to church after I've committed more sins. It's better for me to repent after I've committed them all. What am I supposed to do, if I sin again after repenting?"

Uncle burst into laughter at my husband's clever remarks, and I also cracked a light smile—grudgingly. But at that very moment, Auntie, who was spooning her rice with her head lowered, blurt out in a low but ringing voice, "I've committed no sin."

Auntie was not joking, and as we knew very well that Auntie wasn't the sort of person to kid around, we all tensed up immediately. We continued our dinner amidst the dullest and most awkward atmosphere imaginable. After the dinner was over, Uncle poured water into a glass and handed it to Auntie. I saw her take it without expression and swallow the medicine after opening its packet. My husband seemed to be dying of discomfort as he watched the whole scene.

"Don't worry too much," Uncle said to my husband after a couple of drinks. Auntie was alone in the kitchen preparing some appetizers to serve with drinks, and Uncle said to me, "Migyŏng, I think it's good that you know, too. These days, your auntie is receiving psychiatric treatment."

"What?"

"They say she's got depression—a symptom often occurring in middle-aged housewives. It seemed to me that she has been grieving a lot over the death of your grandmother. The doctor says that she will be all right before long. So, we decided to go to church together. I've done so much to hurt her. Every time she takes the medicine, I feel like I'm being punished for my past deeds."

My hand began to tremble as I held my wineglass. Without my

realizing it, I abruptly turned my face around and looked at Auntie in the kitchen. Auntie was looking at me, too, with those same eyes from which tears had fallen behind the closing elevator doors, the same eyes as when she told me in a high tone, "At that time, I fell in love," and with the same eyes as when she was standing at Grandma's grave like a sorrowful gazelle. On the dinner table at which she had been sitting, the half-empty glass of water was still standing, with the medicine-packet beside it.

I understood that the medicine packet ultimately meant a cleverly wrought compromise between Auntie and Uncle. I had no way of knowing whether Auntie had really confessed to Uncle about her affair of fifteen years ago. And I was determined never to ask her about it in the future. At any rate, the medicine was a successful bargain between them. It seemed to me that, by making Auntie into a mental patient, Uncle made her into a woman only he knew, and by accepting this role, Auntie could again settle into a comfortable life in her own castle. The medicine might even erase her memory of her affair from fifteen years before. At least, Uncle and Auntie were probably hoping so.

But why was I feeling such a violent sense of betrayal? On top of that, I also felt wronged—unbearably wronged. Uncle, who, according to Auntie, was guilty of more than a dozen flings, would emerge spotless after casting off all his sins through offering repentance at church. But what the devil was going to happen to Auntie? Did this mean then that the dagger Auntie had brandished just once hadn't killed Uncle but herself instead? Was this why she was swallowing pills so wretchedly, having found that her own penitent prayers were useless?

I wanted to scream at her, "Auntie! Was that all? Is this all that you could come up with?" I wanted to shout from the bottom of my heart, "Auntie, you shouldn't take those pills! You shouldn't!"

It happened in our car as we drove back home. I had all sorts of mixed feelings. I couldn't stop thinking about Uncle and Auntie's profiles standing in the apartment plaza to see my husband and me off. Standing under the street lamp with their dark shadows to their backs, Uncle and Auntie appeared like a single lump, no longer separable, one from the other. I was wondering whether those two, who had only hurt each other throughout their whole lives, could truly form one entity, while the emptiness in their individual hearts was filled with those wounds.

"Listen," my husband suddenly blurted out, "it occurred to me that I have to be good to you."

"What's with you? Have you done something wrong to me?"

"Please don't bare your claws. You should try to learn to listen in good humor when I say something nice. When I saw Auntie, it began to dawn on me that I too should be nice to my wife, really nice to her. … "

I didn't say anything. I wasn't touched in the least. But my husband looked as if he wanted to make me feel moved. Perhaps he thought I ought to be moved by his words.

"You know, I mean it." My husband tried repeatedly to express his sincerity, and suddenly he blurted out, "Honey, I love you."

He was trying hard to impress me, but I looked at him blankly. In front of me was a guy whom I had no reasons to break up with or hate. Did I love this guy? No. Love is not a tangible entity. Love is only an abstraction created by our decision to believe in it. The love that I need at thirty-four was not the sudden, heart-flooding kind. What I wanted was the belief that I lived with my husband because we needed each other, not simply because we were married.

My husband hummed to himself. Then he stole a look and even winked at me. His effort to restore me to my usual self was pitiable. While watching him trying so hard, I was for a moment tempted to interpret his efforts simply as love. I was almost inclined to believe that we were living together because of just such moments.

But at that very moment, I realized what I had always known—the fact that we had been sharing a life together, even before we needed to believe in something or confirm anything. All of a sudden, I felt a passionate desire to fight. From here on I would fight with him. I would fight fiercely, scratching his face with my fingernails. I would fight shedding blood from my heart to ensure we not live as a woman and a man, but as two partners in marriage. I would never make any compromise and believe that perfection of my life would yield perfection of his. This would at least provide some respectable meaning to this so-called husband-wife relationship, which was by nature bound to be mundane. Ah, isn't life like that in the first place?

I tried not to get depressed. On this way home where my husband and I lived together, I tried to foster a new hope. Even when I noticed my husband increasing the speed of the car, I didn't stop him. This late at night, the Olympic Boulevard was unblocked—

straight all the way.[10] Our car was going faster. Our house would appear at the end of this breathless stretch of speed. Belatedly, I fastened my seat belt. And I made up my mind once again.

"Go ahead! Now break into a run!" At that moment, that was the only shout I could let out.

⋈

10. The Olympic Boulevard is the principal transportation artery in the part of Seoul south of the Han River. Completed in 1986, it was designed as a transport artery between Kimp'o International Airport and the Olympic Main Sports Arena in the Chamsil district for the 1988 Summer Olympic Games in Seoul.

Kim In-suk (b. 1963)

Born in Seoul as the youngest of five children, Kim In-suk at age four lost her father to a long illness. Her widowed mother provided for the family by running a boarding house located in a marketplace, and Kim suffered economic hardship from early childhood on. In junior high, Kim became a member of the school broadcasting team, an experience that inspired her to dream of a career in the field. During her high school years, encouraged by her Korean literature teacher, she participated in a national student writing competition and won the top award. In 1982, Kim entered Yonsei University in Seoul to major in journalism and broadcasting, her dream come true. In her sophomore year, Kim made her literary debut with a short story "Sangsil ǔi kyejŏl" (A season of loss), winner of a literary competition sponsored by the newspaper *Chosŏn ilbo*, which drew a great deal of attention from both the media and the literary world. The work is a graphic account of the uninhibited sexual exploits and other self-indulgent activities by a college couple, who revel in them in total disregard of moral conventions and principles in the name of pursuing personal freedom. Still a college student, Kim went on to publish two full-length novels, *P'itchul* (The blood line; 1983) and *Pulkkot* (Flowers of fire; 1985), both of which embody daring searches for pure and true love by the young generation of 1980s Korea, in defiance of their society's established morals and rules.

In her senior year (1986) Kim took a year leave of absence from school to join the labor movement, which was becoming increasingly radicalized and militant. She became a fervent participant in industrial disputes and strikes undertaken by unionized factory workers and laborers. Based on these first-hand experiences, Kim wrote (after her graduation in 1987) a few short stories, such as "Hana toenǔn nal" (The day we become one; 1988), which won her the Chŏn T'ae-il Literature Award,[11] "Sŏngjogi ap'e tasi sŏda" (We stand again facing the Stars and Stripes; 1988), and "Hamkke kŏnnǔn kil" (The road we walk together; 1989). These stories share common thematic cores with a focus on the struggle of factory

---

11. The award was established to memorialize Chŏn T'ae-il (1948–1970), a sweatshirt-shop worker, who committed suicide by self-immolation in protest of the military government's oppression of the working class.

workers, who, empowered by a firm conviction of their civil rights and group solidarity, succeed in repelling exploitation by multi-national American industrialists and their collaborative Korean managers. Kim continued to produce her work in the same thematic line, which culminated in her novel, '79-'80 kyŏul esŏ pom sai (Between winter '79 and spring '80; 1987). This three-volume novel made its author the most visible woman writer of her generation firmly engaged in a crusade for working-class causes and a champion of the "labor novel." It was through these social activities that Kim met her husband and married in 1988.

From the early 1990s, when the once dominant antigovernment, anticapitalist literary trends of the 1980s began to decline, synchronized with the success of the Korean democratization movement and the reestablishment of a civilian government, Kim In-suk also started to move away from her earlier preoccupation with labor-oriented, dissident activism. Her attention turned inward to explore the private realms of human relations, most notably problematic gender and marital relationships. Her novella, "Kallal kwa sarang" (Love and daggers; 1993), is the outcome of this thematic shift and is the best received among her works of this period. An example of the changing contemporary concept of the conjugal dynamic, "Yangsuri kanŭn kil" (Road to Yangsuri; 1993) points out the gender role reversal in which the wife's self-assertion and financial independence dampen her husband's domestic decision-making ability and even his self-identity and will power. In 1993, her husband's job took her to Australia, where she lived until 1995, and her novel, Sidŭni, kŭ p'urŭn pada e sŏda (Standing in front of Sidney's blue ocean; 1995), which depicts the local Korean immigrant community's reality, evolved out of her foreign travel and sojourn down under.

Kim was the leading explorer of the thematic area of introspective reminiscences, searching for the true significance and implications of the popular movements for democracy, justice, and socioeconomic equality advanced by the radically politicized "386 generation" of her time. Her short stories, "Yuri kudu" (Glass shoes; 1998) and "Kŭ yŏja ŭi chasŏjŏn" (Her autobiography; 2005) are representative pieces of this venture. They vividly reveal Kim's attempt to reassess a variety of emotions: pain, trauma, disillusions, and sometimes remorse as a misused youthful energy retroactively experienced by the politically committed, one-time college population of her generation, both male and female.

From 2002 to 2004, Kim lived in Dalian (Diaren) in China alone with her teenage daughter (Kim was divorced in 1996), spending most of her time learning Chinese at a language institute. Her short story, "Pada wa nabi" (The ocean and butterfly; 2002), winner of the 27th Yi Sang Literature Award (2003), probes the difficulty of genuine conjugal communications and its attendant anguish and even despair, set against a backdrop of the hard-pressed, diasporic life of Korean immigrants in China. The narrative may represent her endeavor to come to terms with her own past marital experience from a temporal and spatial vantage point. Kim's short story, "Kamok ŭi ttŭl" (The prison yard; 2004), is another product of her sojourn in Dalian and recipient of the Yi Su Literature Award (2005). It exposes the unflattering sides of marginalized overseas Koreans by relating a ruinous, short-lived love affair of a divorced Korean man, an escapee from his business failure and debt, with a married woman he met in China, who has also been rejected and divorced by her husband back in Korea.

In 2010, Kim added another award to her successful writing career with her short story, "Annyŏng Elena" (Goodbye Elena; 2009), which won the 41st Tong-in Literature Award (2010). It is a portrayal of a family's dysfunction caused by the father's domestic violence and moral irresponsibility, but Kim underscores the need for forgiveness and compassion by showing the heroine's reconciliation and acceptance of her father before his death. The same year, Kim published *Sohyŏn*, a novel fictionalizing the tragic life of Prince Sohyŏn (1613–1645) of the Chosŏn dynasty, who, after spending nearly nine years in Manchu Qing Empire as a hostage after the second Manchu invasion of Korea in 1636, upon his return home met a suspicious death by poisoning at his father's royal court. The novel, however, focuses on his last two years of life in Qing China before returning to his native land and accentuates the Prince's endurance of humiliation, frustration, and absolute loneliness as a human being and his long-cherished hope of returning and contributing to his country's growing strength and prosperity. In 2011, Kim In-suk was invited as a visiting professor of creative writing at Chung'ang University, Seoul, in recognition of her continuing literary production and contribution to contemporary Korean literature. ଔ

TEXTUAL READINGS

Another first-person narrative, the novella, "Love and Daggers" adds a new dimension to the probing by Korean women writers into the harms of deep-rooted patriarchal gender ideologies and conventions. With the postmodern culture of 1990s Korea as its backdrop, the story is told by Migyŏng, a professional woman in her mid-thirties, about her beloved maternal aunt, Chonghŭi, a homebound housewife and mother of two sons, who is going through a midlife crisis in her mid-forties. The narrator lays bare how long-sanctioned patriarchal gender concepts and familial customs have disempowered her aunt and forced her to carry on a counterfeit life devoid of true purpose or meaning. Veritably, the narrative is a first-hand account of the wrecked life of a modern "virtuous woman" and raises a voice against its unfairness and irrationality.

What sustains and drives the storyline of "Love and Daggers" is the author's narrative scheme and arrangement, which simultaneously develops the two closely interwoven stories of married female relatives: the narrator's and her aunt's. There is a deep and genuine bond between the two women forged from their early years, and they are soul sisters who can understand and communicate with each other even without words. They share basic human decency, affection, and sensitivity, which makes their rapport enduring and without equal among their other family members. These dramatis personae, however, could not be more different in their character traits and conduct, attitudes about themselves and gender/conjugal relations, familial and kin relationships, and decision-making patterns.[12] The contrasting responses to their respective domestic issues and troubles by these two main characters create a medley of cross-generational and tantalizing spousal and family dramas.

---

12. Kwŏn Myŏng-a, "'Tangsin' ŭi kwangye non ŭl wihayŏ: Kim In-suk non" [For the study of the relationship of 'you': on Kim In-suk], in *P'eminijŭm ŭn hyumŏnijŭm ida: 90-yŏndae munje chakka rŭl chindan handa* [Feminism is humanism: diagnosing problematic writers of the 1990s], ed. Han'guk Munhak Yŏn'guhoe (Seoul: Han'gilsa, 2000), 247.

Aunt Chonghŭi is a personification of the traditional "virtuous woman," with a history of submissiveness and self-effacement—perennially accommodating, circumspect, and uncomplaining. Through most of her married life, she has taken her husband's chronic marital infidelity, physical abuse, financial squandering and bankruptcy, and other wrongdoings as male prerogatives. She also puts up with the abuse of the proverbially meddling, spiteful mother-in-law. However, her own unforgivable one-night extramarital transgression results in her sense of guilt, transforming it into a secret weapon ("the dagger"), which she masochistically uses on herself to endure and survive her conjugal and familial difficulties. With the accidental discovery of the death of the man in her hidden past, she loses the basis for her self-negation, silent suffering, and above all, her tolerance of her husband's possible future affairs. Her only alternative is to slip into depression—a pseudo death—which her husband takes as a middle-age woman's illness to be cured by medical treatment and religion. Aunt Chonghŭi's life continues to be a charade, bizarre and almost tragicomic to the all-knowing narrator.

In sharp contrast to her aunt, the narrator Migyŏng is forthright, outspoken, and perspicacious; she quickly grasps what goes on around her, knows what she wants, and speaks her mind. She has a principled uprightness and insists on fairness in human interactions, particularly among family members. She makes it clear that her idea of marriage is one of equal partnership of shared responsibility and openness and insists on upfront and honest dialogue between husband and wife—key to a healthy and constructive spousal relationship. Therefore, she can be confrontational, argumentative, and even unyielding when her husband evades frank and unguarded conversation on domestic issues. "Submission" and "silent suffering" are not in her conjugal lexicon. Furthermore, when it comes to her relationship with her mother-in-law, the narrator draws boundaries and wouldn't accept the elder woman's notion of male superiority as well as her power and authority over her daughter-in-law. Much of the narrator's actions and posture of resistance vis-à-vis her husband and mother-in-law have been reinforced by her resolve not to reproduce the gender domination-submission model personified by her aunt. In fact, the aunt serves as a negative model for the narrator, and Migyŏng's story represents a counternarrative to her aunt's personal tale.

What further bolsters the narrator's position and confidence is the fact that she has a job outside the home in the public sphere—she is a partner in maintaining a dual-income home. Migyŏng's professional and economical credentials lend weight to her insistence on establishing herself as her husband's equal and endow their domestic life with a certain measure of symmetry in gender and power dynamics, something her aunt totally lacks. In this way, the narrator does not have to harbor a self-destructive "dagger" such as her aunt's. The combination of these factors makes the narration of "I" carry authenticity and credibility; it is not a complaint of a vulnerable, apologetic, or acquiescent woman. In short, Migyŏng represents a new, critical gender consciousness by the younger generations of Korean women who are not inclined to submit to their society's female traditions as a given without first challenging them. By drawing the contrasting portraits of Aunt Chonghŭi and Migyŏng, "Love and Daggers" speaks cogently that women's marital relationships and conceptions of self can be realized only through resistance to patriarchal iniquities and the unflagging fight to destabilize them. ∞

Dreams of Butterflies, 1995

Ch'a Hyŏn-suk

Since he had nothing special to do, Zhuangzi took a nap.[1] In his sleep, he became a butterfly and fluttered around the world. But his dream was interrupted time after time, because his wife shook him and woke him up. Zhuangzi became irritated. One day, he told his friend about his dreams, complaining that he couldn't finish them because of his wife. His friend said to him, "You were probably a butterfly in your previous life. While you were collecting honey in the celestial flower garden, the gatekeeper happened upon you and killed you with the sharp end of his spear. That's why you keep dreaming the butterfly dream." Then his friend added that the gatekeeper was none other than Zhuangzi's wife.

Zhuangzi decided to set out on a journey in search of the butterfly dream. He quit his job—nothing to speak of in the first place—and abandoned his crumbling house too. The only thing he couldn't dispose of was his wife. She refused to leave him. He begged her to let him go, but she insisted, "I love you and I can never part with you." So Zhuangzi had no choice but to start out with his wife.

The title of the original is "Nabi ŭi kkum, 1995," and was included in *Yi Sang munhaksang susang chakp'umjip* [Collected works of Yi Sang Literature Award recipients] (Seoul: Munhak Sasangsa, 1995), 19: 317–341. The present translation is based on this text.

---

1. Zhuangzi (370 BCE–301 BCE), or Master Zhuang, is regarded as the greatest Daoist philosopher after Laozi. He is traditionally credited as the author of the work bearing his name, the *Zhuangzi*. For more details, see also footnote 32.

They happened to pass by a graveyard, where they found a woman crying in front of her husband's grave. Zhuangzi asked her why she was crying, and the woman said, "I am grieving here because the dirt on my husband's grave won't dry fast enough for me to remarry." Zhuangzi turned around and said to his wife, "Look, dear, love is like this, so you'd better leave me." But his wife swore her faithfulness, saying that she was not at all like that. Thereupon Zhuangzi died of pent-up frustration.

While they were holding a funeral for Zhuangzi, the prince of the country passed. He fell in love with Zhuangzi's wife at first sight. Zhuangzi's wife also liked him and agreed to marry him. As they were preparing for the wedding, the prince suddenly fell ill. A doctor came running and, after checking the prince's condition, said to Zhuangzi's widow that the prince could be cured if he ate the marrow of a person who had just died. Zhuangzi's wife took an ax and pulled her dead husband from the coffin. Just as she raised the ax high to strike him down, Zhuangzi sat up abruptly and said, "My dear, now may I go my own way?"[2]

The Kyobo Bookstore is no longer the same place where I used to buy books.[3] It has a completely new modern look. To me, just emerging from a back alley on Chongno Street reveals the bookstore as a dazzling sight, as if I'd stepped into an alien land in the twenty-first century. The entire ceiling is a mammoth mirror. I was overwhelmed. Casting a perfectly symmetrical reflection onto this mirror, I am staring back at myself in astonishment.

I once worked in a bookstore as a salesperson, but the experience left me nothing but unpleasant memories. It was my first job after graduating college. The bookstore was not huge like Kyobo, but, as it occupied a large lot on a street near a university campus, it did steady business with students.

At first, I didn't know it was a mistake for me to take a job at a bookstore. This fact finally dawned on me when, after six months on the job, I quit at the owner's suggestion. My first mistake was my miscalculation that I could read a lot of books as a bookstore employee. It was not simply a miscalculation—it was a naïve illusion.

---

2. This part of the story is italicized in the original Korean text.

3. The largest bookstore in Korea, the Kyobo Bookstore is located on Chongno Street in the heart of downtown Seoul.

What the customers wanted from me were the titles of books and their exact locations, and they didn't care whether I'd read the books in the store or not. If a customer asked for *The Zelkova Tree*,[4] the only thing required of me was to go straight to the shelf where the book was neatly placed, quickly pull it out, and hand it over to the customer. My next mistake was my desire to relay the content of *The Zelkova Tree*—and even my own feelings about it—to the customer while I was wrapping it. I had no idea that people did not particularly like to talk about books in the bookstore. The customers couldn't stand me, a salesperson bragging at length about my knowledge of the books I was wrapping for them. Finally, the bookstore owner advised me to find some other job because working in the bookstore didn't suit my aptitude.

However, I hadn't spent six months in the bookstore for nothing. While working there, I met a male college student who had just completed his military duty,[5] married him, and it's now been eight years since I got married. Of course, no one had ever asked me if I had an aptitude for marriage and, so far, no one has advised me to resign from it either. I knew from early on that I can't have everything in life my own way, but these days, I wish someone would ask me about my marriage aptitude.

"After eight years of married life, have you found yourself fit for marriage?"

My ready and simple answer would be, "Nope."

Standing in the middle of the Kyobo Bookstore's main aisle, I raise my gaze high and take a good look around at the books, and then walk toward the display counter with its sign, "Western History." I wonder why I'm suddenly curious about the details of the end of that book—*Lysistrata* by Aristophanes, the ancient Greek comedic playwright.[6] Of course, I remember most of its plot. It goes like this:

The Athenians and Spartans were at war with each other. The warriors were males, and every day they went to the battlefield and

---

4. *The Zelkova Tree* may refer to "The Young Zelkova" (Chŏlmŭn nŭt'i namu; 1960), a major short story by a Korean woman writer, Kang Sin-jae (1924–2001).

5. All South Korean males must complete compulsory military service.

6. *Lysistrata*, written by the Greek playwright Aristophanes (ca. 446 BCE–ca. 386 BCE), is a drama about the extraordinary feat orchestrated by one woman, Lysistrata, which brought an end to the Peloponnesian War. See also footnote 31.

wreaked havoc. The war brought neither fame nor power to women. It simply razed the gardens they had cultivated and smashed their household goods. The women of Athens and Sparta could no longer sit back and watch their painstakingly raised gardens and household furnishings be destroyed. So they decided they would put a stop to the men's war games. One day, women representatives from the two countries met and held a meeting. These representatives, who concluded that none of their nagging, conjugal quarrels, or even tears were of any use, came up with an ingenious proposition. They decided to call a "sex strike" against all men in both countries. Since women of both sides had no other option, they all voted in favor of this strike. The "sex strike" required tremendous determination on the part of the women. There was the danger that the spears and swords of the warring men could be turned on them. And the women also had to work out plans against rape, which might be an adverse side effect of the strike.

These women rushed to the smithy, where spears, shields, and swords were made. They had iron chastity belts made for themselves to prevent rapes. Throughout their cities they hung out placards, which read, "Unite, Women of Sparta and Athens!" Fortunately, even the prostitutes took part in the campaign. Women of both countries were assured of their victory by the fact that the prostitutes, who held the key to the strike's success or failure, cooperated with them. Now the men were absolutely like rats in a trap. In the end, the Athenian and Spartan men stopped their war. The women's "sex strike" had succeeded.

What is prompting me to read *Lysistrata* again is the desire to find out exactly how long the strike lasted. Those Athenian and Spartan women succeeded, whereas I failed. Or rather, I am failing. Above all, my "strike," which is being carried out without other women's cooperation, was probably destined to fail from the beginning. I have been on a "sex strike" against my husband for the past three months, but my husband has shown no physical signs of surrender. I haven't even needed to use the baseball bat I placed in the corner of our bedroom, in preparation for my husband's forced advances. Far from making such a move, he seems to be feeling a sense of liberation from a duty.

Walking these aisles, I can't find *Lysistrata* anywhere. While looking for a book that isn't there, I realize that the duration of the strike doesn't really matter. After all, it is only a one-sided strike on my part, and it's quite possible that my husband lost his sexual desire for me even before I went on strike.

Standing in the bookstore, people are shuffling through books. A man in a necktie and with his suit jacket thrown on his arm drops the book he is holding to the floor with a scowl on his face. He quickly picks it up. Its title is *People Searching for Zhuangzi*.[7] Why Zhuangzi? Grinning, I pass by him.

Feeling further depressed, I poke around here and there, and then stand in front of a bookstand, which was set up for women just like me. *A Woman Dreaming of Divorce*,[8] *A Woman Raising Her Head*,[9] *A Woman Who Stands Alone*,[10] *Women Who Run around the World like Wolves*.[11] Facing the book *Like Wolves*, I suddenly tense up. I feel as if a wolf, which has never been able to raise its head inside me, has cut its way through my chest and is looking at the book. For the sake of that wolf, I pick up the book.

After paying for it, I hold it in my right hand and go over to a fast-food place in the corner of the bookstore. I still have twenty minutes left until my appointment. I have arranged to meet Ǔnhǔi at one o'clock. I was anticipating she'd be running over twenty minutes late, taking into account roughly the amount of time it will take her to get from Inch'ǒn to Kwanghwamun.[12] I walk to the sales

---

7. Obviously an imaginary work created by the author.

8. *A Woman Dreaming of Divorce* may be the Korean translation of *An Unmarried Woman* (1978) by Carol DeChillis Hill, which was made into a movie of the same title in 1978. The Korean translation, *Ihon ŭl kkumkkunŭn yŏja* (Seoul: Ch'ambit, 1993) was done by Ch'oe Sŏn-hŭi and mentions the English original as written by Carol DeChillis Hill, but without mentioning the original title.

9. *A Woman Raising Her Head* (Seoul: P'odowŏn, 1993) is the Korean translation of Terry McMillan's *Waiting to Exhale* (1992). It was translated by Ch'oe Bo-ŭn.

10. As for *A Woman Who Stands Alone,* it is unclear what book this title refers to. The closest to this imaginary title may be Pak Wan-sŏ's novel, *Sŏ innŭn yŏja* (A woman who is standing; 1985).

11. The title, *Women Who Run around the World like Wolves*, is apparently word play by the author Ch'a Hyŏn-suk on a book by Clarissa Pinkola Estés, *Women Who Run with the Wolves: Myths and Stories of the Wild Woman Archetype* (New York: Ballantine Books, 1992). The latter is a collection of multicultural myths, fairytales, folktales, and stories—all related to the author's endeavor to explore the female psyche and unconscious.

12. Inch'ǒn is a port city about an hour to the southwest of Seoul by express rail. Kwanghwamun is a replica of a palace gate of the Chosŏn dynasty located in the center of Seoul, and adjacent to the Kyobo Bookstore.

counter and order a Coke from a female student, who is wearing a blue, part-time-worker nametag on the left side of her chest. Watching her pouring the Coke into a large paper cup, I ask, "What school are you attending?"

She stares at me blankly. She looks unhappy to hear such a question from a woman.

I hope she isn't offended. Why don't women like other women showing an interest in them? Would she feel different if I were a man?

To tell you the truth, my husband approached me at first by asking, "What school did you graduate from?" I shrugged my shoulders and looked away from him, but a number of words were scrambling in my mind, "I graduated from S University. I wasted my time majoring in French literature. And I …" Had I been a man, such words would be crashing about in the salesgirl's mind, too, I thought.

I want to ask her to go out with me, if she is willing, because she is so young and cute. Of course, I know full well that she will have no interest in an older woman, twisted like a dried pollack fish and reeking of household chores. But there is one thing she doesn't know—the fact that this thirty-something woman, to whom not even a dog would give a second look, once had a season of maidenhood like hers.

"Seven hundred *wŏn*, please,"[13] says the salesgirl.

Distracted for a moment by her peach complexion, I briskly rummage around my handbag for my wallet. All the while, from the corner of my eyes I steal a look at her supple skin and mumble to myself that, were she to go out with me, she'd get even seven thousand *wŏn*, not this meager seven hundred. I figure that at her age what she needs is money—money for pretty clothes, perfume, popular novels, and lightweight philosophy books, and a fund for dating.

I also worked part-time throughout my college years to earn money to buy such things, rather than focusing on my studies. The amount of money I earned was absurdly inadequate to satisfy my appetite for spending. Although my friends knew how hard I worked at my part-time jobs, no one knew what I spent my money on. Ŭnhŭi didn't know, either. She always praised my spirit of independence. Since she was from a wealthy family, I didn't feel like

---

13. About fifty cents.

being frank with her. I once accompanied her to a department store on a shopping trip. While she was buying a pricey silk dress, I was just fingering a red half-coat. Because I was then working part-time as a traffic controller at crosswalks, the price was beyond my reach. Ŭnhŭi said, "Why don't you buy it?" and cast a puzzled look at me, as if she couldn't understand why I was just fumbling with the coat instead of taking it home.

My mom always begrudged spending money on me except for my tuition and three daily meals. In fact, she even thought my tuition was a waste. She said, "What's the use of working my fingers to the bone to educate a girl? It'll all be for nothing once she gets married!" At that time, I was so hurt by what my mom–said that I even childishly questioned whether she was my stepmother, but unmistakably she had already seen ahead to what I would become in ten years.

Carrying the Coke tray, I walk over to a table and take a seat facing the salesgirl. When a customer leaves, she puts another paper cup on the tray for the next. I haven't given up on her yet. I picture a scene: I sit her quietly in front of me and ask her, "Do you have a boyfriend? You see, don't ever date a poor guy. And you don't have to get married, either. After you bet your life on a man, all that's left is your body smelling like a dishcloth. What about children? They are thorns in your flesh! You've got to have a job— not this kind of job but some professional work. I mean work that will enable you, as a single woman, to lead a dashing life and gain some fame as well." I am itching with desire to offer up my advice: "You see, at your age I was prettier and more competent than you are. Do you think I ended up this way because I am inferior to you? Nothing special is going to happen to you if you live with an ordinary salaryman, you see. So you must remember firmly what I am telling you."

Back when I was her age, I had no one to give me this kind of advice, logically and point-by-point, easy to understand. If someone had talked to me in this manner, wouldn't I have lived a wiser life? That is what I have always regretted. The angrier I feel about my own misfortune, the more I want to sit the young girl student down in front of me and give her the fortune I didn't have. I gulp down the Coke filled with ice cubes. Standing at the counter, the salesgirl is taking care of her customers, unaware of what is going on in my mind.

I glance at the cover of the *Women Who Run around the World like Wolves*. It shows four Western women, looking intelligent and strong-willed, and laughing radiantly. I can't tell whether it is by chance or the intention of the editor, but all these women are divorced and socially successful. One is an anchorwoman, the other a writer, the third the vice president of a bank, and the last a painter. I begin to turn the pages, a strong curiosity perking up within me. I flip through the pages, turning the leaves of the book noisily. I am looking for something. What has become of their children? No, that's not it. Why did these women get divorced? How could they become successful after their divorce? However, none of this information is what I am looking for. Or perhaps it is, but what I am *really* looking for is advice. I want to know what poor and shabby divorcées, who are not successful as these women are, should do to make it in this world. But in this book, only good-looking and glamorous divorcées are talking and laughing.

Of my college classmates, Chŏnghwa was the first to get divorced. She left her husband three years ago, leaving their son with him. She'd said, "I want to be successful socially, but my husband wants me home by seven in the evening. On top of that, my child wakes up every night and cries. I can't concentrate on my work. No one wants me to accomplish what I want. They don't offer any help, either. They don't want me to achieve anything beyond being a wife and a mother and earning a salary at an ordinary job. They keep giving me their so-called advice: 'What more dreams can you dream? That's greed. A woman's desires destroy the family.' I can't stand it. My nerves are about to snap." In the end, before her nerves snapped, Chŏnghwa became a divorcée. Fortune followed her, too. She cut a brilliant figure in the advertising field and became famous by writing essays about why she had to get a divorce.

I am jealous of Chŏnghwa, not because she divorced but because she became successful afterward. I also despise her because she failed in her marriage. It hurts me to see her appearing in women's magazines every so often. I cut off contact with her, as my complicated feelings of envy and jealousy mixed with contempt and disdain for her are unbearable to me.

As soon as I push the book to a corner of the table, I feel very tired. I calculate in my head the pros and cons of "my divorce," which tell me that I won't profit from it. My child, the apartment with its mortgage still to be paid, and my future all look hopelessly gloomy. Ah! More than anything else, I am fearful for my child. I feel apprehensive about his life.

It's twenty to two. Forty minutes past our appointment time, but Ŭnhŭi still hasn't shown up. In truth, we have little more to talk about even when we get together. Once or twice a day, we phone each other and chat away. Our topics range from that day's cooking to the dowdy ways our husbands conduct themselves, to how bad our kids behave or whether we had done our Pap smear tests. This morning we babbled on the phone for about an hour and, in the end, I called Ŭnhŭi to go out.

"Why don't you come out today?"

"What for?" Ŭnhŭi objected strongly in a drowsy voice. She had been running around every day for the past two months looking for a job. Completely overwhelmed by defeat, she's been cooping herself up at home. To draw her out of such a state, I came up with some serious excuses.

"Something important has happened to me. Otherwise why would I bother you? Normally I wouldn't even think about stepping out of the house because of my kid."

"What about your son, then?"

"I've made arrangements to leave him with the next-door neighbor."

"What's this all about?"

When she asked me this, I thought over "that important matter" again. Although the problem with my husband is important, I wondered if it was something that I should discuss with others. For my pride's sake, I couldn't do it. I had always managed to feign a measure of happiness and satisfaction with life in front of my friends. Wasn't there any other important topic, something that would be safe to talk about to others and still bring me comfort? I suddenly began to regret having asked Ŭnhŭi to come out at the prospect that I'd have to tell her about my sex-life with my husband. But I didn't have enough confidence to roam around the city alone. I find it overwhelming to wander around like a lost child along the art galleries lining Insadong Street,[14] which I hadn't visited for a long time, or to wait in line after buying a single movie ticket—not two—at the box office. For seven years since the birth of my child, I haven't ven-

---

14. Insadong Street, a few blocks off Chongno Street, is lined with small art galleries, antique stores, folkcraft and handicraft shops, cafés, and tearooms— popular among young shoppers and tourists.

tured beyond my neighborhood by myself. Whenever I went out-side the house, either my child or my husband tagged along.

I coaxed Ŭnhŭi, "I'll buy you something delicious. And … I have something really important to tell you." I lowered my voice as if I was about to tell momentous secrets.

For over four months, my husband has been carrying in the inner pocket of his suit a letter of resignation to submit to his com-pany. He has been looking for the right moment to decide whether to submit it or tear it up and throw it away.

That night, as usual, my husband returned home at eight in the evening in his Pride.[15] Come to think of it, that day had been com-pletely ordinary and uneventful. I'd finished getting dinner ready and was waiting with my son for my husband's return. At the sound of the doorbell, my son rushed out shouting "Daddy's home!" Fol-lowing him, I opened the front door. My husband, expressionless, pushed his son aside and went into the main room. Once inside, he slept there through the whole night and went to work the next day after a simple change of clothes. For the next few days, he said noth-ing upon his return home and simply went to bed.

What he told me afterward was bizarre. He'd been driving home from work that night and happened to pass by an art gallery. A huge black-and-white photograph, which was hanging outside the gallery and illuminated by dazzling lights, suddenly appeared in his field of vision. The fellow in the photo stared at him and asked, "Who are you? Where are you rushing to?" And the eyes of this guy, seeing through my husband's daily routine, gave him a good scolding. Those eyes kept following my husband as he drove home, demanding answers to those questions. By the time he reached the front of our house, my husband had barely managed to get rid of the eyes. But when he opened the entrance door, he met those eyes staring at him from inside the house.

I was all flustered, unable to understand the meaning of the eyes that haunted my husband, or our quandary around sex. I didn't intend to solve it together with Ŭnhŭi, though.

I decided that, in my life, all that I wanted was a person by my side—someone not burdensome—while I tried to come up with my own plans and backup plans for whatever life presented. Other-

---

15. The "Pride" was a popular, small-sized car model manufactured by the Kia Motor Company from 1987 to 1999.

wise, I knew I would be returning to my kitchen, frightened and stressed out by my own thoughts. There, in the kitchen, I would scrub away at the surface of the stainless-steel gas range and wait as usual without any alternatives. I would say to myself, "Why should I bother? You see, I have my son, Myŏngho." Then I would hug Myŏngho at play, squeezing him so tightly that tears would well up in his eyes, and I would phone my husband. After sizing him up to determine whether or not he had submitted his resignation, I would say, "Honey, I'm going to make a seasoned and steamed pollack dish for dinner. You're coming home early, right?" After uttering these words—enough to lure him home—I would give up on leaving him.

"Hey, girl, what's going on with you?" Ŭnhŭi, who is wearing white short pants, flings her shoulder bag on the table with a bang and begins furiously fanning her face.

"Why are you so late?" I hold my watch to Ŭnhŭi's face.

"Don't you know there's a subway strike? It took me an hour and a half to get to Seoul Station by out-of-town bus. Then I had to transfer to another bus. I almost went home, so don't complain," says Ŭnhŭi.

"What do you mean subway strike?" I ask. I came by bus as far as Kwanghwamun, since every morning my husband drives our new car to work—with that letter inside his suit pocket. It's not that I don't read the paper. But the extent of my newspaper reading is checking the TV program guide and entertainment articles. I didn't know about the subway strike. Neither did the woman living in apartment No. 305, nor the one living in apartment No. 307, with whom I occasionally have tea, mention anything about a strike. No one who phoned me talked about such happenings in the world. Something like that is not important to me. The most important thing to me is how to lead my husband's lost soul back to him.

"So, they're on strike! I'd like to go on a full strike, too. I'm sick and tired of the same old housekeeping and taking care of my kid—twenty-four hours a day, three-hundred-sixty-five days a year."

If my husband wants to be free from everything, I too want to be liberated from everything and to be left alone. It would be so nice to sleep alone all day long or to go to the river and watch the water flow day and night for three days. Why does my husband think he's the only one with such desires? To have my wishes come true, I should examine myself more seriously and intently today, as I walk around with Ŭnhŭi by my side.

"Let's go," I say.

"Where?" asks Ŭnhŭi.

"I don't know. But let's go somewhere anyway. I've got lots of money today," I say.

I brought my entire emergency cash in my purse, which I had stashed away without my husband's knowledge. That's not all—I gathered up my credit card as well as an installment savings bankbook and left home. I could live without money worries for a few months, even if I got on a flight somewhere just as I am. I want to go away to a place beyond my husband's reach.

We walk as far as the *Han'guk Daily* building.[16] I walk unsteadily, watching the tender leaves of the trees that line the streets and the light footsteps of people coming and going under them. My husband—he changed, to be sure. He openly vents his discontent over just about everything. He knits his eyebrows as he looks by turns at the straight legs of passing women in miniskirts and my body. I sigh, looking down at my two breasts, now of different sizes—the result of breastfeeding my child. My husband frets over the side dishes set out on the dining table and complains about their saltiness or blandness, tapping his chopsticks on the plates. Every morning, he shakes his trousers at me, which aren't creased neatly with an iron, and shakes his head.

Some time ago, he came home after a poker game at the house of his college classmate. He had lost miserably.

"Bastard!" he swore. "He's richer than me. How could he fleece his friend of three hundred thousand *wŏn*,[17] after having invited me over?"

I was shocked at the amount of money he mentioned. Upset, I said, "How could you be robbed of that much money by a friend in just a few hours?"

My husband hurled the glass of water he was drinking and growled, "His wife goes to work and gets a salary higher than his, all while raising two kids. What about you? What have you done for me? If I had a wife who earned money, I wouldn't have cared about

---

16. The *Han'guk Daily* (Han'guk ilbo) building is located in Anguktong Street near Insadong Street.

17. About four hundred dollars.

that puny amount and would've won the game betting a million. Do you know what kind of car he drives?"

Such insults! I shuddered. My husband clearly envied his friend. And my husband was fed up with me, his wife, who racked her brains to get money from him for daily food.

Out of the blue, he began to crave clothes and top-quality possessions. Even his belt had to be Gucci or Michiko London. His new medium-sized car still had twenty-eight monthly payments on it. He took more than half his salary as his allowance, saying he needed it for keeping up his dignity when meeting people. I was always short of money. I bought cheap panties costing only a thousand *wŏn* for three. But I bought twelve pairs of fashionable underwear for him, just as he requested, and put them away neatly in the drawer. For some time now, it has been my habit each dawn to take my husband's wallet from his trousers and open it. Frequently I found it packed with ten-thousand *wŏn* bills. I wanted to steal money from his wallet. Although I had never done so before, today I stole fifty thousand *wŏn* and shoved the money into my purse.

"Have you heard anything about your job applications?" I ask Ŭnhŭi.

"No. If I had, do you think I'd be spending time wagging my tongue with you like this?" says Ŭnhŭi. Ŭnhŭi had sent her three-year-old twin daughters to her in-laws in Taegu.[18]

"What's wrong?" I ask.

"For starters, I'm old. On top of that, I have too little experience for my age," says Ŭnhŭi.

Indeed, we are already thirty-two, and no one will officially hire us.

I say, "But you've got a graduate degree. Besides, you have over half a year's experience with a publishing company, right?"

"Don't you see it's tough at my age to compete with that amount of experience? By now I should have already reached the position of editor-in-chief but my qualifications are not equal to the job now. But, who would hire someone like me as a new employee when they have fresh, young kids moving up aggressively? I've already had over ten interviews. Now I break into a cold sweat as soon as I go out into the world. I've lost confidence."

---

18. Taegu is the largest city in North Kyŏngsang Province located in the souteastern part of Korea.

"Don't you think you should have kept your job after you got married?"

"Who would have thought I'd have twins? It really drives me crazy. Now that my kids are more or less grown, I am eager to work for myself in one way or another, but this stupid society won't co-operate. It won't!"

"Is your husband still worked up about labor movements? He hasn't come to his senses?"

"He says he has bet his life on them, and I've thrown up my hands now. But then what else can that poor guy possibly do? That's all he's learned. These days he doesn't even tutor at night, you know. Every day we get a morning call from the Labor Bureau checking up on him. You see, the strike for the reinstatement of wage earners is at its height now in Inchŏn. My husband is known as the most villainous of them all, and if need be, he'd be the first to be nabbed—so I heard."

"No kidding! Now that times have changed, it seems people are enjoying themselves, taking things easy, so what's gotten into your husband? If he wanted to live his whole life like that he shouldn't have had kids or gotten married in the first place."

"I'll say. It's nothing but egotism. He is good to others but is an egotist when it comes down to his wife and kids. His standpoint is something like this: we should sacrifice our family for our country and its people. So he asks me to get a job right away and buy him a 486-model computer for his labor-counseling office. I'd feel really good if I could beat up every one of those guys who make their families suffer while talking big about their countrymen and society."

It amazes me how Ŭnhŭi has managed to provide for her family up to now. When she announced that she was getting married to an antigovernment protestor fanatic who had been her upperclassman at her college, none of her friends believed her. They concluded that one of them—either Ŭnhŭi or her husband—was a sham. There certainly is no rule that prohibits the youngest daughter of a wealthy family from marrying a demonstration nut. But Ŭnhŭi had never taken part in street demonstrations throughout her college years. Her husband also had thought poorly of girls who wore perfume and miniskirts. Yet they got married and had twin daughters. Yes, Ŭnhŭi's husband has his own clear logic about society, but it seems he hadn't used this lucid logic in choosing his wife.

Once I asked him about Ŭnhŭi. His answer was simple, "As you know, Ŭnhŭi is good-natured and pretty." Of course, that's true. The problem with him was that he pushed "good-natured and pretty" Ŭnhŭi out into the world just as she was. And she became fiercely aggressive—to a surprising degree. Her change, which began with her marriage to a husband without regular income and with raising twin daughters, might be natural. In fact, I became curious about her husband. I had never been interested in why Ŭnhŭi's husband participated in demonstrations, because at that time everybody took to demonstrating, and students like me, who were unconcerned about such matters, were considered incomprehensible. But now, I am dying to know what made Ŭnhŭi's husband pursue his chosen path so single-mindedly. Aren't times going unfavorably against him now?

Ŭnhŭi tells me that her husband won't bat an eye whether the Soviet Union crumbled or not. She can no longer understand her husband, although she had a clear understanding why he had to do what he did in those days when he was in the thick of protests. The only thing clear to her now is that her husband won't ever be able to provide for his family, because, according to him, he will become far busier as labor disputes rise in direct proportion to the advancement of capitalism. So Ŭnhŭi has to carry the burden of feeding her family. Yet her society is not cooperating by refusing to hiring a thirty-two-year-old woman.

Insadong Street is intoxicated with the mellow light of the spring. Green leaves in large flowerpots lined up in front of the shops softly reflect the transparent sunlight. Ŭnhŭi and I look in at the shops, trying hard to divert our minds. While looking at the antique-styled ceramics and silver accessories, we become out of breath.

"Let's go somewhere and have a cold beer," I say.

We exit the ceramics store and search the Insadong alleys for a suitable café. We pass by some cafés with eye-catching names such as "When the Moon Shows Its Face" and "In the Midst of Life," and enter the one named "Primitive Age."

We are the only customers in the café. Indeed, who would crawl into this dark nook at this hour of the day, leaving behind a street full with spring? The proprietress of the coffee shop, who looks over forty, simply darts a glance at us while sipping wine. We request that she play the record, "Love Is Always There" by the Sunflowers.[19] After putting on the record, she thrusts a menu at us. I fling it open. The price for a piece of dried squid is eight thousand *wŏn*. I remember buying one for Myŏngho for one thousand five hundred *wŏn* only the day before.

"Let's order the most expensive items," I say.

"Don't go overboard," says Ŭnhŭi.

"Excuse me, ma'am! We'd like to order beer, a Mexican salad, and a dried squid," I say, and add, "Make it a Hite, please."

"Why Hite?" asks Ŭnhŭi.

"I like the flavor. I can't stand OB anymore," I answer.

"Finally, Crown beats out OB, huh![20] But I wonder if they really use water drawn from five-hundred-feet-deep rock beds?"

"Why question? Just trust and drink."

The proprietress brings us the four bottles of Hite we are to drink unquestioningly, a Mexican salad, and a dried squid.

The first glass of beer tastes tingling good.

"So, what's this important matter all about?" Ŭnhŭi asks. She hasn't forgotten.

I agonize over my pride but, challenged by the look in her eyes, I own up. "It's whether I should go through with my second pregnancy or get a divorce. That's precisely what the matter is about," I say.

"Does your husband know that you're carrying your second child?"

"Well … he doesn't. I haven't told him. He's not even interested."

"Don't you think he's having an affair?"

"Who knows? I wish he were. Then, I'd have a concrete adversary to fight, and we'd reach some conclusion one way or the other."

"How about having your husband go see a psychiatrist?"

"Don't you think your husband needs to go, too?"

Psychiatry … We fell into silence. Which of them has to go see a psychiatrist … ? Embarrassed about staring at one another in silence, we pour the blameless beer down our throats.

---

19. The Sunflowers began in the 1970s as a vocal group consisting of four members—two females and two males. Its members have since changed, but the group has remained popular for its delicate melodies, appealing lyrics, and musical harmony. "Love Is Always There" is the group's trademark song.

20. Hite (pronounced "height") is a top selling beer brand in Korea. OB (Oriental Brewery) beer is the country's fourth top-selling beer. Crown is the brewing company for Hite beer.

"I can't possibly go on living like this! I've got to get a divorce," I say.

"Then go ahead," says Ŭnhŭi.

"But what about my son? And how can I make a living at my age after divorce?"

"Then stick with your husband!" Ŭnhŭi spits out the words, as if she is fed up with me, and swigs her beer. She chews away on the dried squid, telling me that I act crazy because I am not hungry enough. Ŭnhŭi seems to be thinking that I have to get on with my life, without any complaints, content with the monthly salary envelope my husband hands over to me. Come to think of it, she might be right, compared with the way her own husband was carrying on. But Ŭnhŭi doesn't know that my husband hasn't brought his salary home that month.

"Listen! Why did you marry that guy?" Ŭnhŭi challenges me.

"It was simple. I thought at least he wouldn't starve his wife and kids," I say.

He was nothing but an ordinary husband until the day he talked about the eyes in the photo following him. He used to eat anything I cooked and was fine with any clothes I bought for him. My mom was satisfied with him just the way he was. She thought he was not at all the sort of person to starve his family.

My father had always made us go hungry. He ran his business, as if he wanted to prove that he was his own boss and that he'd never stoop to working for someone else. But then he started to lose everything and was eventually cleaned out. By the time the bank repossessed our house he had disappeared. My mom worked as a caterer for other people's parties, and then opened a noodle shop in front of a school. Just then, after two years, my father returned home. After that, he never left the house except to briefly catch a breath of fresh air outside with the allowance he got from Mom. Mom's noodle shop grew bigger into a cold noodle shop and then into a barbecue-rib shop.

Mom was stingy with both her husband and children. She never tired of talking about her hard-earned money. She kept harping at me for not having worked and paid for my marriage expenses with savings from my salary. She treated my old, dispirited father badly, saying how lucky those women are who live on their husbands' earnings. The year before last, when she threatened to divorce him, she gave us siblings a scare as it would mean the responsibility of caring for him would be dumped on us. After that incident, Father grew more crestfallen and found it difficult to even breathe freely.

For a while my husband continued to spend money on fancy outfits, cars, computers, and CD players, and then he suddenly changed the direction of his spending. He bought home books of Van Gogh's and Gauguin's paintings. Some time ago, when I asked him why, he said curtly that it was because he had lost his dreams. When I asked, "What dreams?" he answered that he couldn't even remember what they were and that this made him feel all the more miserable. I asked him in a gloomy tone whether all this was because he was shackled to his family. I had inadvertently gotten pregnant before he'd graduated from college. He had gotten a slap on the cheek from my mom and married me. He barely managed to graduate and found a job through the help of his upperclassman, with little time to think about his own aptitudes or such things. From that point on for eight years straight he had been running the rat race. It was obvious he was looking for traces of the dreams he'd had before he met me.

"So Ŭnhŭi, why'd you marry that guy?" I ask.

"Because he's an egalitarian—isn't he fighting for equality, betting his whole life on it? I thought he would treat me as an equal too. You know my father, a former colonel, right? You remember how tyrannical he was to my mom and me, don't you? He always ordered us around as if we were his subordinates. My only aspiration at the time was to escape from him. He desperately opposed our marriage, but I believed in my husband. But now he's hailed as a feminist by women other than his wife."

"I guess it's not easy living with a man one respects."

"Now it's too much for me to live with a man I respect. To back up the social service of the man I respect, I have to earn a living."

We go on drinking in silence, each absorbed in our separate, sad personal situations.

"Both of you must be over thirty. I guess you're at that age," says an unfamiliar voice. We absently look at the proprietress, who is squeezing in between us with a glass of wine in her hand. How long was she listening in on our conversation?

"I thought I was going crazy at that age." This uninvited woman begins to talk about herself casually, as if talking about someone else. I pour beer into her empty glass.

"… So I left home, though I was worried about my child. I cried an awful lot every night, thinking of him. And yet, imagine, he came to see me as his mother once he grew up! Looking back now, I think I was a delinquent housewife. I couldn't get myself interested in housekeeping no matter how hard I tried, and I always felt suffocated. Each day I was going crazy with an urge to break out of the house and go somewhere. After I had run away from home a few times even my husband, who was very good-natured, agreed to divorce. I have only myself to blame, I guess."

A delinquent housewife—so the woman defines herself, aged thirty at the time. Ŭnhŭi and I steal a look at the shadowy passion hidden underneath her dark eyebrows.

"Male customers coming here are all artists. They have good manners and are filled with a passion for life. A number of painters, writers, movie directors, and professors drop in here. I suppose you have already done the job of raising kids, so why don't you come here at night and have fun? You can enjoy conversations with them, widen your view of the world, and make money, too …"

"You seem to have enjoyed quite a lot of affairs with your customers?" Ŭnhŭi spits out, quickly dropping her eyes.

"Well, I wonder. But they are all just good friends." The proprietress quietly smiles at us with a twinkle in her eyes.

Ah, imagine, these men are painters, film directors—not a salaryman with a one-thousand-dollar monthly wage! Falling in love! How glamorous … I wish I could! Suddenly I pictured myself as a café owner. I could almost hear sweet music playing and stylish men talking about art, even seeming to catch a glimpse of my elegant figure.

"Let's get out of here," Ŭnhŭi's sharp voice reaches me, smashing my reverie. I take a moment to come to my senses and look for Ŭnhŭi, but she is nowhere to be seen, having already gone out the café door. I walk over to the payment counter.

"Just drop in sometime. Think of it as a part-time job. See you again, then," says the proprietress.

Ŭnhŭi, who is standing outside with a ferocious look on her face, says in a loud voice, "What a crazy bitch!"

I let out a deep sigh. Ŭnhŭi destroyed my daydream.

While walking back toward Chongno Street, we hesitate, not knowing where to head. For the first time in a long while my face is burning with alcohol spreading like fire through my veins. I notice a public phone booth on the sidewalk. I know I have to phone home.

I get worried whether Myŏngho is doing okay at the neighbor's. But I can't go back home like this.

"Where should we go?" asks Ŭnhŭi.

Why don't we have any place to go? Where should I go and find myself—away from my husband?

"Isn't there anyone we want to meet?" I ask.

"What hussies do you think would come out at this hour when they should be taking care of their kids—except for crazies like you and me?" Ŭnhŭi glares back at the café we'd just left, evidently still mad.

"Okay. Let's go anywhere then," I say.

We pass First Chongno Street and head toward Second Chongno Street. On the way, we drop in at Wendy's and have a coffee to sober up, and then cold noodles at a Hamhŭng noodle shop.

"Hey, that's a pretty necklace you're wearing, Ŭnhŭi," I say.

"This? The last time I went to Taegu my father-in-law bought it for me to apologize for the hard time his son is giving me. It's supposed to be three carats."

I am standing outside the cold noodle shop waiting for Ŭnhŭi to pay for us, wondering alternately whether she is rich or poor. I grow more and more uncomfortable. I always waited outside stores while my husband paid. At those times, I felt in the back of my mind how my husband took money out of his wallet and got the receipt, but I never understood the source of the discomfort I felt. Now I understand why.

My husband was thinking of our child and me as yokes, so I think he always calculated the burden he was carrying to provide for us in terms of the money in his wallet. He must have borne a deep grudge against us, although I hadn't realized it before. Probably he was thinking that the money he had to hand over to his wife and child cost him his dreams. If he truly thinks this way, it means he lost himself to gain an incompetent wife and a young son. It seems that he is dealing with his hunger for his lost dreams in this manner: when he sees a movie, he feels he should quit his job right away and become a film director; and when he sees photos by a famous photographer, he feels compelled to buy a Nikon camera, even on credit if necessary. The night he bought the book of Gauguin's paintings and came home, he said, "They say that Gauguin quit his job at forty and left home for Paris to paint." My husband is thirty-six. He has four more years until he turns forty.

But I know that my husband doesn't have the talent. I look at this completely talentless man, thinking how unfortunate he is. No matter how eagerly he leafs through the books of Van Gogh or Gauguin or listens to Jim Morrison's music, he just ends up envying their fiery lives—not their works of art. Whatever his dreams, he would face only despair at confirming that he, at age thirty-six, has neither such late-blooming talent as Gauguin's nor even an insane streak like Jim Morrison's. All my poor husband can do is to go back and forth between our home and the office every day, his letter of resignation stuck in his pocket. I don't have the heart to tell him about our second child.

Ŭnhǔi and I just keep walking, now going ahead, now dropping behind, immersed in our own thoughts. We don't even ask each other where we should head, although we go back and forth several times along the alleys behind the Chongno Bookstore.[21] We just shift the straps of our handbags on our shoulders, looking up now and then at the lines of old buildings as withered as our faces. Where should we go on a sunny day like this with no destination in mind, grimaces on our faces, and our hearts full of anger? In the end, beating a hasty retreat, we rush into the Pine Hill Café, cursing this transparent and innocent sunlight.

We sit gloomily facing the draft beer before us, cut off from the spring afternoon by a huge picture window.

I say to Ŭnhǔi, "Have you seen the movie *Blue*, starring Juliette Binoche?[22] Remember she loses her husband and child in an accident? Afterward, she has a one-night stand with her husband's student, and then walks toward a freedom that can make her true to herself, right? Into the intensely blue light, I mean. Do you know how fierce the light in her eyes was at that moment? Throughout the movie, I was thinking that it would be better to be a widow than a divorcée—a widow who neither has to put up with social criticism nor bear the responsibility for a broken family. Yet I get so scared of myself, who could imagine such things."

I'm not sure if Ŭnhǔi is listening to me. She is just gazing out the window in silence, while wiping the beer foam from her lips.

---

21. Chongno Bookstore, now gone, was one of the major bookstores along a busy section of Chongno Street.

22. It refers to the 1993 French film, "Three Colours: Blue." Juliette Binoche won the Venice Film Festival Award for Best Actress for her performance in the movie.

Because I am getting tired of my own story, I drink my beer and absentmindedly turn my eyes toward what Ŭnhŭi is looking at. The bluish evening light, which has stolen upon us, is spreading among the buildings and people. The streetlights are turned on and people freed from their work briskly fill the back alleys of Chongno Street.

I become more and more uneasy. In my mind looms the image of my son playing at the neighbor's, my husband at his office hurrying to get home with no chance again to take out his resignation letter from his suit pocket, and my own empty figure, wandering from one café to another all day long. Leaving Ŭnhŭi, who is silently heading for her own inner world, I walk toward the phone on the payment counter.

My husband answers the phone, "What's up?"

I say, "I'm calling from outside. When you get home from work go straight next door and pick up Myŏngho and take care of him, would you? I'll be a bit late."

"Are you crazy? Are you out of your mind or something? What's with you? You must come back home first and then we'll talk."

"I said I'll be late a bit. Make sure to have Myŏngho pee before he goes to bed. And you … you're an idiot! All you do is run from reality."

"Listen you! Have you gone crazy?"

Even without my husband having to say so, I really want to go crazy, if only I could.

My husband's dreams are now overtaking me. I was good at French in high school. At that time, I thought I could at least become a French professor. None of my classmates was better than I was in French pronunciation. The French teacher always praised me for my linguistic ability. I dreamed of being an intellectual and elegant woman who could read Marguerite Duras's *The Lover* in the original French and teach at college.[23] When I got the job at the bookstore after graduating college, I intended to save money to go to Paris. I wanted to visit Nice and Algeria—if only once. I also

---

23. Marguerite Duras (1914–1996) was a French novelist, playwright, screenwriter, and film director. She was born in Saigon, Vietnam, as the only child of her parents, who, encouraged by the French colonial government, settled there and worked as teachers. She left a number of plays, films, interviews, essays, and short fiction. Her bestselling autobiographical novel, *L'Amant* (1984), was awarded the prestigious Prix Goncourt in 1984, and was adapted to film in 1992 as *The Lover*. See also footnote 9, p. 181.

wanted to study at the Sorbonne. But fortune didn't smile upon me. Before I had time to save money, I was kicked out of the bookstore and ended up getting pregnant. Instead of going to France, I moved into my husband's boarding room on Sillimdong Street with a bundle of bedding.[24] Then, I gave birth to my child, prayed everyday in front of the statue of the Holy Mother for my husband's employment, and then bought an eighteen-*pyŏng* apartment.[25] After a long lapse of time, I became a "missus," leading an uneventful daily life, and only once in a while watched a French movie on video.

After leaving the Pine Hill Café, Ŭnhŭi and I, with nowhere else to go to and nothing specific to do, stand with vacant looks on our faces in the hazy darkness of the spring day, which is becoming more and more crowded with people.

Ŭnhŭi bursts out, "Those bitches, raving about getting a divorce or not getting a divorce for stupid, shit reasons!" I glare at her, baffled as to whether she is directing these words at me or herself. Completely ignoring my scowl, Ŭnhŭi, immersed in her own thoughts, goes on spitting out curses aimed at no one in particular.

"Maybe I should get a job as an insurance saleswoman. Will you open an account to help me out?" she says.

I gasp, "My goodness, an insurance saleswoman? You?"

I decide to send Ŭnhŭi, who is getting more restless than I, back home. We take a taxi together to Seoul Station, where Ŭnhŭi can catch an out-of-town bus back to Inch'ŏn.

"By the way, tell me who started the strike," says Ŭnhŭi.

"What?"

The taxi driver throws a quick glance back at us.

"I am asking you who started the strike between you and your husband," says Ŭnhŭi.

"It's a simultaneous strike," I say.

"Listen, think carefully. You know these days divorce is running riot among women like you, as if it were a hot fashion. Who among women wouldn't get a divorce for reasons like theirs? See, women like me are still sticking it out," Ŭnhŭi says, sounding as though she were a woman in her fifties.

---

24. Sillimdong Street in the Kwanak Ward of Seoul is most noted as the location of Seoul National University, the top-ranking university in Korea.

25. Approximately 216 square feet.

I glare at the diamond necklace on her neck, paying no attention to what she is saying.

Ŭnhŭi leaves. While loitering about the Seoul Station Plaza, I begin to worry whether my husband has gotten home yet. Should I call home to check or … ? I shake my head. I don't want to go home to where my husband is. Then, where should I go? To my parents? My mom would kick me out right away without listening to what I have to say. To a friend's? My friends would keep asking me questions. After their curiosity were satisfied, they'd pity me. Should I just leave on a night train for somewhere? But then, what will I do in a strange city once I get there?

Seated on a worn-out plastic bench in the lobby of Seoul Station, I look up at the train schedules for the Kyŏngbu and Honam lines and then watch people heading purposefully toward the gates.[26] There is no place where I will be greeted with welcome. Well, there *is* one place where I would be welcomed. "Be sure to come … all right?" The voice of the proprietress of that café whirls in my ears. I lightly bite my lips. How can I possibly work in that café with my bulging, pregnant belly? I want to go home … to my house, where my child and the furniture I polished with my own hands are. But … anxiously, I look up at the clock in the lobby, which is pointing to eleven o'clock.

I have become alone … A desperate feeling strikes me. As if for the first time in my life, at thirty-two, I have become an orphan—trembling all over with fear, curiosity, and intense desire, like a child abandoned in this Seoul Station lobby. I rummage through my memories to retrieve my unrealized dreams of going to Paris and my passion for life before I met my husband, but those already bleached memories don't rush back to life. Only the clock in the lobby keeps rapidly running forward. Its hour hand is passing twelve. Blankly and without emotion, I keep looking at the train schedules and watch the sparse footsteps of people heading toward the gates. Without the heart to stand up, I simply remain seated on one of the empty, dirty plastic benches.

 beginor8

---

26. The Kyŏngbu train line runs between Seoul and Pusan, while the Honam line connects Seoul to Mokp'o, a major city in South Chŏlla Province.

Ch'a Hyŏn-suk (b. 1963)

A contemporary Korean woman writer whose literary career blossomed in the early 1990s, Ch'a Hyŏn-suk was born in Sangju in North Kyŏngsang Province. From her early childhood, Ch'a felt uneasiness and anxiety about her parents' marital situation (she and her younger brother were born before their parents' respective previous marriages had been legally dissolved), about which they were secretive.[27] At the time of her entrance into primary school, she learned to her shock that she was listed in her official family register as the daughter of her father's former wife. The discovery was a devastating blow, imprinting in her young, defenseless, and sensitive mind shameful feelings and a sense of moral inferiority. These emotions turned into anger and resentment toward her parents for putting themselves above others, including their children, which came to darken her view of marriage, conjugal relationships, concepts of family, and life itself.

Eventually Cha's family moved to Seoul, but because of its financially straitened circumstances, she chose a commercial high school instead of a regular one. She neglected her studies, however, as she was constantly dogged by a crippling sense of life's purposelessness, anxiety, and self-doubt, which in large part stemmed from her obsessive sense of stigma about her family background. The only way for her to manage these emotionally and mentally trying years was to cling to works by Friedrich Nietzsche and Arthur Schopenhauer. This absorption in Western philosophical masters led her to major in philosophy at Tongguk University in Seoul, but her college years were also haunted by the same gloomy questions on the meaning and purpose of life. Yet her exposure to basic ideas in women's studies, part of the university curriculum, provided her with substance, inspiration, and perspectives vital for her later production of stories dealing with the interrelationship of society, family, marriage, and women's identity.

---

27. See Ch'a's interview, "Chungjŭng uuljŭng ch'ehŏm tamŭm sosŏlchip p'yŏnaen chakka" [An author who published a collection of stories about her experience of severe depression], *Yŏsŏng tonga* (June 2008): 420–422. The following biographical information about Ch'a is derived from this source.

After her marriage, encouraged by her husband, who recognized Ch'a's literary talent, she began to try her hand at creative writing. In 1994, she made her debut with "Tto tarŭn nal ŭi sijak" (The beginning of another day), which problematized the new post-democratization era in Korea of the 1990s characterized by the easy compromise of principles, selfish pursuit of individual gain, and materialistic obsession, in disturbing contrast to the societal idealism of the 1980s with its faith in truth, passion for justice, and allegiance to a larger public good. Ch'a depicted the deplorable development through the inner conflicts and outrage of the female protagonist—a victim of betrayal by her former college boyfriend, now transformed into the epitome of the era's lamentable social and cultural trends—and her determination to stand on her own by devoting herself to writing.

Since then, Ch'a's primary thematic areas have covered pressing social issues, such as gender and family conflicts, family institutions, husband-wife relationships, established sexual mores, politics of women's education, job, and society—all related to her generation's gendered quandaries and polemics. Most of her literary protagonists are college-educated, urban, middle-class homemakers—usually in their early thirties with small children who, isolated in their homes, are dispirited and suffocated by the drabness of their daily routine and feeling trapped in their marriage. Though they are recipients of a college education, they have neither outlet to relax and express themselves beyond their household roles as mothers and wives, nor jobs outside the home that might allow them to make use of their specialized knowledge gained through higher education. These housewives want to be more than helpmates to their husbands and perfect mothers to their children; they want to lead their lives as they once dreamed of doing during their college days. But their society does not offer such opportunities. As Ch'a once observed, in most cases, they are helplessly stranded between the feminist appeal for independence and self-reliance and Korea's traditional restrictive gender notions about women.[28] "Nabi ŭi kkum, 1995" is one of the most illustrative cases in point. The female protagonist's malaise and dilemma can be considered analogous to that of an American suburban housewife's, so piquantly labeled "the problem that has no name" by Betty Friedan in her *The Feminine Mystique*—

---

28. See her interview with the newspaper, *Chosŏn ilbo*, November 14, 1999.

only with the Korean cases separated by the temporal lag of about three decades.[29]

A series of Ch'a's works, "Nabi, pom ŭl mannada" (A butterfly meets spring; 1996), *Pulu pŏtŏp'ulai* (Blue butterflies; 1996), and "Nabihak kaeron" (Introduction to the study of butterflies; 1997), whose titles share the word "butterfly," are variations on the theme of the impasse and malady plaguing career housewives as they face early midlife crises. Marriage was the only choice their society gave to these women after college, and that marriage turns out to be a systemic shackle and a dead-end street. They find themselves imprisoned in domesticity, forever occupied with the mind-deadening routine of preparing meals, doing laundry, housecleaning, and grocery shopping, while disputing their uncompensated household labor as unacceptable and choking personal growth. What makes matters worse is that their husbands are clueless about their wives' frustrations and desire for change and make no effort to understand them.

The "butterfly" series stages these women's desperate attempt at self-transformation using the metaphor of butterflies, with the women hoping for personal makeover by leaving behind their unfulfilling marriages, unsatisfactory motherhood, sterile domestic life, and the loneliness all of these bring. For instance, "Nabi, pom ŭl mannada" presents an ingenious, experimental family arrangement made by a young, childless housewife, who agreed to a divorce requested by her womanizing husband. The heroine befriends a younger woman she calls "Spring," who used to be her husband's lover, has multiple boyfriends, and has rejected the family institution after experiencing the damning abandonment of her parents. "Spring" becomes pregnant without really knowing the identity of the child's father, and the narrator/protagonist decides she and "Spring" will raise the child together with a sense of value and purpose of life. The narrative represents the authorial deconstructive challenge to the traditional gender order, marriage system, and conjugal power structure, branding them mechanisms of women's oppression. At the same time, it embodies an attempt to invent and advocate alternative meanings of family organization and child rearing.

---

29. Betty Friedan, *The Feminine Mystique* (New York: W.W. Norton & Company, 1963), 15.

The narratives in Ch'a's short-story collection, *Ohu 3-si ŏdi edo haengbok ŭn ŏpta* (No happiness anywhere at three o'clock in the afternoon; 2000), all deal with the problems of young couples who, faced with marital stalemate or deadlock, choose extramarital affairs and/or divorce as a way out of their conundrum. But stories such as "Sesang e pit i issŏra" (Let there be light in the world) make the point that such choices do not constitute real breakthroughs, as they hurt and damage children and result in dire economic deprivation for divorced women without regular incomes. In some cases, women's love affairs after divorce bring disappointment, more emptiness, and even deeper unhappiness, as illustrated in "Yuri kudu" (Glass shoes) and "Ibŭ ŭi kŏul" (Eve's mirror). The ultimate recommendations suggested by these works are the necessity of changing society's systematic devaluation of woman's potential, education, and individual worth, and of fundamentally modifying and realigning society's gender and family structure.

A recent work of importance to the understanding of Ch'a Hyŏn-suk's literary trajectory is her short-story collection, *Chayuro esŏ kil ŭl ilt'a* (Lost in liberty street; 2008). Of these stories, most informative and edifying is "Chong'i inhyŏng" (A paper doll)—her autobiographical narrative. This story returns to the author's tortured and estranged relationship with her parents after her marriage, focusing on her parents' deaths in 2002 and her subsequent severe depression. In the narrative, she underscores the moment of her insight into the fact that she was not the sole victim of her parents' anomalous marriage: other members of her family were equally wounded and humiliated. This new perception of her birth origin and its ramifications brings her years of anguish, self-alienation, and despair full circle and signals the closure she has long sought. Ch'a proffers this latest work as a message of healing to those who have experienced longstanding, agonizing depression like herself.[30] ∞

---

30. Ch'a Hyŏn-suk obtained a psychological counseling certificate in 2005, and encourages people to acknowledge their depression and seek treatment. See Ch'a's June 2008 interview in *Yŏsŏng tonga*, p. 422.

TEXTUAL READINGS

Presented in a humorous, witty, and even self-deprecating tone, and in shifing memories and interior monologues, "Dreams of Butterflies, 1995" is a serious plea for a closer look at the conjugal and personal troubles of young, college-educated, middle-class housewives in the changing sociopolitical and cultural environment of mid-1990s Korea. The first-person narrator and her college friend, Ŭnhŭi, find themselves battling with their respective husbands, who, preoccupied with their own personal issues commitment, pay little attention to their wives' needs, desires, and dreams. These women find their current domestic circumstances and marital relationships disappointing and demoralizing, and their lives are pervaded with a sense of frustration and uncertainty about their future.

Although the narrative line of "Dreams of Butterflies, 1995" is primarily led by "I," Ŭnhŭi's story runs in close parallel to the narrator's and adds diversity, color, and reinforcement to the frustration and predicaments the two women share. The two female characters come from different socioeconomic backgrounds, but they are united in their quest for a breakthrough to a personally fulfilling, nourishing, and satisfying life. Sharing streaks of sassiness and feistiness, these young women with small children are basically caring, straight-thinking, and no-frills individuals, who possess a full and down-to-earth awareness about themselves and their own familial situations. As revealed in their candid, genial, and often sparkling dialogues (in which both characters serve mutually as confessor and confessee), the twosome long to be more than just stay-at-home wives and mothers.

As the narrator's self-account illustrates, her domestic storm is triggered by her husband's abrupt midlife crisis, which leads her to review her own married life only to find a lack of personal fulfillment and a dissatisfaction and restlessness no less serious than that of her husband, if not more so. Marriage has dampened her expectations, burying her in the monotonous, paltry, stifling routine of home, completely cut off from the changing world outside. Domestic household work has negated her higher education and destroyed her dreams of an academic vocation as a French literature professor. "I" yearns to be more than an attachment to her husband and a caregiver to her son—to be an individual possessing her own time, space, and identity apart from the preset gender-role expectations for a married woman.

To aggravate their situation, Korean society has no realistic prospects for these women to use their education outside the home—except for jobs catering to men, such as the one held by the café woman. This systemic abandonment of or discrimination against women has nullified their college education and disenfranchised their dreams and career opportunities, stranding them in stagnant domesticity and deadlocked spousal relationships. They are also gnawed by the sense that they are falling behind the times and being pushed out of their rapidly modernizing society by its competitive and competent younger generations. The story thus posits that the two women's disenchantment, exasperation, and insecurity as wives are no less real, serious, and valid than their husbands' midlife crises and frustrations; indeed, that such crises are not a male monopoly, as popular perceptions or myths would have it. In so doing, it raises a pressing and difficult question about what needs to be done about these women's predicament.

The gender wars of "Dreams of Butterflies, 1995" are augmented by the author's direct references to well-known classics from both the West and East: *Lysistrata*[31] and *Zhuangzi*.[32] In a whimsical manner, the allusion to these two texts suggests that the author's modern Korean narrative is a variation on the perennial gender squabble, a recurrent drama that transcends time, space, and culture. Especially, Ch'a's literary originality in adopting the Zhuangzi story reaches a virtuoso level. She twists the original Zhuangzi's dream

---

31. *Lysistrata* is a comedy written by Aristophanes (c. 446 BCE–386 BCE), an ancient Greek playwright hailed as the Father of Comedy. Basically an antiwar drama, it has as its heroine the Athenian Lysistrata, an exceptional woman of intelligence, courage, and ingenuity. She persuades her country women to withhold sexual intimacy from their warring husbands as a means of coercing the men to negotiate a peace for the Peloponnesian War between Athens and Sparta.

32. *Zhuangzi*, by Zhuangzi (late 4th century BCE), is considered one of the most influential texts in Daoism. Perhaps the best-known part of the work is Zhuangzi's dream narrative for its profound Daoist metaphysical inquiry into the mystery of human existence. The text reads: "Once upon a time, Zhuangzi dreamed that he was a butterfly, flying about enjoying itself. It did not know that it was Zhuangzi. Suddenly he awoke, and veritably was Zhuangzi again. He did not know whether it was Zhuangzi dreaming that he was a butterfly, or whether it was the butterfly dreaming that it was Zhuangzi." In this original book, the wife does not exist.

episode by inventing the character of the wife, who has the upper hand in her marriage, and morphs the story into a comic skit between husband and wife. In this imaginative parody, the reversal of gender roles is played up to function as a facetious and surreptitious commentary on the dispirited state of modern Korean female characters, who are not allowed such advantages in their own home or society. In contrast to the happy endings of these foreign texts, contemporary Korean married women, who, like butterflies, want to fly away from their oppressive reality, remain in limbo.[33] They are unable to either go back or move forward—utterly unlike their counterparts in Aristophanes's masterpiece, who form a spiritual unity for a common cause, or the wife in Zhuangzi's dream narrative reimagined by the author Ch'a, or other female characters and heroines in contemporary Korean and Western literary texts.

Additionally, the frequent references to Western artists, writers, the real title of a foreign movie and its stars, and a Korean vocal group and their songs, show the glaring time lag in women's societal usefulness and self-fulfillment, a sharp contrast to the internationalizing Korean cultural trends and entertainment amenities of the early 1990s. Most of all, the deliberate teasing posture taken up by the narrator to poke fun at herself and her husband, which is mixed with jesting quips and informal, curt dialogue, makes the story not only amusing but an eye-opening reading of the pressing gender questions and the predicaments of married women of the author's generation. The last scene of "Dreams of Butterflies, 1995," where the protagonist sits forlorn in the deserted train station at midnight, cries out for the urgency of redressing outdated gender role expectations in the sociocultural milieu of a Korea rushing breathlessly toward globalization. ೞ

---

33. See Kim Mi-hyŏn, *Yŏsŏng munhak ŭl nŏmŏsŏ* [Beyond woman's literature] (Seoul: Minŭmsa, 2002), 185–187.

In Front of the House

Yi Hye-gyŏng

[1]

Standing in front of a long, full-length mirror, a woman ponders her reflection. The narrow mirror is barely able to show a person's whole body, and she looks as if she is locked within its frame. It appears as if the mirror is compressing her figure and hemming it in. Her gathered skirt, edged with white lace, and the white T-shirt with the blue cardigan thrown over it make her seem at first glance like a young girl. But a more careful observation reveals the plump lines of her shoulders rounding the T-shirt and the wrinkles on her neck that make it look thicker than it actually is. Her coarse and colorless facial skin doesn't take makeup well. She is old, much older than her clothes suggest. Worse still, the slightly frayed lace on her skirt makes her look pitiful. It's inconceivable that she hasn't noticed the worn lace on her skirt—her favorite clothing for casual outings, because she feels comfortable with its rubber-banded waist and voluminous width. She strangles the sighs threatening to burst out and, cutting them bit by bit, lets them out through the gaps between her clenched teeth.

"You look fine, Big Sister. Haven't you noticed the way those married housewives dress themselves up? I can't even tell whether they're young singles or middle-aged women. I like the way they looked, though, full of vitality," says my younger sister-in-law, the wife of my husband's younger brother, appearing from behind the

---

The title of the original is "Kŭ chip ap," and was first published in her collection of short stories of the same title, *Kŭ chip ap* (Seoul: Minŭmsa, 1998), 32–78. The present translation is based on this text.

mirror and pushing up the cardigan that slipped down my shoulder. Although she deliberately uses a playful tone to hide her intention to cheer me up, I can't help but feel her caring heart trying to soothe my hopelessness. She is the kind of woman who, because of her boundless consideration of others, ends up giving the impression that she has hidden away her true feelings somewhere else.

The moment I see the carefree look in her eyes, I feel self-conscious. I wonder if the real "me" looks more ludicrous than the way I see myself. But my younger sister-in-law smothers my surging doubts.

"You look far brighter, Big Sister. When you go out, which handbag are you going to take with you?" She attends to this and that as if she were an older sister sending her younger sister out on her first date. Her innate nature is attracted to the weak more than the strong and her wisdom keeps her empathy for others' pain from showing it off. Her warmth, like newly picked cotton, is hidden one layer beneath her usually detached demeanor.

Recalling that I too had an inner glow like hers in the past, I look at my younger sister-in-law with yearning, as if trying to recall something I once cherished but lost without realizing it.

"Big Sister, I will be on vacation for a week from next week," my younger sister-in-law said happily through the phone. "I will be free once I come back from a visit to my parents' home on the weekend. Do you have anything you want to do then?"

I listened to my sister-in-law's bouncy voice and carefully opened the can of beer I had taken from the fridge just before the phone rang, making sure the sound of the can opening wouldn't reach her ears.

I usually have a can of beer—as if watering a dry tree trunk— when I feel blighted like shriveled autumn leaves, when wind blowing from somewhere else deposits sands inside me, and when I feel as if those very sands suck up all the moisture in my body. The moment I have the first sip, I feel moisture seeping into the walls of my intestines, just like how the dry soil around the base of a tree soaks up water and turns itself black.

As I do this, my eyes are usually directed toward the bonsai pots on the decorative furniture in the living room or on the display stand on the veranda of my apartment. There is the juniper tree on whose branches, as white as bleached bones, densely grow small and pointy leaves. The cedar is growing straight up quite nicely even in the small pot, as if it kept in its cells the memory of the forest towering against the sky. The zelkova spreads its leaves sideways, its roots tracing back to its ancestor, the shade tree, which, standing near the entrance of a village, used to cast a shadow over the people going in and out and listened to their stories. These are trees that my mother-in-law raises with painstaking care.

What kind of reactions will these trees show if I pour beer over them? Although I've never tried it, each time my eyes fall on these trees while I'm drinking, I am badgered by such a temptation: After mixing in a spray bottle a cocktail of *soju*, beer, and even hard liquor, I would mist it on the leaves and branches. The thin, delicate, and threadlike roots that I saw during repotting would swallow up the alcohol, mistaking it for water. But, before long, they would be shocked by the foreignness of the liquid touching their roots. The alcohol would seep into the tree's water ducts. ... It's at this point that, sitting immobile on the sofa, I usually stop myself, shaking my head.

"What's this all about? Is your husband going somewhere?" I asked my younger sister-in-law.

She answered, "He'll be going on a business trip to China. I probably showed too much joy at the news. He got all cranky and left the house, saying that I should take out a large life insurance policy on him, that I should be happy because someone told him, after reading his palm, that his life span is short, and so on. No matter what he said, I still feel happy. Don't you think I can spend some time in peace while he's gone?"

Her husband, who recently developed a great interest in martial arts movies made in Hong Kong, stayed up all night watching them on weekends. Obviously, my younger sister-in-law had gotten sick of the yelling in the movies. She wrinkled her nose in distaste, saying that she felt the bloody scenes were turning her hair gray.

"So, Big Sister, why don't you share the vacation with me? I will take care of Inyŏng, and you go wherever you want to go alone. Or, you can go see a movie with your husband. Aren't you expecting Mother to come back soon?"

Mother, that is, my mother-in-law, was out of town looking after her daughter during her childbirth, and I felt restless, as if I were a soldier on furlough, counting the number of days before going back to base. Empty beer cans piled up in the utility room that my husband rarely peeked into, marking the number of days on the calendar.

On the day of the memorial service for my father-in-law, we three daughters-in-law were busy preparing pan-fried dishes and seasoning vegetables. We chatted among ourselves about this and that, and when the wife of my husband's older brother heard that my husband was planning to come back to his native town and settle down, she stopped ladling the batter of chives into the frying pan and said to me: "It's just until Inju finishes his entrance exam—only two more years to go. You see, as a mother of a student preparing for college entrance exams, I am no different from the test-taker himself. It's not that Mother gives me a hard time, but as Inju's school has moved, it takes much longer for him to commute. Why don't you take living with Mother during this period as paying your dues? She will be taking care of her own living expenses, so it will help you with the cost of living too."

Hot oil spattered onto the back of my hand, probably because of drops of water that fell into the frying pan.

"Don't you think it's necessary for Inyŏng to live with her grandma too? These days, we hear people making a big deal about boosting their morale, and don't they say that three generations living together under the same roof helps mix the young and old energy together and form harmony in the home, right? What do you think, Littlest Sister?"

Sitting on the dining chair, my younger sister-in-law was skillfully seasoning vegetables, and then put some into my mouth, saying "Please taste these to see if they are seasoned properly." To our elder sister-in-law's words, she said, "Yes, so I heard. I sometimes feel sorry for kids these days. In our younger days, when our parents scolded us, we could take cover behind our grandmother's skirt. But these days, kids have no one to lean on. If anything, this seems to make them so selfish. But, Biggest Sister, do you think Mother would agree?"

"Oh no, it's not that we decide the matter here, but just to talk about it among us in advance. Frankly speaking, we don't have any power, do we? Yet as Mother knows well the ways of the world, she would understand." My older sister-in-law was outspoken in the way she talked. As it's been said that women wait until their husbands' retirement to get a divorce, such toughness exuded from her. Her voice began to carry weight recently, ever since her husband got a job in a rather large architectural firm, having worked at his mother's dry-goods store after his failure in every other business he tried his hand at. Taking this as an opportunity, my older sister-in-law seemed to be intent on pushing her plans all the way to moving out of our mother-in-law's house.

On the delivery day of the household belongings we had packed after cleaning out our old place in Seoul, my older sister-in-law, who had already moved out into an apartment, patted me on my shoulder and said, "Don't try to be an angelic daughter-in-law, just do as much as you can. If you push yourself too hard, you will make yourself crazy. To tell you the truth, it's not always easy to live under the thumb of our high and mighty Mother."

I felt fogginess descending upon me, tickling my forehead. The veil of a "good-natured daughter-in-law" was about to fall over me. I hurriedly brushed it off. Then I said, "Big Sister, because the circumstances have turned out this way, we are moving in to live here. It seems to help us financially too. You see, as urgent as your situation might be, we also need to consider our own convenience." She seemed to be thinking that I was trying to acquire the title of a "well-mannered sister-in-law" as well as being a good-natured daughter-in-law.

As soon as Inju entered a decent university, my older sister-in-law, by taking over a discount cosmetics store in the neighborhood, made it clear that she had no intention of living with our mother-in-law again. By then, I was struggling with my inability to remove the veil that had unceremoniously fallen over me. The veil, though cumbersome, at first had an enjoyable glitziness as it came with other's recognition of my dutiful serving of my mother-in-law but it turned into the sticky stuff made of old dust, moisture, and my own distress.

"Big Sister, when you go out today, please ask your husband to buy you lots of delicious food. If it gets late, I can sleep in Inyŏng's room, so don't try to come back early. You won't mind me staying over, would you?"

I watch my younger sister-in-law in the mirror and feel her concern for me. "Of course not, but how about your husband, who calls you every night, as you said? Don't you think he'll be very worried if he can't get in touch with you?"

In the back of my mind, I have a sneaking feeling that my day out today will turn out to be long, prolonging my younger sister-in-law's stay in our apartment into the late evening. I know that her husband, even for a man, has a jittery personality. So I am concerned, once he finds out that his wife isn't home even late at night, that he'll be calling her every thirty minutes to check if she's gotten into a traffic accident.

"I told him I'd be coming here today, so, if he can't get a hold of me for a couple of days, he'll call here. As you know, given his impatience, he won't just sit still. Don't worry about me, and have a great time," my younger sister-in-law assures me.

I detect a guarded concern in my younger sister-in-law's talk, as she picks up a strand of hair that fell on my shoulder. My mother-in-law has compared the two of us endlessly: "Now you see why people talk about the importance of family background. Look at your younger sister-in-law. No one can find any fault with her." It is due to my younger sister-in-law's virtues that I have no resentment toward her.

"Hey, Inyŏng, tell your mommy to have a good time with Daddy, and then you play with Auntie. What shall we do for fun? But, first say goodbye to your mommy, okay?"

"Okay. Bye, Mommy. Come back home with lots of yummies," my kid shouts with a ringing, childlike voice. On occasions like this, she looks like a child, but other times, I realize that she already has an adultlike emotional sensitivity within her.

Some time ago, while folding the laundry, my fingers touched a worn part of an old cotton pillowcase, and the threadbare cloth ripped away. The pillowcase would be useless anyway. I put my fingers into the torn part again. Every part of the cloth my fingers touched ripped away. I kept saying to myself, "Why am I doing this, why," but I didn't stop the movement of my fingers.

Just then, Inyŏng, who was playing with her toys on the other side of the dining table, rushed toward me and clung to my arm. "Mommy, don't do it, I say, don't do it."

To me, it was an unexpected reaction, as I was not at all aware that she was watching me. "Don't worry. This is old and useless. I will throw it out and buy a new one."

My kid, with a tearful face, twisted my arms. "Anyway, don't do it, I say, don't do it." She grimaced. Her eyes were filled with pain and fear—unlike a child's.

Horrified, I dropped the cloth and hugged her. "I'm sorry, honey. Mommy made a mistake."

As soon as the phone rings, my kid quickly runs toward it and picks up the receiver. Recently, her vocabulary has increased remarkably, and she has begun to enjoy phone conversations. Some time ago, she asked me to call my younger sister-in-law, and once the answering machine began running, she knew how to talk about what was on her mind: "Auntie," she said, "what am I supposed to do? I think I am too pretty. People say I am too cute. Auntie, when are you coming over to see sweet Inyŏng?"

As I watch my child and my younger sister-in-law, who has no child yet, having married late, play together, they appear to me like sweethearts.

"This is Inyŏng's house. Yes, Daddy! Okay. Daddy, I am going to play with Auntie. What will we be playing? Umm … I don't really know. Mommy, this is Daddy!" She hands the receiver over to me, a habit of hers when asked a question that is difficult to answer.

"Hello."

"Hi, is that you, dear?"

"Yes. Has something happened to you?"

"It's good that you haven't left home yet. I think you should leave a little later. You know Ch'ŏlyŏng, right? He's here. He wants to see me since he's come all the way down here. And I guess I'll have to."

"Okay. Leaving plenty of time, then, I'll meet you in two hours. I guess I should leave home around five o'clock. See you later."

I have been hesitant about this outing, and this reluctance almost makes me give up on it. There is something unsettling about the two-hour window, just like when one receives a notification, while busily preparing food, that the invited guest can't make it for some reason. Unsure about what to do, I head toward the sofa but my younger sister-in-law pushes me away from it, embracing my shoulders in her arms.

"Big Sister, please don't! Since you're already ready, why don't you go out early and get some fresh air? You need to stroll around the street when you look so elegant as you do now, don't you see? Who knows, a nice-looking bachelor may ask you for a date? Hey, Inyŏng, doesn't your mommy look pretty?"

Ding! The moment my apartment elevator stopped on the first floor, my heart sank for no reason.[1] An exaggerated sense of crisis surged in my mind, as if I had no business to enter this front entrance again or, if I did leave, I wouldn't be able to see my child's sweet face again. It felt like the anguish one feels when witnessing one's child, who, having learned for the first time how to ride a bicycle, speeds along the narrowing road and grows smaller and smaller, receding into the distance. It just felt like that sense of remoteness when one quietly mumbles the name of the child, as if she, who presses down the pedals, wiggling her upper body this way and that to keep balance, may never come back. It felt like something one can't bring back, something that once stayed nearby but is now gone.

The street felt so distant. Prompted by the desolate feeling that I might not be able to see it again, I stopped after taking a few steps and looked up at the apartment. The twelve-story apartment building felt like it would collapse on me. The building looked stern, like someone behaving coldly to disengage themselves from those they love.

"Hello!" A child who was slowly riding a tricycle greeted me in a voice full of endearing coquetry.

"Hi!" I replied, thinking it was Inyŏng's friend, but she turned out to be an unfamiliar child. Having taken my eyes off the back of the child, who was wobbling with her hands off the handlebars, I called out to an empty taxi just leaving the apartment compound. Just at that very moment, an idea about a place to go hit me.

[2]

It's the first time I have visited my old school since graduation. This city, which is my husband's native town, is also the place where I stayed for three middle-school years to prepare for the high school entrance exam. It's been more than two years since I came to live

---

1. To smooth the flow of the narrative, I have shifted the order of the paragraphs beginning from "Ding" and ending with the sentence in the next section [2], "I do believe it is this tree." These sections, therefore, differ from the textual order of the Korean original. This segment of the story represents an example of the author's idiosyncratic literary technique that departs from the conventional practice of presentating the sequence of events in a chronological manner.

here, but this is the first time I've thought about visiting this old school.

The school on Saturday afternoon is quiet, as students seem to have all gone. When I climb up the hilly road, I can see the trees, those still in my memory. A stand is in place on the hills dense with shrubs, and around it, a line of acacias and sycamore trees stands in a row. Different from the acacias that are thick with leaves, the sycamore trees, whose small twigs are trimmed off, have new leaves growing only on their upper trunks and looking awkward. They look like a young girl who has grown noticeably while going through puberty, or an overgrown middle-school girl lost in secret sorrow. Underneath them, the tender leaves just sprouting from the tussock grasses are red. Is it because they are so tender that they look transparent? Their redness reminds me of the pink color of a baby just broken loose from amniotic fluid.

As soon as I lean on the tree, a groundless conviction grabs me: "This is the tree. This is the very tree that embraced me every night a long time ago." I recognize the tree because of its tilted shape. This slanted tree held me comfortably like a recliner when I leaned against it and looked up at the stars shining far away. The touch of my body against the tree removes the uncertainty of my memory. I do believe it is this tree.

"Go! Go out to the city and study. And live freely. In the world today, if a woman is educated, she can live the way she wants," Big Mother said to me as she padded the liner spread on the floor with newly whipped cotton. Mom, seated diagonally across from Big Mother, remained silent, just working busily with her hands, padding the cotton. The light brown color of the freshly whipped cotton felt snug, as if one could fall asleep right away just looking at it. When I put pressure on the fluffy cotton with my hands, my handprints appeared momentarily, only to disappear in no time. The pillow decorated with rainbow-colored pillow-ends was also completed. The two mothers were always affectionate with me, but I increasingly felt a distance between us as they decorated new bedding and fitted an ample amount of new underwear. Such devotion wasn't something to be repeated several times over. It was once-in-a-lifetime devotion befitting the occasion someone is sent away to a very faraway place. I, who got lonely like a baby laid in a willow-woven basket to be floated down the river, buried my face in the soft new cotton.[2] "Look at her, what a childish thing to do!" Mom scolded me.

The women stealthily float a basket on the river, away from others' eyes. Inside the basket they had placed a baby who was born after the mother's belly was cut open, and sent it away. The teary-eyed women watch the river glitter with waves, hoping that the basket holding the baby gets caught in the tree roots or water plants exposed on the riverbank while drifting down on the current and that the baby be found and brought up by some kind-hearted soul. Why did such thoughts occur to me?

"You, Tree, give me strength!"

The tree trunk is just warm enough for me, as it has absorbed the sunlight during the day. As I stand leaning my back against it, I can feel the coolness of the tree sap flowing beneath the bark—the moisture that the roots, stretched out like threads, suck up from the depths of the earth; the long, unblocked, powerful flow of the water, which the soil and the water, mixed with the fire in the earth and the energy of the metals, push up to the veins of leaves.

A long time ago with the high-school entrance exam ahead of us, I used to sneak out during the nighttime study period and stand leaning against this tree like a tired American Indian sojourner. At night, the classroom smelled musty as a result of the smell of side dishes from packed lunch boxes and the smell of the floor crumbling into decay by the humidity and dust. The fluorescent bulb cast a pale light, but occasionally sizzled, making the feelings of desolation intransigent.

When I raised my head from the book, the stagnant atmosphere of the classroom was suffocating, its air torpid, noiseless, and rotten. The moment I thought I was trapped, I felt choked. When I imagined that the other senior-class classrooms would be lethargic with this same monotony, I feared wild screams would burst out of me. In the end, I stood up from my seat and slipped out of the hall-

---

2. This passage and the following paragraph are likely a reference to the episode about infant Moses in book 2 of Exodus in the Bible. It depicts the efforts of Moses's mother and sister to save him from the Egyptian pharaoh's decree of death for newborn Israeli males by secretly floating him down the river in a basket.

way, escaping the eye of the teacher on duty, who was dozing off at the end of the corridor.

I felt the cool night wind the moment I stepped on the playground. Wrapped up in that wind, I climbed up the hill, quietly leaned my body against the tree, and finally took the deep breath I had suppressed until then. My palms, which I put behind my back, touched the bark, and while I stood leaning like that, even the recklessness of my youth was gently calmed, diluted by the tree sap.

"You, Tree, give me strength!"

As I absentmindedly stand leaning against the tree, a middle-aged man—very likely a teacher on duty—passes by, staring at me with a searching and suspicious look in his eyes. There seems to be a huge incongruity between the school campus on Saturday afternoon and the image of a middle-aged woman wandering around alone. Such irreconcilability may resemble the contrast between the rallying cry, "Absolute Victory," that the students shouted during the high-school military drill session while winding compression bandages, and the sweet melody of the theme music of the movie *Romeo and Juliet* taught to us by the curly-haired English teacher, who had vaguely impressed me as a good tap dancer. Feeling the glance of the teacher on duty on my neck, I lower my eyes toward the playground below.

The playground is empty. There is only one middle-aged woman, wearing a white T-shirt, sweatpants, and a red sun-cap, walking briskly on the track. The woman, who is neither walking slowly nor running but goes around the track at a quick pace, seems to emanate dark and damp repressed passion rather than vitality. It appears nothing would be able to control her rapid walk—she was a woman who seems to be possessed by something.

I step down to the playground stands, take a seat, and open a can of beer from my handbag. The beer that I bought at the corner store before coming into the school tastes cool—just right. Conscious of the teacher who may show up anytime or anywhere, I wrap my hands around the beer can in hopes that it would look as if I were drinking water out of it, if by chance the teacher sees it from a distance. The can in my hands makes me feel like a delinquent student. I chuckle. Just like a woman who goes out forgetting to wear underpants but wears a modest expression, while rustling her long, ankle-length skirt; just like a woman who despairs at her forgetfulness but, satisfied with the decadence that the forgetfulness brings, wanders off giggling.

I have a sip of beer, raising my hands gracefully in a deliberate manner. A slightly bitter taste twines around my tongue. Still, I decide that no matter what, today's beer tastes sweet. The subdued sunlight is comfortably mild, and as the alcohol spreads in me, my stiffened body relaxes, making me feel good. The alcohol caresses me tenderly. I feel drowsy. I wish I could lie down, get a good sleep, and then get up. I wish that, when I wake up, everything will have changed, and I will live in an unfamiliar place and as a different person; I wish some thirty years will have passed by then.

I was a third-grader when I had my first taste of alcohol. When holidays or occasions to entertain guests approached, a jar covered with a blanket nestled in the warm spots on the *ondol*, the heated floor.[3] At that time, it was strictly forbidden to brew alcoholic beverages at home, so there was always a secretive air in my house surrounding brewing. The well-dried, hardened malt was pounded and mixed with the steamed rice, and the mixture was poured into a jar, which was then draped with a blanket. When the surface of the mixture bubbled up, a rice-wine filter was inserted in the jar. First, *yakchu*, the clear rice-wine, was filtered and ladled out, and next, *makkŏlli*, the unrefined, milky rice liquor. Then the lees were buried in the backyard. It was a secret as solid as my father's silence.

The silence of my father, a man of few words, endowed him with a weighty authority that wouldn't be swayed by any winds. That authority occupied the center of gravity between Big Mother and Mom, like the pendulum of a scale.

That day, Big Mother was filtering *makkŏlli*, after taking care of the *yakchu*. From the filter, the milky, sour liquor was dripping, and the floury lees were piled up in a bucket. Seated next to Big Mother,

---

3. Traditional Korean houses had rooms with floors made of pieces of flat stones and then papered over with sturdy oiled paper. As the smoke of burning firewood passes through the tracks underneath the stones and then out of the chimney, the floor is heated and the room becomes warm.

who was sipping *makkŏlli* now and then to adjust its consistency, I asked, "Does it taste good?"

"I wonder, but, anyway, it makes you feel good, even though overdrinking can be a poison. Why, would you like to try, Chuyŏn?"

I nodded. Big Mother used to let me get away with almost anything, but not a chance with Mom.

Big Mother poured the filtered *makkŏlli* into a small enamel bowl and, after mixing in a spoonful of sugar, handed it over to me. I sipped it one spoonful after another. It tasted like the condensation of the smell that was wafting around the room when the rice wine was fermenting. A soupy, sweetish, and tart taste clung to the tip of my tongue. One spoonful at a time, I emptied the bowl and held it out, asking for a little more. "My goodness," said Big Mother, dumbfounded, but she poured about half of the earlier amount into the bowl and gave it to me. Making the most of the chance while she was gone for a moment, I scooped up another bowl of *makkŏlli*. Upon drinking it, I felt loosened and limp. Just like the furrows that are formed when a thick liquid is stirred, heavy waves rose inside of me.

When I woke up, it was a cozy dusk with the dimmed sunlight lingering on the paper sliding door. My head felt vacant, empty winds swirling around it. As I tried to raise myself, I felt as if a heavy rock were rolling inside my head and knocking against it. I barely sat up and leaned against the wall with my head spinning. When I looked out of the window, the blossoms of the silk tree in the garden were burying their feverishly crimson stamens in the dim twilight. The stamens wedged between the leaves looked dreamy and glorious, but the blossoms looked ominous, as if they would shake up our peaceful daily routine. Their leaves, which usually fold up at night like insects falling asleep with their wings folded, remained still open. I heard the chorus of children playing a game in the yard ouside of the fence.

"Let's build a snail's house. Let's build it pretty. Let's make it big, bit by bit, make it small, bit by bit. Let's make it big, bit by bit, make it small, bit by bit."

On the empty lot, children drew an outline in the shape of a snail and circled within it, grabbing the ends of each others' clothes. The tagger, standing outside the drawn outline, tried to snatch the children. Each time the tagger's hand charged through the air, the petrified shrieks of children trying to dodge it rose up to the skies.

A vague feeling divided me and the children's monotonous melody. I loved to play this game, but I felt separate from the other children now. It was just like the case of the woodcutter in the fairy tale, who, after having napped leaning against a tree, found that a long time had passed, turning his hair white. The conviction that I wouldn't be able to cut in that game again soon permeated me like an evening haze. I turned my head around and rested my forehead against the wall. I saw my paternal aunt who lived in Seoul enter the open gate, dragging a boy—about a couple years older than I—by the hand.[4]

Way below the playground stands, two middle-school girls are seated, sharing their friendship on the deserted campus on a Saturday afternoon. All that I can see are the dark head of one girl and the two knees of the other girl, who seems to be leaning far back— her black, round head and the white, smaller knees. Occasionally, these teenage girls would stretch their legs, waking up from sleep amid their dream that they were falling from some place. Some of them with muscle aches from growing pains. Girls who would feel from time to time the sting of innocent anguish in their small bosoms. I feel an urge to go over to the girls and, holding them in my arms, I would like to soothe their agonies embedded in the countless hours coming their way. But instead of approaching them, I arch my neck back and take another swig of beer.

I drink up the beer quickly. When I press down on the middle of the empty can, the silvery, firm, and shiny cylinder caves in defenselessly. As it collapses with crackling sounds, its two circular surfaces—top and bottom—come together, facing each other.

"Right, you two, after completely emptying your contents, your surfaces, which appeared to have no chance to meet, can be aligned side by side. I bet you are happy to have met," I mumble. "If one empties one's mind of the very thought that keeps saying, 'empty it, empty it,' two minds separated from each other may connect," I wonder.

---

4. This boy would be the one adopted by the protagonist's father as his son. While not explicitly stated here in the story, close readers of this scene understand that this child will be adopted as the protagonist's brother to fulfill the need for a son in the family. See also p. 294 for confirmation that the protagonist's father adopted a son when she was a third-grader.

The two circular spaces of the beer can, which seem to enjoy the impossible encounter, look up together at me. I put the can away in my handbag. I take out my compact and look in the mirror. The light reflected by the mirror stings my eyes. It feels as if my retina will burn off in a second. I carefully peer at myself in the mirror. On my face, there is a reddish tint like a mild fever from the beer, but it might look like a sunburn from early summer heat. Who cares if people notice? I get absurdly bold—the bravado of a drowning person, who surfaces momentarily only to sink into the water deeply in no time.

The woman is still walking briskly along the track. It is the same pacing gait, which will continue eternally, unless someone goes over and drags her off the track. She appears to be chanting an incantation, "Someone, please drag me off. I can't get off this orbit by myself." Out of fear that I might run down the stands and violently drag her off, I hastily leave the place.

The Himalayan cedar is still there in the flower garden in front of the main school building, drooping its dense branches—just like kelp—at an awkward, horizontal angle. The branches of that tree are all fragile, but at least they won't all be cut off, I imagine. Those branches drooping with a sentiment of pity and with heartfelt sorrows! I gaze for the first time at the Himalayan cedar that I have never found beautiful.

"There are weak branches and strong branches, even though they grow from the same tree. The branches shooting up vertically are the strongest. Look at these! These branches that grow droopingly are weak, and they need to be cut off mercilessly. They only block the other branches' growth. They also lower the dignity of the tree." My mother-in-law callously cut off the branches of the Korean hornbeam—the edges of the leaves were soft and serrate— and flung them into the waste bin. My husband was standing beside her, nodding his head like a submissive student. My mother-in-law must be tenderly looking at the hornbeam, which looked far more distinguished after its horizontal, weak branches were trimmed. While looking at the backs of the two figures—my mother-in-law and my husband, who seemed like cedars planted side by side in a pot—I felt pain as if I were the branches thrown into the garbage bin for the sake of the tree's dignity, or the branches twisted with aluminum wires to mold the shape of the bonsai trees.

The schoolgrounds have been dug up in places. Small signs, "Under construction," can be seen here and there. The wooden dance building has been changed into a two-story cement structure—probably some time ago. On our way home from school, we used to hear the melody of "Isadora" performed by the Paul Mauriat Orchestra flowing from within the wall built with coal-tar-treated wood stacked up in layers.[5] That melancholy tune used to sweep my bosom clean, like a green and fine-textured broom does. The melody commemorates the death of a woman strangled to death by her scarf entangled in a car wheel, the end of life that came at a totally unexpected moment.[6] The girls in tights fluttered as they were carried on the rhythm, and the dance teacher, who looked like a Westerner with her deep-set, large eyes, raised her voice, tapping her palm noisily with the ruler she always carried, "Is it dance or gymnastics? Even a wooden stick will dance better than you do."

The dance hall is clearly visible through the window above the locked door. Its front wall is the mirror, and the bars on both sides of the glossily polished floor are shining like silver. The sunlight, having entered aslant into the hall from the west-facing window, has formed on the floor a bright square of light in the shape of the window. What would Suja be doing now? The buried name springs up in a familiar way as if I had seen her yesterday.

Suja used to perform ballet on the stage during the school arts festival in my primary school days. She wore a featherlike dress, and her body soaring high was as nimble as a bird's. Yet people in my hometown who watched her agile body couldn't rid from their minds the image of large chunks of red meat hanging on hooks from the ceiling or the image of her father holding a sharp carving knife in one hand and, in the other, a knife-sharpener that looked like a fencing sword.

With a slender build like an overgrown blade of grass, a high nose, and her sharp face like an inverted triangle, Suja who resem-

---

5. Paul Mauriat (1925–2006) was a French musician, orchestra leader, and composer who specialized in jazz and popular music. "Isadora" is one of the most popular pieces in his copious musical repertoire.

6. Isadora Duncan (1877–1927) was an American dancer who lived in Western Europe and the Soviet Union from her early twenties until her death. She was an innovative dancer, obtaining fame throughout Europe during her lifetime. Her signature mark was flowing scarves, and she died in Nice, France, in an open car accident strangled by the silk scarf she was wearing.

bled a bird, was one of the students who came to study in this city. Given her school record, ranked near the bottom of her class, it was a known secret that she was admitted as a special dance student with a large sum of money donated to our private school. Kids whispered about her among themselves, but I felt close to her because it occurred to me that she was also a child stealthily floated away on the river to avoid other people's eyes. In that town, Suja was the daughter of the butcher no matter how well she danced on the stage. And, no matter how well I performed at school, I was the daughter of a household where two women lived with a man under the same roof.

It was on the riverside that the ideas to settle down near a river and to build my own nest dawned upon me. For the first time, I met a man with whom I wanted to greet the morning. It was during a retreat held by my company by the South Han River over four days and three nights. The camp was organized partly as a rally to build unity among the company employees and partly in commemoration of the company's foundation day. It was a retreat in name only. Its program, which adopted a grueling type of Japanese training, was arduous enough to make me long to lie down by early evening. In spite of that, the reason I—compared to other participants— didn't feel like it was hard work was that I had become aware of a man who was from another department.

Tall and reserved, he had left his image in my heart by staining the edge of his clothes. One day, my department members and his staff had accidentally gotten together in a drinking place near our company. He went out of his way and tried to pass the glass over to me, sitting two tables diagonally across from him, but his shirt edge brushed against the kimchi bowl and ended up getting smeared. His colleagues kidded him, saying, "See what happens when you do something so unlike you!" His face, already warmed up by alcohol, got redder. That day, he came into my mind and settled there.

At the final party on the last night of the retreat, he was not present. His colleagues said that he had to leave early due to some unexpected circumstances. Upon hearing these words, my mind, which had been tense for the past three days, suddenly relaxed, as if loosened from a shackle. Finally, I felt free, and the freedom that was brought by his absence paradoxically made me realize how important his presence in my heart was. At dawn after that night when I felt at ease and empty at the same time because of his absence, I went out to the riverside alone. As the mist over the river lifted, the waves rippled in the sunlight. A dredger ship was going back and forth, interminably making heavy, jarring mechanical noises. The furrows created on the river each time the ship passed by left the same cleavages in my mind.

I would like to be with him. In the morning, I would quietly slip out, while he was still asleep, and prepare breakfast, making as little noise as possible while chopping, lest he should wake up. Someday, we would buy a house with a garden, where I would plant plantain lilies, afternoon ladies, and garden balsams. In autumn, I would collect the seeds and put them in small paper bags. While indulging in visualizing my future garden, I felt a dull ache weighing down on my heart. It was deep like the pool created by a dredging ship that had scooped away the sand. And yet, the pain was tinged with the softness of the water collected in the pool.

Where have the dredged-up sands gone and what kinds of houses would they have built? Since then, how much time has passed? How far have I traveled from the time when I couldn't even dream of days that would turn out to be like the dried-up river—the dry river about which I learned in geography class? When the teacher, who sniffled all the time because of sinusitis, said that "wadi" is a dry river,[7] a sandy wind swirled in my bosom. He said that it is also called "dry basin" in the United States—a river with no water, with its bed exposed under the scorching sun. I turned my head toward the window as my heart rustled like dried leaves. The leaves of the Himalayan cedar were hanging droopily like a bunch of hair hanging at the tip of the pole that was used to retrieve the soul of a woman drowned in the river. Between these leaves, I could see students in white gym clothes playing dodge ball in the playground, gasping hard.

Was the wadi a river in the desert or was it the vestige of a river? Why do such rivers come into being? How I wish I could know! I clench my fists, getting edgy for no reason. Suddenly, I come to myself and look at my watch to find out that the appointed time to meet my husband has already passed. Hurriedly, I go

---

7. Wadi means the riverbed or valley in regions of southwestern Asia and northern Africa, which remains dry all year around except during the rainy season.

down the hill. As I walk down quickly like the woman going around the track, more unanswered questions come to my mind: Didn't they say that if it rains in the dry river, water flows temporarily? Then, would aquatic plants grow there? When the rain stops, what will happen to those fish that flowed into the river by mistake? When only a dry riverbed remains, will it remember that it used to be a river?

[3]

"How did you know about this place? It even has corn wine, huh?" asks my husband, as he walks up the steps of the restaurant and notices the advertisement, "Corn wine" displayed on the entrance door. His eyes sparkle. I feel a sort of lonely elation.

My husband, who spent his army days on the front, occasionally talked about the corn wine he drank then. Every time he did, there was a hint of yearning in his tone, like winds brushing against the corn stalks—the corn wine he used to drink alone, while waiting for the bus on his furlough day. My husband, who is not particularly into wine and is usually calm, would show a delicate longing whenever he talked about corn wine, as if he were talking about a spring hidden in some forest known only to him. Some time ago, I went to a clinic because my child had caught cold. In the waiting room, I read an article in the regional newspaper about a house that brewed corn wine using traditional methods. I called the place and found out its location.

The restaurant is bright. Even though it is in a building on the main street, they built the rooms cozily with a narrow wooden porch running along the outside. We get a room near the entrance. A woman in a modern Korean dress brings wet towels, water, and the menu.

"I heard that this place is known for its fixed set of delicious Korean dishes and acorn-jelly salad. What did you have for lunch?" I ask my husband.

"I had a bowl of handmade noodles. Are you hungry? How about ordering corn wine and acorn-jelly salad first and rice a little later?"

"Okay, go ahead. Then we can have the regular, full meal afterward."

My husband carefully looks at the article on the wall. It is one of those articles clipped from the regional newspapers or magazines and laminated. He is always quiet, but as I look at the profile of his face directed toward the wall, I feel embarrassed at my silly suggestion to meet him here, even leaving our child at home. Is he the same man? Am I the same woman who pledged to herself that she would greet morning together with him, when she saw the fog rising under the morning sunlight from the surface of the river, cooled during the cold night? Wasn't that day a dream, perhaps? My heart, from which love for him disappeared without a trace, fills me with emptiness, even hardening my fingertips. I know that words, although spoken after deep reflection by a person who is not given to baring his soul, may sound abrupt to someone else. Even so, I want to put this question to my husband pointblank, "Choose! Is it your mother or me?" Shocked by my own childishness, I gulp when the owner of the restaurant comes in with dishes on a tray.

Thankful that she came just when I had run out of patience to keep silent, I say to her, "You won't believe how much my husband harps on corn wine. I was happy to read an article about this place."

The woman replies with a smile, "Yes, I have had a few guests like you. Thank you."

The tiny earthenware bowl contains a ceramic dipper in the shape of a gourd. The brownish wine has a limpid transparency, and on its surface oil floats while bubbles snap up from within it mischievously.

"Look at the oil floating on the wine, honey!"

"Don't you know they even make oil out of corn? Here it is, you go first." My husband ladles the wine. I lift the cup in front of me and receive the wine and then pour the wine in his in turn. We toast each other ceremoniously.

"How is it compared with the one you drank before?"

"It tastes about the same, but a bit bland. It would be more so to you, since you can hold four times more alcohol than me." My husband laughs, "four times." Before, I would have laughed together with him, but now, instead of laughing, I quietly peer at the cup. I watch the bubbles soar up from the wine and burst the moment they are exposed to the air. I feel that even the intimate affection between people, the only people who share the memory linked to a single word, seems to be as ephemeral as these bubbles.

It happened after we made love for the first time. As we were looking up at the ceiling, lying side by side with our bodies touching, my husband suddenly chuckled. It was unexpected laughter for me, still immersed in the lingering effect of our lovemaking. In spite of the playfulness I felt in his laughter, I was tense.

Sensing my nervousness, my husband, playing with my hair, said, "You have no idea how anxiously I wanted to hold you like this whenever you walked arm in arm with me. Each time we walked together, I could feel your bosom with my elbow."

I liked to walk arm in arm with him, and, when it was cold, I enjoyed the warmth that was transmitted to me when I put my hand under his arm. But I had little inkling that such an expression of intimacy could stimulate a man's sexual desires.

"You silly, you should have told me so. I wanted you to hold me, too."

"Well, you know what, I couldn't do it sober, so each time I felt like it, I asked you to go drink. I thought I needed to set the mood. Why did you think I drank so much, even though I am not a drinker in the first place? But it was of no use, because I always got drunk ahead of you, as you know. You won't begin to guess how bad I felt because you could hold about four times more alcohol than I."

In the old days, when my husband said while drinking that I could hold four times more alcohol than he, a touch of secretiveness was nestled in those words shared only between us. But now, I can't look him straight in the eyes, as I am trying to keep myself from taking his words as criticism, "How come a woman drinks so much?" But he doesn't know that I drink during the daytime. My guilt makes me flinch. My husband, who has been looking at my cup just as I have been, goads me, "You have something to tell me, right? These days, you don't talk at all at home, and there is something keeping you silent."

"Was I that obvious?"

"I'll say. Even though I haven't said so, you sometimes feel like dry ice."

"That can't be right! You could call me ice, though," I chime in quickly. But I can't figure out where to begin. I am at a loss how to tell him—why I feel so weighed down when I step into the house, why I can't talk, why I feel he is drifting away from me, and how I am coping with all this.

I calculate the amount of time my mother-in-law needs to leave the front door, dressed up without a single strand of hair out of place, and gets in the car. Once she is gone, I rummage through the fridge. Some days it's wine, other days, it's beer. If there's none of these, I even look for *ch'ŏngju*, clear rice wine—left over from cooking a fish dish and tucked away under the sink. The first glass was for the breathing spell made possible by my mother-in-law's absence. It didn't take much alcohol to relax my nerves, every inch of which were strained and pressed down by my constant awareness of my mother-in-law's eyes while she was at home. As my taut nerves began to loosen and become supple, a phrase surfaced in my mind like a buoy, "kitchen drunk." The word "drunk" always called to my mind the sinister smile of a woman who opens a trunk filled with all kinds of alcohol hidden away in a secluded room. I couldn't believe that I was such a woman, drinking in the kitchen and enduring her daily routine with intoxication.

My mother-in-law once said, while cleaning her face with a tissue paper, "I heard that your husband is going deaf, because your horoscopes don't match. What can we do now? My fault is great, too, because I let you have your way, believing that you two would live happily since you liked each other." As her fine makeup was removed, I saw her bare face exposed. After my father-in-law passed away, she built up a huge dry goods store all by herself. Once she could afford it financially, she began to enjoy various hobbies and put on weight befitting her elderly physique.

My mother-in-law's remark at first sounded like self-reproach for allowing us to get married without confirming the compatibility of our horoscopes. But its pitch was targeted at me, blaming me for my husband's hearing loss.

The bradyecoia specialist at a university hospital whose consultation we had sought with slim hope before we left Seoul calmly said: "It's an aging process. As you well know, it's just like the differences in timing among people for developing presbyopia. For instance, some people need to get reading glasses as soon as they turn forty. I would say that the same symptom appeared to you earlier than other people. As it is a phenomenon caused by dying auditory cells, we can do little about it. There is no effective treatment either." Certainly, for an ENT doctor who deals with patients with all kinds of ear, throat, and nose diseases, the fact that a patient whose nerve cells are dying earlier than others would be no different from looking at a tree among other trees standing outside the window that sheds its leaves exceptionally early. The doctor's composure regarding a matter that was beyond his control appeared professional—something that he had to let go as he couldn't do anything about it. Compared with other doctors in private clinics who had vaguely declared that my husband's case was weak hearing, his diagnosis was far more professional, and because of that, it sounded far more hopeless to us.

My husband's auditory cells were dying! He was having difficulty in hearing, as if the dead cells, like the earwax inside his ears, hindered his eardrum from vibrating. With the same kind of sense of remoteness and uncertainty that I had had when I dove underwater after stuffing my ears with cotton, I looked at my husband. With no inkling about his condition, I sometimes thought that he didn't answer me on purpose.

"If you find it too inconvenient for your daily living, you have no other choice but to wear hearing aids. These days, there are products that don't look noticeable."

I comforted myself that it's better than losing eyesight, but the future looked dark, nonetheless. Someday, my husband would turn into a person who would withdraw from society. Then, I would have to be responsible for our livelihood. The only experience I had was working at a company for about three years after college, and I knew nothing about society. What could I do, a stay-at-home wife, who does housekeeping with her husband's monthly salary deposited in his bank account? Besides, I have a daughter to take care of. Delivering home-study materials? Working as an insurance sales representative? Pyramid merchandizing? All these made me feel as if I was running into a blank wall. The moment I realized that I was imagining these things while my husband was falling into despair alone beside me, a chill ran down my back. Ah, this was why people say a husband and wife are strangers!

I remained optimistic up until my husband applied for a transfer to the branch office in this town. As the saying goes, "Even foxes turn their heads toward their birth place when they grow old." I thought he'd feel more at ease working in a smaller-scale branch office. And I felt such change was better than looking at him crestfallen, beat up by a sense of crisis as if he'd be eliminated right away from competition because he misunderstood other people's words during a meeting. There, he might be able to let people around him know about his hearing difficulty and ask for their assistance.

My husband's hometown is a metropolitan city, but there is a forest within easy reach by car, and what's more, it was a familiar place for him because he finished college there. I also expected that we'd be able to save money with more ease once we moved in with my mother-in-law, just as my older sister-in-law had said. It wasn't such a miscalculated expectation, until my mother-in-law and I slowly began to fall out with each other, making people around us feel uncomfortable when this situation became known to them.

My sisters-in-law eventually heard about my mother-in-law's remark that the onset of my husband's condition was due to the incompatibility of our horoscopes. My younger sister-in-law was the first to respond: "Please don't mind such talk. One of my friends was even forced by her mother-in-law to have double-eyelid surgery even before she got married. We didn't go through anything like a horoscope check, either." The response by my older sister-in-law, who had lived with our mother-in-law, was more forceful: "That old woman! She can't get rid of her old sick habit of gnawing away at others. Don't keep quiet. Snap back at her, 'If your son is losing his hearing, your fault is great too because you married us without checking our horoscopes in advance.'" But my older sister-in-law's words were of no help either.

My mother-in-law came back with, "I didn't blame you. I just said that I made a mistake." I realized that the intonation of one's speech can completely overturn the meaning of a sentence without changing a single word.

It was the mother of the first friend I got to know upon entering primary school who taught me that the usage of the term "Big Mother" in my house was different from the way other people used. When I went over to my friend's home to play, her mother asked my name and how many family members I had, just as usual.

"I live with my father, Big Mother, mother, and an uncle who helps around," I answered.

My friend chimed in, "Mom, Chuyŏn doesn't have an older sister or older brother. She doesn't even have a younger brother. She's so lucky!" While she was saying these words, her younger brother closed in on her desk and ripped a page out of her notebook spread on it.

"Is that right? Your Big Aunt lives with you? Has your Big Uncle gone somewhere?"[8]

"Big Uncle? I don't have Big Uncle living with us."

"If he doesn't live with you, he must have gone somewhere far away."

"No. I haven't seen him even once."

My friend's mother scrutinized my face while I was eating the barley flour, scooping it up with a spoon made with a piece of paper ripped from a notebook. Her widened eyes told me that the absence of Big Uncle meant something serious. Big Uncle? No matter how much I burrowed into my memory, there was no such vocabulary in my dictionary. It contained only words like paternal aunt, and her children's use of words like maternal uncle and maternal aunt. That day, when I returned home, I asked Big Mother, of all people, "Big Mother, why don't we have Big Uncle?" I vaguely remember Big Mother's face stiffening.

When I talked to my husband before our marriage about my family, I was not so much worried about the possibility of his giving up on the idea of marrying me once he learned about it. The bigger concern for me was that my story could make him pity my childhood as worse than it really was and plant in him prejudices against my family members.

Upon learning that I was a concubine's daughter, people tried to shower pity on me. When I told them that the concubine lived together with the legal wife under the same roof, my home was transformed in their minds into a den of jealousy and scheming. Furthermore, once they learned that even the concubine couldn't bear a son and that the husband was its cause rather than her, my father, who had been considered as an incarnation of greed and virility up to that point, suddenly fell into a pitiful state of a seedless watermelon. My father, the heir of the senior branch of his family, who had waited for the birth of a son until I became a third-grader, went through a complete medical and learned that he had such a serious physical defect as to make my birth a near miracle.

---

8. In Korean, Big Mother (kŭn ŏmŏni) is the same as Big Aunt (kŭn ŏmŏni), a designation for the wife of Big Uncle (kŭn abŏji), that is, the older brother of one's father. The regular and common usage of these terms throws the heroine off, as she is accustomed to use "Big Mother" as a term for the woman who was her father's legal wife, not the way her friend's mother meant.

This led him to adopt a son. My father indeed had endured a long wait, given the traditional values inculcated in the minds of his generation.

Although my husband used to talk about his longing for corn wine, of which I would never hear the end, he is now more absorbed in scooping up the *toenjang*, soybean-paste, stew and cooked rice. And the speed of his drinking is ridiculously slow. A dark premonition that our time together, which my younger sister-in-law provided, would end up wasted like bubbles slips into my mind, dimmed with tipsiness. We will just have to go back home after finishing the rice, I think. A sense of resignation begins to wrap around me comfortably like old clothes, and the moment I am about to bury myself in it, an old memory from the past pops up.

"Honey, do you know how *sanja* is made?"

In the middle of separating bones from fried fish, my husband raises his head with a quizzical expression, wondering what I mean.

"*Sanja*," I repeat more loudly, now that I have brought the topic up.

"*Sanja*? What's that?"

"It's a traditional Korean pastry. Why, you know the crispy biscuit that crumbles if you chew it. It's a honey pastry coated with popped rice, the same as those our younger sister-in-law brought for Mother a while back."

"Yes, I remember. Why?"

"During the holiday season when I was young, we used to make them and then go around delivering them to the houses of my father's friends. I don't know why, but suddenly, I remembered *sanja*. I wonder if it's because the table setting here looks like that of the holiday," I mumble. I don't mean to end our conversation on *sanja* in this manner, though.

I eat seasoned aster without savoring it. Just as the corn wine represented my husband's youth now gone—youth gone with no trace left behind, like a scarf fluttering briefly in the wind, the youth undefiled like a sesame leaf, youth that was mixed with raw pain like hot pepper—*sanja* was a word that brought back my warm memory. Yes, before another memory was added to it.

As the holiday season approached, one of the biggest events in my house was making *sanja*. In the courtyard, Mother and Big

Mother sat facing each other with a brazier placed in front of them. Over the brazier, the lid of a large, traditional cast-iron caldron was hung upside down, and my mother, who was holding chopsticks, looked like a little kid beating a drum. The aromatic smell of oil filled the courtyard.

Placed in the boiling oil, the solidly dried rice-dough was making lots of tiny bubbles around the cast-iron lid. The dough, the size of an adult thumb, easily stretched to three, four times bigger when rolled out with the back of a spoon. Although I saw this all the time, it always struck me with wonder. Come to think of it, that was not the only wonderful thing. It seemed to me that the whole process of making *sanja* was intended to show how raw material goes through various transformations until it becomes a completed dish.

The water-soaked sweet rice, pounded in the mill, is changed into white flour. After it is steamed, it becomes a plump chunk of sweet-rice dough. When it is placed in a large, round earthenware bowl and whisked with a smooth, round wooden stick for fulling cloth,[9] tiny bubbles are formed around it. Then, this incredibly soft and sticky dough is rolled out flat and spread on the wooden floor to dry. It becomes so hardened that, if struck, it breaks with clear, clanking sounds. When this glutinous dough is dropped into oil, it churns out any number of wafers. These wafers are then coated with honey and with flowery popped rice, which is made by frying roasted sweet rice, and the *sanja* is complete. The *sanja* is finally put in paper boxes, which are then piled up in the main floored room. What captivated me was not only the flavor of the sweet and crispy *sanja* but also the process of continuous change it underwent, each erasing its former form. In the end, the *sanja* boxes were loaded on our house-helper's bicycle and delivered to the homes of my father's friends as holiday gifts. I recall with fondness the sunlight reflecting from the heads of Big Mother and Mother, who were frying the wafers as if they were beating a drum, seated across from each other.

After my younger sister-in-law, the daughter of a high-ranking government official, was married into the family, my mother-in-

---

9. Traditional Korean women used a pair of finely polished sticks to beat starched cloth on a flat stone, a fulling-block, to give it the final glossy shine.

law's litany about the family background increased. "A person's roots are important, you see. As the saying goes, deep-rooted trees are thick with leaves." Even during the hottest summer days, I couldn't wear sleeveless clothing. Not that my mother-in-law told me not to, but I couldn't pluck up the courage, even when she said nothing about my younger sister-in-law's clothes that bared her round shoulders—so round as to tempt me to touch them.

Each time my mother-in-law mentioned family or birth, my loving memories of my mothers became shabby, and I even had doubts as to whether I had embellished those experiences myself. I wondered if the way I remembered my past days in my old home as something lonely but warm was like covering a dirty dining table with a tablecloth. Wouldn't it be like discovering chipped bowls containing scraps of kimch'i or stuck with grains of cooked rice when one lifts a finely starched, linen tablecloth covering them? Unbeknownst to me, didn't my two mothers fight, grabbing each other's hair?

It was on the day—of all days—the *sanja* was delivered that I learned that Big Mother and Mother could be called Big Wife and Small Wife, respectively.[10] After school, I met Uncle Kyŏngdŏk, our house-helper, and got on the front of his bicycle. He was about to go to the house of my father's friend near the school and was planning to go back home after delivering the box that had been carried on the back of the bicycle.

"Is anybody home?" Uncle called out, standing in front of the main room with the *sanja* box in his hand. A woman familiar to me came out of the backyard.

"Hello. I am from Saet'ŏ, and it's a small gift for your family."

"Oh my goodness! I don't know what to say, as we keep receiving this all the time. I was just about to bring some fully ripened soybeans from our vegetable garden to your house. Please have something to drink and wait a while—I was right in the middle of picking them."

---

10. In colloquial Korean, Big Wife (kŭn puin) and Small Wife (chaggŭn puin) imply legal wife and concubine, respectively.

While Uncle Kyŏngdŏk was waiting, seated on the wood floor and drinking the beverage, I headed toward the backyard to which the woman had disappeared. As soon as I went around the corner, I could see the woman and another woman squatting amidst the soybean leaves on the furrows.

"You know what! We feel obliged to receive the gift every year, as they took so much trouble to send it over to us. But, I am totally at a loss for words when I imagine the big wife and the small wife made it with their heads put together."

"Big wife, small wife." The moment I heard the words, a mass of cloud fell on the scene in which Big Mother and Mother were facing each other.

The sweet rice dough wouldn't have been the only thing my two mothers rolled out with a spoon. While living together in the same space serving as wives of one man, they would have pushed, pulled, steamed, and fried the feelings of wretchedness, feelings of pity, knots of resentment, regrets, and the like—all piled up in their hearts coil after coil, knowingly and unknowingly, and in the end, created such fabulous *sanja*. If I have tried to coat the familiar scene with a gentleness of resignation, my mother-in-law ceaselessly tried to turn its bottom over and show it to me.

I had no idea when my mother-in-law's initial words of comfort, "While you were growing up, you must have gone through a lot of heartache," changed into snubbing. So I used to rewind the film of my memories about my daily life with her to find out when and what mistakes I made to cause such a change in her. When her guests, who had been chatting cheerily, all at once fell into silence upon my entrance into the room, I tried to soothe myself by saying, "It's no big deal." But my heart smarted as if boiling oil had been splashed on it. Unable to tell my husband about such wounds, I began to be submerged in silence.

One afternoon during my mother-in-law's absence, I fell asleep overcome by the effects of alcohol. When I awoke, the midday sunlight was baring every part of the living room, and I could hear clear chirpings of birds on the veranda. The moment I slipped out of the slumber and heard the birds singing, I cried without even moving one fingertip. I felt my body stiffening with fear, as if I were stuck to the floor stretched out and wouldn't be able dislodge myself unless someone came and lifted me up. I was the animal skin, stripped of flesh and fixed to the wall with thumbtacks to dry. I was the hide, slowly drying but not completely dried up and hardened yet, while the body scent of the animal that once ran around the forest, was carried away on the the wind. I was the skin stuck flat on the wall, prematurely stiffening, driven by a foreboding that it will be completely hardened before long like an untanned animal hide.

It was the phone call from my younger sister-in-law that tore me—utterly stiffened and unable to budge an inch—off from the wall. "Big Sister, I will be on vacation from next week, and I wonder if you have anything you want to do." Earlier she had dropped by our apartment to share some of the potatoes she bought at the wholesale fresh produce market and then go out with me for lunch. She saw my tipsy, droopy eyes and the flatly crumbled beer cans piled up in a plastic bag in the utility room, to which she went to put away the potatoes.

"I don't know if it's right for me to tell you, but …" says my husband finally, after he finishes his dinner with a heavy heart, as if the food he ate remained stacked up in his stomach.

I look at him indifferently.

"I don't know whether my older sister-in-law or younger sister-in-law knows it or not, but you don't need to tell them. My mother, like you, is the daughter of a concubine. I didn't hear it from Mother, though. Sometime ago, her sister from Suwŏn, my auntie, blurted it out—by mistake, I guess. I don't know why it is a matter that should be hidden so carefully. At any rate, that may be why Mom demands so much more from you. As you know, people can't stand the part of others that resembles themselves, right?"

[4]

What am I supposed to do now? I feel lost standing beside my husband, who is paying the bill. It is an awkward situation—I can neither go back home in this unsettling state nor talk about something anew.

It's getting dusky outside as we leave the restaurant. The sunlight has become dim, and it's the time of day when the trees, sensing the approach of the night, gather their own light in and shut themselves in silence. At dusk, the streets are bustling more than during the bright daytime. The trees on the street that have absorbed the sunlight during the day exhale through their wind-pipes an acrid, fishy smell that floats in the air. It is a whiff of something like the aroma of freshly cut grass that adolescent boys give off.

Young boys brush past me carrying bouquets of flowers in their hands, their faces confused by passion that hasn't found an outlet. The bouquet will serve as proof of love and move a girl's heart. Will they know how many quagmires are in their paths of love? Will the girl remember today's bouquet when love fades away?

"I parked my car over on the other side. I'll bring it back, so why don't you sit here and take in some fresh air," my husband says.

"Are you sure you can drive?" I ask.

"You are the one who hit the bottle. I'm okay," says my husband.

My husband has me sit down on a bench in front of the department store and walks toward the parking lot. It feels as if I am look-ing at his retreating figure for the first time. From behind, he is tall and lanky and lonesome.

What am I supposed to do now? Should I ask him to drive out to the suburbs for a cup of tea? By tomorrow, my mother-in-law will be back. My marriage, which I believed would complete my love for him, the love aroused at the riverside by his absence on that day … Does my mother-in-law's presence expose other parts of marriage that the veil of love has concealed?

"Where shall we go now? Do you have some place in mind?" asks my husband.

"Whatever." I bury myself deep in the seat next to him, feeling resigned.

"I know of a nice tea house near the Sunsun Farm. How about going there for a drive?"

"Okay. How do you know such a place?"

"We went there last month after a company get-together. It's out-doors with a good view of the forest. It's quite nice, though it's bus-tling with young people."

Like his timid character, my husband's driving is rather cau-tious. He drives carefully through the unfamiliar dusk. "Young people"—my husband and I have excluded ourselves from that designation before we knew. Now the rest of our life is only a downhill slide. Suddenly, it dawns on me that the slightly uphill road we are driving on looks like the one I used to take during my younger days.

"Honey, you won't mind stopping off somewhere for a moment? I think this looks like the street. Would you drive to that side street ahead over there?"

The street seems narrower than before. Probably it looks that way because the buildings on the street are bigger, making the street appear smaller in contrast. After asking my husband to drive a little more slowly, I try to find the part that overlaps the scene in front of me with my memory.

I am amazed that this neighborhood, a residential area, has stayed largely unchanged. It was a neighborhood with a lot of two-story houses with high walls. One day when the fragrance of the lilac tree was wafting in the air, I roamed around this neighborhood with my roommate, Ŭnju. We had to look for another place to stay because the owner of our boarding house had moved away. Was it a Sunday morning? We could hear our footsteps, as the street, rather broad, was very quiet, as if it had sunk in silence. I was quite exhausted as we made rounds around the school area, looking for a notice that said, "Boarders Wanted," usually posted on fences or electric poles.

"Look! That house over there! How about ringing its doorbell?" Ŭnju was pointing to a two-story house that, even seen from the outside, looked like it had a large garden. The brown gate looked massive, and the upstairs windows enclosed in the security wire-netting impressed me as if they had never been opened through-out the year. A house that was like a long silence.

"Why would such a house take in boarders?" I said.

"You know what? I think there is only an old couple living in the house. All their children either left for school or got married. So the upstairs is all empty. Look at that window. Don't you think it's never been opened, even once? The old people living in the house must be lonely. What's more, they aren't in need of money, either, so they wouldn't want to rent the upstairs out to anyone. They should be missing their granddaughters, so let's ring the doorbell and politely ask them, "Would you by any chance like to take in boarders?"

Ŭnju's face looked wistful as she was dreaming of being a little princess. My legs ached, threatening to stiffen up, and while I kept an eye on her, I sensed an expectation slowly rising in me. Who knows, I might get a lucky break at least once, a fortune that I had never dreamed of! Like the kind of luck that I had during my childhood as the result of my random scissoring of a folded sheet of writing paper, which I intended to paste on the the door as decoration! Without any idea about what shape it would take, I haphazardly cut the folded paper, and when I unfolded it, there emerged patterns spreading out gloriously and in an orderly manner.

Now I notice that most of the big houses Ŭnju and I walked past without the guts to ring their doorbells have been converted to multi-household residences. But there remain a few old ones, as if they were the stepping stones to my memory. There is a house with a well whose tin lid has rusted dark red and fallen through the cracks between the wooden slats it straddled, reflecting the skies in it. On the top of the wall of another house, rolls of rusted and crumbling wire-nettings are resting.

"Would you park the car somewhere around here?" I ask my husband.

Without a firm conviction that this is the right street, I lock my arm in his. I walk swingingly, led by the blurring—the collusion between my memory and this street. I am floating, carried away by the effects of the alcohol that swirl warmly inside me. Wondering whether this is the same old street, I peek in. I have a glimpse of a fence covered with verdant green appearing way up there at the end of the gentle slope. The narrow alley leading to that house is long and deep. From a distance, the house standing at the end of the sloping alley comes into vision. Recalling that the house looks like it stands at a dead end but is not the last house there, I grab my husband's arm, squeezing it hard. "Look, the house is still standing there."

Pop! A light sound, like a champagne cork popping, streaks a white vapor trail across my mind.

In those days, the popping sound of cheap champagne on someone's birthday, mixed with the cheerful shouts and shrieks of young girls, used to cross over the fence of the house. The house is now completely covered with the ivy. The tree towering over the green fence must be the persimmon tree. If the sycamore trees in my old school pushed me away, here the persimmon tree greets me. I wonder if these wordless trees, having gotten together, prepared the path for me and led me here. I seem to see the conspiracy of the trees, their exchange of knowing glances in the air: "Has she dropped by there? Okay, then, I will send her over there now." I feel as if I have come here following the dots that their glances placed on my unconscious map.

Here is that house. Time, sliced just like a soil-mudded radish is chopped off to bare its clean cross-sections, shows the house to me. It is as if the long flow of time over the years has been scrubbed with water and washed clean. The water that has rinsed time flows, wetting my feet. In the center of the metropolitan city, where things change every minute, a corroded house is standing undaunted, bearing the burden of its own crumbling. Even some ten years ago, the house was very old, and stinkbugs, only seen in my country home, used to crawl out of it.

I draw close to the house and peek in through the cracks in the eroding gate. The dirt yard remains the same, and the old wooden floor where we used to get together to play the guitar is totally filled with junk. The desolation of a house with the number of its family members shrunk … The melody, "My lips, parched because of your silence / My steps, frozen because of your cold glance,"[11] which was the first tune the schoolgirls living in this house practiced when they started learning how to play the guitar, wraps around the trunk of the persimmon tree. When we sang the song, sitting on the wooden floor after dinner, the coronet-like persimmon blossoms that were scattered all around at the foot of the tree shined dimly.

How would it feel to love an unattainable love? Even though schoolgirls sing together, they can't rid themselves of something empty, something false in their feelings. It's because they haven't experienced love. What is love like?

Now I can answer those girls. Love—it is like a completed doll. While it is being made, your heart flutters the whole time, and it feels like dreaming. But once the doll takes shape, it insists on its own independent life. It is not something to be controlled by its maker. When I was a young girl my mother brought out the sewing machine, sewed pieces of rainbow-colored cloth together, and quilted them. Then she used them to make pillow ends or clothes

---

11. These are part of the lyrics of the popular Korean pop song, "An Unattainable Love" (Iruŏjilsu ŏmnŭn sarang; 1973). It was sung by a female lyricist and singer/guitarist Yang Hŭi-ŭn (b. 1952). A graduate of Sŏgang University, Yang has been one of the most popular musical entertainers, especially for young Koreans, since the early 1970s.

for me. I sat beside her and made a doll with the scraps. The cotton cloth or calico often used for bedclothes or pillow cases were suitable for making the body of a doll. I copied the pattern with a pencil and sewed the doll's torso, head, arms, and legs with a needle. I stuffed them with cotton, if I got lucky, and if not, cut the scraps of cloth into small pieces with scissors and pushed them into the parts with a knitting needle. Then the doll's body was completed. I made its head and I made the hair using wool threads with a parting in it. After I drew eyes and lips with a ballpoint pen and clothed the doll, it was born as a living human being, as if it had never been a piece of cloth.

The feeling of happiness stopped there. The moment the doll was completed, it acquired a life, a life that shouldn't be treated carelessly, which made me feel uncomfortable. What I wanted was to have a feeling of fulfillment during the process of making it. It meant the joy experienced during the time collecting scraps of cloth, mulling over how to best copy the pattern on them, and witnessing the birth of life with its own bright eyes that emerged from the useless things to be thrown away. But once the doll was finished, I didn't know what to do with it. So I gave it right away to whoever wanted it, and if not, the doll was bound to be stuck in the corner of the attic. And by some chance, when I went up to the attic and saw the doll stuck among the junk, I felt ill at ease, as if I were a mother who had run away, having abandoned her child. My marriage was like that too. I married for love, but the marriage often presented me with a feeling of dismay, just as if I were holding in my hand a completed doll. Why on earth have I made something like this?

"I lived in this house with an older girl, Sunjŏng," I say.

Two grandmas, who are having a friendly chat sitting on a low-backed, wooden bench brought out in the alley, look over at us, an unfamiliar couple, in the dusk.

My husband looks at me as if to prod me on.

"Sunjŏng was one-year senior to me and very pretty. She had almond-shaped eyes. Sometimes when I looked at ther, even between girls, I felt frightened, because she was too beautiful."

"I doubt she was prettier than you," my husband blurts out as though humoring a child. I look askance at him for the first time in a long while.

Why did I bring up the story of Sunjŏng so suddenly? I can't figure it out as my mind is all jumbled up. I shake my head from side to side. Then, a black stocking hung on the laundry line in the middle of summer abruptly appears in front of me from nowhere.

"She was not only pretty but also good in school. One of her legs was artificial."

So? My husband nudges me on with his eyes.

I detach myself from the fence and look up at the pole adjacent to it. It was originally an electric pole but is now a bare post with all the electric lines gone. The ivy vines, having crept up the fence, have now coiled themselves around the post up to the top, turning it into a green, cylindrical column. The column looks suffocated.

I can't remember why I slept over in Sunjŏng's room that day. It was probably because my roommate Ŭnju's mother came for a visit. Sunjŏng was the only student in the boarding house who lived in a room by herself. When I entered her room through the narrow wooden veranda, she was sitting on a chair, reading a reference book.

"Hi. Why don't you sleep over there?" said Sunjŏng to me. It was a rather cold and plain greeting to a fellow boarder, who came for an overnight stay. I quietly spread the bedding and opened my book. The night deepened with the rustling sounds of Sunjŏng's turning the pages of her book and the sounds of her scribbling in her notebook. Unaware, I fell asleep, and when I woke up in the morning, Sunjŏng was changing her clothes with her back to me. It was a few days after we'd begun wearing our summer school uniforms. She put on a skirt over the pants she was wearing at home and then dropped the pants down through the skirt. Her pants slipped down like a snake sloughing off skin. I don't know why she turned her body around, but I ended up looking at it—it was a smooth, shiny leg without a single downy hair. While she put a stocking on the leg, her back remained stiff.

"I heard that her toe was hit by a bicycle. But it rotted away and was removed. Some years later, her foot was cut off, and as her flesh gradually started to rot away, she had to go through repeated operations. When she lived in this house, she had a thigh-length artificial leg. She wore a black stocking even during the midsummer, so it was easy to spot her among the students pouring out from the school."

Her almond-shaped eyes, her high nose, her tightly closed lips—her face was neat and pretty but sometimes looked frighteningly cold. Her eyes in her expressionless face were so clear as to show the iris. Her face gave off an impression of stagnation with nothing flowing. The kind of hopelessness when a stream loses its bend and comes to a dead-end ditch. The consternation when the blood continuously circulating through the blood vessels reaches a dead end and is blocked. Muscles that ferociously suck in the blood when it slowly resumes its circulation after a standstill. Similarly, Sunjŏng's face was stiff and hardened. Even if I didn't have a chance to see Sunjŏng's leg that day, would I remember her face this way?

Suddenly the street lights are turned on, and the quiet and peace disappear from the desolate alley off the main street and things come alive brightly. The tips of the ivy leaves, thick and green in the dusk, look sharp. The kind of bleakness and chill that comes at the end of a party blends with the nocturnal air, spreading everywhere. Even though it is not chilly, I get goose bumps and feel as if I were a vessel sprawled out on the yard after the departure of party guests. I wish someone would wash me in the soapy sink and rinse me with clean water. Would someone drain me to remove these seething feelings that refuse to subside like dishwater mixed with scraps of food and soap!

At the thought of dishwater, I become uncontrollably queasy, feeling like vomiting. Something sour surges up from inside of me. As I am about to double over, my husband helps me up. I scramble up to the end of the alley and squat in the empty lot behind the building.

The food not yet digested gushes out, smelling sour. My husband pats me on the back. With gurgling sounds, the undigested foods gummed with mucous gastric fluid crowd out. I feel the spoiled milk, the lumpy texture of milk clots that cover the surface of a clear liquid after they are separated from it. The moment I feel it is like curdled milk, I throw up violently.

"Honey, you seem to have grown weak. You didn't even drink much," my husband pats me on the back. Each time he pats, the cavity between my backbone and chest reverberates loudly. As I vacantly look at the vomit spattered on my skirt clutched in my hands, tears gather pointlessly in my eyes, and I call out "Mother!"

I get curious to know which mother I meant. Although I uttered it in dead earnest, I am not sure whether it meant Big Mother, Mom, or even my mother-in-law. In my teary eyes amidst vomiting, scenes from the courtyard unfold.

My mother passed away first, followed by my father, heir of the senior branch of his clan, whose members died young with few descendants. Big Mother stayed on in that house with my adopted older brother. When I visited Big Mother in my native town after my marriage, I asked her if she hated Mom and me, and how she could remain in my memory simply as such a peaceful face.

"Of course, I did. How could a woman live in peace all the time while serving her husband! When your mother was expecting you, I earnestly wished it was a son. But if I carefully looked at the bottom of my heart, I saw I was badly hoping that the baby was not a son. As a human being … I could never get rid of the thought that, if your mom bore a son, the space for me to occupy would shrink that much more. My mind also ran off ahead to figure out what your mom was thinking. As I pored over things in this way, the first thing that grew dark was my own heart, you know. How could I fathom someone else's mind when my mind changed all the time! It occurred to me that the more I checked out my heart and looked at it, the more it would hurt. So I covered it up and coddled it, and that's the way I have lived." Ah, ah, Mother!

A man, his clothes soaked with filth and smelling foul even from afar—a salty, rancid sewage stink. A stench that was mixed with the smell of hair unwashed for a long time after a sweaty sleep. The smell was so fetid that the color of the blossoms of the trumpet creeper climbing up the fence would suddenly fade away, I thought. The beggar came through the gate, and after having taken a few steps inside, stopped and stood there with his hands open. Even though there was no one to block him from coming in further, it seemed as if it was the beggar's courtesy to remain there. Mom gave me money and said, "Give it to him with two hands."

The closer I got to the beggar, the more the stench reeked. It was really a stinking smell. Even on that hot day, he was wearing an old soldier's hat. The words "two hands" barred me from dropping the money. I quietly placed the money on his open hands. The next day, I asked, "Mom, why should I give money to the beg-

gar with two hands? I saw Sŭngja's mother at the drugstore toss-
ing money to the beggar."

Mom was silent. When I looked at her again with a questioning
eye, she said, "Who said that a beggar is not a human being?"

That's all that she said. Those words were etched in my mind—
a child's—far more plainly because they had no modifiers or ex-
planations. Just my father and Big Mother are human beings, and
Mom and I are human beings, the beggar is nothing but a human
being. Ah, ah, Mother!

Every morning, my mother-in-law stands on the veranda and
stretches herself toward the sun as if she were praying. The sun is
wrapped around in the misty air and shines like a silver circle,
like the homopolar moon.

When I first started living with my mother-in-law, her sunward
ritual every dawm impressed me as reverence for life, a sense of
relief that a day has gone by and a new, fresh day has just begun
again. When I, lying in bed, felt drained as if dragged down by a
hopelessness whether I would be able to wake up tomorrow, I
could understand my mother-in-law's rite toward the sun. Given
her old age, I could more than feel for her. But now, as she goes
through the morning sun ritual and then completes her daily ten-
thousand-steps walk without exception, I see in her neat orderliness
only the ugliness of old age and greed—an obstinate desire, a refusal
to obey the natural providence that everything withers in its own
season and that one has to make way for the next generation.

This change in my view toward my mother-in-law roughly coincided with the time when I began to look at the bonsai pots with
a pathetic feeling and aversion—the trees that I used to think so
adorable. It was just like looking at the animals bred in the labora-
tory for experimental purposes, whose growth was stunted.
Whatever caused something like this to happen to me?

"Are you done? You didn't seem to have eaten much, but look what
a feast you've had! It must hurt inside. Rinse your mouth with this."

I rinse my mouth with the mineral water my husband hands
over to me and roughly cover the vomit with dirt I scrape up with
the tip of my foot. "Bury one's head in the sand like an ostrich!"
How could I remember the expression amidst this mess! I awkwardly smile. My attitude, which has tried to cover up all the hurt-

ful memories and remember the unseemly love only, as if trying to paint color over a black-and-white film! In the eyes of my mother-in-law, who suffered through her own pain by embracing it, such an attitude on my part would have appeared just like that of a cat, which, after covering up its own poop, acts dumb. Like a cat that lightly shakes off the dirt from its paws and elegantly leaves the site, I grab my husband's arm and say, "Let's go down."

"You know, I saw Sunjŏng once after graduation. It was during my college days, and can you guess where I met her?" Each time I talk my breath smells sour and I can't come close to see my husband's face.

"Well, at the municipal library, or, at a movie theater?" my husband replies.

"Wrong! It was a nightclub in It'aewŏn,"[12] I answer.

Sunjŏng was dancing with a guy. The reason I could recognize her under the flashy lighting and among the people bumping each other was the degree of her slanted shoulder that was different from others. I approached her awkwardly, swinging my body. Her almond-shaped eyes full of smiles, Sunjŏng was dancing with her partner, paying no attention to anything else—not even once. Although I left without exchanging greetings with her, I felt forever grateful that I could remember her with that bright smile on her face. I had no idea at the time how much she would have paid to acquire such a smile.

"Honey, be patient just for a while. As you have fed me up to now, I will feed you from now on," I magnanimously assure my husband, like a bum who makes an empty promise. My head still spins.

My husband chuckles, "How are you going to feed me? Are you too going to make corn wine and sell it?"

"Either by making ramen noodles or *ttŏkpokki*, spicy stir-fried rice cakes ..."

After a few years, my husband would be completely cut off from sounds, like pine trees oozing resin in the depths of mountains. I wonder whose poetic line this is: "There's little time left to love." Before it gets too late, before my husband sinks into deeper silence.

---

12. It'aewŏn is a section of Seoul well known for its clubs, bars, restaurants and clothing stores, popular among young Koreans and tourists.

I saw for the first time a closed school during my trip with my husband before we moved down to this city. I noticed a sign, "Traditional Teahouse," on the roadside near the entrance to a mountain temple, and we walked up the wooden steps. To my surprise, the teahouse was at the corner of the school playground. I caught sight of a wooden cabinet that stood brightly on the hill above the school playground. Then I saw pieces of tree trunks that had been cut crosswise to the size of an adult's forearm hanging inside the cabinet.

When I approached the school building, I finally realized it was a school that had been closed down. About six classrooms seemed to be used as someone's studio, and the place was messy with the utensils for trimming the wood scattered all over. The wooden floor of the hallway, thickly covered with dust, squeaked. When I walked through the corridor and came out on the opposite side of the building, a fragrance struck me, and I felt as if it were washing my body clean. It was the fragrance from the fir tree, which was spreading all over the deserted school campus with no traces of students to be found. Low-pitched traditional song melodies from the teahouse slowly filled the absolutely silent, empty playground. I wished I could live in a place like this.

It was a college classmate who gave me the idea of buying a closed school and turning it into a campground for teenagers. I was told that my classmate's father had a cousin who bought a closed school in Chŏlla Province and had already built camping facilities. Without even knowing how much it would cost to buy a closed school, I was already cherishing such a dream: my husband would tend the garden and I would open a store with a snack corner in it. We would meet youngsters and then say goodbye to them—that's the way we would grow old.

At night, the insects among the grasses would chirp, rubbing their wings together and letting out sounds that are finer than the filaments of their own wings. The youngsters, full of vitality with no hint of death, would have fallen fast asleep. The playground, on which they romp around, would be brimming with the moonlight and evening primroses would fully open their bosoms to embrace this moonlight. When the moonlight, having hastened from far away, falls on the flower petals, I would be able to hear, if I quietly listen, the sounds of petals popping open. I would then probably tell my husband that I love him, using sign language. Abandoning words, I would convey my love with the patterns made in the air by my hands.

Yes, once again, I will mange to survive. Urgently, I pledge to myself. I don't have the confidence to remove the temptation of the silver-colored can at once or to open my heart wide and show it to my mother-in-law in whose presence it keeps shutting itself. Yet I would at least be able to quietly settle the muddy water in me—with the love of the river, which, before it gets murkier, cleanses its impure body by itself and embraces the lives within it.

☙

Yi Hye-gyŏng (b. 1960)

Yi Hye-gyŏng is one of the most awarded and highly regarded fiction writers of Korea today. She is widely known for her distinctive thematic orientations, which include a sympathetic perspective on human and gender experiences and a spirit of acceptance that embraces life's contradictions, imperfections, drawbacks, and even tragedies. Yi has been especially noted for her consistent focus on love/hate relationships within the framework of the family.[13]

A native of Taech'ŏn, a well-known sea resort town in South Ch'ungch'ŏng Province, Yi was the youngest of eight children.[14] Since her childhood, her mother's compassion and care for those in need in spite of her own busy work in the family store, on their farm, and within the home, left a lasting impression on the perceptive Yi. Yi's observation of her mother's skill in making *sanja* also became invaluable and unforgettable parts of her adolescent years.[15] Because her home was always bustling with people, Yi used to seek quiet and privacy by hiding in a closet. As soon as she learned *han'gŭl*, she committed her thoughts to writing, and this early practice led her to experiment with a diary and letter format by the time she became a primary school pupil.

Yi majored in Korean literature at Kyung Hee University in Seoul, graduating in 1982. Her debut short story, "Uridŭl ŭi tt'ŏlk'yŏ" (Our new beginning; 1982), was the result of her hard work during the summer of her senior year (1981). It is a family-centered narrative, revolving around the father whose naiveté and financial bungling bankrupt his family and drive his wife, unable to cope with the situation, to a cult religion, while provoking hatred and anger in his children. The narrative's resolution, however, suggests the indispensable value of blood ties and mutual support between parents and children, a narrative structure to be readopted and refashioned in her subsequent narratives.

---

13. See Kong Chong-gu, "Yi Hye-gyŏng sosŏl ŭi kajok chuŭi" [Familism of Yi Hye-gyŏng's novels], *Hyŏndae munhak iron yŏn'gu* 19 (2003): 5–24.

14. Much of this information on Yi Hye-gyŏng's biography has been provided by the author herself through our correspondence. I deeply appreciate her thoughtfuness and generosity.

15. For instance, the episodes in "In Front of the House" that describe the biological mother's *sanja* making and her treatment of the beggar are from Yi's first-hand observations of her mother.

For nearly fifteen years after college, Yi had to put her creative activities and production on hold as she taught in high schools or worked as an editor and a journalist. The publication of her first full-length novel, *Kil wi ŭi chip* (The house on the road; 1995), which earned the Today's Writer Award, finally provided her with the much-needed incentive and momentum to resume her creative writing. The novel shows a variety of portrayals of women mired in destructive familial and gender dilemmas caused by the domination, cruelty, and immorality of their male family members. Yet the novel also underscores the author's fundamental faith in family morality—the family as a communal zone for intimacy, respect, and nurturing.

In 1998 Yi's first short-story collection, *Kŭ chip ap* (In front of the house), was published, and her short story, "In Front of the House" (Kŭ chip ap), included in the anthology with the same title, received the Han'guk ilbo Literature Award in 1998. The year 1998 also marked a new departure in her career. Yi left Korea for Indonesia as a volunteer for the Korea International Cooperation Agency (KOICA), and taught Korean language in the Korean Studies Center at Gadjah Mada University on Java until 2000. After returning home, Yi received two highly esteemed literary awards: "Kkot kŭnŭl arae" (Under the shadow of flowers; 2001) earned the Yi Hyo-sŏk Literature Award; and "Kogaet maru" (The hilltop; 2001) became the recipient of the Hyŏndae Literature Award. Soon followed the publication of Yi's second short-story collection, *Kkot kŭnŭl arae* (2002), titled after her short story. The narratives in this anthology illustrate the authorial penchant to uncover the reality of the Korean family today, which is still nightmarish for women as victims of patriarchal tyranny and inhumanity. Still, the durable undercurrent of the injured females' sharing of their pain and their quiet, empathetic bonding also warms many of these stories.

In 2004 Yi's *Kil wi ŭi chip* won the Encouragement Award from the Liberaturepreis in Germany. Her third short-story collection, *T'ŭmsae* (*Cracks*; 2006), winner of the Tong-in Literature Award, showed its author's expanding thematic and literary horizons. It calls attention to the misunderstandings and isolation that postmodern Koreans experience, the concealed male violence inflicted on its members in the name of family, the ills of uniformity and conformity coerced by communal apartment living, and the harsh, alienating social, economic, and ethnic divide between "us" (Koreans) and "others" (foreigners) that illegal immigrant workers feel in Korea, to name a few.

In 2007 Yi's fourth collection of short stories, *Nŏ ŏpnŭn kŭ chari* (The place without you) garnered the Muyŏng Literature Award. The representative stories in this anthology deal with betrayal, infidelity, and deception in familial, interpersonal, and gender relationships. However, Yi's discerning view that there are neither flawlessly pure human beings nor totally wicked villains—we are all mixtures of these traits—demonstrates her increasingly deepening insight into and acceptance of human reality.

Yi's second full-length novel, *Chŏnyŏk i kiptta* (Deep is the night; 2014), marks a turn from her usual thematic path.[16] The novel traces the vicissitudes of the lives of a group of male friends in a rural town from their adolescent days to the present. In doing so, the work casts light upon Korea's most turbulent social and political history from the 1960s, taking the fictional characters as its symbols and indexes. Here, Yi assumes the role of cultural and sociopolitical chronicler of her generation and calls readers to remember the rite of passage Koreans have gone through to become what they are today.

In 2014 Yi went to Cuba under the sponsorship of the Arts Council Korea for a three-month residency program at the Cultural Society Jose Marti. In December 2014 she moved to Ecuador on her own and returned to Korea in September 2015 to prepare works based on her Latin American sojourn, adventures, and experiences. In April 2016 Yi went back to Ecuador and has been living in Imbabura Province. While Yi continues her creative writing projects, she has been enjoying her close relationship with local Ecuadorians, deepening her understanding of their traditions, culture and custom, and way of thinking. She also travels once a month to the capital Quito to work with the second generation of Korean teenagers on Korean composition at the Korean Language School as a volunteer.[17] ଔ

---

16. Under the title "Sagŭmp'ari" (Shards), the novel was originally serialized in the quarterly journal *Munhak kwa chisŏng* (Literature and intellect) from August 2009 to August 2010.

17. I would like to thank Yi Hye-gyŏng for sharing this information in her e-mail to me in September 2017.

TEXTUAL READINGS

The last story in this anthology, "In Front of the House," is an evocative critique of persistent, Confucian, male-centered concubinage that reduces women to the status of second-rate human beings. The heroine/narrator, Chuyŏn, a college-educated housewife and mother of a young daughter, experiences an affliction that stems from the Confucian obsession of her father, who commits polygamy to continue his clan's patrilineage by having a son and heir. The patriarch's doomed transgression subjects his primary wife (Big Mother), the protagonist's biological mother (Mother), who is a concubine, and the protagonist—all perfectly decent and respectable individuals—to social discrimination and prolonged personal torment and angst. The portrayal of the two mothers as consummate craftspersons and transmitters of the living Korean traditional arts of winemaking and confectionery speaks volumes about how unjust and wrong it is to demean and cheapen them as mere physical and material tools for producing male children in the interest of patrilineal succession. At the same time, the two mothers jointly incarnate traditional Korean women's inner strength, self-control, forbearance, and dignity, which were forged in the crucible of humiliating bigamy but unmarred by its debasing effect. The narrator's drawn-out revisit with her women kin in memory is a long-overdue tribute to them as well as a therapeutic process.

The stigma of Chuyŏn's birth carries over to her married life. She becomes the abject target of her mother-in-law's high-handed browbeating. The older woman even blames Chuyŏn for her son's health problems. It is noteworthy here that the mother-in-law's cultivation of bonsai trees—her manipulation of dwarfed trees with their leaves and roots forcefully twisted—is symbolic of her callousness, artificiality, and indulgence in control. The narrator, who has felt a close affinity with nature and finds freedom and restorative energy in trees, flowers, plants, and other vegetation from her adolescent years, feels keenly the same kind of suffocating oppression exerted on her by her mother-in-law. This is revealed in her equating herself with a piece of dried animal skin—shriveled to a subhuman level. The effect is so insidious and poisonous that Chuyŏn feels prematurely old and depleted. She is even unable to relate these bottled-up feelings openly to her husband, even though they still love each other deeply inside.

As a means out of this unbearable situation, Chuyŏn resorts to furtive alcohol consumption, only to feel guilt-ridden and often lethargic. Indisputably, the protagonist's ongoing in-law relationship reproduces the axiomatic oppression of a daughter-in-law by a mother-in-law, and is a textbook example of a woman's victimization of another woman, even though both are victims of the same patriarchal system. The surprising revelation of the mother-in-law's well-kept secret about her own birth identity, that is, she herself is the offspring of a concubine, therefore, is effective in bringing out the punishing impact of concubinage on its victims, while pointing out her two-facedness and absurd posturing toward Chuyŏn. In contrast, Chuyŏn's younger sister-in-law, who becomes privy to her secret drinking issues, breaks down the unnatural walls of sister-in-law rivalry constructed by the mother-in-law and functions as a psychological and emotional outlet for Chuyŏn. The younger sister-in-law's empathetic discerning and sagacious attitude introduce a whiff of fresh air to the household as well as to Chuyŏn's otherwise self-inhibiting daily routine. Here we see the author's deconstruction of conventionally popularized notions about the rivalry and discord among women in the patriarchal household.

"In Front of the House" closes on a reconciliatory and even uplifting note in that the protagonist resolves to sublimate and transcend vicious gender traditions, which have degraded and cheapened her existence and that of the most important women in her life—her two mothers—and even her mother-in-law. In this context, the narrator's vomiting can be interpreted as a symbolic ritual act of purification—the purging of her wronged past and present. Empowered by such a will to settle with her past and its weighty burden once and for all, the protagonist offers her project of rebuilding a new life course, although she is realistic and level-headed enough to foresee that her effort will not be all smooth sailing. Especially appropriate is that her reconstructive venture is to be undertaken in the bosom of nature, as it idyllically fits with her habitual, intuitive perception of the intimate correlation and connection between the unfolding of nature and human affairs, as they coexist in the same continuum.[18] She even readily embraces her husband's physical im-

---

18. Some critics consider Yi Hye-gyŏng's association of woman with nature as part of her inclination toward eco-feminism. See Kim Mi-hyŏn, *Yŏsŏng munhak ŭl nŏmŏsŏ*, 283–286.

pairment in full understanding of its challenges and difficulties, showing her maturity and sense of responsibility in total disregard of her society's gender role divisions or specifications. Finally, her pledge to repurpose an abandoned school campus and there to nurture young generations of adolescents perfectly corresponds to her constructive spirit to chart a wholesome, balanced, and, most of all, unpretentious future from the other-imposed ruins of her past and present.

Here, it is illuminating to take note of the implications of the story of Sunjŏng, the narrator's fellow boarder during her middle-school days in "In Front of the House." The episode about Sunjŏng serves to circuitously underscore the positive possibility for starting one's life anew, giving oneself a second chance. The young woman's personal transformation illustrates the human ability, strength and will that enable individuals to soar above their limits, obstacles, and prejudices, whether they are physical, psychological, social, or even gender-related. In this sense, Sunjŏng plays an exemplary precedent for the narrator, reinforcing her resolve and vow to pursue her new life project—to go beyond her current domestic, psychological, and conjugal difficulties, to claim a new life for herself by rejecting her sense of victimhood, and make a difference to her own world, as demonstrated at the end of "In Front of the House." Indeed, the protagonist, having lived through all of those various homes and houses at different stages of her life, is now standing "in front of the house" of her own that she is planning to build by herself."

Technically, "In Front of the House," which is presented primarily in present tense, is distinguished by its slow and nonlinear narrative arrangement. It frequently intersects with the narrator's retreat to overlapping memories, flashbacks, self-reflections, speculations, and interior monologues and musings, which create abrupt trans-temporal shifts, leaps, and fluctuations between past and present, and even future. In addition, stylistically the narrative is marked by repeated use of ellipses, inversions, and linking of incomplete sentences. These nonconventional narrative strategies and temporal manipulations demand the reader's close attention to and participation in the thought flow of the narrator, and even textual rereading. ∞

Bibliography

Bernstein, Susan David. *Confessional Subjects: Revelations of Gender and Power in Victorian Literature and Culture*. Chapel Hill: University of North Carolina Press, 1997.

Ch'a Hyŏn-suk. "Chungjŭng uuljŭng ch'ehŏm tamŭm sosŏlchip p'yŏnaen chakka" [An author who published a collection of stories about her experience of severe depression]. *Yŏsŏng tonga* (June 2008): 420–422.

———. Interview. *Chosŏn ilbo*, November 14, 1999.

———. "Nabi ŭi kkum, 1995." In *Yi Sang munhaksang susang chakp'umjip* [Collected works of Yi Sang Literature Award recipients], ed. Munhak Sasangsa, 19: 317–341. Seoul: Munhak Sasangsa, 1995.

Chandra, Vipan. *Imperialism, Resistance, and Reform in Late Nineteenth-Century Korea: Enlightenment and the Independence Club*. Berkeley: University of California, Institute of East Asian Studies, Center for Korean Studies, 1988.

Cho, Haejoang. "Male Dominance and Mother Power: The Two Sides of Confucian Patriarchy in Korea." In *Confucianism and the Family*, ed. Walter H. Slote and George A. De Vos, 187–264. Albany: State University of New York Press, 1998.

Cho'e Ch'ang-gŭn. "Pak Hwa-sŏng sosŏl ŭi yŏsŏng insik yŏn'gu—'Sinhon yŏhaeng' kwa 'Pit'al' ŭl chungsim ŭro" [Study of Pak Hwa-sŏng's female consciousness—focusing on "Honeymoon" and "The slope"]. *Honam munhwa yŏn'gu* 58 (2015): 363–387.

Ch'oe Chŏng-hŭi. "Sanje" (Mountain rites). In *Ch'oe Chŏng-hŭi sŏnjip* [Selected works of Ch'oe Chŏng-hŭi]. *Sin Han'guk munhak chŏnjip* [Complete works of new Korean literature], 12: 332–345. Seoul: Ŏmungak, 1973.

Ch'oe Ki-suk. "Chungch'ŏp toen sam ŭl ŭngsi hanŭn tugae ŭi kŏul" [Two mirrors intensely looking at the layers of life]. In Yi Ho-gyu et al., *Han Mu-suk munhak segye* [Han Mu-suk's literary world], 197–228. Seoul: Saemi, 2000.

Ch'oe Myŏng-p'yo. "Somun ŭro kusŏngdoen Kim Myŏng-sun ŭi sam kwa munhak" [Life and literature of Kim Myŏng-sun constructed on rumors]. *Hyŏndae munhak iron yŏn'gu* 30 (2007): 221–245.

Ch'oe Yun. "Pŏng'ŏri ch'ang" [A Mute's Chant]. In *Chŏgi sori ŏpsi hanjŏm kkonnip i chigo: Ch'oe Yun sosŏlchip* [There, a petal silently falls: collection of Ch'oe Yun's short stories], 147–177. Seoul: Munhak Kwa Chisŏngsa, 1992; 1999.

―――. *Sujubŭn autsaidŏ ŭi kobaek: Ch'oe Yun sanmumjip* [Confessions of a shy outsider: collection of Ch'oe Yun's essays]. Seoul: Munhak Tongne, 1994.

Choi, Hyaeweol. *Gender and Mission Encounters in Korea: New Women, Old Ways*. Berkeley: University of California Press, 2009.

Choi, Kyeong-Hee. "Impaired Body as Colonial Trope: Kang Kyŏng'ae's 'Underground Village.'" *Public Culture* 13, no. 3 (2001): 431–458.

Chŏn Tae-ung. "'Sinyŏsŏng' kwa kŭ munjejŏm" [New women and their issues]. *Yŏsŏng munje yŏn'gu* 5–6 (1976): 351–362.

Chŏng Ch'ung-nyang. *Ihwa p'alsimnyŏn sa* [Eighty-year history of Ewha]. Seoul: Idae Ch'ulp'anbu, 1967.

Chŏng Hye-yŏng. "Sinsosŏl kwa woeguk yuhak munje—Yi In-jik ŭi 'Hyŏl ŭi nu' rŭl chungsim ŭro" [New novel and question of studying abroad—focusing on Yi In-jik's *Hyŏl ŭi nu*]. *Hyŏndae sosŏl yŏn'gu* 20 (2003): 193–213.

Chung, Kimberly. "Proletarian Sensibilities: The Body Politics of New Tendency Literature (1924–27)." *Journal of Korean Studies* 19, no. 1 (Spring 2014): 37–57.

Deuchler, Martina. *The Confucian Transformation of Korea: A Study of Society and Ideology*. Cambridge, MA: Council on East Asian Studies, Harvard University, 1992.

―――. "Propagating Female Virtues in Chosŏn Korea." In *Women and Confucian Cultures in Premodern China, Korea, and Japan*, ed. Dorothy Ko, JaHyun Kim Haboush, and Joan R. Piggott, 142–169. Berkeley: University of California Press, 2003.

―――. "The Tradition: Women during the Yi Dynasty." In *Virtues in Conflict: Tradition and the Korean Woman Today*, ed. Sandra Mattielli, 1–47. Seoul: The Royal Asiatic Society, Korea Branch, 1977.

Duncan, John. "The *Naehun* and the Politics of Gender in Fifteenth-Century Korea." In *Creative Women of Korea: The Fifteenth Through the Twentieth Centuries*, ed. Young-Key Kim-Renaud, 26–57. Armonk, NY: M.E. Sharpe, 2004.

Eckert, Carter J. et al. *Korea Old and New: A History*. Seoul: Ilchogak, 1990.

Friedan, Betty. *The Feminine Mystique*. New York: W.W. Norton & Company, 1963.

Haboush, JaHyun Kim. "Private Memory and Public History: The Memoirs of Lady Hyegyŏng and Testimonial Literature." In *Creative Women of Korea: The Fifteenth Through the Twentieth Centuries*, ed. Young-Key Kim-Renaud, 122–141. Armonk, NY: M.E. Sharpe, 2004.

Han Mu-suk. "Wŏrun" (Halo around the moon). In *Han Mu-suk munhak chŏnjip* [Collected literary works of Han Mu-suk], 6: 228–240. Seoul: Ŭllyu Munhwasa, 1992.

Han'guk Yŏsŏng Yŏnguso Yŏsŏngsa Yŏn'gusil. *Uri yŏsŏng ŭi yŏksa* [History of Korean women]. Seoul: Ch'ŏngnyŏnsa, 1999; 2006.

Hiratsuka, Raichō. *In the Beginning, Woman Was the Sun: The Autobiography of a Japanese Feminist*. Trans. with an introduction and notes by Teruko Craig. New York: Columbia University Press, 2006.

Hong Yang-hŭi. "Ilje sigi Chosŏn ŭi yŏsŏng kyoyuk—hyŏnmo yangch'ŏ kyoyuk ŭl chungsim ŭro" [Education of Chosŏn women during the period of Japanese rule—focusing on "wise mother, good wife" education]. *Tong Asia munhwa yŏn'gu* 35 (2001): 219–257.

Hwang, Kyung Moon. *A History of Korea: An Episodic Narrative*. New York: Palgrave, 2010.

Hyŏn Nu-yŏng (Hyŏn Ch'ŏl). "Yohaksaeng kwa tongsŏng yŏnae munje: tongsŏng ae esŏ isŏng ae ro chinjŏn hal ttae ŭi wihyŏm" [Girl students and the problem of lesbianism—the danger when their lesbian love advances to heterosexual love]. *Sinyŏsŏng* (December 1924): 20–25.

Im Og-in. "Huch'ŏgi" [Chronicle of a Third Wife]. In *Han'guk hyŏndae taep'yo sosŏlsŏn* [Selections from representative modern Korean fiction], comp. Im Hyŏng-taek et al., 6: 406–418. Seoul: Ch'angjak Kwa Pip'yŏngsa, 1996.

———. *Na ŭi iryŏksŏ* [My personal history]. Seoul: Chŏng'u sa, 1985.

Kang Kyŏng-ae. "Chasŏ sojŏn" (My short autobiography). In *Kang Kyŏng-ae chŏnjip* [Collected works of Kang Kyŏng-ae], ed. Yi Sang-gyŏng, 788–789. Seoul: Somyŏng Ch'ulp'an, 1999.

———. "Wŏngoryo ibaegwŏn" (Manuscript payment of two-hundred wŏn). In *Kang Kyŏng-ae chŏnjip* [Collected works of Kang Kyŏng-ae], ed. Yi Sang-gyŏng, 559–567. Seoul: Somyŏng Ch'ulp'an, 1999.

Kim In-suk. *K'allal kwa sarang: Kim In-suk sosŏlchip* [Daggers and love: collection of Kim In-suk's short stories]. Seoul: Changjak Kwa Pip'yŏngsa, 1993.

Kim, Kichung. *An Introduction to Classical Korean Literature: From 'Hyangga' to 'P'ansori.'* Armonk, NY: M.E. Sharpe, 1996.

———. "Hŏ Nansŏrhŏn and 'Shakespeare's Sister.'" In *Creative Women of Korea: The Fifteenth Through the Twentieth Centuries*, ed. Young-Key Kim-Renaud, 78–95. Armonk, NY: M.E. Sharpe, 2004.

Kim Ki-jin. "Kim Myŏng-sun ssi e taehan konggaechang" [An open letter to Miss Kim Myŏng-sun]. *Sinyŏsŏng* (November 1924): 46–50.

———. "Kim Wŏn-ju ssi e taehan konggaechang" [An open letter to Miss Kim Wŏn-ju]. *Sinyŏsŏng* (November 1924): 51–54.

———. "Kyŏron kwa ihon e taehayŏ" [On marriage and divorce]. *Sinyŏsŏng* (May 1924): 30–37.

Kim Kyŏng-ae. *Kŭndae kabujangje sahoe ŭi kyunyŏl* [Cracks in modern patriarchal society]. Seoul: P'urŭn Sasang, 2014.

Kim Kyŏng-il. "Ilje ha chohon munje e taehan yŏn'gu" [Study of the early marriage issue during the Japanese colonial rule]. *Tong asia munhwa yŏn'gu* 40 (2007): 363–395.

Kim Kyŏng-mi. "18segi yangban yŏsŏng ŭi kŭlssugi ŭi ch'ŭngwi wa kŭ ŭimi" [Levels of writings by upper-class women of the 18th century and their significance]. *Han'guk kojŏn munhak yŏn'gu* 11 (2005): 5–50.

Kim Mi-hyŏn. *Yŏsŏng munhak ŭl nŏmŏsŏ* [Beyond woman's literature]. Seoul: Minŭmsa, 2002.

Kim Pok-sun. *"Na nŭn yŏja ta": pangbŏp ŭrosŏŭi chendŏ* ["I am woman": Gender as a method]. Seoul: Somyŏng Ch'ulp'an, 2012.

———. *P'eminijŭm mihak kwa pop'yŏnsŏng ŭi munje* [The problems of feminist aesthetics and universality]. Seoul: Somyŏng Ch'ulp'an, 2005.

———. "Pundan ch'ogi yŏsŏng chakka ŭi chinjŏngsŏng ch'ugu yangsang: Im Og-in non" [Features of pursuit of sincerity in women writers of the early division period: on Im Og-in]. In *Peminijŭm kwa sosŏl pip'yŏng: hyŏndae p'yŏn* [Feminism and criticism of the novel: contemporary period], ed. Han'guk Munhak Yŏn'guhoe, 26–65. Seoul: Han'gilsa, 1997.

Kim Pyŏng-ch'ŏl. *Han'guk kŭndae pŏnyŏk munhaksa yŏn'gu* [Historical study on translation of literature in modern Korea]. Seoul: Ŭllyu Munhwasa, 1975.

Kim Su-jin. *Sinyŏsŏng, kŭndae ŭi kwaing: singminji Chosŏn ŭi sinyŏsŏng tamnon kwa jendŏ chŏngch'i, 1920–1934* [New woman, excess of the modern: the new woman discourse and gender politics in colonial Korea, 1920–1934]. Seoul: Somyŏng Ch'ulp'an, 2009.

Kim Tong-in. *Kim Yŏn-sil chŏn* [Biography of Kim Yŏn-sil]. *Munjang* March 1939, May 1939, Feb. 1941.

Kim Tu-hŏn. *Han'guk kajok chedo yŏn'gu* [Study of Korean family systems]. Seoul: Sŏul Taehakkyo Ch'ulp'anbu, 1969, 1989.

Kim Yang-sŏn. *Kyŏnggye e sŏn yŏsŏng munhak* [Woman's literature on the border]. Seoul: Yŏngnak, 2009.

Kim Ye-rim. "Pulhwa ŭi hyŏnsil kwa hwahae ŭi tang'wi: Kim Hyŏng-gyŏng non" [The reality of discord and the mandate for reconciliation: on Kim Hyŏng-gyŏng]. In *P'eminijŭm ŭn hyumŏnijŭm ida: 90-yŏndae munje chakka rŭl chindan handa* [Feminism is humanism: diagnosing problematic writers of the 1990s], ed. Han'guk munhak yŏn'guhoe, 297–321. Seoul: Han'gilsa, 2000.

Kim Yong-suk. *Chosŏnjo yŏryu munhak yŏn'gu* [Study of women's literature in the Chosŏn dynasty]. Rev. and enlarged. Seoul: Yejin Sŏgwan, 1990.

Kim Yun-jŏng. *Pak Wan-sŏ sosŏl ŭi chendŏ ŭisik yŏn'gu* [Study of gender consciousness in Pak Wan-sŏ's novel]. Seoul: Yŏngnak, 2013.

Kim Yun-sŏn. "1930 nyŏndae Han'guk sosŏl e natanan sŏngdamnon yŏn'gu—Kang Kyŏng-ae ŭi *Ŏmŏni wa ttal* e natanan yŏsŏng ŭisik ŭl chungsim ŭro" [Study of gender discourses in Korean novel of the 1930s—focusing on feminist consciousness in Kang Kyŏng-ae's *Mother and daughter*]. *Hansŏng ŏmunhak* 22 (2003): 135–170.

Kim, Yung-Chung, ed. and trans. *Women of Korea: Women of Korea: A History from Ancient Times to 1945*. Seoul: Ewha Womans University Press, 1979.

Kim, Yung-Hee. "Creating New Paradigms of Womanhood in Modern Korean Literature: Na Hye-sŏk's 'Kyŏnghŭi.'" *Korean Studies* 26, no. 1 (2002): 1–86.

———. "A Critique on Traditional Korean Family Institutions: Kim Wŏnju's 'Death of a Girl.'" *Korean Studies* 23 (1999): 24–42.

———. "Dialectics of Life: Hahn Moo Sook and Her Literary World." In *Creative Women of Korea: The Fifteenth Through the Twentieth Centuries*, ed. Young-Key Kim-Renaud, 192–215. Armonk, NY: M.E. Sharpe, 2004.

———. "From Subservience to Autonomy: Kim Wŏnju's 'Awakening.'" *Korean Studies* 21 (1997): 1–30.

———. "In Quest of Modern Womanhood: *Sinyŏja*, A Feminist Journal in Colonial Korea." *Korean Studies* 37 (2013): 44–78.

———. *Questioning Minds: Short Stories by Modern Korean Women Writers*. Honolulu: University of Hawai'i Press, 2010.

———. "Re-visioning Gender and Womanhood in Colonial Korea: Yi Kwang-su's *Mujŏng* (The Heartless)." *The Review of Korean Studies* 6, no. 1 (June 2003): 187–218.

———. "Under the Mandate of Nationalism: Development of Feminist Enterprises in Modern Korea, 1860–1910." *Journal of Women's History* 7 (1995): 120–136.

Kong Chong-gu. "Yi Hye-gyŏng sosŏl ŭi kajok chuŭi" [Familism of Yi Hye-gyŏng's novels]. *Hyŏndae munhak iron yŏn'gu* 19 (2003): 5–24.

"'Tangsin' ŭi kwangye non ŭl wihayŏ: Kim In-suk non" [For the study of relationship of 'you': on Kim In-suk]. In *P'eminijŭm ŭn hyumŏnijŭm ida: 90-yŏndae munje chakka rŭl chindan handa* [Feminism is humanism: diagnosing problematic writers of the 1990s], ed. Han'guk Munhak Yŏn'guhoe, 233–265. Seoul: Han'gilsa, 2000.

Kwŏn Podŭrae. *Yŏnae ŭi sidae: 1920-yŏndae ch'oban ŭi munhwa wa yuhaeng* [Age of love: culture and fad in the early 1920s]. Seoul: Hyŏnsil Munhwa Yŏn'gu, 2003.

Kwŏn Yŏng-min. *Han'guk kyegŭp munhak undongsa* [History of the Korean class-literature movement]. Seoul: Munye Ch'ulp'ansa, 1998.

———. "Sinsosŏl ŭi munhaksa jŏk sŏnggyŏk chaeron" [Review of the literary and historical character of new novel]. *Inmunhak yŏn'gu* 17 (2010): 5–40.

Lanser, Susan Sniader. *Fictions of Authority: Women Writers and Narrative Voice*. Ithaca, NY: Cornell University Press, 1992.

Lee, Ann Sung-hi. *Yi Kwang-su and Modern Korean Literature*. Ithaca, NY: East Asia Program, Cornell University, 2005.

Lee, Ji-Eun. *Women Pre-scripted: Forging Modern Roles Through Korean Print*. Honolulu: University of Hawai'i Press, 2015.

Lew, Young I. "Korean-Japanese Politics Behind the Kabo-Ŭlmi Reform Movement, 1894 to 1896." *Journal of Korean Studies* 3 (1981): 39–81.

Lowry, Dina. *The Japanese "New Woman": Images of Gender and Modernity*. New Brunswick, NJ: Rutgers University Press, 2007.

Lukács, Georg. *The Theory of the Novel*. Cambridge, MA: The MIT Press, 1978.

The Modern Girl Around the World Research Group. *The Modern Girl Around the World: Consumption, Modernity, and Globalization*. Durham, NC: Duke University Press, 2008.

Mun Hŭi-sun. "Hosŏ chiyŏk yŏsŏng hanmunhak ŭi sajŏk chŏngae" [Historical development of literature in Chinese by women of Ch'ungch'ŏng province areas]. *Han'guk hanmunhak yŏn'gu* 39 (2007): 85–116.

Myers, Sylvia Harcstark. *The Bluestocking Circle: Women, Friendship, and the Life of the Mind in Eighteenth-Century England*. Oxford: Clarendon Press, 1990.

Ŏm Mi-ok. *Yŏhaksaeng kŭndae rŭl mannada: Han'guk kŭndae sosŏl ŭi hyŏngsŏng kwa yŏhaksaeng* [Girl students meet the modern era: formation of modern Korean novel and girl students]. Seoul: Yŏngnak, 2011.

O'Rourke, Kevin. "Demythologizing Hwang Chini." In *Creative Women of Korea: The Fifteenth Through the Twentieth Centuries*, ed. Young-Key Kim-Renaud, 96–121. Armonk, NY: M.E. Sharpe, 2004.

Paek Nak-ch'ŏng. *Minjok munhak kwa segye munhak II* [National literature and world literature II]. Seoul: Ch'angjak Kwa Pip'yŏngsa, 1985.

Pak Hye-gyŏng. "Kang Kyŏng-ae chakp'um e natanan yŏsŏng insik ŭi munje" [The issue of women's awareness in Kang Kyŏng-ae's works]. *Minjok munhaksa yŏn'gu* 23 (2003): 250–276.

Pak Sŏn-mi. *Kŭndae yŏsŏng, cheguk ŭl kŏch'yŏ Chosŏn ŭro hoeyu hada: singminji munhwa chibae wa Ilbon yuhak* [Modern women returned Chosŏn by way of the empire: cultural dominance in the colony and studying in Japan]. Seoul: Ch'angbi, 2007.

Pak Tal-sŏng. "Yosai haksaeng kip'ung: namnyŏ haksaeng ŭi yŏnbyŏng kwa munjil" [Recent trends among students: love-sickness and literary diseases of male and female students]. *Sinyŏsŏng* (July 1924): 54–57.

Pak Wan-sŏ. *Chŏmun nal ŭi saphwa: Pak Wan-sŏ sosŏljip* [Episode at dusk: collection of Pak Wan-sŏ's short stories]. Seoul: Munhak Kwa Chisŏngsa, 1991.

Pak Yong-ok. *Han'guk yŏsŏng kŭndaehwa ŭi yŏksajŏk maengnak* [Historical contexts of modernization of women in Korea]. Seoul: Chisik Sanŭpsa, 2001.

Park, Chan E. *Voices from the Straw Mat: Toward an Ethnography of Korean Story Singing*. Honolulu: University of Hawai'i Press, 2003.

Park, Sunyoung. *The Proletarian Wave: Literature and Leftist Culture in Colonial Korea, 1910–1945*. Cambridge, MA: Harvard University Asian Center, 2015.

Pohl, Nicole, and Betty A. Schellenberg, eds. *Reconsidering the Bluestockings*. San Marino, CA: Huntington Library, 2003.

Robinson, Michael E. *Korea's Twentieth-century Odyssey: A Short History*. Honolulu: University of Hawai'i Press, 2007.

Rodd, Laurel Rasplica. "Yosano Akiko and the Taishō Debate over the 'New Woman.'" In *Recreating Japanese Women, 1600–1945*, ed. Gail Lee Bernstein, 175–198. Berkeley: University of California Press, 1991.

Sato, Barbara. *The New Japanese Woman: Modernity, Media, and Women in Interwar Japan*. Durham, NC: Duke University Press, 2003.

Sievers, Sharon L. *Flowers in Salt: The Beginnings of Feminist Consciousness in Modern Japan*. Stanford, CA: Stanford University Press, 1983.

Sin Myŏng-jik. *Modŏn ppoi kyŏngsŏng ŭl kŏnilda* [Modern boy strolls through Seoul streets]. Seoul: Hyŏnsil Munhwa yŏn'gu, 2003.

Sin Sik. "Yŏllyŏ rŭl nonhaya—mŏnjŏ yŏsŏng ŭi chonjae rŭl ch'ajira" [On virtuous woman: find woman's self first!]. *Sinyŏsŏng* (July 1926): 11–16.

Sŏ Chi-yŏng. *Kyŏngsŏng ŭi modŏn kŏl: sobi, nodong, chendŏ ro pon singminji kŭndae* [Modern girls in Seoul: colonial modernity seen through consumption, labor, gender]. Seoul: Tosŏ Ch'ulp'an Yŏiyŏn, 2013.

———. [Suh, Jiyoung]. "The 'New Woman' and the Topography of Modernity in Colonial Korea." *Korean Studies* 37 (2013): 11–43.

Sŏ Yŏng-ŭn. *Ch'oe Chŏng-hŭi chŏngi: kangmul ŭi kkŭt* [Biography of Ch'oe Chŏng-hŭi: the end of the river]. Seoul: Munhak Sasangsa, 1984.

Song Hyŏn-ho. *Han'guk kŭndae sosŏllon yŏn'gu* [Study of theory of modern Korean novel]. Seoul: Kukhak Charyowŏn, 1990.

Song In-hwa. "Hach'ŭngmin yŏsŏng ŭi pigŭk kwa chagi insik ŭi tojŏng: Kang Kyŏng-ae non" [Tragedy of lower-class women and their path to self-recognition: a study on Kang Kyŏng-ae]. In *Peminijŭm kwa sosŏl pip'yŏng: kŭndae p'yŏn* [Feminism and criticism of novel: modern period], ed. Han'guk Yŏsŏng Sosŏl Yŏn'guhoe, ed., 251–285. Seoul: Han'gilsa, 1996.

———. "Sŏng'ae ŭi sŭng'in kwa ch'egwan ŭi sisŏn" [Endorsement of sexual love and visional perspicuity]. In Ku Myŏng-suk et al., *Han Mu-suk munhak ŭi chip'yŏng* [The horizon of Han Mu-suk's literary world], 184–209. Seoul: Yerim Kihoek, 2008.

Songjae Munhwa Chaedan, ed. *Tongnip sinmun nonsŏljip, 1896.4–1899.12* [Collection of editorials in the Independent Newspaper, 1896.4–1899.12]. Seoul: Songjae Munhwa Chaedan Ch'ulp'anbu, 1976.

Spivak, Gayatri Chakravorty. "Translation as Culture." *Parallax* 6, no. 1 (2000): 13–24.

Stanzel, F.K. *A Theory of Narrative*. Trans. by Charlotte Goedsche with a preface by Paul Hernadi. New York: Cambridge University Press, 1984.

Tieszen, Helen Rose. "Korean Proverbs about Women." In *Virtues in Conflict: Tradition and the Korean Woman Today*, ed. Sandra Mattielli, 55–60. Seoul: Royal Asiatic Society, Korea Branch, 1977.

Tomida, Hiroko. *Hiratsuka Raichō and Early Japanese Feminism*. Leiden: Brill, 2004.

U Chŏng-gwŏn. *Han'guk kŭndae kobaek sosŏl ŭi hyŏngsŏng kwa sŏsa yangsik* [The formation of modern Korean confessional novel and its narrative modes]. Seoul: Somyŏng Ch'ulp'an, 2004.

Wells, Kenneth M. "The Price of Legitimacy: Women and the *Kŭnuhoe* Movement, 1927–1931." In *Colonial Modernity in Korea*, ed. Gi-Wook

Shin and Michael Robinson, 191–220. Cambridge, MA: Harvard University Asia Center, 1999.

Yi Hye-gyŏng. *Kŭ chip ap* [In front of the house]. Seoul: Minŭmsa, 1998.

Yi Hye-sun. *Chosŏnjo hugi yŏsŏng chisŏngsa* [Intellectual history of women in the late Chosŏn dynasty]. Seoul: Ihwa Yŏja Taehakkyo Ch'ulp'anbu, 2007.

————. *The Poetic World of Classic Korean Women Writers*. Trans. by Won-Jae Hur. Seoul: Ewha Womans University Press, 2005.

Yi In-yŏng et al. "Chŏnjaeng, kiŏk, yŏsŏng chŏngch'esŏng: Ch'oe Yun ŭi 'Pŏng'ŏri ch'ang' kwa 'Krista Polp'ŭ ŭi 'Krista T. e taehan ch'unyŏm' pigyo" [War, memory, women's identity: a comparative study of memorial writings by Ch'oe Yun's "A Mute's Chant" and Christa Wolf's "The Quest for Christa T"]. *Kap'ŭka yŏn'gu* 12 (2004): 271–291.

Yi Kwang-gyu. *Han'guk kajok ŭi sahoe illyuhak* [Social anthropology of the Korean family]. Seoul: Jimmundang, 1998.

Yi Kwang-nin. *Han'guk kaehwa sasang yŏn'gu* [Study of Korean enlightenment thought]. Seoul: Ilchogak, 1979; 1981.

Yi Kwang-su. "Chanyŏ chungsim non" [On Children-centered ideas], *Ch'ŏngch'un* [Youth] no. 15 (Sept. 1918). In *Yi Kwang-su chŏnjip* [Collected works of Yi Kwang-su], 17:40–47. Seoul: Samjungdang, 1962.

————. "Chohon ŭi aksŭp" [Evil practices of early marriage], *Maeil sinbo*, Nov. 23–26, 1916. In *Yi Kwang-su chŏnjip* [Collected works of Yi Kwang-su], 1:499–503. Seoul: Samjungdang, 1962.

————. "Chosŏn kajŏng ŭi kaehyŏk" [Reforms of Korean family], *Maeil sinbo*, Dec. 14–22, 1916. In *Yi Kwang-su chŏnjip* [Collected works of Yi Kwang-su], 1:490–498. Seoul: Samjungdang, 1962.

————. "Honin non" [On marriage], *Maeil sinbo*, Nov. 21–30. In *Yi Kwang-su chŏnjip* [Collected works of Yi Kwang-su], 17: 138–148. Seoul: Samjungdang, 1962.

————. "Hyŏnsang sosŏl kosŏn yŏŏn" [On selecting award-winning novels]. *Ch'ŏngch'un* 12 (March 1918): 97–102.

Yi Pae-yong. "Chosŏn sidae yugyojŏk saenghwal munhwa wa yŏsŏng ui chiwi" [Confucian life culture and women's status during the Chosŏn period]. *Minjok kwa munhwa* 9 (2000): 25–37.

Yi Sang-gyŏng. *Han'guk kŭndae yŏsŏng munhaksa non* [On the history of modern Korean woman's literature]. Seoul: Somyŏng Ch'ulp'an, 2002.

————, ed. *Kang Kyŏng-ae chŏnjip* [Collected works of Kang Kyŏng-ae]. Seoul: Somyŏng Ch'ulp'an, 1999.

Yi, Sŏng-mi. "Sin Saimdang: The Foremost Woman Painter of the Chosŏn Dynasty." In *Creative Women of Korea: The Fifteenth Through the Twenti-*

eth Centuries, ed. Young-Key Kim-Renaud, 58–77. Armonk, NY: M.E. Sharpe, 2004.

Yi Tong-ha. "*Hyŏl ŭi nu* wa *Mujŏng* ŭi pigyo koch'al" [Comparative study of *Hyŏl ŭi nu* and *Mujŏng*]. *Kwanak ŏmun yŏn'gu* 8 (1983): 357–370.

Yŏm Sang-sŏp. *Nŏhŭidŭl ŭn muŏt ŭl ŏdŏnnŭnya* [What have you gained?]. *Tonga ilbo* (Aug. 27, 1923–Feb. 5, 1924).

Yoo, Theodore Jun. "The 'New Woman' and the Politics of Love, Marriage and Divorce in Colonial Korea." *Gender and History* 17 (2005): 295–324.

Yu Chin-wŏl. *Kim Iryŏp ŭi 'Sinyŏja' yŏn'gu*. [Study of Kim Iryŏp's *Sinyŏja*]. Seoul: P'urŭn Sasang, 2006.

Yu Hong-ju. "Kobaekch'e wa yŏsŏngjŏk kŭlssŭgi—Na Hye-sŏk ŭl chung-sim ŭro [Confessional style and female writing—focusing on Na Hye-sŏk]. *Hyŏndae munhak iron yŏn'gu* 27 (2006): 197–216.

CORNELL EAST ASIA SERIES